THE HONEST ASSASSIN

THE HONEST ASSASSIN

C.J. Carver

This first world edition published 2010
in Great Britain and in the USA by
SEVERN HOUSE PUBLISHERS LTD of
9–15 High Street, Sutton, Surrey, England, SM1 1DF.
Trade paperback edition published
in Great Britain and the USA 2010 by
SEVERN HOUSE PUBLISHERS LTD

British Library Cataloguing in Publication Data

Carver, Caroline, 1959 -
  The Honest Assassin.
  1. McCaulay, Jay (Fictitious character) – Fiction.
  2. Assassination – Investigation – Fiction. 3. Suspense
  fiction.
  I. Title
  823.9'2-dc22   2895

ISBN-13: 978-0-7278-6909-8   (cased)
ISBN-13: 978-1-84751-251-2   (trade paper)

All Severn House titles are printed on acid-free paper.

Severn House Publishers support The Forest Stewardship Council [FSC], the
leading international forest certification organisation. All our titles that are
printed on Greenpeace-approved FSC-certified paper carry the FSC logo.

Mixed Sources
Product group from well-managed
forests and other controlled sources
www.fsc.org Cert no. SA-COC-1565
© 1996 Forest Stewardship Council
FSC

Typeset by Palimpsest Book Production Ltd.,
Grangemouth, Stirlingshire, Scotland.
Printed and bound in Great Britain by
MPG Books Ltd., Bodmin, Cornwall.

For Steve

ACKNOWLEDGEMENTS

For their invaluable help with this novel, I thank Lieutenant Colonel Peter House, Royal Military Police (RMP), Major Phil Hagues, Special Investigation Branch RMP, Colonel Baber, RMP, and the Trinity Road Police in Bristol.

Thanks to my favourite scientist, Dr Michael Seed, for his ongoing and invaluable input into my books. Any mistakes, as usual, are mine.

I would also like to thank Amanda Stewart and the team at Severn House for their support, and a special thanks to my assiduous copy editor, Rachel Simpson Hutchens.

ONE

J ay McCaulay was half dressed, eating toast and marmalade, when she thought she saw a man slip across the garden. She could hear Tom upstairs, singing along to a song on the radio, so it couldn't be him. She doubted it was a burglar doing the rounds at seven a.m. on a Sunday, but something about the way the figure moved – as sinuous as a cat – made her nerves tighten.

Cautiously, she walked across the kitchen. Peered through the French windows. She almost jumped out of her skin when the man stepped right in front of her, inches away.

He wore a pair of combats tucked into black boots and a jacket with its collar turned up. Broad shoulders tapered to a narrow waist. A pair of deep brown eyes held hers.

Her jaw dropped.

He glanced at the window handles, then back. Raised his eyebrows questioningly.

Jay flung open the windows. 'What are you doing here?'

'You have marmalade in your hair.' He reached a hand towards her face, but she batted it away.

'Max!' she protested. 'You're supposed to be in South America!'

'Aren't you going to ask me in?'

She glanced over her shoulder. She could hear the shower running, thank God. The last thing she needed was for Tom to come downstairs and find his nemesis in his garden.

'No,' she said. 'I'm not.'

Before she could move, he plucked the slice of toast she'd forgotten she was clutching and ate it in three swift bites. 'Nice,' he said. 'Although I prefer honey.'

'Max . . .' she said warningly.

'I'm hungry.' A smile inched into his eyes. 'You wouldn't deny a starving man food, would you?'

Jay checked behind her again. The shower was still running. She stepped outside and closed the door. Damp winter chill immediately wrapped around her bare legs, making her shiver. 'That's not what I meant, and you know it,' she hissed.

He held up his hands. 'I'm here because I need your help.'

'What?' Her brain couldn't compute what he'd just said. Max Blake, MI5 officer and general all-round superman, wanted help? Sure, she was ex-Services, but she'd been a civvy for four years and was as soft as a goose-down duvet.

'Please, Jay.' He spoke softly, and suddenly she saw how tired he looked. His normally tanned skin was pale, and he had purple rings beneath his eyes. He hadn't shaved for a while either. 'Just this once, OK?'

They had enough history for her to know something serious was going on. She didn't think she'd ever heard him plead before. Despite her misgivings, she opened the door and let him inside.

'How hungry?' she asked.

'Very.'

He ran a hand over his face. That was when she spotted what looked like blood on the underarm of his shirt. It wasn't old blood either. It was bright red and wet.

'Max?' She pointed it out.

He twisted his arm, had a look. 'A plaster would be good.'

Jay hesitated a second, then hared upstairs. The bathroom was steamy and smelled of shaving cream. Tom had a towel wrapped around his middle. His hair was wet and slick, his cheeks pink.

'Hey, gorgeous.' He reached out an arm and scooped her close, nuzzling her neck. 'Hmmm. I don't have to be at the squash court for another hour . . .'

She opened her mouth to tell him Blake was downstairs, but the words jammed in her throat. Things had been so good between her and Tom over the past few months . . . Could she bandage Blake, hear his story, and get him out of Tom's house before Tom came downstairs?

Tom and Blake had held an uneasy truce ever since they'd worked together on an op in the summer. There was a mutual respect between the two men, both of them professionals – Blake with MI5, Tom with the Bristol police – but Tom didn't trust Blake an inch with Jay. Although nothing had happened between Blake and Jay during their past two missions, she found it harder and harder to convince Tom of this fact, and when Tom had found out that Blake had accepted a job in Brazil, he would have opened a bottle of champagne had there been one in the fridge.

She dived for the bathroom cabinet. Grabbed a roll of bandage, some Micropore surgical tape, antiseptic cream and a box of plasters. 'Back in a minute,' she said.

Tom looked at the medical supplies in surprise. 'Are you OK?'

'Fine. I just thought they'd be more useful in the kitchen.' She zipped downstairs.

Blake, in the meantime, had folded on to the tattered old couch in the corner of the kitchen. His eyes were closed, but when she sank next to him, they opened. He let her roll up his shirtsleeve. The wound was a couple of inches long, jagged and deep, and although it had been stitched, two stitches had torn. She smeared the area with cream and wrapped a bandage around his forearm. Secured it with Micropore.

'Thanks.' His voice was faint.

'Tell me what's going on.'

'I need a favour.'

'Go on.'

'My sister's sick.'

Jay blinked. She never knew Blake had a sister.

'Her name's Emilie.'

'And?' she prompted. Although she was aware of Blake, the pallor of his skin, her senses were focused on Tom upstairs. She heard him pad across the corridor into the bedroom to get dressed. Time was running out.

'She's just been rushed to hospital.'

All thoughts of Tom vanished. 'Oh, Max.'

'I have to go to her. She's in Brussels. But I have a meeting in Paris tomorrow that I can't miss.' He turned his head and looked at her straight. 'I want you to go to that meeting for me.'

'Paris?' she repeated blankly. 'Tomorrow?'

'You speak French.'

'Can't someone else go? Like one of your colleagues?'

'No. You're the only person I trust with this.'

'But I have a meeting with the Home Office at nine,' she protested. 'There are five girls from Kosovo who've been trafficked into the UK, and I need to get permission for them to stay otherwise they'll be sent back and possibly re-trafficked. Then I'm in Manchester, meeting with the police about some Nigerian kids who are being used to scam the social services. They think they've been kidnapped in Lagos and sent here as slaves . . .'

She trailed off.

Blake surveyed her steadily.

'Sorry,' she mumbled. 'You know my job.'

'His name's Solomon Neill. His friends call him Sol. I've told him you'll meet him at a café in the Marais at eleven a.m.' Blake gave her the address.

'Why can't he come to London?' She hated the plaintive tone in her voice. She'd have to reschedule the whole day, and the Home Office wouldn't be impressed after her badgering them for a meeting.

'I've booked you on Eurostar.' He passed her a piece of paper upon which was written a reference number. 'Go to the desk an hour before, and they'll give you your tickets. And here's some cash.' A padded envelope joined the piece of paper. He rose to his feet. Swayed slightly.

'I don't even know what Sol looks like,' Jay said. 'He might be late. I might get stuck in the tunnel . . .'

'He'll approach you.'

'Max, I need to know what this is about.' She stood in front of him. 'I can't just jump on a train on a whim . . .'

'Keep an eye on him, Jay. He's a good friend of mine.'

'But—'

'I appreciate it.' Before she could move, he ducked his head and pressed a kiss on her lips.

At that precise moment, Tom walked into the kitchen.

'What the—'

'Detective,' Blake said. He flicked a finger in a casual salute. 'Sorry I can't stay.'

With that, Blake moved to the French windows, slipped outside, and was gone.

Jay stared at the garden, her lips still tingling from his kiss. As usual, Blake had impeccable timing. Anyone would think he'd planned the entire scene to send her currently stable love life into free fall.

'What was he doing here?'

Although Tom's voice was calm, the muscles in his cheeks were jumping.

'He, um . . .' *Please God, don't let us have a row.* 'He needed a favour.'

'Why didn't he ring you? Why turn up at *my house*?'

'I don't know.'

'Jesus Christ.'

'He asked me to meet a friend of his in Paris tomorrow. It's urgent and—'

'No, Jay.' Tom shook his head warningly.

'We're not going together or anything. He's headed to Brussels. His sister's there. She's been rushed to hospital, apparently. Which is why he's asked me to go to Paris and—'

'Why can't someone else go? Why *you*?'

'He doesn't trust anyone else.'

'Jesus.' Tom flung up his hands. 'Don't tell me you said yes.'

'I owe him, Tom.' Her fingers gripped Blake's envelope. 'Considering what he's done for me in the past . . .'

Tom's expression was hard, uncompromising.

'I'll only be gone a day,' she begged.

'Like I haven't heard that one before. You attract trouble, remember?'

'It's a day return.' She waved the piece of paper with its reference number at him. 'I'll be home for supper, no worries.'

Tom didn't look the least bit mollified, and she desperately tried to think how to change his mood. Out of nowhere, a light bulb switched on in her head. 'How about you invite Sofie?' Jay moved casually to the bread bin and pulled out a granary loaf. 'It's time I met her. Maybe she can stay over for the night. Save her mother from having to drive back and forth.'

Tom's eyes widened. 'You want Sofie to have a sleepover? Here? Tomorrow?'

'I've been thinking about it for a while,' she lied. She'd been purposely putting off meeting Tom's twelve-year-old daughter, more to avoid Tom's exquisitely pretty ex-girlfriend Heather than anything else. 'I'll bring some croissants back with me. They taste totally different to the ones we have here. Does she like croissants?'

'She loves croissants.'

'That's settled then.'

Tom ate his toast in silence, but when he left to play squash ten minutes later he wasn't looking annoyed any more. Just bemused.

TWO

Jay drove back to London on Sunday evening to find her housemates sitting in front of the TV and polishing off plates of lasagne.

'Help yourself.' Denise waved a fork at her. 'There's loads in the kitchen.'

Angela poured Jay a glass of red wine and, plate on her lap, Jay ate while they watched a rerun of *Top Gear*.

'Gorgeously gorgeous rang earlier,' Denise said. 'Looking for you.'

'He turned up at Tom's,' Jay said. 'No phone call. No warning. I was eating breakfast, and there he was.'

Denise's eyes rounded. 'Bloody hell. How did Tom take it?'

'Not well.'

'I can imagine.' Angela's voice was dry.

'So I invited Sofie to stay tomorrow night.'

Both Angela and Denise paused, forks raised. 'Bloody hell,' Denise swore again. 'Some diversionary tactic. Did it work?'

'Yup.'

Swearing came naturally to the girl squad, as Tom called them, thanks to their army background. Both women were ex-special reconnaissance soldiers supporting 1 PARA who Jay had met on her tour in Kosovo. They'd all left the army around the same time, and when the girls had set up house in Fulham, they'd invited Jay to join them. Not for the first time, Jay looked around at the high ceilings, the open fireplace and glass doors that led to the patio and barbecue area, and blessed Angela's ex-husband. Without his generosity during the divorce, they'd probably be living in a squat in the outer reaches of London, rather than in one of the most prestigious suburbs in the heart of the city.

While they cleared the kitchen Jay told her housemates about her trip to France. 'I won't be home tomorrow night. I'll stay over with Tom and Sofie, and then train back the next morning.'

'You're not cooking, are you?' Denise eyed her carefully.

'I'll go to M&S first. They have some really good ready meals.'

'Good girl. You don't want to put little Sofie off for life.'

Jay wondered if she should do a cooking course of some sort. The domestic gene seemed to have passed her by and, unlike the rest of her family, she had trouble making even the simplest dishes. So far, Tom had been tolerant, almost amused at her amateur efforts, but if they were going to get married – they'd been unofficially engaged since July – perhaps the time had come to get her housewifely skills in order. Tom couldn't cook either, and the thought of feeding their kids – she'd already decided she'd quite like two – on nothing but takeaways didn't appeal. Her mind drifted to wonder what their kids would be like. Grossly fat if she didn't learn to cook. Jay resolved to look up cooking courses when she returned from Paris.

Before she headed for bed she made sure she had all the phone numbers she needed to cancel her appointments the next day. Nick, her boss, wouldn't be happy at her sudden change in plans, but then she remembered Blake and Nick knew each other from previous lives. Apparently, they'd done an op together near Tripoli years ago, but what sort of op, she'd never found out. All Blake had said when she'd asked him about it was that it had been 'hot', and Nick hadn't been any more forthcoming. He'd simply said, 'Messy,' and had changed the subject by asking her when she was going to set a wedding date – a subject guaranteed to distract her.

Blake wasn't just tight-lipped about his past. He was tight-lipped about everything. What she knew of his family, girlfriends, friends, she could write on a pinhead. Except now she knew he had a sister; Emilie, who was in hospital. Jay climbed into bed, switched out the light. The familiar sounds of London drifted through her open window: cars starting up, buses groaning down Fulham Road, airplanes coming to land at Heathrow. She wondered what Emilie did and if she was, like her brother, employed by the Security Services. Jay drifted into sleep thinking she'd quite like to meet Blake's sister.

She awoke to the sound of a blackbird singing. Rolling over, she plucked her mobile phone off her bedside table to see her internal alarm clock had kicked in three minutes before the alarm was due to sound. Nice to know some army instincts were still alive.

She showered quickly, pulling on her usual uniform of skinny jeans, stretchy sweater, and a pair of cosy, sheepskin-lined boots. A pair of hooped earrings followed, and a jade heart pendant Tom had given her for Christmas that nestled in the hollow of her throat. A lick of mascara, some lip gloss, and she was good to go.

It didn't take long to cross London for St Pancras, nor to collect her Eurostar tickets. Come seven a.m. she was leaning back in her business premier seat and watching London slide past. She could get used to this sort of travel, she thought, tucking greedily into breakfast. Smoked salmon, fresh ciabatta, croissant, butter, a little pot of marmalade, and coffee on tap. It certainly beat grabbing a takeaway doughnut and a cappuccino served in Styrofoam.

Jay sent Blake a text to let him know she was en route, then wondered if he still used the same number. They'd had no contact since he'd left for Brazil five months ago. The fact he hadn't telephoned her, but had turned up at Tom's house, continued to bother her.

The remainder of the journey was spent making calls and rearranging her week. Frustrating, but the sting was eased by her luxurious surroundings. Clever Blake . . . and even cleverer of him to give her a huge wad of euros, the size of which made her eyes water. She wasn't going to have to travel by the Métro when she hit Paris, but could take a taxi – which, she supposed, had been Blake's plan. Thumbing through the euro bills, she reckoned she could live happily in Paris for a week, no expense spared. Shame she had to return that afternoon. She loved Paris.

The Café de la Poste was set in the heart of the Marais, a residential area comprised of medieval, narrow streets and winding alleyways, and was typical of the area, with tables and chairs on the pavement, tucked beneath gas-burning heaters, and a team of languorous waiting staff who served their clientele at a snail's pace. Jay had been there for ten minutes, and nobody had yet taken her order. She checked her watch again. Sol was five minutes late. She didn't know if he had her mobile number, but she put her phone on the table next to the ashtray, easy to grab, just in case.

She was thinking about going inside and chivvying a waiter when a man approached the café. He wore jeans and a blue jacket, tan belt, and leather shoes. Despite his casual air, his eyes flicked over the pedestrians, the vehicles driving past, the elderly man and his dog crossing the road. He was alert, constantly aware of everything around him. Immediately, she knew he was Blake's contact. He looked as fit and lean as a wolf.

His eyes travelled over her, seemingly without recognition, and for a moment she thought he was going to walk straight past, but at the last second he pulled out the chair beside her – facing the street – and sat down.

'Jay,' he said.

He didn't offer a hand for her to shake. Just studied her with a steady grey gaze.

'Solomon Neill,' she said.

'Sol.'

'Sol,' she repeated.

He gave a nod. She guessed he was military, or ex-military, not just from his erect bearing, but from his haircut, shorn close to his scalp. While she surveyed him, he did the same, his gaze travelling from her boots and up five feet ten inches to her wavy, conker-coloured hair. She took after her grandmother in looks, tall and athletic, and her father in character, fiercely independent and strong minded.

He said, 'Max tells me he trusts you with his life.'

'As I trust him.'

Another nod. 'Impeccable credentials.'

Since she had no idea what the meeting was about, she didn't say any more. It was up to Sol to take the lead. A moped buzzed past, its rider shaking out a leg, indicating his muscles were stiff. The sun had warmed a little, and Jay leaned back, but she couldn't enjoy the heat on her cheeks. She was tense, and would be until she knew what was happening.

'You ordered yet?' Sol asked.

She shook her head.

'Slow service, huh.'

'Very.'

'You mind chasing them up? I'd quite like a coffee today, rather than next week.'

Jay cut him a glance. He didn't seem to be the type to expect a woman to jump to do his bidding, but she wasn't going to quibble. This wasn't a normal meeting. 'Sure,' she said. Handbag over her shoulder, she stepped inside the café. Not a single waiter looked her way. She had to stand virtually on top of one man before he took any notice. After ordering, she returned to her seat.

'Do you know Max's sister, Emilie?' asked Sol.

'No.'

'She's pretty sick.'

'So Max said.'

Sol reached into his breast pocket and popped on a pair of sunglasses. 'I wanted to marry Emilie, but she fell in love with someone else.'

Jay couldn't think what to say to this, and opted for silence.

'That's why I'm here.' He turned his head, but although he appeared to be looking straight at her, she couldn't see his eyes behind his glasses. 'For Emilie.'

Jay gave a nod to show she'd heard.

'And the others.'

She wanted to ask what he meant, but at that moment Sol's phone gave a chirp, indicating he had a message.

He passed it across so he could see. *Just arrived in Paris. See you in 30. Max.*

The muscles in his face were tight. 'He doesn't say anything about Emilie.'

'You could ask him.'

'No.' Sol held up a hand. 'He'll be here shortly. He can talk me through it.'

Sol withdrew. Jay let him be. Their coffee arrived, but Sol didn't touch his. He was staring down the road, but she didn't think he was seeing anything. Talk about a man with much on his mind.

A small boy, no more than eight, came to their table. He didn't say anything, just passed Sol a note and ran off. Sol frowned as he read it. He pocketed the note. Rose to his feet. He said, 'Back in a minute.'

Jay watched him walk to the side of the café and disappear around the corner.

Keep an eye on him, Jay. Blake's words echoed in her mind.

Jay flung some euros on the table. Grabbed her phone and shoved it in her handbag. Set off after him. She rounded the corner, but Sol was nowhere to be seen. Her heartbeat picked up. Blake had entrusted her with his friend. Where was he? She kept walking, turning her head from side to side, studying the pedestrians, occupants of cars. No Sol.

Fifteen yards along, she paused at the entrance to an alley, glanced inside. Saw two figures, just yards away. It took a moment for her brain to process what it was seeing.

Sol was sprawled on cobblestones. He appeared to be unconscious. A lithe blonde woman was bent over him. She had what appeared to be a stiletto in her hand. It looked custom-made, with a bone handle and four inches of needle-sharp steel. Jay took a breath and opened her mouth, a shout forming in her throat, and at the same time the woman rammed the stiletto behind Sol's ear and into his skull.

THREE

Jay's shouts reverberated against the brickwork. 'Stop! STOP!'

But it was too late.

The woman glanced at Jay. She withdrew the stiletto.

The alley was a dead end. The woman would have to get past Jay in order to flee.

Jay braced herself as the woman rushed towards her. She didn't want her to get away. Her heart was thudding, her pulse rocketing. Every sense was heightened. She could see the woman's dark roots, showing she dyed her hair. The gold chain around her neck. The tiny mole at the corner of her mouth. Her man's watch. Its sturdy brown leather strap.

The woman hissed as she ran.

Jay kept her eyes on the stiletto.

At the last second the woman dived left. Jay lunged after her. The woman was fast – much faster than Jay – and lashed out, kicking Jay's right leg from beneath her. She followed this with a karate blow to her throat, which Jay managed to deflect. Off-balance, dropping to her knees, Jay felt her hair being grabbed, and the next instant her head exploded with pain.

The woman had rammed her skull against the alley wall.

Dazed, Jay slumped forward. She heard the soft rush of feet as the woman ran away. She heaved herself upright and staggered to the road. Saw the woman climbing into a taxi. It was too far to read the number plate. As the taxi drove away, an arm appeared out of the rear window. The woman was waving goodbye.

Bitch.

Jay stumbled for Sol.

He wasn't breathing. She couldn't feel his heartbeat, or a pulse.

Oh, sweet Jesus.

Fingers fumbling, she pulled out her mobile phone. Dialled 112. Asked for an ambulance. Asked for the police. Gave the operator directions.

Then she tilted Sol's head back, pinched his nose, and started resuscitation. She gave five full breaths fast before checking his pulse.

Nothing.

Quickly, she found the lower end of his breastbone. Found the midline. Placed the heel of her left hand on his chest. Interlocked the fingers of both her hands and began compressions, counting out loud.

The last time I did this, she thought, *I was on a sodding training exercise in Wales.*

No rain here, though. Just an unmoving body sprawled on cold cobblestones. Blake's friend. She couldn't, *wouldn't*, let him die.

Fifteen compressions. Two breaths. Fifteen compressions. Two breaths.

After a minute, she checked his pulse.

Nothing.

Come on, Sol! Don't give up!

Fifteen compressions. Two breaths.

In the distance, she heard the wail of a siren. *Please God, let it be the ambulance.*

Fifteen compressions. Two breaths.

She didn't stop until a paramedic caught her hands and drew them aside. While he bent over Sol, checking his breathing, another checked his pulse. She scrambled sideways, rose unsteadily to her feet. She said, '*Une femme l'a attaqué.* A woman attacked him. *Elle a utilisé –*' Jay fumbled with her French for the word 'stiletto' – '*un stylet.*' She then told them the woman had shoved the stiletto into the base of his skull.

One of the paramedics glanced at her, shocked, but the other

tilted Sol's head slightly, took a look. He swore. *'Merde.'* His
fingers came away with a tiny smear of blood.

She began to tremble as she watched them work. Her fingers
felt numb. The van's blue lights continued to twirl above its
insignia – SAMU, *Service d'Aide Medicale Urgent* – making
people stare as they walked past. Not long afterwards, the police
arrived in a rush. They paused at the alley entrance when they
saw Sol, the paramedics' concentration.

Finally, the paramedics leaned back. Shook their heads.
'Desolé, Madame,' they said. *So sorry.*

Jay felt as though she was having an out-of-body experience. She'd travelled to Paris to meet a friend of Blake's, a
good friend, and he was dead. Murdered on her watch.

She covered her eyes with her hands.

The police moved in. Began taping the area. Walkie-talkies
spat and crackled. The atmosphere became brisk.

'Madame?' It was one of the cops. He moved her out of the
alley. Began asking questions. He spoke in French, but when
she stumbled with the language – she wasn't entirely fluent –
he switched to English. Jay answered him as accurately as she
could, but her mind was woolly, her head throbbing from being
smacked against the wall.

No, she didn't know the woman who had attacked Sol. No,
she didn't know if Sol knew the woman. No, she'd never seen
the woman before.

She was describing the woman's dyed hair when two men
muscled their way into the alley. They wore suits and reflec-
tive sunglasses and expected the cops to defer. Jay's spirits
sank. She knew the type. She'd met enough of them.
Government agents. The paramedics let the agents search Sol's
body, recovering his wallet, his phone, and the note the boy
had given him. There was lots of talk between the agents and
the police and paramedics. A gendarme began photographing
the body.

The two agents backed out of the alley. Came and stood in
front of Jay. Showed her their badges: DCRI, *Direction Centrale
du Renseignement Intérieur*, the French equivalent of MI5. The
larger one was called Mafart; the smaller, with a pointy beard
the colour of consommé, Prideaux.

'Please, Madame.' Mafart indicated a black Audi parked
behind the ambulance. 'If you wouldn't mind coming with us.'

'A friend is on his way,' she told them. 'Can we wait for him? He's a friend of Sol's. The dead man.' She glanced at her watch, to see that barely twenty minutes had elapsed since Blake had texted her. It felt much longer. 'He should be at the Café de la Poste shortly.'

'His name?'

She could see no reason not to tell him. 'Max Blake.'

Mafart walked to one of the cops, had a word. Came back. 'The police will wait for him. They will bring him to us.'

Before she climbed into the rear of the DCRI vehicle, she scanned the street. Three cop cars, the agents' Audi, and the ambulance. A crowd had formed on the opposite side of the street. She couldn't see Blake anywhere.

Prideaux joined her on the rear seat. Mafart started the car, pulled out. Neither man spoke.

She leaned her head against the headrest to feel a bruise had already formed, continued to throb. The journey felt surreal. The silence inside the car, the way Mafart drove uncompromisingly fast, with his hand on the horn. They passed the *Gare du L'est* in a flash, barrelling north-east. Instead of turning off on the *Boulevard Périphérique* – the inner ring road – as she expected, Mafart pushed north on the same road, past the airport. As the city fell away, Jay felt the first inkling that something was wrong.

'Where are we going?' she asked. The last sign had read *Senlis*, which was well north of the city.

'Our debriefing office is outside Paris,' Prideaux said smoothly. 'Sorry it's taking so long. If you want something to read, there's a magazine in the pocket in front of you . . .'

He leaned across as if to show her a magazine, and at the same time he brought up his right hand and plunged something into her right thigh.

'Ow!' She reared back. 'What the hell . . .?'

Prideaux withdrew a hypodermic needle. 'Goodnight, Ms McCaulay.'

Jay reached for the door handle, but her movement was futile. Her hands were already so heavy that she couldn't lift them. Her legs too leaden to move.

Her last thought before the world turned black was that Tom would be furious when she was late for supper that night.

*　*　*

Jay tried to open her eyes.

They were taped shut.

Fear rushed through her.

Mafart and Prideaux. What was going on?

She told herself to forget about the agents. She had to concentrate on the here and the now. Her survival.

She reached up to remove the tape.

Our debriefing office is outside Paris.

Shut up, she told herself, battling to stop her fear from blossoming into full-blown panic.

Focus. Assess the situation.

Her hands were shackled together with what felt like plasticuffs. Her feet were free.

She felt groggy. She didn't know what Prideaux had injected her with, but it had worked incredibly quickly. She wondered how long she'd been unconscious.

She peeled back the tape from across her eyes. It was pitch dark. She could see nothing. As she moved, she heard a chinking sound. Her cuffs were attached to a chain. She pulled on the chain, but it held fast. On her hands and knees, she tracked it to find she was locked to what felt like a brick wall. The distinctive shape of a large padlock made her spirits plummet even further.

Her body was sluggish, but she forced herself to her feet. As she breathed, she became aware of a thick stench. Oddly, it reminded her of Norfolk, when the wind blew from the south and across the pig farms. Was it pigs she could smell? Or something else?

Wherever she was, it was icy cold and damp. She shivered.

Think! How are you going to get out of here?

Again, she checked the ring on the wall. No way could she pull free.

Her hands were tied, but her feet were unbound . . . A plan sprang to mind.

Pretend you never regained consciousness. Play dead. And when they get close enough, kick them, knock them to the ground. Snatch the key to the padlock, free yourself . . .

Although part of her knew this scenario was unlikely, it was the only plan she could come up with, so she manoeuvred herself back to the ground. Scrabbled around until she felt the tape. Carefully, she placed it back over her eyes.

What position had she woken in? She tried to remember. On her right side. Knees drawn up.

She practised a couple of times until she was sure she could get into position quickly. Then she rose and quietly began pacing. She needed to keep her body moving. Keep it warm and ready for action. Keep a clear head. She tried to keep track of time, but it was impossible in the dark. Eventually, perhaps two hours later, she thought she heard something. Footsteps echoed in the darkness. Had she imagined them?

She froze.

They were faint at first, but gradually became louder.

Fear flooded her.

It sounded like two people. Prideaux and Mafart? Quick. She had to get into position.

Jay tumbled to the ground. Wriggled on to her right side. Drew up her knees. Made sure the tape was firmly over her eyes. She didn't want to risk her captors being alerted she might be awake.

She concentrated on steadying her breathing.

Be still. Don't move.

She heard a bolt being snapped back. The sound of the door opening.

Her heart thumped as someone stepped inside.

Quiet, quiet. Steady breaths.

She heard a click. The blackness behind her tape turned to brown. She guessed a light had been switched on.

Footsteps crossed the room. Quick and light. She smelled something cloying and sweet, like rotting honeysuckle. A brush of fabric told Jay someone was crouching beside her. She had to force herself not to hold her breath in fright, but continue to breathe gently, in and out. In and out.

'Shit. She's still out of it.' A woman's voice, exotic and husky. She sounded irritated.

'Leave her,' a man said. 'I'll check on her later.'

Jay nearly jumped when she felt a pair of cool fingers settle against her neck, checking her pulse.

'Strong and steady,' the woman purred. 'Just how I like it. Shall I leave her some reading material? Get her in the mood?'

'You can leave her with a picture of the French president naked, for all I care. Come on, Nahid. It's bloody cold down here.'

'Promise you won't play with her until I get back tomorrow?'

'I promise.' He sounded weary, as though he'd been asked this a hundred times before.

Jay hastily reviewed her options. Quickly decided it would be better to wait until the man returned alone than take them both on now.

'She intrigues me,' the woman said. She was still crouched over Jay. 'Her passport shows she's travelled to Kosovo and Macedonia. Do you think she's a spook?'

'She might be.'

'Was she a friend of Neill's, do you think? Was that why she was there? Or is she something else? Something more dangerous?'

'We'll find out soon enough,' the man responded.

'She tried to stop me leaving the alley.'

'So you said.'

'It's not often I come across a woman like her. I want to get to know her. See what makes her tick. What her darkest fears are. I wonder which she'll fear more: losing her sight or her speech? I want to know, Tivon.' Her voice rose impatiently.

'Soon,' said Tivon.

'Soon,' Nahid murmured.

There came the sound of paper being rifled. Jay couldn't think what the woman was doing.

'There,' Nahid said. She sounded satisfied. 'I've put my favourites in the middle.'

'Very nice,' the man said neutrally.

Jay had to force herself not to recoil when the woman brushed her lips against Jay's cheek.

'Sweet dreams.' Her voice was a husky whisper. 'My sleeping beauty.'

Nahid's feather-light footsteps tapped away.

The instant Jay heard the door close, the bolts slide into place, she tore off the tape. It took a few seconds for her eyes to adjust to the light from a single bare bulb, dangling from the ceiling. She was in a windowless room. Bare cobbles covered the floor. Bare brick walls with half a dozen metal rings. Mould grew from the mortar between the bricks. Was that what she could smell?

Then she took in the photographs laid before her. Snapshots of people. All naked. Men and women, a couple of children.

They were bruised and battered, their faces shattered and bloody. Skin had been flayed, and limbs broken. There was the occasional flash of creamy white where a bone poked through torn flesh. There was a lot of blood.

Jay closed her eyes.

Nausea rushed through her.

Dear God. Please don't let these be real.

Shall I leave her with some reading material? Get her in the mood?

Calming herself, she opened her eyes. She made an effort to lock her emotions in a box inside her and look at the photographs with a dispassionate eye. Swallowing, she ran her eyes over them. There were forty-three pictures. None of them appeared to be of the same person.

She couldn't look at the ones of the children.

In the centre were two larger photographs, which had been enlarged. One was of a man who had had his eyes sewn shut. The other was of a woman who had had her lips sewn together.

I wonder which she'll fear more: losing her sight or her speech?

Fear roared through her veins. She couldn't help the whimper that escaped.

Shit.

She was in trouble.

Big trouble.

She had to get out of there.

FOUR

Sofie Lore looked out of the window for the umpteenth time, but the car she'd heard pull up on the street wasn't Tom's. She knew he worked hard – he was a policeman, a detective inspector – but even so. It wasn't like they saw loads of each other, and she'd expected him to be a bit keener and get himself home on time, if not before.

Wrong.

Sighing, she turned back to her room. God, it sucked. She'd put a couple of posters up to try and make it feel a bit more like home, but she might as well have tried to wallpaper a cow barn. What a dump. The sooner Tom and her mum got back together, the better. Then Tom could move into their nice big house near Dyrham Park, and she wouldn't have to stay here any longer. Also, she wouldn't have to leave her cat Smokey behind either. She missed Smokey's furry warmth on her bed at night. Where was Tom? God, she was bored. Restless, she moved back to the window.

How on earth did people live here? Twin rows of identical houses facing one another across an identical patch of lawn. It was so unimaginative, so *dull*. What did her father see in the place? She knew he had to live close to the centre of Bristol because he worked there, but couldn't he have found somewhere nicer? Odd that she didn't think of her father as dad, or daddy, but as Tom. She called him daddy though, because he seemed to like it. Her mum did too.

Sofie wondered what bridesmaid's dress she'd wear at their wedding. She liked pink, but it might be a bit too cutesy. Yellow, maybe? Her mind drifted, and it was only when a tall figure unlatched the gate at the end of the front path that she came to.

Tom, she thought. At last!

She ran down the stairs and swung open the door just before he could put his key inside the lock.

'Sofie?' He looked startled.

'Hi, Daddy.' She beamed. He really was the most fantastic father you could wish for. Tall, good looking, and as easy-going as she could want. Not like her mum, who was a complete control freak.

Her mum had never kept Tom a secret, and had told Sofie she could contact him when she was older – maybe eighteen or so – but Sofie hadn't seen any need. He'd sounded pretty awful the way her mum had described him. Not that she'd *meant* to make him sound awful, but Sofie could read between the lines, no problem. They'd gone out for six months, apparently, while her mum was at uni, studying for her law finals. Tom had been a couple of years younger and a bit of a tearaway, a rebel, and when he'd got in trouble with the police – wasn't that an irony considering he was now a cop! – her mum had decided enough was enough and had finished the relationship.

He was a nice guy, she remembered her mum saying. *Handsome and smart, but he was too wild for me. I was destined to be a lawyer, and there he was, getting arrested for fighting . . .*

The month after her mum split from Tom, she'd discovered she was pregnant, but she'd never had any doubts about keeping Sofie.

I loved you the moment I knew you existed.

Tom had popped up in their lives in the summer, when Sofie had fallen ill with a heart-valve disease and the doctors had needed to know the family history. At least being sick had had some positive points. She now had a real-live father.

'Is Heather here?' Tom asked. The puzzled expression was still on his face.

'Mum couldn't stay. She said to say hi.'

'How long have you been here?'

'Oh, a couple of hours. You gave me a house key, remember?'

'You're alone?' He looked horrified.

'It's OK, Daddy. I'm twelve, not two. Mum leaves me alone all the time.'

'Does she?' He looked doubtful.

'Yup. It's fine, honestly. I do puzzles on the computer and things. I love puzzles.'

He leaned down, and she reached up, letting him scoop her into a hug.

'When's Jay coming?' She purposely kept her tone light, not wanting her father to know she wasn't looking forward to meeting his girlfriend.

He twisted his wrist to look at his watch. 'She's due any time now.'

Sofie ducked her head out of the door and looked up and down the street. 'I can't see anyone.'

'I'll text her.' He smiled. 'She'd better not be late. She's bringing supper.'

Sofie followed Tom down the hall, watched him drop his briefcase to one side and kick off his shoes. He pulled out his mobile and dialled. 'Hey gorgeous,' he said. 'Sofie and I are at home . . . Are you on your way? We're getting hungry.' He sang the word *hungry,* making Sofie smile. He hung up and yawned. 'Now,' he said. 'I'm going to get a beer. What would you like?'

I'd like you to chuck Jay and marry Mum, she thought.

Instead, she said, 'An apple juice would be great.' Then, 'Is Jay usually late?'

'Sometimes. Not always.'

'Mummy's never late.'

'Jay usually has a good reason,' he responded. 'She'll be here, don't worry.'

However, when Jay still hadn't turned up come seven p.m., and they had to eat a make-do supper of baked beans on toast, Tom was frowning.

'Perhaps she forgot about us?' Sofie said. She wanted to start putting doubts in his mind about his *gorgeous* girlfriend, but Tom looked at Sofie so hard for a moment that she thought he could read her mind.

'She wouldn't forget,' he said. 'She wanted to meet you, remember? Tonight was her idea.'

'Maybe she got caught up with something more important,' she said.

'Maybe she did.' Tom's expression turned distant. 'I hope she's all right.'

FIVE

Two hours passed before Jay heard footsteps echoing, rapidly increasing, coming her way.

She glanced at her watch. Six p.m. local time. Please God it was Tivon. Just Tivon.

She flinched at the metallic thud of bolts being drawn back. Quick. She had to be quick.

Jay wriggled on to her side. Pushed the tape back over her eyes. She didn't disturb the photographs.

The door opened. Someone stepped inside the room.

The footsteps come closer. Just one set this time. Nahid or Tivon?

'Ah, shit,' Tivon said.

Be still. Still. Still.

Her heart pounded as he approached.

'You awake?' He prodded her with what she guessed was the tip of his shoe.

I am a corpse, she told herself. *I am dead, dead, dead.*

'Shit,' he said again.

Sweat prickled her hairline, the base of her spine.

A small pop as a joint cracked. He was bending down to check on her.

Come closer, she willed.

She breathed steadily. Her mouth was open, her lips slack.

He touched her neck with his fingers, checking for a pulse.

Don't move. Don't move.

His knee cracked again. He was kneeling beside her.

Her heart thumped louder.

'Hey, wake up.'

He lightly slapped her face.

'Wake the fuck up, will you?'

He slapped her face again, harder.

Don't move!

She felt his fingers on her face, picking at the corner of the tape across her eyes.

Wait. Wait.

He stripped back the tape.

Jay's eyes snapped open.

She sprang for him, ramming her cuffs into his throat and toppling him backwards, slamming his head against the floor.

He was so surprised his eyes bulged. His mouth opened into a huge O.

Jay didn't hesitate. She grabbed his hair – nice and thick – and slammed his head against the cobblestones again and again and again.

His eyes rolled back, showing the whites. His body went limp, but she couldn't help herself. She slammed his skull three more times against the cobbles before she got herself under control. She was gasping, her adrenalin in full flow.

'Shit, shit,' she said. 'Shit.'

She was shaking violently, her pulse rocketing.

The keys.

She fumbled through Tivon's clothes. Found a jumbled variety of keys on a brass ring.

OK, OK. Which one was it?

She tried the first key in the padlock. Didn't fit.

Fingers trembling, terrified Tivon was going to wake, she tried the next.

No luck.

Third time lucky.

The key slid into the padlock smoothly. Jay turned it. The lock sprang free.

Immediately, she stumbled for the door. Stepped outside and shut the door behind her. Slammed home the bolts.

She was still cuffed. She had to find something to break the plastic. A wire cutter or cigarette lighter would do. The corridor was dotted with pieces of straw and manure. She increased her pace. Came to a door. Opened it.

Suddenly, she was outside. In a farmyard. More straw, more manure.

Darkness had fallen, but the sky was clear. A rising moon shed enough light for her to make out the shapes of buildings and fences.

She looked for a car, but couldn't see one.

Fuck it.

She wanted to break into a run, get as far away as she could, but she needed to get rid of the cuffs. She also needed a phone. Was there one in the farmhouse?

She crossed the yard. Peered into one of the windows.

All was dark. Silent.

Jay tried the front door. Unlocked. She slipped inside and paused, listening. Could she risk turning on a light? Cautiously, she crept down a flagstone corridor, checking each room she passed. Nobody seemed to be there. She fumbled for a light switch. Holding her breath, she flipped it on, ready to flee, to fight . . .

Nothing happened.

Jay moved fast.

The first room she came to was a sitting room. Overstuffed sofa and armchairs. A big TV. No phone.

The second room was empty, along with the third. At the end of the corridor, she came to a kitchen. When she saw what was on the table, her heart lifted.

Her handbag.

Everything inside appeared intact. Her phone, her passport, her driver's licence and credit cards.

Call Blake. Call for help.

She grabbed her phone. Pressed the 'on' switch, but nothing happened. The battery was dead.

Slinging her bag over her head and across her chest, she began opening drawers. No wire cutters. No cigarette lighter.

Sweating, heart knocking, she moved down the corridor and into a boot room. A coil of garden wire lay on top of an ancient dresser. She pulled open the top drawer to see a jumble of hammers and nails, garden twine, and a small pair of secateurs.

Perfect.

With two snips, her hands were free.

She hesitated, listening for the slightest sounds.

Don't hang around. Run.

She tore out of the house. Turned away from the rutted, muddy drive – she didn't want to meet Nahid head on – and started running. She didn't care which way she went. The fields were muddy, slowing her down, but she kept plugging away.

The third field she came to was full of pigs. Big white pigs, some asleep on their sides, some already tucked up in their wooden shelters. That explained the smell. . . .

Jay skirted the pig field, swinging west. Occasionally, she glanced over her shoulder at the farm, checking to make sure nobody was following. The area was almost flat, barely undulating. She felt as exposed as a beetle on a bed sheet.

She kept running.

After half an hour she halted. Put her hands on her waist and let herself catch her breath.

The farmhouse was still visible. She wondered if she'd killed Tivon. She hadn't seen any blood, but that didn't mean she hadn't cracked open his skull. She'd been so frightened, she'd completely overreacted . . .

Her pulse leaped when she saw a car's headlights appear like pinpricks in the distance.

Oh, God.

The car came closer. Swung into the farmyard. Switched out its lights.

A figure appeared. It was too far away to see properly, but from the light, almost ethereal, way the figure moved she could guess who it was.

Nahid.

There were no hedges for Jay to hide behind. No ditches or woods or forests. It was an arable wasteland.

She could do nothing but run.

Across the next field . . . Up an incline and into another field, this one boggier and harder to negotiate because it had been ploughed. She was forced into a walk. The next field was firmer, covered in soggy stubble. Doggedly, she kept running until she ran out of breath and was forced to walk once more. Run, walk. Run, walk.

A pair of headlights cut the darkness in the distance ahead, and then vanished.

Fear made Jay pause. She stood still, every sense alert, aware. Another pair of headlights followed. Then another.

Thank God. It was a road.

When Jay stumbled on to the tarmac, she had mud up to her knees and was exhausted.

She held up a hand to the first vehicle and waved.

An old Renault pulled up. A round-faced man with a scruffy little dog sitting in his passenger seat rolled down his window. '*Aidez moi*,' Jay said. *Please, help me.*

The man's name was Michel Fuduli, his dog's Aceline, which apparently meant 'noble'. They both were, she told them sincerely, very noble for stopping and giving her a lift.

'No problem,' said Michel in French, looking pleased. 'Aceline likes you.'

Aceline was now sitting in the footwell, looking disgruntled at being booted off the passenger seat. When Michel asked where Jay was going, she avoided answering. She didn't want to leave Nahid and Tivon a trail to follow.

'*J'ai besoin d'un téléphone*,' Jay said. She explained her battery was dead.

Michel passed her his mobile. Waved at her to go ahead, as long as she wasn't going to call Australia.

'*Non. Il s'agit d'un appel local*,' she assured him. *It's local.*

After ascertaining where Michel could drop her – at a village called Ully St Georges – she made a call.

'It's me,' she said when he answered. 'Can you come and get me?'

'Where are you?' His tone was clipped.

Using Michel's local knowledge, she organized a rendezvous at a bus stop in the village. Passed back the phone. '*Merci, Michel.*'

SIX

Blake arrived in a Mercedes sports coupé. He wrapped her in his arms and held her close.

He said, 'Hon.'

'She scared the crap out of me.' She began to shake at the memory. 'She left me a bunch of photographs. One guy had his eyes sewn shut . . .'

He led her to the car. Made sure she was buckled up. Switched on the engine, and turned up the heating.

She continued to gabble. 'Two men who said they were from the DCRI took me and knocked me out with some kind of drug. I woke in a stable. I was tied to the wall . . . Her name's Nahid. She wondered if I was a spook, or something more dangerous. She said she wanted . . .'

She couldn't say the words.

I wonder which she'll fear more: losing her sight or her speech?

He said, 'It's OK.'

She took a breath. Calmed herself. She was safe now.

Blake switched on the satnav screen. 'Describe them,' he said.

Detailing Nahid wasn't a problem, but Tivon was more difficult. All she could recall was his thick black hair and the way his eyes had rolled back in his head when he'd lost consciousness. 'Swarthy,' she said. 'Mediterranean. Middle Eastern. Hard to say, I was so busy bashing his head against the floor.'

'Way to go,' he said approvingly. Then, 'Which farm?'

She peered around the village. 'I came in from over there –' she pointed south – 'and since we drove about two miles to get here . . .'

Jay calmed as Blake talked her through her escape – the direction she'd initially taken, the fields she'd crossed – until they'd pinpointed the correct property.

'Shall we call the police?' she asked.

'Not yet.'

She looked at the side of his face. 'Why not?'

'It's complicated.' He put the car into drive and pulled out.

'Like how?'

'Sol.' He said the name quietly.

'Max, I'm sorry . . .' She put Nahid and Tivon aside as she tried to work out how to break the news that she'd messed up. That she'd let him – and Sol – down.

'Sol's dead,' Blake said before she could speak. It wasn't a question.

'Yes.' She swallowed. 'How did you know?'

'I was part of the crowd opposite the alley.'

'I didn't see you.'

'You weren't supposed to.'

Blake paused briefly at the next crossroads before accelerating across. They were, she saw, north-west of Chantilly and barely an hour's drive from the centre of Paris.

'I'm sorry,' she said. Her voice was small.

'You saw the assassin?'

Jay remembered what Nahid had said in the stable. *Was she a friend of Neill's? Or is she something more dangerous . . . She tried to stop me leaving the alley.*

'I'm pretty sure the assassin and Nahid are the same woman.'

Blake mulled this over for a second before asking, 'Is your phone on?'

'No. The battery's dead. You think they might try to track me?'

'Yup.'

'Is that why you didn't ring me, but turned up at Tom's? So you couldn't be tracked?'

He glanced at her. 'I could have used a phone box to ring you.'

'So why—'

'I had to give you the tickets, the cash. Brief you.'

She suddenly realized her not going to Paris had never been an option.

It didn't take long before they reached the outskirts of Paris, and Jay thought the city had never looked more beautiful. There was nothing like having a near-death experience to heighten one's appreciation of a place. Thanks to the car's efficient climate control system – as well as its heated seats – her jeans were finally drying out. She'd have to give them a good wash later. They smelled of pigs.

She glanced at the clock on the dashboard. Seven thirty p.m. Six thirty p.m. in England. Had it only been twelve hours since she'd left London? It felt as though she'd been away – on the run – for a week. Then she remembered what she was supposed to be doing this evening. Where she was supposed to be *right now*.

Shit.

'I have to call Tom,' she said.

'How urgent?'

'Very.'

He passed her his phone. 'Be quick.'

She tried to remember Tom's mobile number. She never dialled it. Just used speed dial, or picked him out from her list of 'most recently used' numbers.

Feeling stupid, she said, 'I have to look it up.'

'Try this charger.'

He flipped open the central console and withdrew a lead, along with an assortment of connectors. To Jay's relief, one fitted her phone. She watched the screen come alive. Hastily, she scrolled to Contacts. Pressed T, for Tom. He wasn't there. She looked again. Did a double take. She didn't recognize any of the numbers.

'Max . . .' She passed him the phone. 'They're not mine.'

At the next lights he had a quick look. 'They're Sol's,' he said.

She stared.

'You left him with your phone,' Blake said. 'He must have switched SIM cards.'

Jay remembered going to chivvy the recalcitrant waiting staff at the café. She'd taken her handbag with her, but not her phone, which had been on the café table. With Sol.

'Yes,' she said.

It had been Sol who'd told her to try and rustle up some service. Had he planned the swap earlier? How would he have known he could gain access to her phone? Or had the swap merely been opportunistic?

'Did he swap memory cards?' Blake asked.

Jay had a quick look at the media gallery, the assortment of pictures stored. Once again, she didn't recognize anything. 'Yes.'

Just south of the *Gare du Nord*, they hit a traffic jam. Jay leaned back and watched a policewoman pulling cars over for trying to venture up a road that was marked for taxis only.

Blake said, 'Tell me what happened.' His voice was quiet.

She gave him every detail she could remember, from Sol's arrival at the café, to the lackadaisical waiting staff, the amount of money she'd left at the café – even which bills – and the gendarme's questions. It was as though by listing each particular point she could atone for messing up. Would he ever forgive her?

'I'm sorry,' she said again. 'I didn't follow him immediately. If I had, then maybe I could have alerted him, stopped the woman—'

Blake switched his head round. 'Stop there.'

She looked away. Her throat thickened. Tears began to rise.

'You know there are no "maybes" in our game,' he said.

Jay knew this wasn't the case. She played the "maybe" game regularly – not just over operational errors, but in her personal life as well, with Tom and Sofie. And Blake too, but she'd rather nail her foot to the floor than let him know that.

'You weren't to know a professional assassin was on Sol's tail.'

True, but it didn't stop the waves of guilt washing through her.

Gradually, the traffic began to move. They inched their way into town before sweeping west.

'Where did you get the car?' she asked.

Blake gave her one of his looks that she knew meant *don't ask*.

'Where are we going?'

'Somewhere safe.'

Somewhere safe was a beautifully appointed apartment in the heart of the 16th Arrondissement, one of the richest parts of Paris. Spacious, lofty and elegant, it had wallpaper in blues and greens, of lakes and feathery willows and long-tailed fish. The furniture was French antique, lacquered gold. There was a Louis XIV chest of drawers that could have been a copy, but Jay doubted it. The whole place reeked of old money.

Framed photographs were everywhere and featured a beautiful woman with angular features and long dark hair. One picture showed the woman and Blake at the helm of a yacht. They were tanned, and their eyes were creased with laughter. They looked happy. Out of nowhere the knife of jealousy stabbed Jay, leaving her feeling breathless. She'd never seen Blake on holiday, or seen him looking so carefree.

'Who lives here?' she asked casually.

Blake shrugged.

'Come on, Max.' The knife of jealousy made her uncharacteristically pushy. 'Tell me.'

'A friend.'

'What sort of friend?'

Blake opened a cabinet in the corner which hid a television. Using the remote, he switched on the news and wound up the volume.

Jay forgot about Blake's 'friend' when she saw the reporter was on *Rue du Temple*, a stone's throw from the alley where Sol had been murdered. He said the police were looking for a man to question, and at the same moment a picture of Blake filled the screen. It was an old photograph, slightly grainy. Blake's hair was shorn so close to his scalp that it was hard to tell his hair colour. He was squinting slightly, his expression closed. He looked dangerous and mean.

The reporter came back on the screen. He said the murder weapon had been found – an assassin's stiletto that had been rammed into the back of the victim's head – and that Blake's fingerprints were all over this stiletto. Blake was considered highly dangerous, and the public were warned against approaching him.

'They think you're the murderer?' Her voice came out high-pitched and filled with horror.

Blake held up a hand. She fell quiet until the section ended.

'But I saw her!' Jay protested. 'I told the police it was a woman!'

Blake sank on to the sofa. He was white.

'What's going on?' Jay swept to his side. Took his hand in hers. It was icy cold. She threaded her fingers through his. 'Max, talk to me.'

The gaze he sent her was blank.

'Max . . .'

In one swift movement he was on his feet. He picked up her mobile phone with Sol's SIM and memory cards still inside. 'I'll be back in an hour.'

'Max,' she protested.

'Stay here. Don't go outside.' He was looking at her, but he wasn't seeing her. 'Promise?'

She crossed her heart. 'Promise.'

And then he was gone.

Shakily, Jay rose and walked to the kitchen. Opened the fridge. Without looking at the label, she withdrew a bottle of wine. Searched the drawers until she found a corkscrew. She didn't think she'd ever needed a drink so much. Or a cigarette. Despite the fact she'd given up smoking two years ago, the urge for a hit of nicotine was almost overwhelming. Good job she didn't have any ciggies with her, or she'd have smoked the entire pack. After a couple of slugs of wine, she felt stronger. She took her wine on to the balcony. Looked at the street below, the cars scurrying like beetles around a statue of a man on a horse. Napoleon, probably.

When she finished her wine, she didn't pour another glass. She didn't want her senses to be blurred with alcohol in case Blake returned and she needed to be fully aware. Instead, she watched TV to see Blake was the hottest story in France. She wondered why a local Paris murder had been reported so extensively. Was someone pulling strings?

Using the apartment's landline, Jay called overseas directories. She couldn't access Tom's mobile or his home numbers – both were ex-directory – but his parents were listed. She spoke to Tom's mother – an active sixty-year-old addicted to golf – who rattled it off by heart.

'Jessica, when are you and Tom coming to see us again?' Tom's mother, along with her own, were the only people who could use her given name and get away with it.

'Soon,' Jay said. 'Sorry, Diana, I'm in a bit of a rush . . .'

'Of course. See you soon, OK?'

They hung up. Jay redialled.

'Sutton,' he barked.

'It's me.'

'Is this the me racing to Bristol laden with shopping bags bulging with French produce for a late, if fantastic, supper, or the me who's ringing to say something's up?'

Jay closed her eyes. Some days, she wished he didn't know her quite so well. 'The latter,' she admitted.

Silence.

'It's complicated,' she added. 'I'll be back as soon as I can.'

'But not tonight.'

'No. Sorry.'

Another silence while she imagined him rolling his eyes to the ceiling. Or tearing out his hair. Probably both.

'It's OK,' he said on a sigh. 'We had baked beans on toast.'

'I'm sorry.'

'Why can't I be engaged to a normal woman?' Tom mused. 'Someone reliable would be nice.'

'I am reliable! Well, most of the time,' she added hastily.

'Sofie was really looking forward to meeting you.'

Jay cringed. 'Sorry. I'll make it up to her, I promise.'

'Do you think you'll be here tomorrow?'

She dithered briefly before realizing any further uncertainty on her part would only reignite his irritation. She said, 'Yes.'

'We'll have a rerun. I'll let Sofie know.'

'Great.' Her shoulders slumped in relief.

'Is everything OK?' His tone changed slightly as his cop voice inched in. 'You make your Paris meeting OK?'

'Yes.' Which was true. It was only after the meeting that everything had turned pear-shaped.

'Anything I need to know about?'

'I'll tell you about it when I'm back.'

Jay hung up. She hated not telling Tom everything, but caution made her circumspect, especially regarding the fact she was with Blake. She spent the next half an hour alternately prowling through the apartment and flicking through the TV channels. She wanted to wash and dry her jeans, but didn't dare in case Blake suddenly returned and they had to go. In the kitchen she was disconcerted to see several jars of honey from around the globe: Uruguay, Mexico, Italy. Where some people collected postcards or stamps from their travels, Blake collected honey. These were gifts for the apartment's owner.

She closed the cupboard, fighting the blade of envy. Blake had asked her out on several occasions, and she'd always said no. If Tom hadn't been around she wouldn't have hesitated though. Or would she? Blake wasn't exactly great boyfriend material, whizzing off on dangerous missions around the globe at a moment's notice, and his taciturn nature would probably drive her insane. But she couldn't deny the chemistry between them. Little wonder Tom didn't trust her with Blake. Some days she had trouble trusting herself.

SEVEN

Thirty seconds before he'd said he would, Blake let himself back into the apartment. Some colour had returned to his cheeks, and this time when he looked at her, his gaze was alert and clear.

'OK?' he asked.

She gave a nod.

He padded into the kitchen and opened the fridge. 'I see you've already found the Premier Crus.' His voice was wry. 'Any good?'

'Excellent,' she lied. She hadn't tasted the wine through her anxiety, but the alcoholic content had been pretty good.

He refilled her glass, poured one for himself.

'Max, I have to go to the police. Set the record straight.'

His head jerked round. 'No,' he said.

'But I saw the assassin—'

'No,' he said again. His voice was hard.

She was opening her mouth to protest when he added quietly, 'I don't want them to come after you.'

Jay gulped.

'I want them to think you're too scared to come forward.' Hips against the counter, he added, 'It's the only way to keep you safe. Agreed?'

It went against every grain of Jay's sense of loyalty and justice, but she nodded. She didn't want to tangle with Nahid a second time. 'Won't they come after me anyway, though?'

'If you return to the UK without making a peep, they'll leave you alone.'

Somehow, his certainty didn't sit well with her. Not after what Nahid had said. *Promise you won't play with her until I get back tomorrow?*

'How come you were in Paris today?' she asked.

Blake cradled his glass against his chest. 'Emilie's in a coma. There seemed no point in staying.'

Her heart contracted. 'I'm sorry.'

'Her illness has something to do with Sol.'

'Sol told me he wanted to marry Emilie. But she fell in love with someone else.'

'True.' Blake walked into the sitting room. Picked up the photograph of him sailing with the beautiful dark-haired woman. 'Emilie's a freelance translator.' He showed Jay the picture.

The sense of relief that the woman wasn't Blake's lover, but was his sister, made Jay look away in case he could read her expression. She said, 'This flat's Emilie's?'

'It belongs to a mutual friend.'

Jay wanted to ask more about this mutual friend, but now wasn't the time.

'Emilie was on a conference with her boss in Brussels when she rang me.' He touched Emilie's face briefly before putting the picture back. 'She was in a panic over something she'd overheard. She wouldn't tell me what – she didn't trust the phone line. She mentioned the name of what she thought was a private security company, the Garrison. She was really scared . . .'

He pinched the bridge of his nose. 'Before I got to her, she fell ill. Emilie's normally in top condition . . . She's a marathon runner. But when I got to the hospital, she could barely speak. She managed to tell me that she suspected her virus had been introduced. She thought she was being murdered to stop her revealing what she'd overheard.' Blake closed his eyes. 'She lost consciousness at that point. She's remained unconscious ever since.'

'"Introduced"?' Jay repeated. She tried to keep her tone steady, but it was threaded with alarm.

'If she hadn't called me, I'd have assumed she'd caught the virus on her travels. It's the perfect assassination tool.'

Aside from a stiletto, thought Jay, but didn't say so. 'She never told you what she'd overheard?' Jay asked.

'She tried . . . but the effort was too much . . .'

She could see he was struggling to keep his emotions in check, and the urge to go to him, wrap him in her arms and hold him tight, comfort him, almost overwhelmed her. She forced herself to take her wine across the room. Sit on the sofa.

Blake moved to stand near the French windows leading to the balcony. As usual he didn't stand in full view, but to one side, the soldier in him always wary. 'Sol knew about Emilie's illness and demanded we meet to talk about it,' Blake said. 'He mentioned an antidote. A cure.'

Jay's eyes widened. 'I didn't think such a thing existed for viruses.'

'I'm just telling you what he said.' Blake rubbed his eyes. 'And the fact that he was murdered today, before he could help Emilie, means there's someone out there with a serious agenda.'

'Jesus, Max. What a snake pit.'

He came to sit next to her. When his thigh brushed hers, she shifted slightly, breaking the contact. He didn't seem to notice, just passed her a brand-new iPhone. 'Thought you could use an upgrade,' he said.

This had to be the fifth mobile phone Blake had given Jay. She wondered if he had shares in the company.

'Nice,' she said admiringly. 'Now I can get emails on the hoof as well as weather reports around the world.'

'I've copied Sol's stuff on to it.'

'But—'

'If someone wants to track you they won't have your new number, so you'll be safe.' He scrolled through Sol's contacts list. Unlike Jay's, which had had over two hundred entries, Sol's was succinct, with only twenty.

'I don't know any of these names,' Blake said. 'Only three numbers are operative – Richard Walsh, Rachel Jones and Eddie Wright – but none of them are answering. The other numbers are all disconnected.'

'Sol didn't have your number stored?'

'He did, but under another name. He was taking precautions.'

'Which one?'

Blake pointed.

'Cuba?' she said.

'I used to smoke Cohibas.'

'Where did you guys meet?'

'Training.'

Jay turned and studied the side of his face. 'What sort of training?' she prodded.

He gave an infinitesimal shrug and remained silent.

'Like advanced driving training?' she said, continuing to needle him. 'Or training to be a chef? Or perhaps it was dog training?'

A flicker of a smile reached his eyes. 'Survival training in Belize.'

'Thank you.' She smiled sweetly.

He flipped menus. 'There are a lot of photos. And music.'

The photographs were of paintings, CD covers, and a handful of sculptures. One in particular caught her eye. 'Wow,' she said.

'Hmmm.'

They studied the life-sized polar bear, which appeared to have been hewn from white marble. Its outlines were smooth, the carriage of its head low and predatory. Jay took the phone and flicked through the pictures again. She recognized two paintings by Monet, but the others, mostly eighteenth century, were unknown to her.

'Was Sol into art?' she asked.

'About as much as I am.'

She rolled her eyes at him. 'Which means?'

'As much as the next person.' He was frowning. 'I wonder if they're a code of some sort.'

Jay scrolled through the photographs again, and then the pieces of music: Robbie Williams, Mozart, Lily Allen and Beethoven. It was an eclectic mix.

'Any ideas?' she asked.

He shook his head. Stretched. 'I'm going to make supper. We'll leave for London tomorrow morning. Rush hour. Safety in numbers.'

Although Jay wasn't hungry, she knew Blake wouldn't take no for an answer. He believed in not just fuel for the body, but for the mind. Today he served seared steak with a pink peppercorn sauce and a freshly tossed green salad.

'What about the border guards?' she asked as they ate. 'Won't they be looking out for you?'

'I have more than one passport,' he said.

Knowing Blake, she thought, he probably had a cupboard full of alternative IDs.

After they'd washed up, Jay sent Tom a text, giving him her new number. He texted straight back. *What is it with you and phones?*

She decided against responding in case she let something slip and it got her into trouble.

Blake downed a brandy. Set the glass in the sink. He said, 'Let's get some shut-eye.'

From somewhere Blake rustled up a new toothbrush for her, and a fresh towel. After she'd used the bathroom she padded into the sitting room to find Blake standing motionless with Emilie's photograph in his hand. He snapped his head round, and in that moment she caught him for the first time with his expression unguarded, his defences down. The pain in his eyes made her heart squeeze.

'Oh, Max,' she whispered. This time she couldn't resist her natural urge to comfort. She went to him and put her arms around him. Rested her head against his chest. 'I'm sorry.'

His embrace was hard. She could feel the lean length of him, could smell soap and toothpaste. His lips brushed her hair, moving to kiss the sensitive skin behind her ear. Every hair on her body stood upright.

She tried to take a step back, but he reached out a hand and hooked a finger into her waistband, held her still. She saw his eyes darken and soften. She'd seen that look before, and she wasn't sure if she could escape a second time.

'Stay with me tonight?' His voice was husky.

Her heart was thumping like a piston engine. Could he hear it? It sounded deafening.

'Max . . .' The word came out on a rush of breathlessness.

'Please.'

'I can't.' It was a bleat.

'Please,' he said again, and there was such a note of entreaty, of vulnerability, that she nearly cracked.

'Max, I'm sorry,' she gasped. 'I'm engaged to Tom. Remember?'

They locked eyes.

Jay held her breath, part of her wanting him desperately, the other part petrified of the consequences.

Slowly, he pulled her close. Tucked her against his chest. She felt him press a kiss against her hair.

'Goodnight, hon,' he murmured.

As she watched him pad out of the sitting room for the master bedroom at the other end of the apartment, she didn't know whether to sigh with relief or scream.

The next morning at six, sleepy, still befuddled after a restless night of dreaming that Nahid was coming to sew her eyelids shut, Jay showered and dressed, pulling on her muddy jeans with a grimace. She then headed to the kitchen, where Blake was making coffee. Barefoot, he wore a pair of faded jeans, no shirt. His hair was tousled, his skin tanned biscuit brown. Her eyes latched on to the length of his spine, the muscles on either side lean and defined. One scar ribboned his ribs, another created a starburst below his shoulder blade.

'Coffee?' he asked.

'Sure.' Jay cleared her throat and strode for a cupboard to search for a cup and to distract herself from looking at his naked torso.

Coffee poured, Jay took her cup to the sitting room and flicked on the news to see that the story about Blake had been usurped by the death of the Mayor of Calais. Jay's breath caught. She'd met Madeleine Gal last year, at a Prevention of Human Trafficking conference. Tall, flame-haired, Gal had been passionate about human rights, and Jay had liked her enormously. As she watched the section, she learned that Gal had, apparently, as many friends as enemies, thanks to her devotion in trying to sort out the mess of refugees wanting to cross to the UK from Calais. Gal was more sympathetic towards refugees than many people liked, but the general consensus was that she'd had a good heart and it was a national tragedy that she'd suffered a fatal heart attack in the small hours of the morning.

'She's young, to die of heart disease,' Blake remarked from behind her.

'I met her last year,' Jay said sadly. 'I liked her.'

'I'm sorry, hon,' said Blake. He squeezed her shoulder gently. 'You OK?'

'Yes. It's just a waste. She was only thirty-six.'

His voice was gentle when he said, 'We leave in ten minutes.'

Blake drove swiftly for Calais and the Eurotunnel. He'd already booked the Mercedes on to the train, planning to be in London before midday.

Neither said much on the journey. Blake had no trouble at border control thanks to a passport in a different name. There seemed to be nobody looking out for them . . . that they could see. Before they'd boarded, Blake had tried the three remaining numbers on Sol's phone, but they'd all been disconnected. He'd said, 'Someone knows Sol's SIM card is missing. They're covering their tracks.'

They shared their train carriage with a white Toyota. They didn't bother getting out. Blake tipped back his seat and napped through the thirty-minute ride. Bored, Jay squirrelled through the Merc's glove box to find the car was registered to a Francoise Fournier. The address shown on the insurance document was the same as the apartment they'd stayed in. Jay gazed at the name for a long time before putting the documents back. Whether Blake had a relationship with Francoise Fournier was none of her business. She'd do better to try and work out where to buy some decent food for supper tonight, she thought, but her mind couldn't stick with anything domestic.

As the train pulled out of the tunnel and pale winter sunshine leaked through the windows, Blake sat up. 'Miss anything?'

'No.'

Traffic was light into London, the rush hour long past. Blake dropped Jay at Paddington Station.

'You pretend nothing happened in Paris, OK?' he said. 'You haven't seen me or heard from me since I dropped by in Bristol.'

'What if the police come asking questions?'

'Doubtful.'

Jay did an eye roll.

'You tell them the truth,' he said.

She nibbled the inside of her lip. 'What about Tom?'

'Your call, hon.'

He reached out and tucked a strand of hair behind her ear. 'Eyes in the back of your head.'

'Where are you going?'

He faced forward, put the car into gear. 'To find the antidote for Emilie.'

Jay arrived at Tom's weighed down with three carrier bags of M&S's finest food, including croissants, stuffed chicken breasts, and individual chocolate mousses. Just in case Sofie didn't like chicken, she'd added a pizza. All kids liked pizza, didn't they? Dumping the bags on the doormat, she scrabbled in her bag for her keys. Tom would still be at work, not home for a couple of hours. Plenty of time to read the instructions, make the kitchen table look presentable. She was reaching for the lock when the door swung open.

Startled, Jay stared at the girl standing in front of her. Whippet-thin, she wore leggings and a purple striped T-shirt. Acid green eyes looked Jay up and down.

'Who are you?' the girl asked.

'I'm Jay. You must be Sofie.' Jay smiled, holding out a hand, but the girl ignored it.

'You were meant to be here yesterday.'

Jay let her hand drop. 'I know. I'm sorry, but something came up. I'm here now, and—'

'Do you normally not turn up when you've promised to be somewhere?'

'No, I don't. This was exceptional. I had to do a favour for a friend.'

'Mummy never lets people down.'

Bully for mummy, Jay thought, making an effort to keep her expression bland.

'I brought supper.' Jay hefted the bags. Sofie didn't move, but stood blocking the doorway. 'If you wouldn't mind, these are quite heavy . . .'

Sofie stepped aside with obvious reluctance. Jay walked to the kitchen. Began unpacking the groceries. Sofie stood to one side, watching.

'It's all ready prepared stuff,' she said.

'With no additives though.' Jay flipped one of the cartons over. 'Nothing but food ingredients. No E-numbers, preservatives, added salt or sugar. Just good old chicken and vegetables, olive oil and seasonings.'

'Can't you cook?'

'Not very well, no. Which is why I thought I'd play it safe. I didn't want to serve you one of my burnt offerings.'

'Mummy went to Venice to learn how to cook. She says gastronomy is the supreme art of creating, giving, and making others happy.'

Jay clenched her teeth. She had a quick look at the cooking instructions on the pack of stuffed chicken breasts in order to see when she should turn on the oven.

'Is that for supper?' Sofie demanded.

'Well, that's what I was thinking, but if—'

'I'm allergic to chicken,' Sofie announced. And flounced out of the kitchen.

EIGHT

When Tom walked through the front door, Jay swept to greet him, but she wasn't as fast as Sofie.

With a squeal of delight, the girl shot past Jay and jumped into his arms. 'Daddy!'

'Hi munchkin.' He was beaming ear to ear over his daughter's head. Jay forced a smile back. 'How have you two been getting on?'

Sofie took his hand and led him towards the kitchen. 'I helped Jay unpack the groceries. She says she can't cook, but I don't mind. It was really sweet of her to buy stuff she thought I might like. She's really nice. I can see why she's your girlfriend.'

Jay's eyebrows shot into her hairline. Tom blew her a kiss as he passed. He mouthed, 'OK?'

Trying not to stare in disbelief at Sofie, she gave a nod.

'Great,' he said. He was still beaming.

Sofie was all smiles while Jay heated supper, telling Tom all about the games she'd played on her computer, which friends she'd chatted to, what her mother had achieved for the day.

'Mummy managed to get a bank to reveal disclosure,' she said brightly. Jay switched off when the child began detailing an incredibly long and tedious court case to do with an exchange company going bust and a bank losing all its clients' money. Tom, however, seemed riveted.

Finally, Jay lit candles for the table, poured wine for her and Tom, apple juice for Sofie, and served supper.

'How come Sofie's not having chicken with us?' Tom was frowning at the pizza Jay popped in front of the girl.

'She's allergic to chicken,' said Jay.

'No, she's not.'

Jay looked at Sofie. 'Sofie told me she was. Didn't you Sofie?'

Sofie looked straight back at Jay. 'I never said that. I swear it. But it's OK. I don't mind pizza.' Sofie looked longingly at the juicy chicken pieces, glazed golden brown.

'Here, have mine.' Tom swapped his chicken for Sofie's pizza.

'No, it's fine, Daddy. Honestly.'

'I've got an idea. Why don't we go half and half?'

'Would you?' Sofie managed to look hopeful and pathetically grateful at the same time.

'Come on. Snuggle up.'

Jay sat opposite, forced to watch father and daughter sitting cosily together, sharing their meals and laughing. Although she wanted to face Sofie head on about her lie, Jay knew she'd be better playing a long game. The trouble was, patience wasn't her strongest point, and when she jumped the gun in a situation like this, it rarely worked.

After supper, Jay pleaded a headache and went to bed, leaving Tom and Sofie playing chess at the kitchen table. Chess, for God's sake! Shouldn't the child be doing something normal, like watching *Hollyoaks* on the TV?

Jay was pretending to be asleep when Tom came to bed.

'Hey,' he murmured.

He slipped an arm over her ribs and pulled her close. Kissed her shoulder.

'Hey,' she responded.

'Sorry we didn't have any time together,' he whispered.

'It's OK.'

'What do you think of Sofie?'

I think she's a poisonous snake, Jay wanted to say, but held her tongue. 'She's OK,' she managed.

'Yeah, isn't she just.' He sounded pleased. 'Really OK.'

Brushing her hair aside, he trailed his lips to the nape of her neck. His hand gently cupped her breast, his thumb stroking her nipple. Despite the immediate heat that flooded her – Tom always managed to turn her on with a single touch – Jay moved infinitesimally away. She knew Sofie's behaviour wasn't Tom's fault, but she didn't feel like making love. She was too pissed off.

'Anything bugging you?' he murmured. He moved his hand from her breast to stroke her neck and shoulders.

Tom and Jay had made a pact that they would never go straight to sleep without talking if something about the other was annoying them. It could be as trivial as Tom's not putting out the rubbish when he said he would, or it could be a more serious issue, such as Tom's jealousy of Blake, but clearing the air meant they both slept easier.

'Nothing's wrong,' Jay mumbled. 'I'm just tired.'

'Fancy a massage?' His hands were moving rhythmically over her shoulders and down her back. He had beautiful hands, broad and strong, and they gave the best massages this side of the Channel. The only trouble was that she invariably ended up having sex with Tom halfway through, and she was too angry to relent.

'Tomorrow,' she said. 'I need sleep.'

'First thing? You're too sexy to leave alone for any longer.'

'Hmmm.' She was non-committal.

'Sleep tight, sweetheart.' Tom yawned and stretched his length along hers, spooning her close. She tucked his hand between her breasts. Closed her eyes.

Jay fell asleep with Tom's breath rolling in warm waves across her neck.

Jay struggled awake the next morning to find Tom standing over her. He was fully dressed.

'Hell,' she said. She jackknifed up in bed. 'How late am I?'

'What's this about Blake being wanted for a murder in Paris?'

Jay felt herself balancing on a knifepoint about whether to tell Tom or not, but she knew she couldn't withhold something so important. 'Blake didn't kill Sol.'

'By Sol, you mean Solomon Neill. The dead man.'

'Yes. But Sol was killed by an assassin. A woman . . .' Jay clambered out of bed and grabbed Tom's bathrobe from the back of the door, belted it tight. 'I saw her kill him.'

Tom's expression was appalled. 'You were *there*?'

'Well, yes.'

'Why the hell didn't you tell me this yesterday?'

Because I knew we'd have a fight, and I didn't want to give Sofie the satisfaction, she thought. 'I wanted to get to know Sofie. I didn't think it was the right time.'

Tom stared at her. 'Sofie tells me you weren't particularly friendly when you turned up yesterday.'

'That's not true!' Jay protested.

Tom scrubbed his face with both hands. 'Look, I know you just about had a fit when I sprang Sofie on you, but she's a good kid. She's trying hard to fit in, and if you could just make a bit of an effort—'

'*Me* make an effort?' It was a job to keep her jaw from dropping to the floor. 'Jesus, Tom. You have no idea what went on yesterday!'

'And I have no idea what went on in Paris,' he ground out. 'Did you and Blake spend the night together?'

'No. I mean we shared an apartment, but not a bed, if that's what you mean.'

Blood rose to Tom's face.

'He's innocent, Tom. Someone's set him up, but Blake's worried that if I go to the cops I might be in danger. So I'm keeping my head down.'

'In danger from whom?' His tone was strangled.

'We don't know. But it gets worse. Blake believes his sister has been targeted . . .' Jay hastily ran through the story.

'These people *kidnapped* you?' His eyes just about popped from his head.

Jay decided to downplay the entire event. 'I played dead so they'd leave me alone. Then I escaped. No problem.' She moved right along, finishing by saying, 'As long as I keep quiet, I should be OK.'

She stepped forward, hands raised pleadingly, but he took a step back. His expression closed.

'Tom . . .'

'I can't deal with this right now. I have a meeting in thirty –' he turned his wrist, glanced at his watch – 'make that ten, minutes. Will you be here when Heather arrives?'

'What?'

'She's due here at eight thirty. Sofie's packed and ready to go.' He strode out of the room.

Jay stood and listened to his footsteps pounding down the stairs. The faint sounds of him and Sofie talking. The front door slamming.

She sank on to the bed. Put her head in her hands. She should have talked to him last night. What an idiot. And what about Sofie and her lies? Feeling emotionally wrecked, Jay rose and began to head towards the shower. To her dismay, the doorbell rang.

Please God it wasn't Heather. She didn't want to meet Tom's perfect ex-girlfriend looking as though a flock of birds had nested in her hair.

'Sofie!' she yelled down the stairs. 'Can you get it?'

'Sorry.' Her voice was faint. 'I'm in the loo.'

Jay mentally flung her hands in the air. Brilliant.

The doorbell rang again.

'I'm coming!' she yelled.

Barefoot, flushed, still wearing Tom's bathrobe, Jay answered the door to a woman wearing a sharply tailored suit, belted to accentuate her tiny waist. Shiny black killer heels. Pearls at her neck and in her ears. A silver Porsche Boxter was pulled up to the curb outside the front gate.

'Hi,' Heather said. Her voice was warm. 'I'm Heather. You must be Jay.'

'Hi.'

They shook. Heather's hand felt as small and fragile as a sparrow. Her nails were manicured, her skin unblemished. Jay's hands felt like saucepans in comparison and were covered in scars where she'd been caught near a bomb blast in Basra. She put them quickly behind her back.

'Sofie's already packed,' said Jay. 'Would you like to come in?'

'That's OK. I'm in a bit of a rush. It's kind of you to have Sofie to stay. She was really excited to meet you.'

At that moment, Sofie appeared, a small rucksack over one shoulder. 'Thanks for having me, Jay,' she said, sweet as can be, passing her rucksack to her mother.

'My pleasure,' said Jay, struggling to keep the sarcasm out of her voice.

When Sofie came and gave Jay a hug, Jay nearly stepped back she was so surprised. Sofie made to whisper something in Jay's ear. Jay ducked down. Sofie's voice was as soft as a feather. She said, 'Daddy's not going to marry you. He's going to marry Mummy.'

Jay reared back. Stared down at Sofie.

'I had such a lovely time, Jay,' Sofie said brightly. 'Can we do it again soon?'

Jay opened and closed her mouth.

'Mummy's going away this weekend. Maybe I can come and stay?'

'Er . . .' Jay stammered.

'Sofie,' Heather admonished. 'They may already have other plans.'

'No, they don't.' Sofie's eyes were innocently wide. 'Daddy already said it was all right.'

'Well, if they're sure . . .' Heather looked at Jay questioningly.

'Great.' Jay managed a weak smile.

'You're really kind.' Heather's expression was warm. 'Thank you.'

It was all Jay could do not to tear her hair as she watched them climb into the Boxter and roar down the street.

NINE

'What happened to you?' Jay's boss, Nick Morgan, peered into her face. 'You look like hell.'

'Don't ask,' she said.

'Had a fight with Tom?'

'None of your business,' she told him tartly.

He grinned. 'As long as it doesn't affect your inimitable tracking skills.'

Nick was an ex-marine who'd set up TRACE in the belief he could help more people that way than by being a soldier. Deployed in the Falklands and the first Gulf War, Nick felt most comfortable with ex-Service personnel, which was why out of the twenty-three TRACE employees worldwide, only two were from civilian stock. This suited Jay perfectly, since they all worked pretty much on the same page, with similar outlooks and no-nonsense attitudes.

He passed her one of their green FC forms: First Call. Jay ran her eyes down the page to see an all too familiar story unfold.

Irina Dolohov was a sixteen-year-old high school student from the Southern Russian Federation. A family friend proposed a quick trip to London, offering five hundred dollars for her help in bringing back antiques to sell in Russia. Irina was introduced to a man called Anton and within days she received a passport, a tourist visa and a plane ticket.

In the meantime, Anton 'improved' Irina's travel agenda. She was now to work as a waitress in a local café for one thousand pounds a month. Irina's mother became suspicious, but was quickly assured that her daughter was in good hands. Anton also warned Irina's mother that the travel arrangements had cost him a lot of money, and that if her daughter cancelled the trip, she would owe him over a thousand dollars.

'She left Russia over three weeks ago, and her mother hasn't heard a squeak since,' Nick said.

'Anton's known to us?'

'He's part of a trafficking ring, yes.'

Jay flicked through the paperwork. 'She was flown into Stansted. She could be anywhere by now.'

'That's never stopped you before.' Nick grinned. 'But the main reason why I've given you this one is because her mother is sure the city of Bristol was mentioned. That's your patch.'

'Sure is,' she agreed.

'Gill's out until tomorrow,' Nick informed her. 'And I'm out for the rest of the day. Meeting at Whitehall.'

Whitehall wasn't anything to do with TRACE, she knew, but occasionally he was asked for his expertise on matters military by old buddies.

'See you tomorrow,' he added.

After he'd left, Jay reread the form, grateful for the sense of normality it brought. It was a relief to put Blake and her terrifying ordeal at the farmhouse out of her mind and concentrate on Irina. She had no doubt that when the girl had arrived in Bristol she wouldn't have become a waitress, but a prostitute. Her passport would have been confiscated, and she would have been threatened with beatings if she refused to obey or tried to run away. Her life now would be a series of hotel rooms, boarding houses, 'madams' and clients, until either she escaped – which was highly unusual – or turned to drugs, committed suicide, or was found by TRACE.

She looked at the photograph Irina's mother had provided. Irina, unsurprisingly, was heartbreakingly beautiful. Reed slim, she had glossy chestnut hair that hung to her waist and a happy smile. What the girl was going through now, Jay refused to contemplate. A lot could happen in three weeks. She just had to hope the girl was strong and had survived so far.

First, Jay checked Irina's name was in the Interpol missing persons file. Next, she registered Irina with the International Organization for Migration (IOM) and the Russian Embassy. Nick had already alerted the Missing Persons Bureau and the Bristol police. All Jay had to do now was get her backside to Bristol and start asking questions on the street.

After checking her diary, Jay scribbled on the communal

calendar that she'd be in Bristol on Friday the thirteenth of November. The day after tomorrow. She couldn't go immediately, much as she'd like to – the sooner she started searching the better and before the girl got shipped to another city – because she had wall-to-wall meetings all day Thursday.

Jay ate her lunch at her desk, studying Sol's photographs on her phone. Some of the images – especially the ones of paintings – were small, making it hard to make out any features, so she copied Sol's phone folders on to her computer. On a large screen the first CD filed was as clear as day. The artist was James Blunt, the album *Back to Bedlam*.

Jay scrolled through the other photographs. Blake had thought they might have been a code. Each picture was dated. She noticed that the most recent was dated the day before Sol had died. Eighth of November. She studied the picture showing the stone polar bear. Jay googled polar bear sculptors to come up with so many hits, she was forced to refine her search. She added the word 'Paris' and clicked on the first item: *Francois Pompon: the white polar ice bear – photo.*

Her nerves quivered when she saw the photo matched the one on Sol's memory card. The sculpture was in the *Jardin des Plantes*, in the Musée d'Orsay. What did it mean? Had Sol met someone at the museum? Did the bear represent the meeting place?

She flinched when the intercom buzzed. The office was on the first floor of a converted town house, which they shared with a secretarial service on the ground floor and an accountant on the third.

'Who is it?' She spoke into the intercom.

'We'd like to talk about Irina Dolohov,' a man said. 'We have some information for you.'

For a moment she thought she recognized the voice. Puzzled, Jay said, 'Who are you? Which organization are you from?'

'We're from the police. Sergeant Thorpe and Constable Webb.'

Jay's heart sank. Was the girl dead? She'd never had the police turn up in person before. She buzzed them in. 'Second floor,' she told them. 'Door's open.'

She was totally unprepared to be faced with Blake.

'You didn't ask for any ID,' he told her. His face was stern. 'I could have been anyone.'

'But you said you were a cop!' she protested. 'Wanting to talk about Irina!'

Blake just looked at her.

'How do you know about her?' Jay narrowed her eyes suspiciously.

'Ways and means. Just as our opponents will find ways and means.' He moved past her and into her office. 'I said to be careful, remember?'

Getting a lecture from Max Blake was the last thing she needed. 'You tricked me,' she said.

'As they will.'

'Jesus, Max.' She flung her hands in the air. 'What is this?'

'I'm keeping you on your toes. I want you to be vigilant, not opening the door to anyone. I suspect they know you have Sol's SIM card. They might be watching you to see what you do with it.'

Jay digested this with a shudder. The last thing she wanted was to see Nahid or Tivon again. She said, 'Where have you been?'

'Lying low.' Hip propped on one corner of her desk, he added, 'I'm thinking you should do the same. Go away, maybe, until this is sorted.'

'I can't do that,' she protested. 'I have way too much going on.'

'I'm worried they might use you to get me.'

'They don't know we're in touch, do they?'

'Hmmm.' His gaze turned inward. 'You tell Tom about what happened?'

'Yes.'

'Tell him to be careful. I'm sensing a lot of fingers in a lot of official pies. You reported anything to anyone?'

'No.'

'That's what's keeping you safe.'

Jay said, 'Have you had any luck with the antidote?'

He shook his head.

'How's Emilie?'

'Still comatose.'

'I'm sorry.'

'Ask Tom if he's heard of the Garrison. I tried security companies, but there's nothing by that name that I can find. I'm thinking it could be a code word, or maybe a secret organization of some sort . . .' He brought out his phone. Briefly studied the screen. 'Sorry, hon. Got to go.'

After Blake had left, Jay copied Sol's photographs and music to a USB device, which she popped in her handbag. Then, with the instruction book of her new phone to hand, she inputted her contacts before letting everyone know her new number. She worked through the afternoon, heading home just after six p.m. As she drove, she looked to see if anyone was following her, but with such busy traffic it was hard to tell. She could hear Blake's voice echo in her mind.

I want you to be vigilant . . . They might be watching you.

On her street she saw a middle-aged man with a newspaper tucked beneath his arm. A young woman with a fluffy white dog. Both could be watchers, both were bland, and if they wore wigs or glasses then they could change their looks easily, but still, Jay tried to make a mental note of their features.

Inside the house it felt beautifully warm, and Jay guessed Angela had finally managed to persuade Denise that it was winter and so the heating should be timed to come on before they got home. Kicking off her boots, she padded upstairs and brought her computer into the kitchen. She emailed Tom, asking him if he'd heard of the Garrison. She didn't give it a context, and hoped he'd think it was to do with her work. He probably wouldn't touch it if he thought it had anything to do with Blake. She warned him to *tread carefully* and finished her message by saying she'd be in Bristol on Friday, searching for Irina.

He rang three minutes later.

'Can I help with Irina?' he asked.

'Nick's already alerted you guys, but thanks.'

'Look, Jay,' he said at the same time as she said, 'Tom—'

'Sorry,' he said. He cleared his throat. 'Look, I know I went off half-cocked this morning, but God . . . Finding out Blake was wanted for murder while I was eating my cornflakes kind of flipped me out. And then you said you were *kidnapped*—'

'It's OK,' she told him. She massaged her temples. 'It was terrible timing with Sofie staying over. And I was so tired . . . It was a mistake to put it off. I'm sorry.'

She heard him sigh.

'And I was like a bull in a china shop, as usual. Are you all right? I mean you said you did CPR on the victim . . .'

'I'm fine,' she assured him.

'I've heard that a million times before,' he said, 'and funnily enough, it's never a comfort.'

Jay smiled. 'You know me too well.'

'Sometimes,' he sighed, 'I wish you weren't quite so sexy.'

'Ditto,' she admitted.

He dropped his voice. 'Can you stay for the weekend?'

Her body warmed inside. 'Yes, please.'

He said, 'Look, would you mind if Sofie stays over with us on Saturday? Heather will collect her Sunday afternoon.'

'Sure.'

'There seemed to be some tension between you.'

'It's nothing,' she lied. 'It would be nice to see her again.'

'See you Friday,' he murmured. 'Can't wait.'

She was humming when they eventually hung up, and, feeling more settled, she returned to her computer and continued working until the girls came home.

'Risotto OK with you?' Denise asked Jay.

'Wonderful.'

The deal was that since Jay couldn't cook, she supplied the wine. Not that they drank every night, but when Jay told her housemates about what had gone on in Paris, they got stuck into the Rioja. Jay wanted her housemates to know everything, so that they'd know exactly what they were faced with should anything happen.

'Do you really think they're watching you?' Angela asked.

'I don't know, but I just want you to be aware.'

'If you need us as backup . . .' Denise gave her a meaningful look.

Jay smiled. 'I'll call. Don't worry.'

In the morning, Jay made sure she arrived at the office slightly later than usual, and to her relief Nick was already ensconced in his office, making phone calls. Having a grizzled ex-marine nearby helped dispel her feeling of vulnerability, and after she'd made coffee, she settled at her desk. Even with Nick barely ten yards away, however, she couldn't stop thinking about Nahid and Tivon. The way Nahid smelled.

I want to get to know her . . . See what makes her tick. What her darkest fears are.

She thought about Blake and his sister, Emilie, and then her

mind turned to the Garrison. Despite the fact that Blake probably would have done something far more sophisticated, Jay
searched Google, which came up with several Garrisons – a
wedding events company, a gastropub, a post-punk rock group
and a motel – but nothing along the lines she was looking for.
She refined her search over and over again, but came up with
nothing more exciting than a forest heritage society.

When Nick had finished his calls, Jay slipped into his office.
'We need to be careful about security,' she said.

'How come?'

She filled him in. She knew Blake wouldn't mind, since the
two men already knew and trusted one another. She finished
by telling Nick why she hadn't gone to the police.

'Jesus,' he said.

'Can you warn Gill?'

'Yup. We'll take extra precautions. Anything else I can do?'

She shook her head.

'Call me if you need me?'

'Yes.'

Jay spent the remainder of the day ducking in and out of
meetings with the Home Office. At every opportunity she
checked the area, looking for any watchers, but didn't see
anyone who bothered her.

She slept badly that night. She dreamed Sol was at the end
of her bed, pleading with her to save Emilie, and when she
awoke, she could still hear his voice inside her mind.

It was bitterly cold outside, her VW Golf sprinkled with tiny
crystals of frost. Traffic was relatively clear since she was
heading out of the city, and by the time Jay had parked outside
Tom's house and begun walking into the centre of Bristol, it
was just past eleven a.m. She texted Lily as she walked, asking
if she was up for a coffee. Lily texted straight back.

Make it brunch, I'm starving.

Jay met Lily at her usual greasy spoon near Old Market
Street. The air was steamy and warm against the autumn chill
outside, and filled with the scent of frying bacon. Lily's real
name was Ljiliana, and today she was wearing a fluffy pink
top with a short black skirt and mustard thigh-length boots.
Her cleavage was spectacular, her dyed blonde hair teased into
a wild beehive. Not for the first time Jay marvelled at men's
tastes in prostitutes, but since Lily believed that men went for

women who were total opposites from their partners, it made perfect sense. Lily's regulars were, she said, decent white and blue collar workers who simply didn't get what they wanted at home.

'Take Dave, for example,' Lily had told Jay when they first met. 'Self-employed builder with a Catholic prude of a wife. He nearly went through the roof when I gave him his first blow job.'

'Lucky Dave.'

Lily had smiled, showing a set of strong white teeth. 'He gets as many as he likes 'cos he pays half my mortgage. He's all right, is Dave.'

Jay didn't know how many regulars Lily relied on, but considering she owned a Ford Fiesta, her own house and garden, and managed two holidays a year in Spain, she was doing OK. Better than Jay, who rented her house and managed one holiday a year. Mind you, since Jay had a weakness for designer jeans and Italian boots, she thought she might do better if she took a leaf out of Lily's book and bought her clothes in charity shops.

Jay ordered a full English breakfast. Lily did the same. Fried bread, fried eggs and bacon, deep-fried chips, fried mushrooms, and a ladleful of baked beans. Great for the arteries.

'So, who're you looking for?' Lily asked.

Jay brought out a photograph of Irina and pushed it across the Formica-topped table. Lily studied it closely. Shook her head.

'She's from Russia,' Jay said. She didn't say any more. Lily knew the form. She'd ask around, keep her ear to the ground, and if she heard or saw anything she'd let Jay know. And Jay would reward her with cash from TRACE's informant's fund.

After Jay had settled their brunch bill, she joined Lily outside.

'You want some sexy underwear to wow your man tonight?' Lily asked. 'I've some leopard-print G-strings in my bag. Blokes love G-strings. Wives never wear them, you know.'

Jay tried to keep a straight face. 'Thanks, Lily, but I'm fine.'

They parted on the pavement with a hug.

TEN

Sofie turned on Tom's laptop in the kitchen. She knew she wasn't supposed to use his computer – it had loads of cop stuff on it apparently – but she was bored witless. Her mum had dropped her off ages ago, and she was fed up with doing puzzles. If she looked at another online sudoku she'd scream. She'd done her homework – boring – and there was nothing on TV except reruns.

And what about Facebook? She wasn't allowed an account until she was thirteen. What a joke! She'd created an account a while back, lying about her age, but her mum had found out and gone totally ballistic. Anyone would think she was about to be murdered via the Web the way she'd carried on.

She had a sneaky look at Tom's emails to see he had one from Jay. She longed to open it, but didn't dare in case it gave her away. Instead, she trawled through Tom's files, but few were of any interest. There was no mention of the mysterious Max Blake that Tom and Jay had rowed about. She'd heard their raised voices – God, Tom had sounded angry – and, unable to resist, she'd tiptoed along the corridor until she could hear every word.

Had Jay really been with that guy when he'd died? Had she really been kidnapped? It sounded like something out of a movie, nothing to do with real life. Sofie wished she'd get kidnapped herself. Imagine the stories she could tell at school! Even Jaz would be impressed. Raising her shirt, she peered at her stomach. Jaz had said she was fat. Jaz was ten months older than Sofie and the most popular girl in her class. Sofie had told her that her father was a DI, hoping to impress her, and Jaz's response still stung.

'Yeah, right,' she'd snorted. 'Like a DI would have a daughter who's so fat.'

Two other girls with Jaz had sneered, telling her to lose weight, *you fat bitch*.

Sofie pinched her flesh again. She didn't think she was fat. Mum called her a string bean. Even Tom had remarked on her ribs. *I could play a tune on them*. Had they been lying to make her feel better? Perhaps she *was* fat and didn't know it? Maybe the best thing would be to go on a diet . . .

Her thoughts were interrupted when the doorbell rang. Hurriedly, Sofie shut down Tom's computer.

The doorbell rang again.

She trotted down the corridor. She was too short to check through the fish eye set in the door, so she said, 'Who is it?'

A woman said, 'I have a delivery for you.'

'What is it?'

'It's a package for Jay McCaulay.'

Sofie bit her lip. Her mum had told her never to answer the door to a stranger. She scooted into the sitting room and checked through the window to see a slender woman in a red waistcoat standing on the doorstep. The postman. Or rather, postwoman.

'Can you leave it outside?' Sofie called.

The woman turned and waved a small padded envelope at her. 'I need a signature.' She had blonde hair that was black at the roots, but she looked nice. She was smiling.

What harm could it do?

Sofie unlatched the door.

The woman looked her up and down. She said, 'You're very pretty.'

Sofie blushed.

'OK.' The woman pushed out a pen. 'Sign here.'

Sofie signed a form already covered in signatures. She was aware of the woman's scent, sweet and slightly sickly, as she passed her the envelope. Sofie turned it over in her hands. It was so light, it didn't feel as though anything was inside.

'Can you guess what's inside?' The woman's eyes twinkled.

Sofie shrugged.

'Go on. Have a guess.'

Intrigued, Sofie held up the envelope. Belatedly, she realized the envelope just had Jay's name printed on the front. She said, 'How come you know where to deliver it without an address?'

'Because we're clever.' The woman glanced over her shoulder at a thickset, swarthy man standing on the street. He was staring at Sofie. When their eyes met, he slowly licked his lips.

Slightly unnerved, she took a step back. 'I don't get it.'

'Don't worry.' The woman smiled again. 'You're not supposed to. Just give it to Jay. And tell her to keep her mouth shut.'

Sofie felt alarm shiver over her skin. 'What?'

'You heard me,' the woman said. 'Now, you'd better get back inside. And don't open the door to strangers again, will you? It could be dangerous.'

Nerves jumping, Sofie watched the woman walk down the front path. What was all that about? What was in the envelope? Squishing it with both hands, she felt something small and hard inside. Had the woman known what it contained? She'd made it seem as though she did. Sofie studied the envelope flap. One edge hadn't been stuck down properly . . . Could she take a peek?

No. She shouldn't. She'd only end up in trouble . . .

She dithered briefly.

To hell with it.

Before she could change her mind, Sofie peeled back the self-adhesive envelope and peered inside.

ELEVEN

Jay purposely dawdled up the hill. She didn't want to get to Tom's place early. Not after his phone call two seconds ago, telling her that Sofie was staying tonight, thanks to Heather having some sort of work emergency.

'I couldn't say no,' Tom had said. 'I'm sorry. I know we wanted some time together . . .' He'd sounded genuinely apologetic.

She just had to pray Sofie would try and act like a normal twelve-year-old, rather than like something from a horror movie. She was wondering whether to put off her arrival until Tom got home, when she took in the woman walking along Tom's front path.

Jay's heart turned cold.

It was the same woman who'd been in the alley. The assassin. The woman who had killed Sol.

Oh, dear God.

Quick check on Sofie, who was standing in the doorway.

She was fiddling with something, absorbed. She appeared to be OK, but Jay wasn't taking any chances. She put her head down and charged.

The woman heard her footsteps. Snapped her head around. Eyes on Jay tearing towards her, she sauntered to a pearly-white Audi, hopped into the passenger seat, and with a mechanical snarl, the car shot down the street. Jay didn't lessen her speed. She almost lost her footing as she swung into Tom's front yard.

'Hey, where's the fire?' Sofie looked startled. She had both hands stuck behind her back.

'You OK?' Jay gasped.

'Yeah.' Her expression turned contemptuous. 'Why? What's your problem?'

Jay scanned the area. As far as she could see the street was empty, but she didn't trust someone to be watching from one of the houses. She hustled Sofie into Tom's flat.

'Get off me!' Sofie pulled herself free. 'God, you're pushy!'

'Sorry.' Jay slammed the door shut and bolted it before going round the flat, making sure every window, every door was locked. 'But I have my reasons.'

'You need Prozac,' Sofie told her when she returned to the kitchen. 'You are *so* uptight.'

Jay wondered how to tackle this. Whether Sofie was the panicking type or not. She didn't think she would be, but you never knew. She might freak the girl out. She'd have to be careful.

'That woman,' she said. 'At the door. Who was she?'

Something flared in Sofie's eyes, something oddly calculating, but Jay didn't know what it meant.

'Why should I tell you?'

Jay put her hands on her hips. 'Because it's important. More important than you know.'

'Who cares? Daddy's going to dump you soon, so you may as well get used to it.'

Despite the jet of anger that lit beneath her breastbone, Jay let that one ride. 'Sofie. This is serious. I saw that woman recently, in not particularly pleasant circumstances. I need to know what she was doing here.'

'She was from the gas board.'

'Did you see her ID?'

'I didn't let her in the house. Mummy says I shouldn't let anyone in unless she or Daddy are there.' Her tone was self-righteous.

'Very wise,' agreed Jay. 'What did she want?'

'To read the meter.' She rolled her eyes, as though Jay was being particularly stupid.

'And you didn't let her in?'

'No, OK? Can I go to my room now?'

Something wasn't right, but Jay couldn't put her finger on it. She decided to wait until Tom got home. She said, 'Sure.'

Sofie walked out of the kitchen, leaving Jay staring at the space where the girl had been standing. What was wrong with this? It wasn't just the assassin's appearance. Something was off with Sofie. She sighed out loud. She was probably overreacting. Which wasn't surprising, considering the circumstances.

She wanted to call the police, but didn't dare until she'd spoken to Blake. She texted him, told him what had happened, but there was no response. After putting on some Cuban music to help her nerves settle – she loved ethnic music and had downloaded some of her favourite songs from her iPod to Tom's system – she made herself a large mug of tea and drank it over-looking Tom's jungle of a garden. Neither of them were gardeners, and even if they were, they never had time to mow the tiny patch of lawn or roll their sleeves up and weed the borders. The wooden bench sat in six inches of grass, growing mould.

When Tom came home, Jay didn't bother going to greet him. The second the front door opened, Sofie was hammering down the stairs with her little-girl squeal of delight. God, how was she going to cope with this long term? It was a bloody disaster.

'Hey, you.'

She turned and her heart gave a bump. His hair was tousled, his shirt sleeves pushed up to his elbows. He was smiling his usual smile, slightly crooked, and his eyes were shining, vivid blue.

'Hey, yourself.'

He came over and folded her in his arms. 'I'm such an idiot,' he murmured. 'God, I love you. I hate it when we fight.'

'Me too.'

She looked past his shoulder at Sofie, who was kicking at

the table leg. Gently, she extricated herself from Tom's embrace. 'We need to talk. About a woman who came to the house.'

Sofie's head jerked up.

'Sofie answered the door to her.'

Sofie's eyes flicked between Jay and Tom. She said, 'Are you sure you want to talk about this?'

'Yes,' Jay said, puzzled. 'I'm sure.'

Sofie sighed. 'OK, then. Well, this woman turned up. She said she was delivering a message from Jay's boyfriend—'

'What?' said Jay. At her side, she sensed Tom's whole body stiffen.

'His name's Max Blake . . .'

'Sofie,' said Jay warningly. 'Tell the truth or—'

The words jammed in her throat when the girl waved her hand dismissively at Jay, a slim platinum-link bracelet winking in the overhead lamps.

'Jay told me not to tell you,' Sofie told Tom. 'She wanted it to be our secret.'

She could feel Tom's eyes on her, accusing, but she ignored him. She was transfixed by the bracelet. Slowly, she walked across the kitchen. Sofie backed away, scowling.

'Where did you get that?' She pointed at the bracelet. From where she stood she could see the distinctive solid platinum oval nestled next to the catch.

'I bought it last weekend.' The girl's stare was defiant. 'Why? What's it to you?'

A high-pitched whistle started up in Jay's head. 'You're lying.'

'Why don't you get a life instead of having a go at me? All I've tried to do is be your friend!' With that, Sofie ran upstairs. A door slammed.

'Jay . . .' Tom began.

'Not now, Tom.' Jay didn't look at him.

She heard him say, 'Christ,' but she ignored it. Grabbing her mobile, she walked up the stairs, knocked on the spare room door. Sofie's room. 'Sofie?'

'Go away!'

'We need to talk.'

'I don't want to!'

Grateful there wasn't a lock on the door, she knocked again, saying, 'I'm coming in . . .' She stepped inside. Closed the door behind her.

Sofie was curled up on the bed. Her look was narrowed, wary.

Jay settled at the foot of the bed. Not too close, but not too far away either. 'The bracelet,' she said. Her tone was gentle.

'I got it at the market.'

'Do you know what it's made of?'

'Silver.'

'It's platinum. Do you know what platinum is?'

Sofie didn't say anything.

'It's a metallic element. Much more expensive than silver. Much more expensive than white gold. If you look at the solid flat oval, on its underside, you'll see something there. Two sets of initials inside a tiny heart. A and R. Why don't you have a look?'

Sofie began to fidget. She didn't look at the bracelet.

'Where did you get it?' Jay asked for the second time.

Nothing.

'I need to know. Because it belongs to my mother. She never takes it off. My father gave it to her when my brother was born. I'm worried how you got it.'

Sofie fiddled with the bracelet. Jay could see she was trying to overturn the oval and look for the initials without making it obvious.

'The initials stand for Alison and Robert.' Jay's voice was still soft. 'It's not your bracelet. I'm right, aren't I?'

Sofie refused to look at her.

Jay dialled her mother's number in Blakeney, Norfolk. 'Hi, Mum.'

'Jessica, darling.' Her mother's voice was warm. 'How are you?'

Jay turned the phone so that Sofie could hear both sides of the conversation.

'I'm fine. Look, I just wanted to know if you've lost your bracelet? The one Dad gave you when Angus was born?'

There was a shocked silence. 'How on *earth* did you know about that?'

'I have it here.'

'You do? Why? I mean, how in the world—'

'Have you seen a woman with dyed blonde hair? Slim and quite pretty?'

'No, darling. But a swarthy, horrid little man came to my door yesterday, saying he was raising money for the lifeboats, and when I said I already supported them, he became nasty. He wanted my engagement ring, but I refused, so he said the bracelet would do . . . I rang the police the second he left . . .'

Tivon, Jay thought. It couldn't be anyone else.

'I'll bring it over tomorrow,' Jay told her. It was a five hour drive to Blakeney, but Jay wasn't going to do this over the phone. She wanted her family to be prepared.

'What's going on?' Her mother's tone turned worried.

Jay moved the phone so Sofie couldn't hear any more. 'I'll explain when I see you, but in the meantime be careful, won't you? Don't answer the door to anyone you don't know, no matter who they say they are. Keep all the doors and windows locked. OK?'

Her mother sighed. 'I do wish you weren't involved in these Eastern Bloc countries. The traffickers. They're so dangerous.'

'Mum, it's got nothing to do with work. This is something different.'

'Oh.'

'I should be with you early afternoon.'

'We could have a late lunch,' her mother said brightly. 'Which would you prefer? Lasagne, or chicken and leek pie?'

Since her mother's puff pastry was legendary, Jay didn't hesitate. 'Chicken pie would be great.'

Jay put her phone away. Looked at Sofie. 'It's not your bracelet,' she said.

Sofie hung her head. Her mouth was pinched.

'Where did you get it?'

'The woman.'

'The woman I saw leaving the house?'

Sofie nodded.

'Did it come with a note? A message?'

'It was in an envelope.'

'Where is it?'

Sofie looked furtively around the room, as though wishing she could escape.

'Please, Sofie.'

Finally, the girl unwound and hopped off the bed. Slid her hand under the mattress and withdrew a small padded envelope. Passed it to Jay. It had *Jay McCaulay* printed in bold black letters on the front. There was nothing inside.

'You opened this, despite the fact it had my name on it?'
Still, Jay kept her voice level, calm.

Sofie bit her lip. Gave a small nod.

'And there was nothing else inside?'

'No,' she whispered. Then, 'You're not going to tell Daddy,
are you?'

'Sofie, I have to. This is serious. Not so much that you stole
something that wasn't yours, but that the woman delivered it
here.'

'I'm sorry.' Her mouth trembled. 'I don't know why I
opened it. Honestly, I don't. I thought she was the postman.
I mean, woman. She wore a red waistcoat . . . She was scary,
though. I thought she'd be nice, but there was something
about her . . . She didn't smell very nice either. Mummy wears
Chanel, but she wore something really sickly.'

The smell of rotting honeysuckle.

It was as she'd suspected. Nahid was the assassin.

She couldn't believe Nahid had come here. *Here!* To Tom's
house!

'She told me to tell you something . . .' Sofie was picking at
her fingernails.

'Go ahead.'

'She said . . . to keep your mouth shut.'

A chill swept over Jay's skin. Blake had been right. Nahid
was threatening her, warning her not to go to the police. Perhaps
also threatening her not to tell Tom, who was a cop?

'Anything else?'

'No,' Sofie whispered.

'I thought you said the woman mentioned Max Blake?'

Sofie seemed to shrink. 'I made that bit up.'

'How do you know about Blake?'

'I heard you and Daddy rowing that morning.'

'What else did you hear?'

Sofie twisted her hands. 'Nothing.'

Like hell, Jay thought, but let it go. 'Sofie.' She waited until
the girl met her eyes. 'Thanks for coming clean. Now, can I
have the bracelet?'

The girl undid the catch and passed it over. Jay slid the bracelet
inside the envelope. 'Let's go downstairs. Talk to your father.'

'Do we have to?' Sofie pleaded. 'You've got the bracelet
now . . .'

'Yes, we have to.'

Reluctant, looking churlish – an expression that Jay was beginning to realize hid real fear – Sofie trailed downstairs after Jay. Tom looked up when they entered the kitchen. He was at the end of the table reading a newspaper and drinking a beer. His expression was wary.

'Sit down,' Jay told Sofie.

Jay sat opposite the girl, where she could watch her face. She said, 'A woman came to the house today and delivered this.' She passed the envelope over. Tom looked inside. Extracted the bracelet.

'Does this have anything to do with your email?' he said.

She'd asked him about the Garrison. 'Yes, it does.'

'Have you reported this woman?' Tom asked. 'Who threatened *my daughter*?'

'Not yet.'

'Why?'

'I wanted to speak to Blake first.' As soon as the words were out of her mouth, she knew she'd made a mistake.

Tom's face flushed. He glanced at Sofie, then back to Jay. 'We need to talk alone. Now.'

TWELVE

R ising to his feet, Tom stalked to the sitting room next door.

Jay didn't look at Sofie as she followed him. She didn't want to see the girl's triumph that she was going to get a dressing down.

Tom swung round as Jay entered the room, closing the door behind her. 'Blake?' His voice had risen. 'You want Blake to advise you about *my daughter*?'

Jay made dampening motions with her hands. 'No, it's not like that. I mean . . . Look, Tom. Blake thought that as long as I kept quiet, they'd leave me alone.'

'Obviously –' Tom's voice was like acid – 'he's wrong.'

Jay ran a hand over her face, feeling shaky. She hated rows. She hated upsetting Tom. She was glad she was headed to

Norfolk tomorrow, where her mother would hug her and tell her everything would be all right.

'What's the Garrison?' Tom asked.

Jay hadn't told Tom the question came from Blake. She suddenly felt weary of standing between the two men, fighting to keep Tom's trust, fighting to keep her distance from Blake.

She said, 'Blake initially thought it was a security company, but he's now thinking it might be a code, or a secret organization.'

Tom was looking at her with an expression of disbelief.

Jay ploughed on. 'I warned you to be careful. He's worried there are a lot of fingers in a lot of official pies.'

'He thinks it's a conspiracy?' He was shaking his head. 'I don't believe this . . .'

Jay fiddled with her watch, unable to meet his eyes. Finally, she heard him heave a sigh.

'Jesus, Jay.'

She looked up to see he was gazing at her. His expression was resigned. 'Run everything past me, would you? I need to know what we're up against.'

He indicated the sofa. Jay sat. Tom took the armchair next to her. His expression switched to his cop face. Cool, calm, professional. Slowly, Tom took her through every step she'd taken since Blake had entered his kitchen five days ago. Finally, he looked at the floor. His hands were dangling between his knees. He was frowning.

'So,' he said. 'Blake's been set up for murder, and there are two nasty pieces of work hanging around making sure you're not going to report anything to anyone official.'

'That's right.'

'And they don't know you've got a copy of Sol's SIM and memory cards.'

'I'm not sure whether they checked my mobile phone at the farmhouse.' She thought further. 'If it's that important, and they knew I had it, wouldn't they be demanding it?'

'How would they know you hadn't copied it in the mean-time? Sent dozens of copies around the world?'

'They wouldn't,' she admitted.

'Which is why they want to keep you scared,' Tom remarked. 'So you don't share Sol's information with the wrong people. Can I have a look?'

'How about I email it all to you later? Then you'll have every-thing on file.'

He nodded. He wasn't looking at Jay, but past her. He was still frowning. He said, 'I asked about the Garrison.'

Jay blinked.

'It's only now,' Tom said slowly, 'that I'm wondering if Nahid's warning was connected to my questions, rather than to my merely being a policeman.'

Jay swallowed. 'Who did you ask?'

'I was careful, as you suggested. I only spoke to two people. Goose and Clarky.'

Goose was a plain-clothes cop who Tom had known and worked with for over ten years. Clarky was Tom's boss; Superintendent Clarkson. Jay liked Goose and Clarky enormously. Tom trusted both with his life.

'If those are the only two . . .' Jay began.

Tom scrubbed his face with both hands. 'Clarky warned me off.'

'*What?*'

'I didn't realize it at the time. It's only now that I can see it . . . He wanted to know why I was asking. I said it was a favour for a friend, nothing serious. I was really casual about it. He said, "In that case, let sleeping dogs lie." But when I didn't let it drop, he asked me if I'd considered moving cities in order to promote my career. He said it jokingly, but now I realize he was serious.'

Jay felt her skin tighten. 'Jesus, Tom.'

They sat in silence for a while. Eventually, Tom said quietly, 'I don't like you being in touch with Blake.' As she began to open her mouth he added, 'It's the fact he's wanted for murder. I really don't want to see you in the dock for aiding and abetting.'

'I can appreciate that,' she said neutrally.

'Dammit.' He clenched his teeth. 'Blake got you into this . . .'

'I didn't mean for Sofie to get involved,' she said.

'I know.' He closed his eyes and rubbed his fingertips into his temples. Gave a wry smile. 'You just attract trouble, right?'

She smiled tentatively back. 'Sorry.'

He raised an arm. Said, 'Come here.'

Jay slipped on to his lap, wound her arms around his neck. Kissed him on the lips. 'I'll go to Mum's tomorrow,' she said. 'Warn the family.'

'And I'll warn Heather.'

'Will you report it?' she asked. She didn't dare ask if he was going to report the fact he knew Blake was in the country.

His eyes narrowed slightly. 'I'll write it up over the weekend, but I won't make it general knowledge. Not until I know more. I'd like to speak to Goose first. He's away until Monday.'

She felt a trickle of relief. She would, she realized, have to tell Blake about Clarky. Keep him in the loop.

'So, in-between consorting with evil assassins and trying to save every victim trafficked into the UK,' he said, smiling, 'what else have you been up to?'

They spent the evening cooking supper and teasing one another. Sofie watched them through quiet eyes, subdued. When Tom made love to Jay later that night, she climaxed so hard, she cried out his name.

Jay's childhood village, Blakeney, was in the grip of a fierce storm when she arrived, the estuary whipped into grey froth. As she slammed her mother's front door behind her, she was assailed by the scent of freshly baking pastry. The next moment, a hairy rocket collided against her shins, whimpering an excited greeting.

'Hello, Tigger.'

She ducked down to pet the miniature schnauzer, who wagged and panted and tore into the kitchen and back, trying to let Jay's mother know she'd arrived.

'Darling!' her mother called. 'I'm in here!'

'Coming!'

The kitchen windows were steamed up, the Aga going full blast. Jay bent to hug her mother, kiss her cheeks. They couldn't look less alike, Jay thought, not for the first time. She felt like a giraffe, all height and long limbs against her mother's rotund, compact body. As usual her mother checked Jay's wedding ring finger. 'Still no ring?' She tut-tutted. 'I guess you haven't set a date either.'

'You guess correctly.'

'Surely Tom's suggested a date?'

'He thought spring might be nice.'

'Spring?' Her mother looked appalled. 'That's six months away!'

'Plenty of time to get your outfit ready,' Jay told her, 'and to order your hat.'

They ate the chicken pie with sautéed green beans, and washed it down with glasses of red wine. Rain lashed against the windows, and Jay was glad her mother had lit a fire in the sitting room. Snuggled on the sofa, coffee to hand, Jay passed over her mother's bracelet. She didn't tell her mother the whole story.

'He wanted to frighten me,' Jay said.

'Like that nasty Russian man did with Cora.' Her mother's lips had pursed.

Earlier in the year, two men had snatched her cousin's necklace outside church, in order to show Jay how vulnerable her family was.

'I guess so,' Jay admitted.

'Oh dear.' Her mother sighed.

Jay didn't say any more. That way, should Tivon turn up again and ask her mother a question, her mother would appear genuinely bewildered. Like Blake with Jay, Jay thought that the less her mother knew, the more it would keep her safe.

They shared the weekend newspapers. Jay dropped off to sleep after a while, only waking when her mother brought in tea and cake and switched on the TV to watch the news. More doom and gloom over the economy. More soldiers dying in Afghanistan. More civilians dying. Jay felt sorrow rise and was grateful when her mobile phone rang.

'Yo,' she answered.

'Yo yourself. What's happening?'

'I'm having tea with Mum in front of the TV. Eating home-made chocolate cake.'

'My kind of afternoon,' Blake said.

His kind of *what*? She couldn't see Blake sitting in front of the fire all afternoon, no matter how foul the weather. He was too active to stay still for long and would probably prefer to be jogging up a mountain with a fifty-pound pack strapped to his back.

'Tom?' her mother mouthed at Jay.

Jay shook her head. 'Work,' she mouthed back.

'More tea?' her mother whispered.

Jay nodded, watched her mother take the tray outside.

'About your text,' Blake said. 'Fill me in.'

Jay told him about Nahid delivering her mother's bracelet to

Tom's house. 'It confirms beyond doubt that Nahid is Sol's assassin,' she told him.

'Agreed.'

'Tom asked about the Garrison,' she added. 'He got warned off.'

'Who by?' Blake's tone was alert.

'His boss. Superintendent Clarkson.'

'Interesting,' Blake said. 'Because I've hit a couple of walls my end. Any chance you could put some feelers out with some old army buddies of yours? Help us get a wider picture?'

'I'll start with the girls.'

'Good idea.' Small pause. 'Sorry. Gotta go, hon.'

He hung up.

Jay rang home. Angela answered the phone. 'A favour,' Jay asked.

'Sure.'

'Could you ask old friends whether they've heard of something called the Garrison? It could be a code, or some kind of underground organization. Be really cautious. I mean *really* cautious.'

'This to do with your possible watchers?'

'Yes.'

'OK. We'll tread carefully.'

Jay's mother returned with a fresh pot of tea, and Jay put the Garrison aside for the moment. Later, her mother served home-made soup and crusty bread in front of an old Agatha Christie movie, and Jay was about to head for bed when her mobile rang. Her mother looked at it disapprovingly. It was after ten o'clock. Her mother considered it the height of bad manners to call anyone before nine a.m. and after ten p.m.

'Sorry, Mum,' she said as she answered. 'Hi?'

'Hi, Jay.'

Her mouth opened. It was her old boss. 'Major?'

'Rick,' he corrected.

'Rick,' she repeated, but after calling him Major for three years it still felt strange using his Christian name. 'Good grief,' she added. She couldn't help herself. Rick Wayland had been central to her being invalided out of the army. He'd been the one to call time out on her, take her weapon from her, and sent her to a shrink for evaluation. It had been, she realized later, a good call, and she never blamed him for her abrupt change in career. If anything, she was grateful. She loved her current job.

'I've just received a call from a friend of mine in Portsmouth,' Rick said. 'RMP. I can't do this by phone. We have to meet.' His tone was curt, all business.

RMP: Royal Military Police. Jay cleared her throat. She hadn't realized she'd jumped to her feet the second she'd heard his voice. Her body was rigidly standing to attention.

'Where are you?' Rick asked.

'Blakeney. On the northern coast of Norfolk.'

'I know Blakeney. Give me a time and place.'

Instinct made her choose somewhere away from her mother's house. 'The Red Lion at Stiffkey, around midday?'

'Midday it is. See you then.'

Without another word, he hung up.

The Red Lion stood overlooking the marshlands. Stone walls, flagstone floors and a roaring log fire in the grate, it was as familiar to Jay as her mother's house. She used to walk here most weekends in her teens, and now the landlord greeted her with a kiss and berated her for living in London.

'You're not a city girl,' he told her. 'Move back home.'

'I like London.'

'London's for pussies.'

Jay took her cider to a table near the fire. It was still blowing a gale outside, spattering rain against the window panes, and although it was relatively early for lunch, the pub was already half full. Few people were out walking today. Most preferred to tuck up in the warmth and socialize.

Jay recognized a couple of faces and said hello to an old school friend, Josie, and Josie's boyfriend, both of whom came and sat with her. Every time the door opened, she flicked her eyes over the newcomer and away. Major Wayland was known for being absolutely punctual, usually early, but not today. After half an hour, she checked her phone, but there was no message, no text. She tried his number. Her stomach tightened at the auto-mated response: *this service has been disconnected.*

When two hours had passed, Jay returned to Blakeney. The harbour was grey and foaming with waves whipped by the wind. Tucked up by the fire, more newspapers to hand, she waited for as long as she could before leaving for London, but the Major never called. Come eight p.m. she decided enough was enough and packed up.

'Bye Mum.' She hugged her mother before stroking Tigger's head. His stumpy tail was down.

'Be careful, darling.' Her mother's embrace was tight.

'I will.'

The drive home was slow, the traffic hard to see through the spray. At one point, she had to slow to a crawl when she passed an accident on the A1065. A black Audi lay upside down on the hard shoulder, crushed against a tree and surrounded with police tape. The ambulances were long gone. Just a police tow truck remained, along with two cop cars.

As usual, when Jay got home, she rang her mother to tell her she'd arrived safely. 'Thanks for the takeaway,' she said. Her mother always sent her home with boxes of Tupperware filled with goodies. Today she had slices of pink roast beef, a whole quiche, and a box of chocolate brownies. The girls had taken one look at the brownies and snaffled them next door. They loved her mother's cooking.

'I heard there was an accident south of Mundford,' her mother said. 'It was on the local news.'

'It was all over when I went past. Someone driving too fast, no doubt.'

Jay didn't know how wrong she was until she listened to the news the next day. Apparently a Major Wayland had been found dead when his black Audi had overturned on a country road in Norfolk. He had been shot through the head.

THIRTEEN

'Which one of you rang the Major?' Jay was looking between Denise and Angela. Both looked neat and smart in their security uniforms. Blue shirts and trousers, epaulettes, shoes nice and flat in case they needed to chase anyone. Jay had driven to Heathrow as quickly as she could after she'd heard the Major was dead.

'Neither of us,' Denise said.

They were sitting in a small windowless room somewhere

in the bowels of Terminal Five. The label on the door read: *Interview Room 3*. Three Styrofoam cups of coffee stood on the table, but no one was drinking.

'But you spoke to someone he knew.'

Angela nodded. 'Colonel Greene. He's with the RMP in Portsmouth. An old buddy of ours. He told us not to ask about the Garrison again, that he was on the job.'

'Is the Colonel OK?' Jay looked between them. 'He's not dead as well, is he?'

The girls shook their heads. 'We checked after you rang us.'

'I need to talk to him.' Jay brought out her phone. 'What's his number?'

When nobody said anything, she glanced up. Both her friends were looking uncomfortable. 'What's wrong?'

'We can't give it to you,' Denise said. 'Sorry, but we promised. He nearly had heart failure when we told him the Major was dead. He warned us against digging any more . . .' Denise paused when Angela held up a hand.

Angela said, 'He said that we must never mention the Garrison again, or it could be us next.'

'Christ,' said Jay. She licked her lips. 'This is serious.'

Voices echoed briefly in the corridor outside. A door slammed.

Jay said, 'I *have* to talk to the Colonel.'

'No way.' Denise was shaking her head. 'We promised we wouldn't pursue this. Not when people are getting assassinated.'

'*You* promised him,' Jay said. 'I didn't.'

'No.' Denise was firm. 'We swore that would be the end of it, OK?'

'But Major Wayland is *dead*.' For the first time since she'd heard the news, emotion rose. She pictured her ex-boss's intelligent brown eyes that could sharpen in an instant, assessing risk, calculating every factor before he barked orders. Then his weary face when he'd taken her weapon that day in Kosovo. He'd been one of the best commanding officers she'd worked with, and she'd held him in high regard. He left behind a widow, Ruth, and two children, aged ten and twelve.

Jay felt the weight of guilt pressing on her shoulders. If she hadn't asked the girls to ask about the Garrison, the Major could still be alive. If she'd left well alone – as Nahid had warned her to – the Major's family might still have a father.

A tight knot of anger balled in her heart. They had killed one of the most decent men she knew. If she could, she would make them pay.

Jay considered going to Portsmouth, but if Colonel Greene didn't want to see her, she'd find it impossible to get past the guards on the gate. She could always lie in wait and follow Greene home after work, but, firstly, she didn't know what he looked like, and secondly, he might live on site. She bit her lip, thinking. Finally, she got to her feet. 'Thanks, guys,' she told her housemates.

'What's the plan?' Angela asked.

'Ring Blake,' Jay prevaricated, not wanting to tell the girls her real plan in case they tipped off Greene. She hated deceiving them, but couldn't see any other option.

'Send him our love.' Denise grinned, but Jay couldn't raise a smile, not with her old boss dead.

Sitting in her car in the multi-storey car park, half-watching a couple trail up and down the rows of cars trying to find their vehicle, Jay rang Blake, but there was no reply. When his messaging service kicked in, she simply said, 'Call me.'

Jay thought about going to the office. Then she checked her map. Major Wayland and his family lived just outside Bosham, near Chichester. She'd been there a couple of times. Once for a barbecue in the summer, the second time for Christmas drinks. It was a great area for bicycling, she remembered. No hills, lots of water and sea air, and great pubs. Pain stabbed at her with the memory of the Major's face. The way he'd held hands with his wife, laughed with his kids.

Turning on the radio, Jay didn't hear what the chat-show host was saying. She felt a numbness in her body. A grey space in her soul. She let the minutes tick past. Finally, she rang Nick, told him she wouldn't be in for the rest of the day because a friend had died. She didn't say any more. She didn't need to. Nick knew her well enough to know she only took time off when it was serious.

The drive south was dull and grey. More rain. More spray. She took the M3 and then the M27, which eventually dropped into a dual carriageway. Exiting at Emsworth, Jay trickled through a handful of windswept coastal villages. Everyone walked hunched in waterproofs, heads down.

Built out of wood, Sea Spray stood overlooking one of the

tributaries off Chichester Harbour. A long swathe of wild grasses rolled to a jetty, where a skiff bucked against its ropes. Several cars were in the driveway, indicating Ruth wasn't alone. She'd have family with her, Jay realized. Maybe some of the Major's colleagues.

Jay pressed the bell. A grey-haired man answered.

'Yes?' he said.

'Can I see Ruth? I'm Jay. The Major used to be my boss.'

'Just a minute.'

Ruth came to the door. Jay knew Ruth wouldn't be looking her best, having just lost her husband, but even so it was a shock to see Ruth's pallor, the way she walked like an old woman. She was barely forty, but she looked thirty years older. She said, 'Jay.' Just the one word was obviously a huge effort.

'I'm sorry.'

'Yes.'

Jay said, 'I know it's not the best time, but I need to know where I can find a friend of Rick's.'

Ruth frowned. Jay could see a cog begin to work in her brain. 'Is it about Rick's death?'

'No,' Jay lied. She'd already decided to tell Ruth as little as possible, to try and protect her.

Ruth surveyed her steadily. 'Which friend?'

'Colonel Greene at the RMP, Portsmouth.'

Something moved behind Ruth's eyes. Suspicion? Misgiving? Jay wasn't sure, but whatever it was it had brought the faintest blush of colour to the woman's cheeks.

'You know something about why Rick died,' Ruth said. 'Why he was murdered.'

'No.'

'You think Colonel Greene – Harry – knows something too.'

Again, Jay said, 'No,' and finally thought to add a cover story. 'I want to talk to him about a case I'm on at the moment. A missing Russian girl.'

A skein of geese flew overhead, honking. Ruth didn't look at them. Nor did Jay. Their gazes were locked.

'Rick was on his way to see you when he was murdered,' Ruth stated.

Jay looked away. Guilt sat in her stomach like a sack of cement.

'Do you know why?' Ruth asked.

'No.' Jay looked back at Ruth and immediately felt her cheeks begin to heat. God, she was crap at this. Some days, like today, she wished she could lie more successfully.

Ruth's gaze was unerring. 'Does Rick's death have anything to do with the Garrison?'

Jay tried not to show her surprise, but it was too late.

Ruth said, 'I'll get my coat.'

Before Jay could move, Ruth had vanished, leaving the door ajar. Jay craned her head inside. She could smell coffee and hear the murmur of voices. Someone said, 'No.'

Another voice said, 'I don't think it's a good idea.'

And then Ruth's voice, quite crisp. 'I won't be long.'

Ruth swept outside. She was wearing a long coat the colour of mulberries, over grey trousers and soft suede boots. 'Where's your car?'

Jay pointed. Beeped the Golf open. Ruth climbed into the passenger seat, buckled up.

'Where to?' Jay asked.

'The RMP, Southwick Park. You know where it is?'

'Just that it's near Portsmouth.'

'I'll direct you.'

It didn't take long to drive there. Twenty minutes or so. As Jay had predicted, there were two marines on the gate, both armed with MP5s.

Ruth told Jay to park on the left. 'Join me in the guard house. I'll start getting us logged in.'

The guard house was a prefabricated box with plexiglas windows and a uniformed security guard called Clive. Clive took their photographs for their passes, and from his gentle and solicitous attitude with Ruth, it was obvious she'd been a regular visitor. He said, 'The Colonel should be out of his meeting now. I'll let him know you're here.'

Jay watched him pick up the phone and dial. She could feel Ruth watching too.

Clive spoke, then glanced round and looked at Jay. He nodded, hung up. Came to the counter window. 'Mrs Wayland, you're good to go. Sorry, Miss McCaulay, but the Colonel can't see you today. If you wouldn't mind making an appointment, perhaps for next week, that would be good.'

Jay knew the Colonel wouldn't see her. Not after what the girls had said. She was about to take Ruth outside and ask for the Colonel's home address, when Ruth drew herself tall. When she spoke, her voice was like steel. 'Get him on the phone.'

'But Mrs Wayland, the Colonel was quite clear—'

'I want to speak to him *now*.'

Even Jay flinched.

'Yes, Ma'am.'

Clive scurried back to the phone. Dialled. Nervously, he checked Ruth when he began to speak. Then he stopped. Swallowed. Glanced at Ruth again. Spoke some more. Finally, he brought over the phone. The cord barely stretched halfway, forcing Clive to bring the phone's base to the counter.

Ruth picked up the receiver. Her voice was hard. 'Harry, if you don't see Jay McCaulay and me within the next ten minutes, I am going to the Press with a story that will make your hair curl. You know which one I mean.' She dropped the phone back into the receiver.

When the phone rang, Ruth looked at Clive, her hand raised like a traffic cop's. 'I'm not speaking to him until he agrees to see us both.' She walked outside, shoulders stiff. Jay followed. Wind hissed through the trees and made the puddles shiver.

'What's this about?' Jay asked.

'Sorry, Jay, but I don't want to say anything until Harry's here.'

Colonel Harry Greene didn't come to the gate himself, but sent his Staff Sergeant. Swagger stick beneath his arm, the sergeant marched them past the marines and down a driveway. He didn't make any small talk, and Jay wondered if he'd been briefed to keep quiet. She took note of the signposts as they walked. *Mess, dining hall, lecture theatre*. At last, they paused outside a museum. A tall man with faded sandy hair stepped outside. He was in uniform, and Jay struggled not to snap him a salute. Old habits died hard.

'Sir,' the Staff Sergeant said with a salute, standing back, awaiting his next order.

'Thank you, Staff. You may go.'

The Staff Sergeant left, leaving the Colonel surveying Jay steadily with cool grey eyes.

'Please.' Colonel Greene stepped back and ushered Ruth and Jay inside the museum. Aside from wall-to-wall artefacts – including a dummy military policeman in full uniform atop a stuffed horse – the place was empty.

Standing next to the horse, he folded his arms. Said, 'What's this about?'

Ruth said, 'Rick was killed because of the Garrison, wasn't he?'

If the Colonel's face was closed before, now it became firmly barred. 'I have no idea what you're talking about.'

'He was *murdered*, Harry. He had a bullet hole in his head.'

'I heard.' The Colonel's face remained like rock. 'I'm sorry, Ruth. Truly I am. But I know nothing about it.'

'You were investigating the Garrison. A secret organization, Rick said. A dangerous organization.'

'I've been investigating nothing of the sort. And I've never heard of the Garrison.'

'You're saying Rick was never approached socially by his superior officer, Lieutenant Colonel Owen, and asked light-heartedly whether he'd join an organization that was dedicated to halting the flood of Muslims into the West?'

'It's news to me.'

'And when Rick told Lieutenant Colonel Owen that he didn't agree with any group acting outside the official channels, he was sidelined for what had been a rock-solid promotion.'

'Ruth . . .'

'Shut up, Harry.'

The Colonel closed his mouth. He looked calm and collected, but then Jay saw the tiny tic at the corner of his left eye. When Blake was stressed, his skin puckered minutely in the same place.

'Rick didn't seriously think it was the work of a secret society until he brought in the RMP to investigate a murder case. He had watertight evidence against one of his men, a Corporal Owen, which subsequently "vanished". Corporal Owen was Lieutenant Colonel Owen's nephew. You remember the case, don't you?'

The Colonel flicked his eyes to Jay, then back to Ruth. He remained silent.

'It wasn't the first case that had been tampered with. Quietly, you began investigating what you thought was a secret society. And then you were warned off. Rick told me.'

'Look,' the Colonel began, palms spread. 'I know it's been a shock losing Rick, but I've never even *heard* of a secret society in the Services.' He looked at Jay. 'Please, can't you see Ruth's under stress here? She's got everything muddled—'

'Then who killed him?' Ruth stepped forward until she was inches from the Colonel.

He looked down at her, expression as smooth and cold as alabaster.

'Who shot my husband through the head when he was driving to see Jay? Who wanted to stop him from getting to Blakeney?'

He licked his lips. 'Ruth . . .'

'I thought you had the courage to follow this through,' she said. 'Rick thought so too. But he was wrong. You're gutless.'

'Now, that's enough.' His nostrils flared. 'You don't know what you're talking about—'

'I'm going to the police with this. The Press. Right now.' As Ruth made to turn aside, Colonel Greene caught her arm. She shrugged it off.

'Don't,' he said. 'Please.'

'Why not?'

'Just don't.'

'I'm sorry, Harry.' Ruth appeared resolute. 'But with Rick dead, I have nothing to lose.'

'What about Lucie and George?'

'They've got their grandparents.'

Greene looked shocked. 'You can't be serious.'

'I have never been more serious in my life,' Ruth flared. 'With or without your help, Jay and I are going to get retribution for Rick.'

Jay was careful not to move, not to speak. Just watched the scene play out.

'You have no idea what you're getting yourself into,' the Colonel said tightly.

'Tell us, then, Harry.'

'I can't.' Despite his military stance, his even tone, Jay realized the man was begging.

'Because you're too scared.' Ruth curled her lip.

The muscles in his jaw jumped. 'I have a wife and children too.'

You could have heard a pin drop.

'Oh, Harry.' Ruth's face crumpled. 'They've threatened your family?'

'Enough.' Both of his hands were raised. 'I have a meeting I'm already late for. I'll see you out.'

Nobody said a word as he walked them to the gate.

The last Jay saw of the Colonel was as he stepped into the guard house. He glanced at her briefly before he vanished inside. In that one moment, she saw an emotion pass his face, but it wasn't what she expected – fear, or perhaps anger. It was despair.

FOURTEEN

Back in London, Jay thought over everything she'd learned, trying to find a way to track Rick's murderer, and preferably without alerting the Garrison.

Sol had been in love with Blake's sister. Emilie was convinced she'd been targeted, perhaps because she'd overheard something about the Garrison. Tom had asked about the Garrison and been warned off, proving that at least one – senior – cop knew the Garrison existed.

Jay's guess was that when the girls called Colonel Harry Greene, the Colonel had then talked to Rick. Rick had been murdered to stop him telling her about the Garrison and confirming the organization existed.

Jay's mind jumped to Nahid, and then Sol's SIM and memory cards. In the kitchen, she switched on her computer and inserted her USB stick. She emailed Tom Sol's pictures before downloading them on to her home laptop. This time, she studied them carefully, trying to think laterally. If they were a code, as Blake thought, how to crack it?

As if her thoughts had conjured him, her phone rang.

'Yo,' he said.

'Hi.'

'What is it?' He sharpened.

'My old boss has been murdered. Major Rick Wayland.'

'Tell me.'

Jay ran through the story. 'It looks like the Garrison has a hold on the Services.'

'And the police,' Blake told her. 'As well as my guys.'

Her pulse jumped. The Garrison had spread into MI5?

'And they don't want it known,' Blake added. His tone was tight.

'Are you all right?' she asked, knowing it was a stupid question considering he was wanted for murder, but unable to stop herself.

'I saw my boss. He told me to lie low for a while. You do the same. No matter what happens. You hear something's happened to me, you ignore it. You get told by a third party I want to meet with you – and I haven't rung you myself – you treat it with the contempt it deserves. I'm on my own out here. Don't trust anyone who says otherwise. Keep safe, hon.' He rang off.

Jay studied Sol's photographs but, despite her efforts, came up with nothing new by the time her housemates came home.

'What's up?' Denise asked her.

Jay considered whether to be straight with the girls or not. It didn't take more than five seconds, because if they discovered she'd lied, it would be the end of their friendship. Jay said, 'I saw your friend, Colonel Greene—'

'Jay!' Angela was on her in a flash. 'We specifically asked you not to bug him.'

'I know. But I had Rick's widow with me. Ruth. She wanted to see him.'

'Oh.' Angela looked slightly mollified. 'How did it go?'

'Ruth got some closure, I think.'

'And the Colonel?'

'He wasn't best pleased to see me,' Jay admitted. 'But I learned a lot from our meeting.' She quickly filled them in. 'Forgive me?'

'No harm done,' said Angela.

To Jay's relief, Denise agreed. 'We won't be invited to Greene's Christmas party, but what the heck . . . You fancy lamb shank for supper? I got some from M&S. Couldn't be bothered to cook. Too long a day.' She yawned.

Glad to be forgiven, Jay mucked in, washing up the dishes after they'd eaten. Their usual evening routine when they were all in. Jay went to bed and fell into a troubled, restless sleep, filled with dreams of Rick Wayland and Kosovan houses pockmarked with bullet holes.

*   *   *

Jay spent the next week doing what she normally did: getting up at seven thirty, hitting the office an hour later, working her backside off liaising with charities and organizations around the world in an attempt to stem the list of missing persons from rising to catastrophic proportions. Lily texted to say she'd heard a rumour that a new Russian-style brothel had opened – the Russia House – prompting Jay to make another trip to Bristol to try and trace Irina, without success. With Nahid at the back of her mind, she kept her eyes open for any watchers, but aside from the woman she'd seen initially, walking her little white dog, there seemed to be nobody suspicious hanging around.

The girls were on nights over the next week, which meant Jay lived on ready meals and takeaways. Some evenings she just had a bowl of soup or a sandwich, but today was Friday, so she decided to spoil herself and head for the noodle house around the corner. She had a scratchy throat, a precursor to a cold, and she hoped their five-chilli chicken and prawn laksa would have its usual effect and blast away any germs. She couldn't eat the laksa in polite company because it was so fiery, making her eyes water, her nose run. She was looking forward to being well and truly messy, with no company but a box of double-strength tissues and a copy of the *Evening Standard.*

Jay's sinuses were well and truly clear by the time she left the restaurant. As she stepped on to the pavement, about to swing right and head back home, a man bumped into her.

'Sorry,' he muttered and, seemingly off-balance, gripped her upper arm. At the same time, she felt something hard and uncompromising rammed against the soft skin below her ribs.

She glanced down. Her stomach hollowed. It was a pistol.

'Into the car,' he said quietly.

A grey Vauxhall was parked against the curb. Its rear door was open. She could see two men inside. The driver, and a man on the rear seat who covertly showed her he also had a pistol.

Oh God.

Jay knew once she was inside the car she would have no chance of escape. She opened her mouth, but before she could scream the man brought back his arm and elbowed her in the stomach. It was like having a mallet swung into her intestines.

The wind rushed out of her. Dizzy, she bent double, staggering across the pavement, fighting to catch her breath. She was amazed she wasn't sick.

'Is she all right?' she heard someone ask.

'Asthma,' the man said. 'She'll be fine in a minute, eh?'

He manhandled her to the car. The man from the rear seat came to help. Jay tried to struggle, but she couldn't breathe. She tried to kick one of the men, but her attempt was feeble. The next second she was on the back seat. *Clunk*. She heard the central locking engage. Gently, the Vauxhall pulled away. No screech of burning rubber, no revving engine to alert anyone that anything untoward had happened.

Her breath returned in a rush. Gasping, she clutched her waist. Her stomach ached from the man's sucker punch. The man next to her wrenched her handbag from her grasp. Dug out her mobile phone and switched it off. Chucked her handbag into the front of the car.

'Where are you taking me?' she panted.

Nobody said anything. She was trembling, her veins alight with panic.

Keep calm. Think. Assess the situation.

She studied the three men. They looked like squaddies. Short and thickset, with close-cut hair and muscular necks. Two were dark-haired, the one in the back was blond.

'Are you from the Garrison?'

The man in the passenger seat twisted to give a nod at the man sitting next to Jay. He immediately gripped her by the neck and forced her to sprawl face down in the footwell. She could see nothing but carpet. Smell nothing but air freshener. He kept his hand on the back of her neck, controlling her.

She heard the man in front say, 'Max Blake?' Small pause, then, 'We have someone here who'd like a word.'

The pressure on her neck was released. She raised herself a fraction. A phone was being held in front of her. Jay raised herself further. Saw they were turning left just before Battersea Bridge. She blurted, 'Grey Vauxhall. We're heading east on the Embankment—'

The man clipped her around the head, making her ears ring. The phone vanished.

'You heard that?' the man up front said. 'Good. Now listen . . . We want you to . . . No, *you* listen . . . We've got your pussy here, and . . . Hey, back off, pal. No . . . Blake, will you shut . . . Jesus.' The man cursed roundly. 'He hung up on me.'

'Ring him again, eh?' the driver said. 'Time's ticking.'

'Keep your hair on . . . It's ringing.'

Jay felt the car slow to a stop and assumed they'd come to a red light.

'Still ringing . . .'

After thirty seconds or so, they pulled away steadily. No sharp pressure on the accelerator. No rush.

'For fuck's sake,' he said. 'He's not answering.'

'Leave a message telling him what we'll do to pussy here if he doesn't cooperate.'

'I can't,' the man growled. 'It's not going to his messaging service. Jesus . . . It just went dead on me. What is wrong with this guy?'

'But everything's set up for twenty-one hundred,' said the man on the back seat. His tone was disbelieving.

The car swung right, shuddering over what felt like cobble-stones but Jay guessed were rumble strips designed to alert drivers to slow down for a junction.

'What if he's buggered off?' the guy with Jay said.

'Then we abort.'

'Christ. The boss will go nuts.'

'I'll keep trying him. The prick.'

What was Blake doing?

Fear knotted her stomach. What if they got fed up with being messed around and decided to dispose of her, dump her body in the Thames? She'd seen their faces. She could identify them in a line-up. Mouth dry, Jay twisted her wrist, looked at her watch. Just past eight o'clock.

Blake's words echoed in her mind.

I'm worried they might use you to get me.

She tried to think what Blake was doing. She visualized him driving his BMW, racing for the Embankment, checking every grey Vauxhall. Except they weren't on the Embankment any more. Blake was on his own. He had no one to help him. No backup.

They continued to drive. The first man kept trying Blake's number and cursing. The minutes ticked past. Ten, twenty, thirty. At eight forty-five, Jay heard the man say, 'Boss? Yeah, it's us. We've got McCaulay, but Blake's not playing ball. As soon as he heard we had her, he went off the radar. Not answering his phone . . . Yeah, I know the boys are in place. Yeah, I know . . . *I know*, OK?' He finally snapped. 'It's not

my fucking fault he's gone AWOL . . . Yeah, OK. You sure?
It's not ideal, but . . . OK.'

Jay heard the metallic click as he snapped shut his phone.
She now thought of him as the Leader. The Leader, the Driver,
and the guy on the back seat she had named Blondie.

The Leader said, 'We've got to keep her until we get hold
of Blake. The boys are going to stand down until we give them
the word.'

'Shit,' said the driver at the same time as Blondie said, 'You're
joking.'

'I suggest we take her to yours. You're closest.'

'No way!' Blondie protested.

'What do you suggest?' snapped the Leader. 'We can't drive
around all fucking night.'

'This is insane,' said Blondie. 'It was meant to be a quick
snatch, a fast delivery, and in bed by ten.'

'Yeah, well, things don't always go to plan. Which way?'

'Jesus,' Blondie said, but he sounded resigned. 'I don't believe
this . . .' He cursed several times before giving a loud sigh. 'OK.
Keep going straight for a couple of miles. I'll show you where
to turn.'

Jay raised herself a fraction. She said, 'If you ring him on
my phone, Blake might pick up. He might think I've escaped.
Want to help me.'

'We're not stupid,' said the Leader.

It was worth a try, Jay thought, in case Blake could track
her using her mobile. But the men had already thought of that.

What else? You must think of something!

There were some ripping noises, and then Blondie forced her
head back and stuck a length of duct tape across her eyes, another
over her mouth. Being stressed, unable to see, made the drive seem
endless. Eventually, Blondie said, 'I'm down there. Turn left.'

Jay felt the car swing left as he'd commanded.

'It's halfway down on the left . . . Yeah, park in the driveway.
Behind the Fat Boy.'

'Nice one,' remarked the driver.

'Yeah. Got it last year. Goes like buggery.'

Jay assumed they weren't discussing an overweight child,
but a Harley Davidson Fat Boy motorcycle. Quite a nice clue,
if she knew where they were. The car stopped. The engine was
switched off. She was less panicky now she knew she was being

'stashed'. She wondered how long they'd keep her for should Blake not emerge. This thought made her feel dizzy. The men might be told to get rid of her permanently.

Jay felt a rush of icy air as the car door opened. 'Out,' said Blondie.

She clambered outside, stumbling, using the car frame to keep her balance.

'This way.' With a man on either side, gripping her upper arms, she was led forward. The ground's surface was hard and smooth, either paved or covered in concrete. She heard a clanking noise, recognized it as a garage door being raised. 'Inside.' She tripped on a step, but they didn't let her fall. The air smelled faintly of oil and was still and cold. While one man held her, the other tied her hands behind her back.

'Lie down,' the Leader commanded. Jay knelt. He pushed her sideways. She toppled on to the hard, cold floor. She felt his hands on her. He tied her feet together, then ran a rope between the two bindings, effectively hog-tying her and making it impossible to stand, let alone walk.

'You be a good girl now,' he told her.

FIFTEEN

Jay heard the heavy clang as the garage door was shut, then the sound of a key turning in the lock. She tried to wriggle out of her bindings, but they were tied firmly. She began scraping her head against the floor, trying to shift the tape over her eyes and mouth. When she found a concrete lip, she concentrated her efforts, gaining confidence when an edge of tape began to catch at the corner of her eye. She scraped her face a few times, making her eyes water. She began to sweat with the effort, her neck muscles straining, but she kept at it. Eventually, she had rolled the tape back enough to see out of one eye. It was pitch dark.

You've got to get out of here.

Again, she tried to loosen her bindings. After what felt like an age of struggling, she turned her mind to the fact she was in a garage. Garages had tools, right?

By this point, Jay was accustomed to the dark. Orange light seeped through gaps around the garage door. She could see the pale square of a light switch near the door, but it could have been at the end of the street considering her hog-ties. She twisted her head around. Identified a variety of darkened outlines. A lawn mower. A leaf blower. A slender, tall appliance that could be a pressure washer. Whoever lived here liked their appliances.

Her eyes clicked back to the lawn mower.

Lawn mowers have blades. So do other gardening implements.

Jay studied the shapes further. Fixed on one in particular, leaning against the far wall. On her side, she levered herself across the floor, ignoring the bruising pain in her hips and shoulders as she ground her joints into unforgiving concrete. By the time she reached the strimmer – industrial sized with eight-inch long blades – she was gasping for breath behind her gag.

Carefully, she inched herself around and kicked the machine to the ground. Thank God she could open her legs wide enough to straddle the machine. Carefully she jammed the strimmer against the wall, gripped it hard between her knees. The blades were now behind her back.

She was sweating hard by now and finding it difficult to breathe. She forced herself to relax. Closed her eyes and let her breathing steady, her heartbeat slow. Her skin was damp, and she was trembling.

Gently, she probed with her fingers until she found a blade. She wriggled some more; she didn't want to slice open an artery and bleed to death. It took a while until she was confident she was positioned correctly. With her wrists pulled as wide apart as possible, she rubbed the tape against the blade. Back and forth.

Each time it slipped, her heart stopped, terrified she was going to cut herself. Finally, she could feel the tape begin to split and her heart lifted, but on the next stroke her grip slipped and the cold blade fell against her wrist.

Jay yelped behind the tape, but although her skin stung, she knew it wasn't life-threatening. A nick, that was all. But she had to slow down, be careful. Not get carried away.

Sweat dribbled down her face. Gritting her teeth, Jay continued to work her hands back and forth.

She wasn't prepared for the sudden release when her hands sprang apart. The strimmer fell against the floor with a thud.

As quickly as she could, Jay stripped the duct tape from her face before untying her feet. Her legs were shaky as she crossed the garage, flicked on the switch by the door. A fluorescent bulb flickered into life. She tried the door, but it was locked and didn't budge.

Jay looked around the garage. Built with breeze blocks, it was a windowless box with a wall of shelves at the far end, filled with tools, and with a concrete floor. She looked up to see a solid ceiling. She checked every corner of the garage to make sure there was no exit. Then she armed herself with a couple of screwdrivers and a Stanley knife. The men would probably frisk her when they returned, but what the hell. She wasn't going to give up at the first hurdle.

She rummaged around until she'd checked every drawer, every shelf. The temperature was dropping. *Come on, Blake*, she thought. *I don't want to spend the night here. Come and rescue me, won't you?*

No response.

So Jay picked up a mallet and swung it at the garage door, yelling, 'Help!' at the top of her voice.

The mallet hit the metal door with a resounding metallic CLANG.

Again she hit the door. Again she screamed for help.

CLANG.

'Help!'

CLANG.

Jay was striking the door for the fourth time when she heard a commotion outside. The garage door began to rise. Jay stood at the side, ready to sprint outside, but the three men blocked her way like a wall of rugby players.

At the top of her voice, Jay screamed again. 'HELP!'

The men came for her fast, tackling her to the ground. One clamped a hand over her mouth, another hit the side of her head with his fist, but not before she saw a light snap on upstairs in the house opposite. Another light went on in the house adjacent. She hoped the neighbours were nosy and would come to investigate, or call the police. She reckoned on the latter now she could see part of the street. Whitewashed terraced houses with paved parking areas at the front. She saw a VW Polo, a couple of BMWs and an old Rover. Middle-class cars for a middle-class suburb.

She felt hands run over her, strip her of her weapons.

'Get her in the car,' the Leader snapped. 'Get her out of here.'

Fight!

Jay struggled as hard as she could, trying to delay the men, but they were bigger than her and much stronger. She identified the hulking form of the Harley Davidson, but it was shrouded beneath a silver canopy so she couldn't see the bike's colour. Jay concentrated on the VW Polo parked outside the house opposite. Luckily it was parked beneath a street light, the number plate clear to read: YCO9 OPD. Hastily, she committed it to memory before she was crammed into the footwell of the rear seats once more, Blondie's meaty hand resting on the nape of her neck.

'Yeah, it's me.' The Leader was on the phone the instant the car pulled out of the driveway. 'We're on the move ... She went nuts, OK? Started trashing the joint. Neighbours got suspicious, so we got out of there. Yeah, we've got her phone ... OK, we'll give it a go. Yeah ... Yeah. OK.'

He didn't say any more. Jay guessed he'd hung up. Then he said, 'Blake. Don't piss me about ... Yes, we've got her here, but we're on the move so don't bother trying to pinpoint our position ... Sure, Blake. Whatever your heart fucking desires. McCaulay, shout something, would you, so your boyfriend can hear you're alive?'

Jay remained silent.

'God, she's difficult,' the Leader said on a theatrical sigh. 'I have no idea how you put up with her ... Hey, Blake, watch your mouth. No, you shut up ... Shit! He fucking hung up on me again!'

The other two men kept quiet while the Leader ranted. 'How the fuck are we supposed to do our fucking jobs when we've got an idiot like this on our hands? Fuck!'

Jay sneaked a look at her watch. For a moment she thought she was seeing things. She thought she'd been in the garage for around an hour, but it had been much longer. It was now past midnight. No wonder she felt whacked, her muscles trembling with exhaustion. She'd spent over two hours struggling to free herself.

'Send him a text,' the driver suggested. 'Give him the RV point.'

'You really think he'll turn up?'

'It's worth a try, eh?'

'Ah, shit. I'd do anything to finish this assignment.'

The car swayed and bumped as it veered around what Jay took to be a mini roundabout.

'Let the boys know, eh?' the driver added.

'And if he doesn't show?'

'Then we do it again later.'

'Christ.'

Jay closed her eyes, wondering if she could catch forty winks. Her body needed to rest, plus she wanted to be alert for any chance to escape. Gradually, the hand on her nape lessened its pressure. She curled on her side, resting her head against the rear seat. No way could she fall asleep like this . . .

She awoke with a start at one a.m.

'The prick's texted back! We're on!'

Things happened quickly after that. The driver stuck his foot on the accelerator, speeding the car across the city. The Leader made calls during the journey. He spoke to someone called Derby, another person called Wade. He discussed backup, weapons, and positions. How to fulfil the assignment safely. That Blake could be armed and was definitely dangerous.

'He killed one of ours in Paris,' the Leader told Wade. 'Solomon Neill. You knew him? Yeah, good bloke, all up. Fucking shame. So let's get Blake and ram him for it.'

Jay filed the information away. She couldn't think about it now. She had to concentrate. See if there was any way she could help Blake when the time came.

When the car pulled over, the Leader said, 'Tie her up.'

'Shit,' Blondie said. 'I left the duct tape in the garage.'

'Find something else,' the Leader snapped.

'Like what?'

'Christ almighty. Improvise, would you? A tie, a belt . . .'

'I'm not wearing a belt. How about you guys?'

'Use mine,' said the driver. 'But I want it back. Julie gave it to me for Christmas.'

'Wade?' The Leader was back on the phone. 'You in place?'

Blondie clicked his fingers at Jay. Said, 'Give me your hands.'

Kneeling, she twisted around. Felt the leather twist around her wrists, but although he seemed to pull the bond tight, the second he released his hands, she felt the belt loosen.

'Get her in position,' the Leader commanded.

Blondie hustled her out of the car. Street lights coloured the area a dull orange. Warehouses lined one side of the street. Opposite stood a variety of industrial buildings and car parks. Past a car park on her left, a wide dark space stretched to strings of lights in the distance. She took in the faintly briny air and realized the dark space was the Thames.

With the driver on one side, Blondie on the other, Jay walked across the car park. As they walked, she worked at the belt binding her hands and felt her pulse leap with hope. The belt was beginning to loosen. If she could widen the gap, slip her thumb through, she could loosen the belt completely.

She heard an engine approaching. When it was close – less than a street or so away – it fell quiet.

Blake? Is that you?

They stopped in the middle of the car park. She might as well have been standing in the middle of a football field for the amount of cover it gave her. Not one tree. Not a single parked car. Just weeds growing through slabs of concrete. A disused warehouse loomed at one end of the car park. Most of the windows were broken, and graffiti covered the lower parts of the walls. At the other end stood a brick building. This one had no windows. The area looked empty, but thanks to the Leader's phone calls she knew Derby and Wade – the 'boys' – were in place. She didn't know how many more men were there, or whether they were trained or not. Unknown quantities always bothered her, and never more so when guns were involved.

Where was Blake?

Her heart was jumping, her mouth dry.

She worked at the belt some more, felt her thumb slip through the gap. Her heart lifted.

Yes!

She could now pull a hand free any time she wanted. Adrenalin tingled through her veins. She was ready.

The Leader came and joined them. He was holding a red plastic jerry can of petrol. A gallon's worth, if it was full. He raised it high. He called, 'Blake, if you don't show yourself,

I'm going to pour this over your girlfriend, and then light a match. You hear me?'

Jay made a sound in her throat – *no!* – and instinctively made to take a step back, but the two men had been ready for her and held her immobile.

'She'll be barbecued in seconds . . .'

For some reason, Jay thought things would play out for longer, maybe Blake would appear and try and negotiate with her kidnappers, but she was wrong. One second the night was quiet and still, the next it exploded.

Whoosh.

They all spun to see smoke pouring from one of the warehouse's broken windows. Flames flickered against the shattered glass.

The Leader took a step forward. 'What the fuck?' He turned to the Driver and snapped, 'Check it out.'

The Driver broke into a jog. He was halfway across the car park when a volley of shots rang out. Instant chaos. The Driver pelted for the cover of the building. Blondie dropped his hands from Jay and spun aside, making to sprint away. The Leader dragged Jay in front of him, using her as a human shield.

Now!

Jay yanked her hands free of the belt. She tried to hit the Leader in the face, force him to release her. Abruptly, a deafening noise made her turn her head. An engine screaming at maximum revs. The next second a huge, gleaming black motorbike bounded on to the car park and hurtled towards them. The rider was in black leathers. Shiny black helmet. His torso lay flat on top of the bike, offering as small a target as possible.

The bike rocketed across the space like a stone fired from a slingshot.

It happened so fast that the Leader was off-balance. The motorbike was already halfway across the car park, the engine howling, the sound ricocheting off the surrounding walls.

Jay flung herself sideways, forcing the Leader to stagger aside. She lashed out at him, catching him on the knee. He yelped and stumbled, and she was turning, preparing to sprint away, but the Leader came for her. He grabbed her and clenched an arm around her throat. Rammed her arm high between her shoulder blades.

The bike was yards away. She couldn't see his face through

his visor, but she recognized Blake's lean length, his swimmer's build.

Jay kicked out desperately, but the Leader's grip didn't break.

Blake kicked down a gear, and at the same time, to her horror, she heard the distinct *crack* of a rifle firing. Just a single shot, it echoed around the empty space.

Smoke poured from the bike's tyres as Blake engaged the brakes. He twisted the handlebars, and the tyres were screeching as the bike slid sideways towards them. Jay knew he wanted her to leap on-board behind him, wrap her arms around his waist, and then he'd accelerate, speed them away to safety.

But then the bike began to topple. Blake tried to right it, but she could see something was wrong. His movements became clumsy, uncoordinated. He put out a foot to try and stop the bike from hitting the ground, but his leg didn't extend far enough, and the machine crashed on to concrete and skidded sideways. Blake was flung forward. He lay crumpled on the ground, unmoving.

Jay's whole body went numb.

'Blake?' she whispered.

For a moment, everything was still.

She felt the Leader's hands drop away. Jay pelted for Blake. Skidded to his side.

Please God he's OK.

She was aware of the Leader walking to the bike. Switching off the engine. She heard him tell his men to put out the fire in the warehouse. He was standing behind her, but all her senses were fixed on Blake.

With trembling fingers, Jay raised his visor.

A rush of relief when a pair of deep brown eyes looked into hers.

'Max,' she said.

'Jay,' he whispered.

'Are you hurt? Where? God, tell me . . .'

'Not . . .' he managed. His eyes were urgent, trying to tell her something. 'Not . . .'

'Not what?' She bent over him, her fingers running over his leathers, trying to find the blood, the bullet hole, his wound. She was gasping as she worked. Please God, she could stem the bleeding. Get him to hospital . . . 'Ring for an ambulance!' she yelled.

The Leader laughed behind her. 'Not bloody likely.'

Blake's eyes continued to burn into hers with a fierce intensity.

'Max,' she pleaded.

Her body was shaking. She could hear the blood pounding in her ears.

Suddenly, she saw a cloud begin to creep across his eyes.

No. Please God, no.

'Max!' she called.

She was dizzy, her movements fumbling. She couldn't find any blood . . . Dear God, was the exit wound in his back? How big was it? She prayed they hadn't used a dumdum, which would have mashed his intestines into pulp . . . She tried to roll him over, but he was a dead weight. He gave a groan.

'Sorry, Max,' she sobbed. 'Sorry.'

She saw the light in his eyes begin to fade behind the cloud.

This isn't happening. It can't be.

'Stay with me, Max!' she pleaded. She tried to breathe normally. She needed to concentrate, to save him.

The cloud thickened.

'NO!' The half-shrieked denial burst from her throat. She felt the blood draining from her head as she realized she was losing him. 'No! No, no, no!'

To her horror, the light in his eyes went out.

'MAX!' Jay screamed his name so hard that her voice cracked.

SIXTEEN

Jay didn't want to leave Blake, but the men bodily picked her up and shoved her back inside their vehicle. She had no idea how long the journey was before they stopped, opened the door, and pushed her outside. Dumbly, she watched the car vanish up the street.

With shaky legs, she began to walk. Her mind was blank as she made her way slowly along. She looked at her watch. Three a.m. Where was she? The sky was brown, coloured faintly orange from the street lights. No stars. It began to rain.

She became aware she had her handbag. She paused, rummaged inside with stiff fingers. Withdrew her phone. At the next street corner, she checked the street names and dialled. It rang for a long time, then disconnected. She tried again.

'Hello?' Angela's voice was thick with sleep.

'It's me.'

'Jay?'

'I need a favour.' Her voice was hoarse from screaming Blake's name. 'Can you come and pick me up?'

'Where?'

'I'm on the corner of Leyborne Avenue and Carew Road,' she said.

She heard Angela talking quickly to Denise. 'South Ealing. We shouldn't be long. Are you all right? Do we need to bring a medical kit or anything?'

'No. I'm OK.'

'We'll be there in –' Jay heard them making calculations – 'less than twenty minutes. There's no traffic, so maybe we'll be there faster. We'll keep both our phones on.'

They hung up, and Jay sank to the ground, clutching to the numbness inside her to keep her mind from absorbing what she didn't want to know. The rain increased. Became icy cold. Jay huddled on the pavement, shivering.

'Jay.'

Jay blinked rain from her eyes to see Denise crouched in front of her.

'Are you hurt?' She gestured at Jay's face, where she'd grazed her cheeks trying to scrape the duct tape free.

Jay shook her head. Denise held out both hands. Jay gazed at them for a second, and then Denise gripped Jay's wrists and pulled her up from the ground and into her arms. 'You're soaked,' she chided, and then she paused, turned Jay's hand over to expose the cut from the strimmer blade, still fresh, still seeping blood.

While Angela drove, Denise put a plaster on the cut. Dabbed Jay's cheeks with antiseptic cream. 'Just in case,' she murmured.

The journey home was a blur. Upstairs, the girls helped her into a pair of striped pyjamas – bought especially for winter nights in her aunt's farmhouse in the country – and helped her into bed. Her hips and shoulders were sore from wriggling across the concrete garage floor, but it was nothing compared to the emotional pain she held inside. Denise made her drink a mug of hot chocolate. When Jay had finished, she said, 'What happened?'

'He's dead.'

'Who?'

'Blake.'

'*What*?'

Denise looked horrified, but Jay didn't want to talk. She pulled the duvet up over her head.

'She says Blake's dead,' Denise whispered to Angela.

'Shit. What happened?'

'She didn't say.'

'Should we ring Tom?'

'No. Not when she's like this. It could jeopardize their relationship if he sees how devastated she is . . .'

'I didn't realize she cared for Blake as much.'

'I don't think she did, either.'

Jay drifted into unconsciousness. Fell into a deep, exhausted sleep.

Jay awoke to hear Angela calling her name, and she immediately thought, *I'm late for work,* but at the same time a memory was clawing to the surface of her mind, something she didn't want to know.

'Jay?'

She looked at Angela, who looked anxiously back. 'You were dead to the world,' Angela continued. She gave a tentative smile. 'You up for some coffee?'

The image of Blake's eyes, the cloud creeping across them, burst into Jay's head. Pain clamped around her heart, tight as a fist. For a moment she couldn't breathe.

Angela eyed her carefully. 'Are you OK?'

She shook her head. She knew that nothing would be the same again.

'What happened?' Angela asked.

She remembered him hooking a finger in her waistband in Paris, asking her to stay with him for the night. She pictured his mouth. She'd only kissed it once, and it had been soft – far softer than she could imagine – and now she wished she'd kissed him unreservedly, held him close and made love to him.

'What happened to Blake?'

Hearing his name was like a blade slicing through her body. She closed her eyes. 'I was kidnapped.' Her voice was still hoarse. 'They used me as bait. They shot him as he came to rescue me.'

'Who shot him?'

Jay didn't reply. It didn't seem to matter any more.

'Do you want to report this?'

Jay shook her head. She curled into a ball. Her throat swelled with tears, but she couldn't cry.

'It's OK.' Angela's voice was gentle. 'We're here. You take your time.'

The girls stayed around all morning and, in-between putting up some shelves in the hallway – something that they'd wanted to do for months, but had never got around to – kept an eye on Jay. Not that Jay cared. She slept most of the time, wanting to escape the pain, but each time she woke it came rushing back, engulfing her.

That afternoon, she was startled to find Nick in her bedroom. She struggled upright.

'The girls rang me,' he said. 'Is it true?'

She nodded. 'I'm sorry,' she managed.

The lines grooved into his face deepened, and for the first time Jay realized she wasn't alone in her grief. Her mind suddenly went to Emilie, lying in a coma in Brussels. Who was going to tell Emilie that her brother was dead?

'Get dressed,' Nick said. It wasn't a request, but an order, and the way it was spoken had the army captain in her responding.

'Yes,' she said.

Nick turned on his heel. She heard him head downstairs and into the kitchen, start talking with the girls, but she couldn't hear what they were saying. She struggled to the shower. Stood beneath it for what felt like an age. She tried not to think of Blake, but then she worried she might forget him if she ignored her memories. Forget the precise colour of his eyes, which were as deep and shiny as the darkest chocolate. The way he teased her. His dry humour, his intense focus on a mission. His strength.

Holding herself tightly together, she peeled the sticking plaster from her wrist to see the narrow cut had healed over. She binned the plaster and pulled on jeans and a sweatshirt.

Barefoot, she walked downstairs. Nick and the girls were sitting at the kitchen table.

'Toast?' offered Denise.

Jay shook her head. Sat down. Angela poured her a cup of tea, but Jay didn't drink.

'You have to tell us what happened,' said Nick.

Jay nodded.

'Start from the beginning. And don't leave anything out.'

Jay thought back to Blake turning up in Tom's garden. As she pictured the way he'd cocked his eyebrow, asking to be let inside, the pain twisted its familiar way through her body. 'He wanted me to go to Paris.' She couldn't say his name. 'To meet a friend of his.'

Jay started slowly, feeling her way, but as she spoke, and Nick asked questions, she gathered momentum. The girls sat quietly, listening. When Jay came to the interview with Colonel Greene, Nick stiffened.

'The Garrison?'

'Yes,' said Jay. 'Why, have you heard of it?'

'There was a rumour, ages ago, going around the Home Office . . .' Nick's gaze turned inward. 'But everyone shrugged it off.'

'What was the rumour?' Denise asked.

'That a bunch of right-wingers were infiltrating the prison system. Rumour had it that anyone in jail who was considered socially irredeemable – paedophiles, murderers, and rapists – and who would end up costing the taxpayer hundreds of thousand of pounds being housed for the rest of their life in our prison system, would be eliminated.'

Even through her pain, Jay felt the shock of it. 'Eliminated?' she repeated. 'You mean, killed?'

'It was so far-fetched, nobody took it seriously.'

'I don't recall a huge amount of prison inmates being bumped off,' Angela remarked.

'Nor I,' Nick agreed. He looked at Jay. 'What happened after you left the Colonel?'

Jay talked them through her driving Ruth back to Bosham, then returning to London. Getting snatched outside the noodle house. The car park by the Thames. The motorbike roaring towards them.

'There was a single rifle shot . . .' She curled inward, hugging her ribs to hold herself together.

'Oh, sweetheart.' Nick's voice was so tender, she nearly cracked. 'I had no idea.'

Jay stumbled back to her room, trying to silence Blake's voice. *Stay with me tonight . . . Please.*

She remained in her room until night fell.

'Jay?' Nick knocked on her door. 'Can I come in?'

She didn't respond.

'I know you're hurting, but we need you. We have to tackle this Garrison issue. We're a team, right? You, me, and the girls. We can find who killed Blake and bring them to justice. Don't you want that?'

Did she? She wasn't sure. She felt as though she was balanced on the edge of a precipice. For some reason, she knew how she responded to Nick would determine her future. By letting Nick in, she'd be forced to live with the pain, because when they went after the Garrison, she wouldn't be able to forget Blake, because it had been Blake – and Sol and Emilie – who had started all this. He'd be on her lips and in her thoughts of every minute of every waking hour.

The other option was to do nothing. This would mean she would be allowed not to think of Blake. She could lock him away in a distant part of her memories and avoid the pain for days, and months, at a time. She'd be numb, unfeeling, and could live her life relatively normally. This option, she realized, was very attractive.

'Jay.' Nick's voice was gentle. 'What would Max want you to do?'

It was the word 'Max' that did it. The pain rose, and this time she allowed the tears to come. *Max, Max, Max. I'm sorry. I never knew how much I loved you.*

She flung open the door. She was sobbing. 'Get the Garrison,' she choked.

Nick opened his arms. 'Good girl,' he said and hugged her close.

SEVENTEEN

Nick insisted Jay make a report to the police.

'What about Nahid and Tivon?' Jay worried as they walked inside the station. 'Won't they go after my mother?'

'We can't leave it like this.' Nick spoke in a fierce, low voice. 'You were kidnapped, Jay. A friend of ours was killed.'

'But Nahid said—'

'They can't have every cop in their pocket. It's not possible.' His mouth narrowed into a hard line. 'Besides, I refuse to be bullied. I want them to know that, OK?'

Deciding to be cautious, Jay rang her mother and warned her.

'I do wish you'd find another job, darling,' her mother sighed. 'So you didn't mix with such unsavoury types.'

Normally, Jay would have defended TRACE to the hilt, especially since it wasn't TRACE's fault they were in danger, but today she had no strength. She suggested her mother go and stay with her sister, Elizabeth, on her farm just outside Bury St Edmunds for the next week or so.

'Duncan's got the dogs,' Jay said. 'They're great alarm bells.'

'So is Tigger,' said her mother stoutly, then softened. 'But I suppose you're right. Toast and Marmite are ten times bigger. I'll go there for a few days. I'll ring Elizabeth now.'

As Jay followed Nick and the duty sergeant down a corridor painted the colour of mouldy cheese, her phone rang. It was Tom.

'Hi gorgeous,' he said.

'Hi,' she said.

'I just wanted to tee-up next weekend,' he said. 'Sofie's with her mother, so I'm free from Friday. Shall I come to you?'

'Sure.'

'I'll take you to Patara Thai. Feed you up.'

The Patara was one of her favourite restaurants, but she couldn't rustle up any excitement. 'OK,' she murmured.

'Are you all right? You sound a bit off.'

'I'll tell you everything when I see you,' she said.

'That sounds ominous,' he said, but his voice was smiling.

'Got to go,' she managed. 'Sorry. Meeting.'

Jay sat with Nick, opposite Sergeant Neuhaus, in a window-less office that resembled a broom cupboard it was so cramped. Nick got the proceedings started. The sergeant, blinking, eyebrows darting up and down, took furious notes before going outside and returning with a woman constable – Constable Robertson – and a tape recorder. Then he turned to Jay and led her through a series of questions, sometimes repeating them twice. What did the kidnappers look like? Their car? Where did they take her? Was there anything she could remember that might help them identify the kidnapper's house?

'The Polo's number plate. YCO9 OPD. If you could trace it, find out where it's registered . . . or where it was that night . . . The kidnappers held me in the house opposite to where it was parked. Another thing – unless they've cleaned up, there'll be some blood on the garage floor, where I cut myself.' She showed the narrow scab on her wrist to the sergeant, who nodded.

The questions continued. Why didn't Blake call the police when Jay was kidnapped? Why did he meet the men alone? Where was the car park? What happened to Blake's body? His motorcycle?

When Jay admitted Blake was wanted for murder in Paris, things got heated. The interview became interminable. Already exhausted, Jay sagged in her chair, her answers becoming shorter and shorter until they were almost monosyllabic.

After Jay and Nick had signed their statements, Sergeant Neuhaus finally rose from behind the desk. Shook their hands. Energy crackled from his curly brown hair to the ends of his square-tipped fingernails. He looked ready to charge outside and start making arrests straight away. He said, 'Do you think you could join us in searching for the car park where Max Blake was shot?'

Although exhausted, Jay nodded. Four of them piled into a grubby Vauxhall Cavalier. Neuhaus drove to the street corner where the girls had picked up Jay. From there, they began casting around the north side of the Thames for any clues. It took two hours until Jay recognized the graffiti on one of the derelict warehouse walls. Neuhaus walked across the car park.

When he saw the fresh scores in the concrete from where Blake's bike had toppled, then the burned-out carcass of an oil drum where Blake had caused his diversion, the sergeant called in forensics.

Constable Robertson drove them back to Fulham, where it was raining, the wind still gusting hard. Pedestrians fought with their umbrellas, their jackets and coats billowing and snapping around them. Nick then drove Jay back to Redcliffe Road. When he'd double-parked outside her house, he turned to her. 'You mentioned Blake's friend Sol was with the Garrison?'

Jay nodded. She heard the Leader's voice echo through her head. *He's killed one of ours . . . Let's get Blake and ram him for it.*

If Sol was part of the Garrison, why had he been meeting Blake? And what about Emilie, who Sol had been in love with? Was she still alive? Jay posed the question to Nick.

'I'll do some checking through some NATO contacts of mine in Brussels,' he said. 'Do you know which hospital?'

Jay shook her head. 'Sorry.'

Nick told Jay to work from home over the next week. 'So you can sleep when you need to,' he told her.

She didn't understand what he meant until Tuesday afternoon, when she found her eyes wouldn't stay open. It wasn't just the trauma of losing Blake, but the kidnapping had taken a lot out of her. She rested her head on the kitchen table, thinking to have a five minute nap, only to wake with a fierce crick in her neck to find she'd been asleep for over two hours.

While keeping an eye on her normal work and her clients, Jay began to research the prison system to try and find if there was any foundation to Nick's Home Office rumour. She studied inquest statistics from the early nineties up to the current year until her head ached, but finally, towards the end of the day, she had a working chart to show Nick when he popped round to visit her.

'Interesting,' he said, staring at the totals.

Beneath the heading *Self-inflicted Deaths*, the national total of deaths in British prisons went from fifty in 1990 to seventy-one in the last year. *Non Self-inflicted Deaths* went from twenty to thirty-eight.

Beneath the heading *Homicide*, the total went from five in

1990 down to one in the last year. *Control and Restraint* dropped from three to zero.

Beneath the heading *Natural Causes*, however, the total leaped from eighty in 1990 to 170 in the last year.

Nick pointed at the figure 170 with raised eyebrows. 'What did they die of?'

'I don't know.' Jay bit her lip. 'The information isn't public knowledge.'

'Probably the diet,' Nick muttered. 'Or drug overdoses.'

He didn't seem to make much of it, but it bothered Jay. How could one statistic increase so much, while the others rose relatively steadily, or dropped?

The week dragged past. Nick spoke to Sergeant Neuhaus on Wednesday, but apparently the policeman had had no luck with the number plate search on the VW Polo. He had, he told Nick, hit a bit of a 'problem', whatever that meant.

'I'll keep pushing him,' Nick promised. 'I want that address. Then we can lean on one of your kidnappers, if you know what I mean.'

Leaning, as Nick called it, was an understatement. He had friends in the Special Forces, hardened soldiers who knew exactly how to extract information. The men who'd kidnapped her weren't in the same league as Nick and his buddies, and if they got their hands on one of them, she had no doubt they'd get the intel they needed.

When Friday arrived, Jay was amazed she'd survived. The aching loss hadn't lessened, but the fact she'd made it to the weekend without losing her mind meant she was strong enough to bear the pain. Tom had texted her saying he'd booked a table at the Patara for eight p.m., but Jay was still at work on her computer, tucked in the corner of the kitchen, when he rang the doorbell. Angela went to answer the door. Denise was in the middle of cooking Moroccan tagine.

'Smells good,' Tom said as he stepped into the kitchen, sniffing the air appreciatively. Raindrops clung to his hair.

Jay felt a familiar surge of happiness at his smile. She realized she was glad to see him.

'You can stay if you like,' Denise said, waving a wooden spoon in his direction. 'We've got loads.'

Tom cocked a questioning eyebrow at Jay. She crossed the room and put her arms around his waist, comforted by the contact. He cupped the back of her head, his thumb gently stroking her nape. They stood like that for a moment before Jay looked up at him. His eyes were sparkling. 'Your decision,' he whispered.

'I'd love to eat in,' said Jay. 'Would you mind?'

'Since you're looking so sexy, no, I wouldn't mind.'

'You think everything's sexy,' she murmured.

'Only because it's you.'

While Tom cancelled the restaurant booking, Jay poured glasses of Chianti and turned the lights low to create a cosy atmosphere against the stormy weather outside. Denise served the tagine at the kitchen table with slices of warmed bread. The conversation was general, Tom asking the girls what they'd been up to, the girls asking him about his latest case – two Somalian youths up for murdering another as retribution for knifing a friend of theirs – until Denise asked Jay for news on her and Nick's investigation into the Garrison. Not that she put it that way, just said, 'What's the news with Nick and Sergeant Neuhaus?' but Jay knew Denise was offering her an opening to tell Tom what had happened last weekend.

Jay pushed aside her plate. Tom frowned. She'd barely touched her food. Since her kidnapping, and Blake's death, she hadn't had an appetite.

'You feeling OK?' he asked.

This was the opening she needed. She took a breath. Willed the girls to stay and not bolt for cover. She said, 'Something happened last weekend.'

Tom's fork paused mid-air.

'Something serious,' she added.

The girls continued to eat and drink their wine, seemingly unperturbed, creating an oddly normal atmosphere against the sudden tension in the room. Slowly, Tom put down his fork. 'Go on,' he said.

'I had to ring Denise and Angela early last Saturday morning. Three a.m. to be precise. I didn't know exactly where I was because that's where the men dumped me . . .'

Tom's expression froze as Jay continued to talk. Having run through the weekend's events with the girls, Nick and the police, she had the story pretty pat by now, and Tom seemed to realize this, because when she finally ground to a halt, he said, 'How many people know this?'

Jay told him.

He pushed back his chair with a clatter. Got to his feet. The girls glanced at him, then away. Concentrated on their wine.

Tom's open, friendly smile was gone, the warmth in his eyes replaced with an arctic chill. 'At least I know where I stand. I don't come first in your life. Not even second or third. But fifth.'

Jay rose and faced him. 'Tom, it's not like that—'

'Tell me what it is like, Jay.' His tone was scathing. 'Tell me why you rang the girls, not me. Why you talked to Nick before you talked to me. Why you went to the police station with Nick, not me.'

He stared at her, his eyes angry.

'You were in Bristol,' she said lamely, but it was a lie. She hadn't been able to bear seeing Tom so soon after watching Blake die. She didn't know why, but it had felt as though by having Tom nearby, she'd be disrespecting Blake.

'And Bristol's on the other side of the world,' he said, his tone dripping sarcasm.

'Tom . . .' Denise spoke tentatively, but he rounded on her.

'Stay out of it,' he snapped.

The girls quietly rose and left the room.

'I wanted to talk to you about it,' Jay said weakly. Another lie.

'So what stopped you?' he hissed.

'I was . . . a mess.'

His face didn't change.

She raised a hand, let it fall. 'I was exhausted. Shocked. I was barely functioning—'

'You were functioning well enough to go to the police.'

'Not really,' she said. 'Nick did most of the talking.'

It was the wrong thing to say. His jaw tightened. He spoke through his teeth. 'That makes me feel so much better. The fact that you called on your boss for help, rather than me, is just great for my ego.'

'Tom, please,' she begged. 'I'm sorry. It's just the way things played out. Please don't take it so hard.'

'How should I take it?' he demanded. 'Jesus, Jay. I'm not your pet dog, able to survive on the scraps that fall from your table. We're engaged to be married, remember? People who get married are *partners*. They're a *team*. From the way you're behaving, I'm not sure you're on the same page as me. I'm not sure you're even in the same *book*.'

He studied her face for a long moment, speculating.

He said, 'I think we should take a break.'

'What?' Her heart clenched.

'Sofie said you didn't want an engagement ring. That you thought having a ring would be like being branded. Now I can see why.'

Her mouth fell open. 'She said *what*?'

'You heard. Now I know why we've never managed to go shopping for a ring,' he said. His hands clenched and unclenched at his sides. 'You don't want to get married, do you?'

Her mouth still hung wide.

'I guess not.' He gave a bitter smile.

Jay shook her head, trying to clear it. 'I never said anything like that to Sofie. She's lying.'

'Why would she lie?'

'She wants you to marry Heather.'

He paused at that. 'That's not possible.'

'Why not?'

'It just isn't, OK?'

'I wish Sofie was as confident,' she said. For the first time since Blake died, she felt some energy return. 'Do you have any idea what it's been like having her pretending to be my best friend while she stabs me in the back? She lies about everything, Tom. From being allergic to chicken, to how she got her sticky little paws on my mother's bracelet—'

'Having a go at Sofie is below the belt.' Tom glared at her. 'Especially since she isn't here to defend herself.'

'Grow up, Tom,' she snapped. 'Your daughter isn't sugar and spice and all things nice. She's a spoiled only child who's always got her own way, and when things don't work out how she wants, she meddles. Look at us now! Fighting over her! You think she didn't plan this?'

He was suddenly right in front of her, eyes tight. 'She's just a *child*.'

'She's a poisonous bitch.'

'Enough!' He walked out of the kitchen, striding for the front door.

'Send her my love!' Jay yelled after him.

The only response she got was the door slamming behind him.

EIGHTEEN

Eight thirty on Monday morning, since it was pretty much en-route to the office, Jay dropped into the police station. She'd had another awful night, and her blood felt sluggish, as though it was pulsing behind a bruise. Every word she and Tom had said on Friday had raced around her head until she'd fallen into a fitful sleep just before dawn, with tears seeping from her eyes.

Jay wasn't sure how she'd function without Tom. Her life had been entwined with his for over three years now, and she cringed away from the idea of life without him. Tom had been her rock since they'd first met, safe and comforting. But it wasn't just about her docking in a safe harbour. They were good together. Truly good.

Even as she recognized this, she wondered how to patch this latest row. She'd have to tell him everything. How deep her feelings had been for Blake. How she hadn't truly known this until Blake had died, when she'd been hijacked by debilitating grief. It was the only way Tom might understand. She'd have to explain everything the right way, so that he'd know that he wasn't second best. She would, she decided, buy him an engagement ring, go down on one knee, and ask him to marry her. Her heartfelt commitment would be the only way to heal this rift. She'd deal with Sofie and her lies another day.

Jay asked the female constable on reception if Sergeant Neuhaus was available.

'The sergeant's not here. Can anyone else help?' Her expression was open and friendly.

'When will he be in?' Jay assumed the sergeant was on a later shift.

'Sergeant Mayer's available,' the constable suggested.

'No, thanks. I want to see Sergeant Neuhaus. When would it be a good time to catch him?'

'Sorry.' The constable's smile became a little strained. 'But the sergeant no longer works at this station. He was transferred. Shall I call Sergeant Mayer?'

The skin at the back of her neck began to prickle. 'Where was the sergeant transferred?'

'I'm sorry. I'm not at liberty to divulge that.'

'OK. When was he transferred?'

The constable thought this over until she evidently came to the conclusion that this information wouldn't do any harm. 'Last Thursday.'

'Was it sudden? Or was it planned? Like a promotion that had been in the pipeline for a while?'

'Er . . .' The constable looked uncomfortable. 'I'm afraid I can't say.'

The prickling at her nape increased. 'What about Constable Robertson? Is she available?'

The woman picked up a phone. Punched in some numbers. 'Hi, Pippa. I have Jay McCaulay in reception for you. OK. Great.' She beamed at Jay. 'She's on her way.'

Constable Robertson arrived, breathless, looking harassed. 'Hi,' she said. She didn't meet Jay's eyes. 'How can I help?'

'I wanted to know how you were getting on trying to find my kidnappers.'

'It's probably best if you talk to Sergeant Mayer. He's heading the investigation.'

'What about the VW Polo that was parked opposite the garage where they held me? Surely you've tracked it down by now?'

'Not yet. Sorry.' Robertson's eyes flicked to the desk constable, who was watching them curiously. 'As soon as we do, we'll let you know.'

'So what are the police doing to find my kidnappers? The men who murdered Max Blake? What about the forensic results from the warehouse car park?'

'You really need to talk to Sergeant Mayer.'

When the phone on reception rang, Robertson flinched. Turning away, the desk constable answered it. Jay took the opportunity to step close to Robertson. 'What happened to Sergeant Neuhaus?'

Robertson glanced past Jay with unconcealed discomfort. 'He got transferred. Look, I'm sorry, but I'm really busy. I must go. I'll get Sergeant Mayer to come and talk to you.'

Jay realized she wasn't going to get anywhere with the constable. She said, 'OK. Send Sergeant Mayer.'

The constable just about bolted from the room.

A mixture of emotions settled on Jay as she waited, but the main one was disbelief. What had Nick said? *They can't have every cop in their pocket. It's not possible.* Or was she being paranoid? Seeing things that weren't there? Police got transferred all the time. Then she remembered the threat to Tom all those days ago when he'd asked his superior officer, Superintendent Clarkson, if he'd heard of the Garrison. Clarky had warned Tom off asking anything further.

Sergeant Mayer arrived within five minutes. In his thirties, with fading red hair and pale skin dotted with freckles, he had an easy smile, but his grey eyes were as hard as flint. He said all the right things: that the investigation was in full flow, that they were searching for the garage where Jay had been held, and that they hoped to find her kidnappers soon.

'And the VW Polo's number plate?'

'We've found the owner, but it was being driven by his son that weekend. The son has since gone to Majorca and hasn't yet returned. He isn't answering his phone.'

'Any luck with the car park? Where the bike's skid marks were?'

He shook his head. 'We found no shells. No blood. We went door-to-door locally, to see if anyone saw anything. A couple of people remembered hearing a motorbike, but nothing else.'

Jay left the station unable to work out if the investigation was going ahead normally, or if it was being stymied in some way. She berated herself for not getting the name of the Polo owner from Mayer. What an idiot! But then she doubted Mayer would have given it to her. He didn't seem the sort of cop who would hand out that type of information to the public, no matter how heavily they were involved in the case.

When she arrived in the office and told Nick what had happened, his mouth tightened. 'Neuhaus got transferred? I don't like the sound of that.'

'You don't think I'm being paranoid?'

'Even if the Garrison exists, surely it can't be that big an organization.' Nick was shaking his head, baffled. 'Otherwise we would have heard of it.'

'We?'

'I've done some asking around. Old muckers. That sort of thing. Not a whiff of anything untoward.' He frowned. 'Do you know any friends of Blake's? Names of anyone he worked with?'

A humourless smile crossed her lips. 'You know Blake. What do you think?'

'He was always a bit of a loner,' Nick admitted. 'I tried to talk to his boss, Jim Turner, but his assistant guards him like a Rottweiler. I doubt my messages are getting through.'

Jay studied the wall chart to see she was due to meet one of her IOM contacts in an hour, just around the corner from Thames House, where Blake used to work.

'How about if I try and see Turner?'

'Sure.'

Jay made a call to Jim Turner's office.

'Brian Keith,' a man said, voice oily and smooth.

'I'd like to make an appointment to see Jim Turner.'

'And you are?'

'Jay McCaulay.'

There was a taut silence, where for some reason she thought she'd startled him.

'Of course,' his silky voice returned. 'He has a space at midday today for half an hour. Would that be convenient?'

Jay just about fell off her chair in amazement. 'Sure. Great.'

'I'll have a pass ready for you at the security desk from eleven thirty. They'll show you where to go.'

Without another word, he hung up. Jay turned the phone in her hand, unnerved at the ease she'd gained access. Where was the Rottweiler Nick had spoken about? Ducking into his office, Jay told her boss what had happened.

'They're obviously partial to a pretty face,' he grumbled. 'Don't care for grizzled old dogs like me.'

'Any luck with Emilie?' Jay asked him. 'Blake's sister?'

'My friend went and saw her at the Hospital Saint-Pierre yesterday. She's still in a coma, but the doctors are pleased she's hanging in there. She's not giving up yet.'

Jay told Nick she'd be back after her meeting with Turner, and he waved her away. 'See you later.'

Her IOM contact, Tina Higgins, a frizzy-haired woman with a figure as flat as an ironing board, managed to distract Jay from her looming meeting with Jim Turner by telling her she thought they had a lead to Irina, the Russian girl who'd supposedly vanished into Bristol.

'We rescued a friend of hers earlier in the week,' Tina said. 'She was shipped to Birmingham the day after both girls arrived at the Russia House. They wanted to split the friends up, you know how it goes.'

Jay nodded. Traffickers tried to keep friends apart in case they encouraged one another to escape. Better for the women to make friends with their captors, who could continue to feed them lies that the British police would beat them senseless if they were discovered without passports.

'Where's the Russia House?' Jay asked.

'Apparently it's in Redfield. Beyond that, I don't know.'

Jay texted Lily to see if she could ascertain anything further. Lily texted straight back saying she was on the case. *Lunch 2morrow?* she added. She'd included a bistro's address.

Sure, Jay texted back. *CU 1 p.m.*

She would, she decided, see Tom that same evening. Try and clear the air. When her meeting with Tina finished, Jay called Tom. His phone rang, and then it clicked to his messaging service. She left a slightly garbled message telling him she was in Bristol the next day, and that she wanted to see him. She *had* to see him. She had things to say, things to explain . . . For the first time it entered her mind that he might not want to see her. A trickle of panic edged into her senses. How to persuade him she loved him?

Jay was so absorbed in her thoughts that she narrowly missed a woman in pointy heels and a smart grey suit.

'Watch it,' the woman snapped.

'Sorry.'

Jay peered at Thames House North, which loomed imperiously on the corner of Millbank and Horseferry Road. She went to the door, where she handed over her driver's licence and identified herself. A security guard asked her to walk through a scanner while her handbag was scanned separately, along with her boots. She stood as her photograph was taken and incorporated in her day pass. Ushered to an echoing marble space, she was told Mr Turner's assistant wouldn't be long.

Jay hung around with two businessmen in pinstriped suits and a woman in a floral dress and grey court shoes. There was nowhere to sit. No newspapers to hand. The three of them stood awkwardly, waiting.

Brian Keith glided in three minutes later. Slender and androgynous, he had an angular face with full lips and dark brows shaped
like upturned wings. His skin was translucent white, accentuating
the darkness of his hair, the piercing blue of his eyes.

He introduced himself smoothly. His grip was as hard and
cold as marble. 'I'm afraid Mr Turner's been held up. He won't
be able to see you today. I'm sorry. What was it concerning?'
With barely noticeable gestures, he effortlessly guided her to
one side and out of earshot.

'It's personal,' Jay said.

He considered her coolly.

'Does it have anything to do with Max Blake?' he asked.

Jay swallowed. She decided to bite the bullet and see his
response. When she spoke, her words were slow and measured.
'Yes. But I also wanted to discuss the Garrison.'

Brian Keith's face altered swiftly. The coolness wavered and
became first concern, then dismay.

'I think you'd better leave,' he said. His voice was low and
flat. 'I won't tell Turner you were here. Blake is not the most
popular person at the moment, and your consorting with him
won't win you any friends, least of all Turner. I suggest you
turn around and don't come back.'

'Don't you dare,' she hissed. 'I will not be fobbed off, OK?
I want to see Turner.'

He put his head on one side as he considered her. She glared
back.

'You have no idea what you're getting into, do you?' He
gave a condescending little smile.

An image of Blake lying sprawled in the car park sprang
into her vision. Outrage made her voice quiver. 'Murder, cover-
ups, conspiracies, and that's just for starters,' she said fiercely.
'You're in it with the *Direction Centrale du Renseignement
Intérieu*, the Metropolitan police, and what about the prisons?
You can't tell me all those inmates died of natural causes. You
can't say that's—'

Before she could finish, he yanked her out of reception,
bundling her along an echoing corridor. He had her upper arm
in a vice-like grip.

'Hey!' she protested. 'Just wait a—'

'I'd rather we take this conversation somewhere private,' he
hissed.

Somewhere private was a cool blue room with an oval table surrounded by eight high-backed chairs. The windows were frosted with minute filaments that Jay guessed were to repel bullets.

Brian Keith dropped her arm only after he'd closed the door behind them. 'Who do you work for?' His voice was flat and icy.

'TRACE. It's a reunion and crisis—'

'I know TRACE,' he snapped. 'I meant who *else* do you work for?'

'No one.'

She could see from his eyes he didn't believe her.

'I swear it!' she insisted.

'If that's true, then you're in big trouble.' He surveyed her, his face clean of emotion. 'And I'm not sure if I can help.'

She wondered what he saw on her face, because he then said, 'I'll give you my private numbers.' He withdrew a business card and a pen, scribbling on the back of the card before passing it over. 'I'd prefer it if you kept them safely and didn't tell anyone you had them. Now, I'll see you out.'

Frowning, Jay pocketed the card. As Keith reached for the door handle, it turned, and the door swung open. A small man with a gaunt face and speckled grey hair, balding at the crown, stepped inside. 'Brian!' he exclaimed with apparent warmth.

'Sir.' Brian Keith was standing as though to attention. 'This is Jay McCaulay. She wanted an appointment with you, but—'

'I know what she's here for. You can go, Brian.'

'Yes, sir.' Brian Keith gave Jay a nod, and although his expression was absolutely neutral, giving nothing away, she sensed his nerves were strung as tightly as piano wire. He slipped out of the room without a sound.

'Jay McCaulay.'

'Yes.'

His eyes swept over her curiously. 'Blake's friend who destroyed his kitchen.'

She was taken aback for a moment.

'You are that friend, aren't you?' His eyebrows were raised. 'Yes.'

'Jim Turner.' He stepped forward and shook her hand. It was firm and warmer than she expected.

He said, 'You're here about Blake?'

'Yes.' Jay didn't know how else to say it, so she said it straight. 'He's dead. I saw him killed.'

Turner blinked. 'I'm sorry?'

'He was shot. I was with him when he died.'

Turner went quite still. 'When was this?'

'Last Friday night. I was kidnapped to lure him out of hiding. He was shot trying to rescue me . . .' She trailed off when he held up a hand.

'Jay,' he said. 'You've got it wrong.'

'What?'

'Blake isn't dead.'

Her eyes flashed to him in disbelief.

'He was shot with a tranquillizer dart. Brought in to us. We've been questioning him over the past week, but now he's in jail. He's safe.' Turner's mouth lifted into a wry smile. 'And very much alive.'

NINETEEN

'Sofie.'

Sofie didn't like the way Tom was looking at her. There was a wariness in his eyes she hadn't seen before. An odd tightness around his mouth.

'Yes, Daddy?'

'We need to talk about Jay.'

Because her mum had been called up to Edinburgh, Sofie was staying with Tom. He'd dropped her off to school this morning, collecting her after school to bring her to the police station, where she was supposed to do her homework. He shared his office with DI McFarlane, a thin Scotsman with sad eyes who everyone called Mac. Mac was nice, and she wished he'd stayed. She didn't want to face Tom in this new, weird mood.

'Jay's great.' Sofie imbued her tone with enthusiasm. 'I really like her.'

Tom took a breath, let it out. 'Jay and I are . . . taking a break.'

Sofie said nothing, but inside, something shrank.

'We had a bit of an argument on Friday . . .' He trailed off, biting his lip.

At last, she knew what was bugging him. When he'd picked her up first thing on Saturday, he seemed to have had a personality bypass. The cheerful, energetic father she'd known had vanished, and in his place was a moody, morose man she didn't recognize. He hadn't smiled once. Nor sung along to the radio, or danced with her in the kitchen.

'Oh,' she said. No other words came to mind.

'The argument . . . Well, some of it was to do with you. Look, I don't want to cast blame, but Jay said you've been lying to me.'

Stomach squirming, Sofie looked away.

'You told me that . . .' Tom cleared his throat. 'Jay said that wearing an engagement ring would make her feel as though she'd been branded.'

Sofie's mouth suddenly turned dry. 'That's why you split up?'

'Put it this way –' his mouth twisted – 'it didn't help matters.'

His eyes were bruised. She knew he hadn't been sleeping because she'd woken up each time he'd padded around the house. He was, she realized, totally and utterly miserable because he'd split up with Jay. He'd stopped singing and dancing because of that. She screwed up her eyes.

Rats.

He was miserable because of her.

She'd lied to try and split them up, and now it had happened she felt awful. Suddenly, she felt like bursting into tears.

'Sofie?' Tom prompted.

She pictured Jay sitting on her bed questioning her about the bracelet. She couldn't think why she'd opened the envelope . . . She'd only wanted a peek, and the bracelet had been so pretty – and the second she'd slipped it on, Jay had charged into the house like a demented buffalo, leaving Sofie no time to put the thing back and pretend nothing had happened. Jay had then been amazingly calm. She hadn't shouted and screamed, not like her mum would have. When Jay'd come to her room later that night to say goodnight, all she'd said was, 'Let's draw a line under what's happened today, hey? Truce?'

Sofie had mumbled something incoherent, and now she regretted not saying, 'Truce,' in return.

'Sofie, I need to know the truth.' Tom's voice was gentle.

'You won't hate me?' Her voice was small. She pulled a thread free from her sweater and balled it between her fingers.

'No, I won't hate you.' He gave a smile that showed in his eyes. 'You're my daughter. How could I hate you?'

She chewed her lip. 'I didn't mean it,' she whispered. 'I swear I didn't.'

'Ah.' He let out a sigh.

She scrunched up her face in mortification. 'I know I shouldn't have said anything, but it just slipped out.' Tears trembled. 'Sometimes I don't know why I say the things I do . . .'

Sofie fidgeted while Tom rubbed the bridge of his nose with his fingers.

'Do you . . .' He cleared his throat, looking oddly embarrassed. 'Would you like me to marry Heather?'

A tear spilled down her cheek. She brushed it away. She said, 'I did. I mean, I used to. I thought that if you weren't with Jay . . .'

'Oh, Sofie.' He closed his eyes.

'I'm sorry . . .' Her mouth wobbled.

'You can't lie about stuff like that,' he said. 'The consequences . . . Well, you've seen what can happen.'

'I know. I'm sorry. I didn't think . . .' She gulped. 'Will you get back with Jay now?'

'I don't know.' His gaze turned distant.

'But you have to!'

'It's more complicated than that.'

They both turned when a voice from the doorway said, 'Tom? You're needed in the incident room.' It was Mac, waving a hand urgently.

Tom groaned. 'I'll be right there.'

Sofie watched him gather a couple of files and a pen. He said, 'We'll continue this later. Will you be OK? I won't be long.'

'I've got loads of homework to do.'

'Don't touch anything you shouldn't, OK?'

'Promise,' she said meekly.

After he'd gone, she looked around the office. Tom's house was scruffy, with mail opened and shoved on surfaces, old envelopes lying around, but he made more of an effort at work. Making sure the door was closed, she had a quick look through some of his paperwork. Missing persons, a knife attack, a boundary dispute . . . Where were the murder books with grisly pictures of tortured bodies?

Last week she'd shown Jaz a photograph of Tom in his uniform. Jaz had taken it and burst into laughter. 'Good God! Look here, everyone!' She raised the picture high. 'Sofie's dad's a Chippendale!'

Everyone collapsed laughing, but Sofie didn't get it. She said, 'No, he's not. He's a Detective Inspector—'

'I bet all he inspects is tits!' Jaz creased up.

'Does he get greased up before work?' Ollie asked. 'Oil or lard?'

More shrieks of laughter. Flushing, close to tears, Sofie grabbed back Tom's photo and fled.

At home, she'd googled Chippendales to find they were male strippers. Humiliation burned her to her core. *Everyone thought her Dad was a stripper?* She had to prove Tom was a real policeman.

Despite her rummaging, Sofie found nothing gruesome. No pictures of dead bodies or corpses being cut up. Zilch. Double-checking the door was shut, Sofie turned to Tom's computer. Surely Tom would have *something* hidden away . . .

She wanted to help herself to some of Tom's chocolate Minstrels sitting on his desk – he'd told her to help herself – but she resisted. She didn't want to get any fatter.

Familiar taunts ran through her head.

Lose some weight, fatty. You're so ugly, don't you realize?

Was that why she found it hard to make friends? Because she was ugly? If only she could find something really gruesome to take to school, everyone would be totally impressed. She opened Tom's Outlook Express and had a look. The instant she saw Jay's email, and that it had been opened, temptation bit. She shouldn't open it. She *mustn't*.

In the Subject bar, Jay had typed, *help*.

Sofie dithered. Could she help Jay? Help Tom? Oh, God. She wished she hadn't lied. Could she get them back together? Then Tom would sing and dance around the kitchen instead of being a misery guts. And Jay wasn't so bad. In fact, she was pretty nice really, even if she couldn't cook.

Before she could change her mind, Sofie quickly read Jay's message. She'd attached a couple of files, which had, apparently, belonged to someone called Sol Neill. Sofie frowned. Wasn't that the man who'd been murdered in Paris?

Sofie checked the Internet to see that yes, Sol had been murdered in Paris.

A thrill ran through her. This was more like it! She was reading about a real live murder!

Jay's final sentence read: *Blake says it might be a code, but I can't decipher it. Any ideas?*

Her excitement grew. What if she cracked the code? Would that help Tom and Jay forgive her?

Sofie opened the attached file to find a selection of music and a bunch of photographs. She scrolled through the pictures, but stopped when she came to one of a life-sized polar bear.

Yes!

She'd seen the bear in Paris last spring, at the Musée d'Orsay.

She scrolled further. Lots of hideous paintings . . . another of which she recognized because, at the time, she'd pointed it out to her mum, remarking on the sad, dead donkey. God, the museum had been dull. Sometimes she wished her mum wasn't so into art and stuff and would take her to Disneyland instead. Disneyland, however, was Heather's *anathema*. When Sofie had looked the word up, she knew she'd never get to Disneyland. Perhaps, if she cracked the code, Tom and Jay would take her?

Enthusiasm in full flow, Sofie reviewed the music collection. She didn't like any of it, except the Jason Mraz track, which was reasonably cool.

Did all this stuff tie together?

If so, how?

Sofie started with the music, but when, after an hour, she still hadn't found a connection, she decided to forward the lot to her own email and work on it later.

It would be *so* cool if she cracked the code. She'd be helping her Dad with a murder investigation! Jaz couldn't help but be impressed with that.

TWENTY

J ay's knees softened. She swayed briefly. Turner was there in
a flash, a hand beneath her elbow.

'Jay,' he murmured. 'I am sorry.'

'Take me to him.'

'Of course.'

Within minutes Jay was cocooned in the rear of a shiny black
Mercedes with darkened windows. A uniformed driver sat up
front, while Jay and Turner sat in the back. Rain hammered on
the windows and roof, and the windscreen wipers swept from
side to side, not making much headway. Visibility was low, and
the roads were awash. It felt as though they were driving along
the bottom of the ocean.

She remembered the urgency in Blake's eyes when she'd
skidded to his side, demanding where he'd been hit. His saying,
'*Not . . .*' He'd been trying to tell her he hadn't been shot. That
he wasn't hurt. Despite this reasoning, part of her couldn't
believe Turner was telling the truth. Something inside her
suspected a trap, but she couldn't help but go along with it.
Just in case Blake was alive.

'Why didn't he ring me?' she asked.

Turner leaned forward and pressed a button, raising the parti-
tion between them and the driver. 'He couldn't.'

'Where did you keep him?'

'I can't say.'

'Who kidnapped me?'

He fell quiet.

Finally, Jay ventured, 'Have you heard of the Garrison?'

'Blake talks about nothing else.' His expression was neutral.
'He has some wild theories, but no evidence. The only evidence
that appears irrefutable is that he killed Solomon Neill and Rick
Wayland.'

'Rick?' For a moment she wondered if she'd heard him
correctly. 'What do you mean, he killed Rick? Rick's my old
boss. He'd never kill him. He didn't even *know* Rick.'

'The gun that killed Major Wayland was found in Blake's garage.'

'You can't believe that.' Jay snorted. 'He'd never be stupid enough to leave a murder weapon lying around.'

'It was hidden in the roof.'

'It could have been hidden in his sock drawer and it wouldn't change the fact *he didn't kill Solomon Neill or Rick Wayland.*' Jay was almost grinding her teeth in frustration.

'The evidence—'

'I *saw* the woman who killed Sol,' Jay hissed. She looked him straight in the eyes as she spoke. Her tone trembled with conviction. 'I was *there*. I watched her ram a stiletto into the back of Sol's head. I tackled her, tried to stop her from getting away . . . Blake did not kill Sol. OK? And he did not kill Rick Wayland.'

The car made a couple of turns, began to head north-west through the burgeoning traffic.

'The prosecution says differently.' Turner sighed heavily. 'They think he went off the rails. They want to subpoena you.'

Jay felt a moment of disbelief. 'Me?'

'They're saying Blake killed Neill and Wayland in a jealous rage.' Turner pursed his lips. 'Blake saw you with Sol Neill in Paris. He thought you were having an affair . . . Then he heard you were meeting Rick Wayland . . .'

'That's ridiculous.'

'Is it?' Turner fixed her with a pale grey gaze. 'Tell me what's been going on, Jay. I'm having trouble understanding.'

Again, Jay told the story of Sol's death, the gendarmes taking down her statement and then the two men who said they were from the DCRI – Marfart and Prideaux – taking her to the farmhouse where Nahid and Tivon were. Blake's collecting her from Ully-St-Georges. The Paris apartment filled with antiques. Blake's shock on seeing his own face on TV, wanted for murdering his old friend. His trying to protect Jay by sending her back to England. Nahid coming to Tom's house to threaten her.

'I was kidnapped last Friday. Nick and I reported it to the police, but when I went and saw them this morning they said they can't find the man who was driving the Polo that night and have no clues from the car park. The sergeant who took our initial statements has been transferred I don't know where . . .' She trailed off. A sense of helplessness trailed through her.

'I would like to ask one question,' Turner interjected. His features remained a cool mask.

'Yes?' Jay said.

'If all this is true, why do you continue to fight? You make the Garrison sound like an all-powerful organization, with eyes and ears everywhere. If it exists, in the way you're beginning to believe it does, do you really think you can win?'

Her whole body went cold.

'I think you should persuade Blake to confess,' he added.

Blood pounded behind her ears. She opened her mouth to say something, she wasn't sure exactly what, and then closed it again.

'Blake will listen to you. Tell him to plead guilty to the charges and I can protect you. Fight any further and I can't guarantee your safety.'

She stared at him for a moment, uncomprehending. He stared back. His eyes were as empty and emotionless as a shark's.

'You're with them.' Her voice was a whisper.

He didn't deny it, simply turned his head to stare out of the window. They didn't say anything more until the car drew up outside the police station where Blake was being held. Leaving the engine running, the driver came to Jay's side of the car and opened the door.

'They're expecting you,' Turner told her. 'And don't forget to tell Blake what I said, will you?'

Blake was standing at the far end of his cell, arms folded, shoulders against the wall. His eyes were closed. He looked as though he was meditating.

'Are you all right?' the guard accompanying her asked.

It was only then that she realized she was shaking. She heard a sound she didn't recognize, a strange whimper, and for a moment she wondered where it came from, but then she realized it was her.

Blake's eyes snapped open. Looked straight at her.

She froze in place, but then he said, 'Jay.'

She pushed past the guard and ran flat out for him, gasping, calling his name.

He moved towards her. She slammed into the widely-spaced

iron bars, but he pushed his arms through and wrapped her against his chest.

'Max,' she breathed.

'I know,' he murmured.

'I thought you were dead.'

'I wish you hadn't gone through that.'

She wound her fingers through his hair, fiercely cupping the nape of his neck. 'Kiss me,' she said. 'God, please. Kiss me.'

He bent his head and touched his lips to hers. She clutched him tightly through the bars, kissing him, half-sobbing, half-laughing as he pulled her tightly against him, so tightly she could barely breathe.

'It's OK, hon,' he told her. 'It's OK.'

Gradually, she regained her composure. 'No, it's not.' She pulled back, wiping her eyes. 'Not with you in here.'

'You bring me any goodies?' He quirked an eyebrow at her. 'The food's terrible in here.'

'Sorry. I came straight over. What would you like?'

'A cake with a file in it would be nice.'

Jay glanced over her shoulder to check on the guard – she didn't want a potential Garrison member eavesdropping on their conversation. She relaxed when she saw him leaning against the wall where she'd left him, and that not only was he out of earshot, but he also appeared absorbed with texting on his mobile phone.

'How long have you been here?' she asked Blake.

'The boys finished with me yesterday. Hand-delivered me to the cops first thing this morning. It seems I have no friends any more.' His eyes glinted. 'Aside from you, that is. You're my first visitor. Looking good, as usual.'

'And you look terrible,' she said, studying the purple rings beneath his eyes, the pallor of his skin. He'd lost weight too, she realized. He was gaunt.

'That's what sleep deprivation does.'

Her heart clenched. 'Turner said they had you for a week.'

'Yup.'

'What did they—'

'Don't ask.' His expression closed.

'Why did they tranquillize you? Why didn't they . . .' She wanted to ask why they hadn't killed him, but couldn't say the words.

'You want to know why I'm still alive?' He looked amused.

'Yes.'

'I'm more trouble dead.'

'I don't understand.'

'If I die, then all hell breaks loose, because my colleagues will think twice about everything I've said. Right now, they think I've gone off the rails, seeing bogeymen in our midst. But if I wind up dead they'll consider the fact I might have been bumped off and will investigate.'

'Oh.' She bit her lip.

'Much safer to have me tucked away, accused of a couple of murders. So when I go down, they can forget all about me. The DNA evidence is tight.'

'Doesn't everyone know DNA is fallible? That it can be planted?'

'Sure, but there's a lot more against me. Like the fact I was in Paris at the right time, in the right place. And the gun that killed Wayland was tucked in my roof.'

He talked her through why he was in a holding cell in the basement of the police station. Apparently, he was waiting to appear at Westminster Magistrates Court the following day, where the authorities would decide what to do with him next – whether he should go to trial by jury in the UK, or be extradited to France. 'I'm hoping to stay in the UK,' he said. 'But anything could happen.'

'What can I do?'

'You say you saw Turner?'

'Yes.'

'Did he have any luck finding the gendarme you spoke to after Sol was killed? He was hoping to persuade him to testify. Once we have one whistle-blower on board, he's convinced others will follow.'

Jay's mind raced, trying to work out what to do, what to say. She replayed Turner's words:

Blake will listen to you. Tell him to plead guilty to the charges and I can protect you. Fight any further and I can't guarantee your safety.

Whether Turner really was with the Garrison or not was a moot point. He wasn't on their side if he wanted Blake to plead guilty. She touched Blake's face. He turned his head and kissed the tips of her fingers. Her heart contracted. No way would she let him spend the rest of his life in jail.

'He said to hang in there,' she lied. 'He's doing everything he can to help.'

'Good man. Work with him, OK? He'll keep you safe.'

Jay gave a nod. She was careful not to meet his eye while she lied.

'Any news on Emilie?' he asked.

'She's still fighting, apparently. Nick's got a NATO buddy out there checking on her daily.'

'Tell him thanks.' Blake scratched his throat with a finger. 'Any luck decoding Sol's stuff?'

'Not yet.' She went on to tell him that Nick was on board, along with the girls. 'Nick said he heard the Garrison might be involved in the prison system, eliminating undesirables so that the taxpayer won't have to waste millions of pounds protecting, say, child killers.'

Blake's expression turned distant. 'There are some people who might agree with that.'

'I studied the statistics of deaths in prisons,' Jay continued. 'The number of deaths by natural causes has almost doubled in the past ten years.'

'How did they die?' His tone sharpened.

'I don't know.'

'Ask Tom to help you. He'll have access.'

Jay's gaze slid aside.

'Everything OK there?' he asked.

'Not really,' she mumbled. 'We had a row.'

'Does that mean I'm in with a chance?' His eyes gleamed.

Jay studied his face, re-memorizing every angle, every plane. She remembered her regret that she'd never made love to him. Unbidden, desire rose, flushing her neck, her cheeks.

His eyes immediately darkened. 'When I get out,' he said, his voice husky. 'Yes?'

'Yes,' she said, putting her hand on her heart. It was a promise.

TWENTY-ONE

Jay rang Tom as she drove down the M4, but once again it clicked straight to his messaging service. Was he avoiding her? He hadn't responded to her message yesterday . . . She left another voicemail, telling him she was heading to Bristol to have lunch with Lily, who she hoped had news about the Russia House. And, she added hesitantly, she hoped to see him later, if that was all right? As she spoke, she trailed off, suddenly confused. Should she see Tom now she knew Blake was alive? Plus there was the small fact that she'd promised to sleep with Blake when he was free . . . She hung up mid-sentence, groaning out loud. Being in love with two men made life unbearably complicated. Emotions all over the place, Jay decided to ground herself by ringing her boss.

She'd texted Nick yesterday to tell him Blake was alive, and he'd texted back saying, *best bloody news*, but thanks to mistiming their calls to one another for the rest of the day, they had yet to speak. This time, Nick answered on the second ring.

'They shot him with a tranquillizer dart?' he said.

'Yes.' She now felt incredibly stupid at believing Blake had died. 'I didn't realize. It worked so fast . . .'

'You weren't to know,' he said. 'A bit of an emotional grinder for you though, going through all that and then finding it was all for nothing.'

Not quite for nothing, she thought, visualizing the scar shaped like a starburst below Blake's shoulder blade. She wondered how it would feel beneath her fingers.

'What else?' Nick asked.

She told him about Jim Turner and Brian Keith. 'I was warned off.'

'We're rattling cages,' he cautioned. 'Means we're on to something. Be careful, Jay.'

Instinctively, Jay parked in Tom's street before walking into town. The brasserie Lily had suggested was near the harbour, overlooking a cobbled street that, in summer, would be wall-to-wall with people dining and drinking outside, but in winter was quiet.

Today, Lily was dressed in a surprisingly conservative blue suit. Her platinum-blonde hair was tied in a fierce chignon, and although a lot of bosom swelled from her white blouse, straining the buttons alarmingly, she could have been mistaken for an office manager.

'Wow,' Jay remarked. 'Very tasteful.'

'Hideous,' Lily snorted. 'But Gary likes it. He's one of my regulars. Fancies I'm his secretary.'

Jay didn't dare ask if Lily had just seen Gary, or was going to see him later, in case Lily went into any more details. Instead she turned to the menu.

'I think I've found your girl,' Lily said. 'She's only been here a month, so she's still fresh.'

'The Russia House?'

Lily nodded. 'Along with four other new girls. You may well find they're trafficked as well.' She gave Jay the address of a street just north of the A420. 'Word on the street is that it's part of a ring. Possibly fifteen hundred clients.'

Jay whistled. 'Big business.'

'It doesn't come much bigger.'

'You are wonderful,' Jay said sincerely.

'Does that mean I can have a glass of wine with my haddock?' Lily said with a smile.

'You can have the whole bottle if you like.'

Lily looked shocked. 'Not when I'm working.'

Jay brought out her phone. 'Do you mind? I want to brief the cops.'

Lily shook her head. She knew the form.

Jay tried Tom again, with no success. After leaving him a message, she spoke with the duty sergeant, Lauren Carter, who she knew. Lauren said that if the prostitution ring was that big, then they'd want to go for the jugular, and with a crack team. This meant they wouldn't go in straight away, but probably later in the day, when they were ready and had social services on board as well, to take the girls into care.

'Do you want to be there when we go in?' she asked Jay.

'Yes,' she said. 'Text me when you're on your way. I'll meet you there.'

Jay hung up. Put the phone on the table where she could

grab it in a second. It reminded her of her doing the same in
Paris. She must, *must*, do some more work on the photographs
on Sol's phone. If it was a code, as Blake thought, it might
help his case.

At two p.m. Lily took a call from Gary. 'Sure, babe,' she
told her client. 'I'll get a taxi. See you in half an hour.'

Jay settled the bill and gave Lily a peck on the cheek. 'I
can't tell you how brilliant you are,' she told her. 'Without you,
we wouldn't help half the girls we do.'

Lily shrugged, but Jay could tell she was pleased.

Jay killed time, waiting for Lauren to call her. Tucked up in
a coffee shop, she studied Sol's photographs and played the
clips of music. No message or code came to her but she kept
at it. Finally, at four p.m., Lauren rang.

There were six uniformed police officers in place when Jay
arrived, along with an armed-response unit, just in case. Last
year, an Albanian pimp had pulled a gun and tried to shoot his
way free, wounding two officers. Today they weren't taking
any chances.

Jay studied the innocuous-looking Russia House. Set at the
end of the street, it looked much like its neighbours – red brick,
two-storey, with a path leading to a front door – and the only
hint that it might not be what it seemed was the fact its neighbours looked after their front gardens and the Russia House
didn't. The paving stones were edged with weeds and covered
in a carpet of cigarette butts.

Jay introduced herself to the social services representative,
a willowy woman in jeans and a black leather jacket. They
stood on the street corner, well out of the way, and watched
the cops go into the Russia House. Everything fell silent. The
armed-response unit remained in position.

After ten minutes or so, two officers returned, muscling a
broad-shouldered woman into the back of the police van. Another
woman followed, along with a man in a pair of pale-brown
trousers. Then came the girls. There were six. Jay recognized
Irina immediately. She was a mess. Her miniskirt was awry, her
skimpy blouse buttoned haphazardly. Despite the darkened rings
around her eyes and the fact she was almost skeletal, the girl
was still hauntingly beautiful.

Jay watched as they were escorted to another van. The social
services rep went and joined them. The girls were shaking and

weeping, obviously convinced they were going to be beaten.
Jay followed the girls to the police station, where she gave
them each her card. Told them who she was, and that she'd
help reunite them with their families back home, if that's what
they wanted. She told them there was a possibility they could
stay in the UK if it could be proved they might be trafficked
again. She added that when she contacted their families she
would keep what they'd been doing in England confidential.
She knew that some girls in the past had been so fearful of
their parents discovering they'd been prostitutes, they killed
themselves. Also, some girls were fearful that if their prostitution became common knowledge, no man would want them,
and they would never marry. Jay had no compunction lying to
some families to protect a particularly vulnerable girl.

It was after six o'clock when she left. She still hadn't heard
from Tom. Tired after an intense afternoon persuading the girls
they were now safe, she trudged up the hill to where she'd
parked her car. Her tiredness vanished when she saw there was
a light on in Tom's flat. She checked her watch. Six forty-five.
He was home early.

Jay rang his home number, but it was engaged. Dragging up
her courage from the soles of her feet, Jay walked to his front
door and pressed the bell. She heard him yell something, and
then it went quiet.

The door swung open to reveal the whippet-thin form of
Sofie.

'Hi, Jay,' she said. She looked strangely awkward.

'Hi. Can I come in?'

Sofie dragged the door open wide. 'Daddy!' she yelled over
her shoulder. 'It's Jay!'

'Coming,' he called back. He didn't sound enthusiastic.

As she stepped into the hallway, Jay said, 'How's your Mum?'

'She got the bank to disclose.' Sofie glowed. 'Which means
they're going to start mediating. They don't have to go to court.
She's saved millions of pounds.'

'Well done her,' Jay managed. The only thing she'd ever
managed to save was a jar of Puglian honey Blake had given her,
which he'd brought back from the foot of Italy last spring. She
was going to crack it open when she next made some porridge.

Suddenly, Tom was there. 'Jay,' he said.

'Hi.'

'Have you come to pick up your stuff?' he asked.

Her stomach immediately rolled, making her feel dizzy. 'My stuff?' she repeated. Her mouth had gone dry.

'Sofie.' He turned to his daughter. 'Would you mind leaving us for a minute?'

Sofie hesitated. 'But—'

'Now.'

The girl vanished.

'Sorry.' Tom ran a hand over his face. 'I thought that's why you were here.'

'Haven't you got my messages?'

'I'm sorry. I've been busy . . .'

'I called you twice, about Irina. Lauren helped bust the Russia House this afternoon. There were six girls. They're with social services.' A wave of tiredness swept over her as she pictured Irina's fear-filled eyes.

Tom immediately softened. 'I'll put the kettle on. Or would you like something stronger?'

'It depends.' She gave him a wan smile. 'Whether I'm driving or not.'

'Tea it is.' He turned brisk. He didn't want her to stay. She felt like crying.

In the kitchen, Sofie was curled on the sofa doing a jumbo crossword puzzle.

'Do you want a box to put things in?' Tom asked Jay.

'No.'

'What, then? A carrier bag won't be big enough—'

'Tom, I'm not here for that. I need a favour.'

His mouth narrowed. 'I'm all out of favours, Jay.'

Sofie looked up, her expression oddly anxious. Jay wished the girl wasn't a witness to her humiliation, but she had no choice but to plough on.

'Please. It's important. I need the VW Polo's number plate run.' She didn't want to say more with Sofie there. 'I want to know who owns it.'

'The Met should be doing that.'

'I'm not sure they're one hundred per cent committed.' She took him aside and, in an undertone, told him about Sergeant Neuhaus being transferred and Sergeant Mayer's apparent professionalism but lack of progress. His nostrils flared as he thought. He wasn't happy with the story, she could tell.

'OK,' he said. 'I'll run the plate tomorrow. Do you have Mayer's number in case I need to check in with him?'

Jay passed him her phone. After punching in the number, Tom placed both phones on the counter, near the fruit bowl, where they usually belonged. He hadn't seemed to realize what he'd done. His expression was closed.

'Thanks,' she said. She wanted to touch him, to show how grateful she was, but didn't dare. She didn't think she could bear it if he turned aside.

'Anything else?' The clipped tone was back.

She considered telling him Blake wasn't dead, but didn't have the courage. 'Just one thing. It's to do with the deaths in Britain's prisons.'

He blinked.

'The national total of deaths in British prisons has nearly doubled in the past ten years. Those dying from natural causes leaped from eighty to a hundred and seventy.'

Even though he didn't move a muscle, she saw the surprise flare in his eyes.

She said, 'I want to know what they died from.'

'If you clear your stuff from upstairs, I'll find out for you. Deal?'

The last thing she wanted was to take her things, because then he wouldn't be reminded of her. She swallowed. 'OK,' she said. She trailed upstairs and began to gather some items from the bathroom. Her deodorant, some moisturizer and shampoo. A stick of mascara, eyeliner pencil, a tube of lip gloss. She refused to take her toothbrush. It would be like saying it was THE END in capital letters. Her throat closed. Tears rose. *Dammit*, she thought. *I won't do this*. She put the whole lot back. Wandered into the bedroom. Sat down on the bed. She could hear Marvin Gaye belting out downstairs. Sofie was probably dancing with her doting Dad. Depressed, she continued to sit on the bed, unsure what to do next. She didn't move until Tom came into the room.

'Jay? Are you all right?'

She slowly rose to her feet.

'Don't worry about your things,' he said quietly. 'We can do it another time.'

She didn't reply. Brushing past him, she padded downstairs and into the kitchen. She paused on the threshold, looking for her mobile phone. Unable to see it, she scanned the kitchen. Sofie was on the sofa, playing with a phone . . . *Her* phone.

Jay stalked across to stand over the girl. Sofie looked up, her expression almost frightened.

'What the hell do you think you're doing?' Jay hissed. She put out her hand. Sofie passed over the phone. It was open at one of Sol's photographs.

'I only wanted to help,' Sofie bleated.

'By poking your nose where it isn't meant to be?'

'It's the same puzzle as Daddy's,' Sofie said. 'It's a code, right?'

Jay blinked. 'What?'

'I think I know how it works.'

Jay stared at the girl in momentary disbelief. *Sofie had cracked Sol's code?*

'It's people's names,' Sofie said. She twisted her fingers in her lap. 'Some are foreign, which is why it was a bit tricky to start with. But once I got going, it was easy. I know I shouldn't have been nosy, but I can't resist puzzles. Shall I show you how it works?'

Jay dropped beside the girl. 'Fire away.'

Sofie brightened. With a few taps, she opened the clips of music on Sol's memory card. Jay instantly recognized James Blunt's *You're Beautiful.*

'You take the first name of the artist,' Sofie said.

'James,' said Jay.

'Then you go to the first picture with the same date as the music. You see, they're numbered to make it easier.'

Sofie opened picture number one, a stark pen and ink painting of what Jay guessed was Don Quixote and a dead mule. The next picture Jay recognized: *Le déjeuner sur l'herbe.* Picnic lunch on the grass, by Claude Monet. The third picture was a portrait of Napoleon, the fourth of two lushly naked women amongst spilled roses, the fifth two naked figures in soft pink light. The sixth picture was a repeat of the second by Claude Monet.

'So we have six pictures, two of which are repeated.' Jay said. 'And the name James.'

'Correct.' Sofie bounced to her feet. 'Now we have to go on the Internet.'

Jay followed Sofie to Tom's laptop on the kitchen table.

Her eyes widened when Sofie opened the Musée d'Orsay's website. She'd looked up the same museum when she'd tried to research the photograph of the stone polar bear. Sofie clicked on to the link to show the museum map.

'*Salle* four,' said Sofie. '*Salle* means—'

'Room.'

'Room four contains the picture of the man with the dead donkey.'

'It's a mule,' Jay murmured.

'Whatever.'

Tom came and stood behind them. Peered over Jay's shoulder.

'OK,' said Sofie. 'The mule is in room four, which is the fourth letter of the alphabet. D.'

Sofie moved the mouse on to another room. *Salle* eighteen, which contained Claude Monet's *Le déjeuner sur l'herbe*.

'The eighteenth alphabet letter,' said Sofie, 'is R.'

She continued to move the mouse across the floor plan. 'This bloke—'

'Napoleon,' said Jay.

'Whoever. He's in room one, which means A.'

'DRA,' said Jay.

'Correct.'

The two lush naked women were in room sixteen, the sixteenth number in the alphabet being P, and the two pinkly naked figures in room five: E. The sixth picture was repeated, meaning they were back to Claude Monet's painting in room eighteen: R.

'Draper,' murmured Jay. 'James Draper. The name rings a bell.'

'He was the Bishop of Bath and Wells,' said Tom. 'He died six months ago.'

Jay and Tom shared a look.

'Show me another?' Jay asked Sofie. 'Say, the latest?'

'Sure!' Sofie wriggled like a joyful puppy before her fingers flew over the keyboard.

There were four pictures dated the day before Sol was murdered. Just the single tune. Sofie played the tune, which Jay recognized straight away since she had the CD at home. 'Madeleine Peroux,' she said. 'Madeleine.'

Sofie nodded. Showed Jay a dark oil painting of a deer fight. *Spring Rut*. 'Room seven,' she said.

'G,' said Jay.

The next picture was one they'd seen before. The portrait of Napoleon in room one. 'A,' Jay said.

The last picture was of an angel with a stave, striking a door. A picture called *Peste à Rome* – the plague – in room twelve. 'L,' said Sofie. She was frowning. 'But I don't get it. Is Gal a name?'

Dear God.

Jay was back in the Paris apartment with Blake, watching the news, watching the report on the death of the Mayor of Calais. Madeleine Gal, a woman she'd met, who had died of a heart attack. 'I know Madeleine,' she said. 'I knew her, I mean.'

'So her name's spelled right?' Sofie said.

'Yes. It's spelled right.' Her head was light. 'Show me some more.'

Once you knew how the code worked it was relatively simple, and soon they had eight names before them: James Draper, Madeleine Gal, Colin Hutton, Leo Roberts, Anne Matus, Richard Huller, Gregory Ergin, and Thomas Campion.

Just one to go, dated the second of September. The week before Sol Neill had been murdered.

Jay's breathing became shallow when the musical artist was revealed: Emilie Simon. She stood rigidly as Sofie decoded the five-letter surname, but she already knew who it was going to be.

Emilie Blake.

TWENTY-TWO

Jay asked Sofie to google Colin Hutton and Leo Roberts. Both men were dead. It was at that point she suggested they take a break, but while Tom and Sofie headed back to the kitchen, Jay googled the remaining names to find that – aside from Emilie – each person was dead.

James Draper had died within three days of contracting a virulent and unidentified virus. Madeleine Gal had died of a heart attack. Colin Hutton and Leo Roberts had also suffered fatal heart attacks. Anne Matus had been overtaken by a strange virus, along with Richard Huller. Gregory Ergin and Thomas

Campion had both also died of heart attacks. And poor Emilie was in a coma, fighting for her life against an unknown virus.

Aside from Blake's sister, nobody had lived more than a week after the date the code had been sent.

'My God.' Jay leaned back, her skin tingling. 'My God.'

She was still feeling unsteady when she returned to the kitchen. Tom was boiling spaghetti while Sofie stirred onions in a pan. When Jay murmured her findings to Tom, he said, 'Christ. I've heard there are drugs around that can cause a cardiac arrest . . . You don't think they've been bumped off, do you?'

'I don't know what to think.'

'Christ,' he said again.

'I need to know how those prison inmates died.'

'They're linked?' He looked appalled.

'They might be.'

He gave a groan. Closed his eyes briefly. 'Don't you think you should leave well alone?'

She nibbled the inside of her lip. She could no more let Blake rot in jail than she could take a chainsaw to her leg. 'I can't,' she said.

'Thought so.' He sighed. 'I'll email you.'

'Thanks.' Normally she'd touch him, maybe squeeze his arm as a way of thanking him, but she refrained. She took a step back, made a vague gesture. 'I've got to go.'

He gave a nod. No farewell hug, no kiss.

Jay walked to stand in front of Sofie. Looked into her eyes. 'You are a truly brilliant, amazing, and wonderful person,' she said. 'I would never have unlocked that code without you.'

To her surprise, Sofie blushed. 'I only got it because Mummy took me to the museum at Easter. I saw the white bear there. It was the bear that gave me the clue.'

'Well, however you managed it, I will be forever grateful, OK?'

Sofie bit her lip. Her gaze was glued to the floor. 'You're not cross with me?'

'If you hadn't cracked the code –' Jay was honest – 'I would have been furious. But as it is . . . You have no idea how much time you've saved us. But please, Sofie. Promise you won't look at my mobile again? It's *private*.'

'I swear I won't, OK?'

The girl looked so anxious, so willing to please, that Jay held out her hand. 'Truce?'

'Truce.' Sofie shook her hand firmly, expression intense.

Jay glanced at Tom before she continued, making sure he was listening. 'Before I go, Sofie, will you promise me something?'

Sofie nodded furiously. 'Anything.'

'Don't tell anyone what you've found. It's very sensitive information, which could be dangerous if it fell into the wrong hands.'

'Is it to do with that woman who came here?'

'Yes.'

'I promise.' Sofie solemnly crossed her heart.

'If you ever need a job with GCHQ, the centre where spooks do all their decoding and eavesdropping, I'll write you a reference, no problem.'

'You think I could be a spy?' The girl's face was alight.

'You already are.'

Sofie beamed.

When Jay arrived home, she was too wired to sleep. Instead, she trawled the Internet for information on the eight dead people.

The Right Reverend James Draper, it transpired, had headed the Church of England Diocese of Bath and Wells, a vast area that stretched from Portishead in the east to Bath, and down to Yeovil and across Dorset to Exmouth. He entered the House of Lords in 2005. He'd had the ear of many Members of Parliament, and of the Prime Minister. He'd also had access to the Queen. A powerful figure, by all accounts.

As Jay dug deeper, she gradually uncovered Draper's vision, his policy of purpose. He'd been a liberal Christian, apparently, who'd believed in integrating the Muslim faith into his Diocese. He'd firmly believed there was room for both faiths and that, one day, for every church there should also be a mosque.

Jay recalled what Ruth had said when she'd confronted Colonel Greene.

You're saying Rick was never approached socially by his superior officer . . . and asked light-heartedly whether he'd join an organization that was dedicated to halting the flood of Muslims into the West?

Surely not, she thought. Disbelief had her shaking her head. Was the Garrison really going around assassinating people who didn't hold their views? It didn't seem possible. Still shaking

her head, Jay researched the next name on her list. Colin Hutton
had also been in the House of Lords. Like Draper, he'd been
a liberal, and had been known for his fierce opposition to the
UK having an army, navy, and air force. Instead, he'd espoused
an integrated European police force, controlled by the EU. Not
something many right-wing voters would agree with.

Leo Roberts was the next in line. A mature student and leader
of a Students' Union, Leo had been against the war in
Afghanistan. He'd organized a variety of student protests and
had appeared firmly pro-Muslim.

And so it went on. Each person on Sol's phone appeared to
have been either left wing or liberal, and in favour of an integrated society, welcoming Muslims into the West.

The only anomaly Jay could find was Emilie. They hadn't
attempted to assassinate Emilie for her liberal views. Blake had
said she'd overheard something that panicked her. And what
about Sol? Emilie's coded name had been sent to him the week
before his meeting with Blake. Sol had known Emilie had been
stricken with a virulent virus . . .

Head overloaded with information, Jay yawned, tears
collecting in the corners of her eyes. She glanced at the kitchen
clock to see it was past two in the morning. Closing down the
computer, she stumbled to bed. She fell asleep as though felled.

Blake's appearance was due to be held at three thirty in the
afternoon at Westminster Magistrates Court, leaving Jay free
to head for the office on Wednesday morning. She'd just come
out of the deli when her phone vibrated, alerting her she had
an email. She checked the sender to see it was from Tom.
Subject: *statistics*.

Of the 230 who died in prison of natural causes, there are 80
that concern me: 52 died of heart attacks, 28 from an unknown
virus. (The remaining 90 died of everything from pneumonia to
liver failure and cancer. I'm not worried about these.) With roughly
80,000 people housed in 150 prisons, the unknown virus is
concerning the authorities, but they haven't hit the panic button
yet. The toxicology guys are wondering if the high number of
heart attacks is due to some new, undetectable drug being pedalled
around – they've found degradation products that concern them.
Interestingly, nearly all of the 80 people who died of heart attacks

or the unknown virus were in jail for either killing or having harmed a child. Where are you going with this?

Heart thumping, she reread the text. Could it be true? Were the Garrison really killing these people?

She shot off a quick email, thanking Tom. Like herself, he must have been up half the night, digging through the prison stats. She'd ring him later, she decided, after she'd talked to Nick. She made two mugs of coffee and took them into Nick's office, along with half a dozen sticky baklava she'd picked up at the deli around the corner. Both she and Nick were addicted to baklava, having been introduced to the syrupy pastries in the Middle East.

'Hmmm,' Nick said, swallowing his first finger-shaped pastry in two bites. 'God, they're good.'

'Sofie cracked Sol's code.' She quickly explained how the code worked, listed the names, and told him that all eight people were dead of supposedly natural causes.

'And?'

She showed him Tom's email. He fell quiet, sipping his coffee. After a couple of minutes, he reached for his ancient Rolodex and flipped through the cards. 'We need to speak to a friend of mine, Dr Cole. Used to work at Porton Down.'

Porton Down, Jay knew, was the UK government and military defence science and technology laboratory.

'He now works in a research lab at Bart's.' Nick dialled, but Dr Cole was in a meeting.

While Nick played phone tag with the doctor, Jay caught up with paperwork. It wasn't until after lunch that Nick called her into his office. He had Dr Cole on speakerphone. He introduced them.

'Jay wants to hear what you've got to say about these statistics.'

'I don't like them,' Dr Cole said. His voice was big and booming, making Jay picture a man the size of a tractor with a beard like a spade. 'If it's true, that they've been assassinated, then the toxicologists need to be looking in this direction. Do you remember the Bulgarian defector Georgi Markov? He was jabbed in the calf by a man holding an umbrella on Waterloo Bridge in 1978. He felt a stinging pain, which he took to be from the tip of the umbrella, and when he arrived in his office, he found a red pimple where the umbrella had jabbed him. He ended up in hospital with a high fever and died three days later. The autopsy showed a pellet the size of a pinhead embedded in his calf. Porton Down found it was sugar coated and designed to melt at body temperature. As it melted, ricin was absorbed into the bloodstream. The Russians were blamed.'

Jay fixed her eyes on the phone. Her flesh was crawling.

'Any pellets in your victims?' Dr Cole asked.

'We don't know,' Nick said. 'But from now on we'll be looking.'

'A heart attack can be brought on by a variety of drugs,' Dr Cole continued. 'It could be injected, or dropped into someone's drink. The virus is a different matter. It has to be introduced via mucosal surfaces, like tissues, towels, and hands. That's how flu and colds are transferred.'

'One of the victims suffering from the virus is still alive,' Jay said. 'She's in a coma, but she's alive.'

'Hmmm,' Dr Cole mused. 'Maybe the virus is aggressive to start with, culminating in a peak, which is when the victim dies. Should the virus stop replicating after this peak, and the victim has reached this stage alive, then their immune system can begin to fight it. Or maybe they've already got some form of immunity for this particular virus.'

He paused briefly to clear his throat. 'You said there might be an antidote, but I've never heard of anything that works like that towards a virus. See if you can get your hands on samples of the virus. Bring them over to me, and I'll have a look. Tell you what they're about.'

After he'd ended the call, Nick sat rubbing his forehead. 'Jesus,' he said.

Jay remained quiet for a while, trying to take it in. Were people in the prison system really killing targeted inmates? It seemed wild, crazy, but having listened to Dr Cole, and the story about Georgi Markov, anything seemed possible.

'Look,' Nick said. 'I've got a meeting I can't miss on the other side of town. Text me Blake's court result?'

'Sure.' Jay rose and fetched her handbag and, when the clock ticked to three o'clock, headed for the tube.

The courtroom wasn't particularly large, and Jay was surprised at how busy it was; solicitors, legal assistants and media were all jostling for space. Murder suspects were obviously a crowd-puller. Jay took a seat in the third row at the end of the bench, in case she needed a quick getaway. Her skin tautened when she saw Jim Turner arrive. He crossed the room and squeezed himself on the bench behind her. He leaned forward. 'How are you, Jay?'

'Fine, thanks.' She was brittle.

'I gather Blake is still protesting his innocence.'

'That's because he *is* innocent.'

'But I thought I asked you—'

She twisted in her seat to face him. 'I know what you asked. You don't have to repeat it.' Her voice was low and angry.

'Look, Jay.' He massaged the space between his eyes. 'I admit I made a mistake. I thought you'd back off after what I said in the car. I should have known better, given your file, but I thought it was worth a shot. Plenty of people have been intimidated by less.'

The muscles in Jay's face felt stiff. Had he helped orchestrate all those people's deaths? Including those of the Bishop of Bath and Wells, and Madeleine Gal?

'There's more going on here than you can realize,' he continued. 'I wish I could show you the bigger picture so you could understand, but it's impossible. It's also very dangerous. If I tell you that I'm on your side, that I'm trying to protect both you and Blake . . .'

She gave a snort. 'Does Blake know the bigger picture?'

'Nobody does.'

'Except you.' Her voice was mocking.

'Except me,' he agreed.

Jay rose to allow a man to inch past her, heading for a space further along.

'What can I say to convince you?' Turner murmured.

'You can't,' Jay said.

'Blake is safe in jail,' he said. 'That's why I want him there.'

'Safe from whom?'

'You know the answer to that.'

'The Garrison.' As she said the word, the pupils in his eyes became pin dots. Once again, she was reminded of a shark.

'You really should be careful about using that word,' he said.

At that moment, there was a commotion to one side, and Turner's water-pale eyes moved to focus behind her. Jay turned to see Blake walking into the courtroom, flanked by two uniformed policemen. He wore a dark suit, white shirt and red tie.

His bearing was tall, his gaze direct. He looked like a solicitor
– which, she supposed, was his intention. She didn't think he'd
find her in the crowd, but as he turned to take his seat he looked
straight at her and sent her a wink.

Jay rolled her eyes at his flippancy. He looked amused. He
didn't seem to notice Jim Turner, but Jay knew things with
Blake were deceptive, and that he'd no doubt pegged everyone
he needed to within seconds.

It didn't take long for the prosecution and the defence to get
into a wrangle over whether Blake should be granted bail or
not. Once upon a time there was an automatic ban on murder
suspects being given bail, but this had been ruled out by the
government because it would, according to the European
Convention, breach their human rights. Plus, there was the fact
that if every murder suspect was sent to jail pending trial, the
jails would be even more overcrowded.

The prosecution said that Blake was dangerous and could
commit another murder if allowed to 'roam the streets'. The
defence said Blake was an upstanding citizen and faithful
employee of the security services, who had never been arrested
before and was no danger to anyone. There was no talk of bail
surety; unlike in the US, there was no financial bond. If a
murder suspect was given bail, no money changed hands.

The judge watched both men impassively before saying,
'Max Blake will be held under house arrest until his trial. He
will be electronically tagged. He steps outside his own four
walls, he goes straight to jail. Clear?'

The prosecution ground their teeth, while the defence clapped
Blake on the back and shook his hand, but Blake wasn't looking
at his solicitor. He was looking directly at Jay, expression
intense. His eyes burned into hers.

He mouthed, 'Tonight.' It wasn't a question.

Her stomach swooped. She hadn't expected to fulfil her
promise so soon. Her mind flipped from wondering how he
was going to get home to whether her local beauty salon would
be able to fit her in for a full-body makeover at two minutes'
notice.

'Jay.'

She tried to drag herself back to reality. God, she was going
to sleep with Blake tonight. *Tonight!* Her belly was doing flip-
flops already. Heaven knew what state she'd be in later.

'Are you all right?' Turner was studying her.

'Fine.' She cleared her throat. 'No problem.'

'I want you to give Blake this.' He passed her a small padded envelope. 'I don't trust the phone, or email.'

'What is it?'

'You'll find out if he chooses to share it with you. Or if you open it yourself.' He paused, watching her speculatively. 'Be careful how you tread, Jay.'

She watched him walk away, and for the first time she noticed he had a slight roll in his gait, like a man used to being at sea.

Jay had just locked her car and was walking to the office when Tom rang. He said, 'Got your number plate.'

She scrabbled in her handbag for a pen. 'Tom, I can't thank—'

'It belongs to an Alan Churton.' He was curt. 'In Mitcham.' He rattled off an address, along with a phone number, which she hastily scribbled down on the back of her hand.

'You're wonderful.' She took a breath. Hearing his voice had sent her emotions all over the place. She wanted to talk about the prison deaths, about Dr Cole's theories on the heart attacks and the unknown virus, but all sense had fled. 'Look, I know you said you wanted a break, but can we talk about it? I know I don't always act how you like—'

'Sorry, Jay,' he interrupted. 'Not now.'

'I just want to talk, that's all. I need to explain why—'

'There's nothing to explain. I need time to think, OK? Bye.'

He hung up.

She stood briefly, wondering whether to text him or not, but then she remembered Blake, that she was supposed to be at his house that evening, and decided against it. God, life was complicated.

Sighing, Jay rang Nick. 'Blake's under house arrest,' she told him.

'Could be worse.'

'And Tom's found the Polo's address.'

'Where?'

Jay told him. 'I thought I'd drive down there now,' she said. 'See if Churton's home. Ask a few questions. See if he knew where his son parked the night I was kidnapped. I don't want to do it by phone.'

'Good idea. When you get the address of your kidnapper, ring me.'

Jay drove out to Mitcham. Later, she couldn't remember much about the journey. Just the fact that every time she thought of Blake, and pictured the lean length of his spine, the scars wrapping his ribs, her grip on the steering wheel tightened until her knuckles gleamed white.

Mitcham was five miles from Fulham, but it could have been fifty the time it took to battle her way through Clapham and Streatham. Finally, she turned off the London Road and into Graham Road. Large terraced houses lined the street – most whitewashed, each with a paved front patio on which to park a couple of cars. In the old days, these paved spaces would have been gardens filled with shrubs and grass. No wonder sparrows were almost non-existent in London. They had nowhere to forage any more.

She was barely twenty yards down the street, head turning from side to side to read the house numbers, when, for no apparent reason, her nerves began to sing a warning. She slowed. Broadened her vision to look at each side of the street, to the end and back. She took in two women with a pram. A young guy on a bicycle. The distant sound of a drill. Nothing to be worried about, but something was wrong; her subconscious knew it, but her conscious mind couldn't work it out.

She slowed further. Heart thumping, Jay inched down the street. Out of nowhere, all the hairs on her body stood bolt upright.

Just past a white transit van on the left hand side, stood the hulking shape of a motorbike shrouded beneath a silver canopy. Parked on the front patio of the house opposite, stood a VW Polo. Number plate YCO9 OPD.

TWENTY-THREE

Sweat springing, Jay drove down the street without braking or changing gear. It was only when she'd put a good mile between her and her kidnapper's garage that she pulled over and rang Nick.

'I've found the house where they took me. It's opposite Churton's place. He must have lied about his son borrowing his car. And lied about his son being in Majorca and out of touch. It's a cover-up. They've got to Churton, they must have. Or he's a friend. Or he's in on it . . .' She had to force herself to take a breath.

'Where are you?'

'Streatham.'

'Good. Don't go back.'

'I won't. Shall I call the police?'

He didn't answer.

'Nick?'

He said, 'What do you think will happen if you do that?'

Jay considered Sergeant Mayer and his steely grey eyes. Then she considered Sergeant Neuhaus and his sudden transferral from the station, along with Constable Robertson's reluctance to talk to her. 'I'm not sure.'

'How about we have a chat to your kidnapper first, then call the police?'

'Hmmm.' She was noncommittal.

'Was anyone in the house, do you think?'

'No idea.'

'I'll set up some surveillance. When we see someone's home, I'll ring you. Get you over to ID them. If they're one of the guys who snatched you, we'll talk to him. OK?'

'I guess so.'

'Where are you going now?'

'Home. Then to Blake's.'

'Give him my best.'

Back in Fulham, Jay showered and washed her hair. Moisturized. Blow-dried her hair. She dithered about what to wear, eventually settling on some peach-coloured satin underwear and her usual stretchy shirt and jeans. Some pretty velvet shoes. A pair of gold Grecian earrings followed. Her watch. No other jewellery.

She checked her appearance and sighed. She looked about as seductive as a traffic warden. Again she dithered, wondering whether she ought to wear something sexier, like a skirt or a dress, but by the time she'd rifled through her wardrobe a third time, the girls were home and demanding to know if she was in for supper. Jeans it was. She decided against packing an overnight bag, just stuffed spare undies and a toothbrush into her handbag.

'Back later,' she called, sailing past the kitchen. 'Maybe tomorrow. Maybe tonight. Don't know.'

'See ya!' they called at the same time as she closed the door behind her.

She exhaled in relief at having left without them seeing her. If the girls got an inkling of what she was up to they'd rib her endlessly, as well as quiz her about Tom. But tonight wasn't about Tom. It was about her and Blake.

When Jay turned off the country lane, and on to the rutted track that was the start of Blake's drive, she suddenly lost her nerve and pulled over. This was ridiculous, she thought. Her hands were trembling. Anyone would think she was about to face a firing squad, not a man she loved. She jumped a mile when her mobile rang.

'Hi.' Her voice was scratchy.

'Having second thoughts?'

'Of course not,' she lied, craning her neck. Had he seen her? His home was tucked in the folds of the next hillside, and unless he had X-ray vision, he'd have no idea she was barely half a mile from him.

'If you do, it's not a problem.'

'No, no.' She was beginning to sweat. 'I'm on my way.'

'I want you with me one hundred per cent, OK? No doubts.'

'No doubts,' she echoed.

Jay hung up and stared blankly through the windscreen.

Of course she had doubts. Yes, she and Tom were on a break, but it wasn't the first time. They'd had a break eighteen months ago, and he'd used that break to sleep with his secretary, Sharon. Despite Jay's jealousy, they'd got back together and things had been so *good* between them . . . Could it happen again? Not if Tom discovered she'd slept with Blake.

And what of her regret when she'd believed Blake was dead? She recalled the pain she'd felt, her sorrow that she'd never made love to him.

Still dithering, a mass of nerves, Jay used a device her sister-in-law had once suggested and pictured herself an old woman, lying on her deathbed. What would that old woman advise her? To turn her back on Blake . . . or not?

The answer was resounding. No doubts.

Go to Blake.

Jay put the car into gear and continued along the track to the rustic farmhouse surrounded by beech trees. The air was filled with the cawing of rooks. When Jay climbed out, the front door opened to reveal Blake barefoot, in jeans and a black T-shirt. She walked to him. His expression was serious as he studied her.

'OK?' he asked.

'Yes.' She swallowed. 'Look, I have a lot to tell you. We've cracked Sol's code . . .'

'Not now,' he said gently. 'Later.'

She reached up and stroked his cheek, feeling the faintest rasp of stubble beneath her fingertips. She stroked his eyebrows, his lips, the silky hair above his ears.

In one sweep his arms were around her, pulling her to him. His mouth was cool and soft. His hands trembled as they cupped her face, making her feel unbearably tender. He stood back. His breathing was hard and fast. He put out a hand, palm up. Jay rested her hand in his and let him lead her inside.

When he laid his naked skin against hers, it set off a tremendous shock of heat.

'Jesus Christ,' he whispered.

She groaned, pulling him close, but at the last second he reared back.

'Oh no you don't.' A smile played on his lips.

'What?' Jay froze.

'I've waited a long time for this,' he murmured.

'I know. Sorry.'

'I promised myself that when we got to this point –' gently, he pinned her wrists above her head – 'I would kiss every inch of you.'

'Really?' Her voice was several octaves higher.

His eyes darkened until they were almost black. 'Really.'

Blake kept his word and come midnight, when they were curled together in front of a log fire, he continued his gentle exploration.

'There's a bit here I think I missed,' he murmured, pressing his lips below her shoulder blade. 'And here.' Another kiss on her nape as his hands skimmed the length of her belly.

Jay twisted to look into his eyes. 'Lie back,' she told him.

He blinked.

'It's my turn,' she said.

She awoke in the morning in his bed, limbs entwined, and for a moment she couldn't work out which limb went where. Her head nestled on his shoulder, one leg between his thighs, the other over his waist. His arms were around her, his breath warm on her cheek. She'd never slept wrapped in a man's embrace like this before. She and Tom would spoon one another, but they'd never slept like a couple of animals heaped together.

'Hmmm,' Blake murmured.

'Hmmm,' she agreed.

She shifted her leg slightly and felt the plastic cuff around his ankle. Gently, she stroked her foot against his.

His hands began to drift over her body. 'Yesterday,' he murmured, 'I hated the idea of house arrest, but with you here, it's not a problem.'

'I won't be here all day.'

'So let's not waste valuable time.'

Later, Blake padded to the kitchen to make coffee, leaving Jay sprawled face down on the bed. Her body felt languorously tired. She tried to think about what she had to do today, but her mind was a haze. She'd have to look at her diary. Vaguely, she heard a mobile ring. It was her phone's tone, but since all Blake's mobiles had the same tone, she didn't move. She closed her eyes and began to drift.

'Jay.'

Something in his tone had her scrambling upright. 'What is it?'

'It's Nick. He says they've picked up a man at the house where you were held. He wants you to ID him.'

'Tell him I'm on my way.'

Jay drove with one hand on the wheel, the other eating a bacon sandwich that Blake had rustled up while she'd been in the shower. They hadn't eaten much last night – just some olives and Spanish almonds – and the sandwich was a godsend. She had given Blake Turner's envelope, but hadn't said anything more than that Turner had passed it to her in court. She hadn't had time to go into things any further. At least she'd managed to give Blake a brief summary of Sol's code as she'd raced to get dressed.

Nick was waiting for her two streets from where the kidnappers had held her. He was driving an innocuous white van with blue *Plumb Centre* logos on its sides. He told her to hop in the back, where two men sat: Dave and Rob. Both greeted her with a handshake and a grin.

'We'll park in the street,' Nick told her. 'I'll angle the van so you get a good view of the house. He started fettling his bike half an hour ago. Let's hope he's still there.'

Nick cruised down the street, pulling up quietly halfway along. The Harley's shroud was folded to one side. Cloths and rags, bottles and tubes lay on a groundsheet, and on the other side of the bike a man was bent over, polishing one of the fairings. Despite craning into the van's cab, Jay couldn't see the man's face.

'No greater love hath a man than for his Harley,' said Rob.

'Give me a Ducati any day,' said Dave. 'They've got soul.'

'Unreliable,' said Rob.

'If Jennifer Lopez was unreliable, it wouldn't stop you dating her,' replied Dave, and at that moment the man straightened up. Jay's stomach lurched. It was Blondie. Same stocky body, squat neck, and shorn blond hair.

'It's him,' she said.

'Hey, cool,' said Rob, sounding as though he'd just received a present he'd been waiting for all year. 'Let's go get him.'

'I'll park around the corner,' Nick said.

As Nick started the van, Dave sang softly, 'We're coming to get youuu . . .'

Even though the lads were on her side, Jay couldn't help her shiver.

The second Nick parked the van around the corner, Rob and Dave opened the rear and hopped out. Rob carried a toolbox, Dave a couple of lengths of white plastic pipe: props to match the plumbing logos on the van. Jay watched them vanish down the street.

'What's the plan?' she asked.

'We drive your kidnapper somewhere nice and quiet, and talk to him.' Nick turned in his seat. 'You OK with this?'

'Not really,' she admitted. 'I know he snatched me, and that he's part of the Garrison, but it worries me we're going off-piste and without the cops.'

'We won't pull out his fingernails or anything.' He gave a humourless smile. 'We're more subtle than that. Now, jump in the front, would you?'

It didn't take long before Rob and Dave reappeared, with Blondie walking between them. Nerves tight, she watched them in the wing mirror. To her surprise, the man looked completely at ease. He was laughing. He didn't appear to see Jay in the front passenger seat. She heard the rear door open, then the sounds of all three men climbing inside.

'*Another Day in Paradise*,' Blondie said. 'That's what I want to call it. What do you reckon?'

'Sounds about right to me,' said Rob.

'Fucking A,' said Dave.

The door slammed. 'Hey, Nick,' called Rob. 'This is Stewart Bradley. He's a Para. Bomb disposal in Afghanistan. He's writing a book about his experiences. We thought we'd have a pint or two down the pub.'

'Hey, Stew,' said Nick and turned in his seat, stuck out a hand.

Stewart leaned forward and shook, saying, 'Great to meet you . . .'

And then he saw Jay.

His mouth dropped open. 'What the—'

'This is a friend of ours,' said Nick. 'Jay McCaulay. She'd like to join us, if that's OK? She used to be with the Sigs.'

Jay copied Nick's light-hearted approach and sent Stewart a brilliant smile. 'Hi,' she said.

'Hi,' he responded. His voice was croaky.

Nick started the engine, pulled out. 'You've met Jay before, haven't you, Stew?'

'Er . . .'

'It's OK. She doesn't hold any hard feelings, do you, Jay?'

Like hell, she thought, but said dutifully, 'No hard feelings.'

'Right.' Stewart's voice turned faint.

'Sit back and relax,' said Nick. 'And tell us about your book.'

'Yeah,' said Rob. 'I fancy writing a book myself. How do you go about it? Do you have to have an English degree, or do you get someone to help out? Like a ghostwriter or something?'

'I've . . . um. Yeah, I've teamed up with someone . . .'

Stewart's voice faded as he retracted into the rear of the van, but during the journey she heard snatches of conversation. Dave asking whether Stewart was going to use his real name, how much he hoped to sell the book for, and what he'd do with the money. After a while, Nick switched on the radio, and she couldn't hear any more, just the occasional laugh – Dave and Rob creating an atmosphere of conviviality, of soldiers together, having a laugh.

They passed Purley and ducked east, past a couple of golf courses and on to the North Downs. A couple more turns and they were on a windswept road with nothing but scrubby grassland on either side. There was no traffic.

Nick pulled over and switched off the engine. Silence fell. Nick turned in his seat. He said, 'Stew. We need to talk. Tell us about the Garrison.'

TWENTY-FOUR

'The what?' Stewart tried to sound surprised, but the nervous click in his throat gave him away.

'We're thinking of joining,' Nick said. 'But first we need to know what we're getting into.'

'Oh. Well . . . er, we're a type of club.' Stewart cleared his throat. 'Like-minded people coming together. Looking out for each other. You're all ex-Services, right?'

'Right,' said Nick.

'Well, we're fed up with things, wouldn't you agree? Not enough helicopters in Afghanistan, rotten kit, crap care for our boys when they return home . . . One bloke I know – he'd lost both legs to an IED – was put in a bed next to a Muslim, who fucking spat on him. What a fucking disgrace. We shouldn't have our men sent to the fucking NHS. We should be in military hospitals, cared for by our own kind, not by a bunch of people who don't fucking care.'

Stewart's voice increased in strength as he spoke, becoming impassioned. 'And what about our regiments? They're all being amalgamated, taking away a soldier's pride in their history, fucking destroying them. The Navy's going tits up. The air force too. One day, this country will be fucking invaded, and we won't have anyone to defend us. We'll be a pushover for every fucking raghead in the fucking world.'

'So you weren't a fan of Colin Hutton, then,' said Jay, referring to the man whose prime objective was to turn the UK's armed services into a European defence force.

'It's people like fucking Hutton who are bringing this country to its knees.'

'You know he died two months ago?'

'And I didn't shed a tear.'

She twisted to look into his face. 'What about Madeleine Gal?'

'You mean the woman who encouraged all those illegal immigrants to come to Britain?'

'Did you know she died two weeks ago?'

'No. But I'm not shedding any fucking tears over her, either. Why, are you?' His tone turned sneering.

She said, 'Stew. What do you know about prisons?'

'The same as you, probably.' He sounded wary. 'That it's a place to be avoided.'

'What about eighty inmates last year meeting an untimely death?'

'And if each of those inmates was a child molester or a child killer –' Stewart suddenly leaned forward, his voice low and hard – 'would you care if they fucking died?'

Before Jay could reply, Nick said, 'No. I'd say good riddance.'

'Good riddance,' Stewart echoed, looking between Jay and Nick.

Nobody spoke as a mud-spattered Land Rover drove past, vanished into the distance.

'How many are in the Garrison?' asked Nick.

'I can't say.' Stewart spread his hands. 'But there are a few of us around the place. Mostly in the UK, but we're spreading overseas, heading east, which is good news for us. Push the fucking Muslims back where they fucking belong.'

'The DCRI,' Jay said. 'In Paris. They're involved, aren't they?'

'Yeah.' Stewart looked surprised. 'I'd heard some of them had joined up. Who do you know?'

'Marfat and Prideaux.'

'Don't recognize the names, sorry.'

'How about Solomon Neill?' Nick asked.

'We all knew Sol. Top bloke. That bastard Blake for taking him out . . .'

'Blake didn't kill Sol,' Jay said. 'A female assassin did, called Nahid. Small, lithe, and blonde. Ring any bells?'

Stewart's expression was baffled. 'What?'

'I witnessed Sol's murder. Nahid rammed a stiletto into the base of his skull. Why was he killed?'

'What comic books have you been reading?'

'I watched him *die*.'

'Max Blake killed Sol.' Stewart was stubborn. 'That's why we went and grabbed him, to make sure he stands trial, and nothing you can say will alter that.'

Jay let it go.

'Who runs the Garrison?' asked Nick.

'I don't know.' Stewart's voice rang with sincerity.

'So how does it work?'

'We belong to chapters. There's one in south London, for instance. We meet maybe three, four times a year for a piss-up.'

'How many of you?'

'Not many.' Stewart looked uncomfortable.

'How many, Stew?' Nick insisted.

'I'd like you to take me home now,' Stewart said.

Nobody said anything for a long time.

'Look, mate.' This time it was Dave who spoke. His voice was deceptively soft. 'Jay said she cut herself in your garage. There's DNA evidence you kidnapped her right there, at your place. You really want us to set the cops on you? Kidnapping's a serious crime, in case you didn't already know it. So why don't you tell us how many other like-minded people are in your chapter?'

Stewart's throat made another nervous click. 'Fifty or so. Not that we all meet every time. Usually it's around fifteen, twenty of us.'

'Are you all with the Services?' Dave's tone was like silk.

'No. We've got members all over. In the police. Some are in Customs. Others are doctors, nurses, secretaries. There are a couple of judges. A solicitor or two.'

Tentacles winding through every walk of life, Jay thought.

'How many chapters?'

With Dave asking questions, they gleaned that there were chapters in most of the major cities, some larger than others, and that they were self-contained and rarely communicated with one another. Each new member had to be proposed by two current members, and there was a probationary period of a year before they were promoted to full membership. Each chapter head collected the annual fee in the New Year and forwarded it to a post-office box in central London.

'How much a year?' asked Nick.

'Eight hundred.'

'Your chapter rakes in forty thousand pounds a year?' Jay was astonished.

'We have costs.' His eyes darted around the van.

'What sort of costs?'

'Join up, and you'll find out.' Stewart was looking between them. Anxiety was etched on his face.

'Not today,' said Nick. 'But thanks for the offer.' He glanced at Jay. 'Any more questions?'

'Loads. Like, how long have you been a member, Stew?'

'Look, I really don't want to say any more.'

'How long?' asked Dave quietly.

Stewart fixed his gaze on the floor. 'Six years.'

'How did you know Sol?' Jay asked.

'He was the head of our chapter. A really good bloke, up for a laugh. Totally professional, though. He's one of you guys.' He looked at Dave and Rob, meaning the Special Air Service, the SAS. 'You knew him?'

'Not personally,' said Rob. 'But we'd heard the name. As you say, totally professional.'

Apparently, Sol used to live in Kensington, and he travelled to Paris regularly. It was Sol who had kept in touch with the upper echelons of the Garrison. Stewart and the others were the Garrison's underlings, its foot soldiers.

Jay asked, 'What are the names of the other two guys who kidnapped me?'

Long pause.

'Stew?' Dave prompted softly.

Stewart cringed. Closed his eyes briefly. 'Jed Weale and Charlie Gabb.'

'Addresses?'

'Oh, Jesus.'

'You know we're going to get everything we need from you,' Dave said. 'One way or the other.'

Jay heard Stewart's dry swallow.

'Jed's in Clapham. Charlie, Brixton.' Stewart rattled off two addresses.

'Who gave the orders to snatch Jay?'

'My chapter head.'

'Their name?'

'Alison Drake.' Stewart almost whispered her address, and, when they dropped him around the corner from his home an hour later, he stood on the pavement, shoulders slumped, watching them go.

Nick drove Jay to collect her car from where she'd left it in Streatham. She followed the white van back to Vauxhall, where they parked outside the office. Nick handed the van's keys to Dave and Rob. 'Thanks guys,' he said.

'Any time, boss.'

They left with a cheery wave.

Puzzled, Jay said, 'What did they mean, boss? I thought you were a marine.'

'It's a loose term.'

'You're SAS?'

'Ex,' he said. 'And I'd appreciate it if you didn't publicize the fact.'

'Cross my heart,' she assured him.

'We have to see Blake,' Nick said. 'My car or yours?'

'Er . . .' Jay wanted to ask if they could take both, but lost her nerve. She may have spent the night with Blake, but she didn't want to assume she'd be spending another night there. 'Yours,' she said. As they headed for his car, she added, 'Should we set the cops on Stewart?'

'He's probably already scrubbed the inside of his garage with bleach. Besides, I'd rather keep him on edge and on our side, so that if we need any more info, or need to send out some disinformation, we can use him.' He beeped open his car. 'Hop in.'

They mulled over the Garrison and its workings during the journey, trying to find a way through the mire to exonerate Blake, but no ideas sprang to mind.

When Blake opened his door, he scooped an arm around Jay's waist and pulled her to his side. Pressed a kiss on her lips. With his arm still around her, he shook Nick's hand. Nick's eyebrows shot up, but to Jay's relief he didn't say a word.

'I just got a call from the Hospital Saint-Pierre,' said Blake. 'Emilie opened her eyes this morning.'

Jay turned in his embrace. 'Max, that's fantastic!'

'She looked straight at the nurse, apparently, but when the nurse tried to talk to her, she sank back into unconsciousness. She hasn't moved since.'

'But that's a great sign, surely?'

'That's what I'm hoping.' He threaded his fingers with Jay's. 'I was just making lunch. Join me.'

Nick and Jay sat on stools while Blake tossed an avocado salad and laid out prosciutto, mozzarella, tomatoes, and fresh basil on plates. Bread baked with sun-dried tomatoes accompanied a shallow bowl of Italian olive oil. They talked as they ate, but when they began to discuss Sol and his role in the Garrison, Blake fell quiet. Eventually, Nick said, 'If Sol was head of a chapter, then he'd be giving orders. It could be that he received the codes and forwarded them to the appropriate person.'

'An assassin,' said Jay.

'Yes,' Blake agreed. He was looking thoughtful. 'But I think it's simpler than that. I think Sol *was* the assassin.'

Oh my God.

What felt like a rush of electricity flashed over her skin. She was picturing Sol at the Parisian café, remembering what he'd said.

I wanted to marry Emilie, but she fell in love with someone else . . . That's why I'm here. For Emilie. And the others.

'What is it?' Nick demanded.

'Max could be right,' she said. She rose to her feet and began to pace. 'Let's say Sol was the assassin. And when Emilie became a threat to the Garrison, Sol was given the orders to kill her. The Garrison didn't know that Sol knew Emilie . . . What if Sol had a crisis of conscience? What if he suddenly saw all the other victims in the same light as Emilie? He wanted to see Blake, why? To atone? To find the cure for Emilie? He gave me his SIM and memory cards. He gave us evidence of what had been going on . . .'

She turned to look at the two men. 'Sol wanted us to know about the Garrison.'

Blake mopped some oil with his bread, popped it in his mouth. He was gazing through the window. He said, 'Which is why he was killed.'

'Makes sense,' Nick said. 'So, with what we know, how do we get the Garrison off Blake's back? Stewart gave us the name of the head of his chapter, Alison Drake. We have the names and addresses of the guys who snatched Jay. Can we use them somehow?'

'Not yet.' Blake slid off his stool and walked across the kitchen. He returned with Jim Turner's padded envelope, which he placed in front of Jay.

'What is it?' she asked.

'Have a look and see.'

Jay withdrew a single piece of A4 paper, folded into four. It was a printed page from a website advertising a Parisian pharmacy on the Rue Soufflot. The head pharmacist's name, Stephanie Legrand, had been highlighted. The name 'Mr Brown' had been handwritten at the top, along with a ten digit number and a note: *collect samples of both prescriptions.*

'Prescriptions?' Jay asked.

'How did those eight people on Sol's phone die?' Blake asked.

'Heart attacks, and an unknown virus.'

'Possibly brought on by administering a drug that causes them.'

Jay looked at the slick, professional-looking home page. 'You think this is where the assassin gets the drugs?'

'I don't think Turner would be sending us on a wild-goose chase,' Blake said. 'I'd like you to go and meet Legrand. I'd send Nick, but he doesn't speak French.'

Jay's mistrust of Blake's boss rose. 'What if it's a trap?'

'Why should you think that?'

'Because . . .' She took a breath. 'I don't trust him. He wanted me to tell you to plead guilty to the charges against you. That if I fought the Garrison, he couldn't guarantee my safety.'

'True,' Blake said. He didn't seem to be at all bothered by his boss turning traitor.

'He's with the Garrison,' Jay said. 'I'm certain of it.'

'You're probably right.' He moved back to his stool and spooned some more salad on his plate. 'Anyone for any more?'

Jay pushed her plate away. Blake could be insufferable sometimes, like right now. He knew something she didn't, but he wasn't going to share it. Compared to Tom, who was always up front about what was going on, Blake was a proverbial clam. Her mind immediately leaped. She'd forgotten to ring Tom.

Hastily, she showed Blake Tom's email and ran him through the prison statistics. Then Nick told Blake what Dr Cole had said.

'Cole doesn't believe there's such a thing as an antidote to the virus.' Nick shifted uncomfortably. 'I'm sorry.'

Blake looked past them, his cheek muscles taut. 'Which means Sol's talk of an antidote was to get my attention. Make sure I got to him quick smart.'

'I'd better call him,' Jay said. 'I mean Tom.'

She wasn't sure what she expected – maybe for Blake to frown a little, show some concern at her ringing her ex-fiancé – but his expression didn't change. He said, 'Don't forget to tell him your anxiety about Turner. Or that you're going to see Stephanie Legrand tomorrow.'

Jay walked into the sitting room to make the call. It rang twice before it was answered.

'Hi, Jay!' Sofie said brightly.

'Hi there.'

'How's it going with the code? Did you know all those people are dead? I looked them up on the Net. Weird, huh?'

Why Jay had tried to shelter the girl earlier, she now couldn't think. 'Yup. Weird.'

'Can I do anything else to help?' Sofie sounded keen.

'Not right now,' Jay said. 'But can I keep you on standby? As my special undercover spook?'

'Great!' Sofie's tone dropped to a whisper. 'I won't tell Mum, OK? It will be our secret.'

Unsure whether this was a good idea or not, Jay's tone was hesitant, but the girl didn't seem to notice. 'OK.'

'Brilliant! Do you want to speak to Daddy?'

'Yes, please.'

'Hang on a mo'.'

Barely ten seconds passed.

'Jay,' said Tom.

'Hi.'

Tom said, 'What are you going to do with the prison statistics?'

No 'hello, thanks for ringing'. Just straight to the question, using his cop voice.

'Nothing, as yet. They're sitting in the pot of stew called the Garrison.'

'The pot of stew including Blake.'

Oh, God. She never had got around to telling Tom that Blake was alive. Things had been moving so fast. She wondered how Tom had found out and knew it wouldn't have been difficult. All he had to do was read his newspaper, or check the news on the Web.

'Yes,' she said. 'He's under house arrest.'

'And you're with him.'

She closed her eyes. 'Yes.'

This time, she couldn't jump in saying there was nothing going on between her and Blake.

'I see. Goodbye, Jay.'

He hung up.

Her heart hollowed at the finality in his tone. Tears began to rise, and she forced them down. She swallowed. Opened her eyes. Blake was standing in front of her. He took her phone and put it to one side, then wrapped her in his arms. He didn't say a word. Just held her.

When she felt stronger, she pulled out of his embrace. 'I couldn't tell him anything. He didn't want to talk.'

'Come.' He took her hand and walked her back into the kitchen, where Nick was sipping coffee. 'Nick and I have made a plan for tomorrow. We want to know what you think.'

TWENTY-FIVE

Once again, Jay found herself in the plush surroundings of a Eurostar premier carriage. More smoked salmon, fresh ciabatta, and coffee on tap. Nick was at the other end of the carriage. He was travelling with her as her minder, and having an ex-SAS soldier shadow her was a huge comfort.

The day before, Blake had made Jay an appointment with Stephanie Legrand. He'd pretended to be Mr Brown, and had told Legrand that a colleague would come and collect samples of both prescriptions at eleven a.m. When the woman had protested, he'd recited the ten-digit number. The woman had fallen quiet, then had started a low, angry tirade.

'This has never happened before,' she'd said. 'Why now? Why do you demand—'

'Just do it,' Blake had said. And had hung up.

Jay wondered if he'd been wise. It was a far more direct approach than she'd have thought prudent, and when she'd voiced her doubts he'd leaned back, interlacing his fingers behind his head, and said, 'So what's your plan?'

'Talk to her on the quiet?'

'And if she refuses to give you any answers?' He'd put his head on one side. 'What are you going to do? Strap her to a rack and torture her?'

Jay had nibbled her lip. 'Um . . .'

'This way,' Blake had said decisively, 'we nail her straight up. We get the evidence she's involved, and later we can threaten her with going to the cops.'

Jay prayed the woman hadn't smelled a rat and set a trap for her.

The pharmacy stood to the east of the Pantheon, an enormous edifice that Jay had always promised to visit one day, to see where Joan of Arc lay. Now, however, the last thing on her mind was playing tourist. All her concentration was centred on the pharmacy. It didn't look any different to any other Parisian pharmacy, with its green flashing cross and signs stating *homeopathie* and *herboristerie*. Jay slipped inside to see the Pharmacie du Drugstore was more of a medical centre, offering aromatherapy remedies as well as medical advice. There was a beautician on hand, along with a podiatrist and skin specialist. The shop sold everything from headache pills to foot baths and magnetized cushions.

After she'd introduced herself, one of the shop assistants showed Jay into a cool blue waiting room towards the rear, which boasted enlarged photographs of flowers on the walls. She didn't know exactly where Nick was at that moment. She'd seen him climb out of his taxi and cross the road to a café, and she assumed he'd stake out the pharmacy with a cappuccino to hand.

Please God, it's not a trap.

Stephanie Legrand appeared bang on time, looking harassed. A small, round woman, her air of anxiety was exacerbated by her jerky and bird-like movements. She came straight to Jay, talking fast in an undertone. 'Why do you need samples? It's the first time I've been asked for this. What's going on?'

'I'm just following orders.'

'This is most irregular, you coming here. I don't like it. I hope it won't happen again.'

'It won't,' Jay said.

'Follow me.'

Jay lengthened her stride to keep up with the woman, who was almost running down a long blue-painted corridor. Halfway along, she pushed open a door on her right. Inside, a chrome laboratory bench ran the length of the room. Four workstations housed computers. Computer printouts were stacked neatly on top of the filing cabinets set between the workstations. Refrigerators and freezers stood against one wall.

A young black man was standing in front of the bench, carefully scooping soft white powder on to an electronic balancer. He glanced up and gave them a nod. Jay nodded back, but Stephanie ignored him and marched past, heading straight for one of the refrigerators. As she pulled it open, she said, 'I can't believe you're here. It's unforgivable.'

As Blake had advised, Jay remained silent.

Legrand pulled out several ampoules and marched across the room. Put the ampoules in a small blue Styrofoam box, along with half a dozen hypodermic needles, and passed it to Jay. 'No point in adding dry ice. Both lots will last a couple of weeks, even if you go somewhere hot.'

Jay took the box. 'Thank you.'

'You can shove your thanks,' she snapped. 'I was promised this would never happen, yet here you are, demanding samples in person. *Samples!*' Legrand looked ready to burst a blood vessel. 'Why couldn't you get to the museum?'

'It wasn't possible,' Jay said. 'I can't say why.'

'*Merde.*' Legrand swore. 'Will we have to find another place?'

'Perhaps. We'll let you know.'

Legrand snorted. 'You can tell your masters that if this happens again, they can find another pharmacist to do their dirty work.'

With that, Legrand marched Jay to the front door. 'Make sure we don't meet again.'

Styrofoam box in hand, Jay and Nick returned to London and delivered the ampoules to Dr Cole at Bart's. As Jay had guessed from the boom in the man's voice, he was big and raw boned, and although he didn't have a beard, his cheeks were dark with stubble. She'd expected his office to be messy, with papers spilling everywhere, perhaps some old food wrappers, but instead it was obsessively neat. The books on the shelves were perfectly in line and arranged in alphabetical order, and every object on every surface was squared away. Even his pens were lined up in a perfect row.

The moment Jay placed the box on his desk, he snapped it open and picked through the ampoules. 'It might take days to identify the contents.' He snapped the box shut. 'Or weeks. I can't say until we start work on them.'

Jay felt a protest begin to rise.

'I'm aware Max's sister is in a critical condition,' he added briskly. 'I'll be cracking the whip over this and will get the results to you as soon as humanly possible.'

'Thank you.'

'Can you tell me where you got them from?'

'A pharmacy in Paris,' Jay said. 'Look, before I go, could I borrow your computer?'

'Sure.'

Jay had worn a high-definition micro camcorder watch for her meeting with Legrand, and now she downloaded the film on to Dr Cole's laptop. The recording was shaky, but the sound was clear.

'I can hear every word,' Jay said, pleased with the result. 'And she didn't suspect a thing.'

'Boy, she sounds pissed off,' Dr Cole remarked as the footage moved along.

'Her anonymity's been blown, that's why.' Jay looked up at Cole. 'Would you mind if I forwarded the video to Blake? And saved the clip for safe-keeping here?'

'Go ahead.'

By the time Nick and Jay caught the tube, it was rush hour and the trains were packed. Jay found herself rammed between Nick's spare frame and a young woman in a too-tight business suit. Body odour and stale perfume filled the carriage. Copies of the *Metro* littered the floor and were wedged behind the seats. It felt a long way from Eurostar's premier luxury. At Holborn, Jay switched from the Central Line to Piccadilly, leaving Nick to head for the Northern Line and his flat in Tufnell Park, and by the time she exited at

South Ken she was overly hot and glad to be in the cool air again.

She stopped at Tesco's on Brompton Road and bought a bottle of Chianti and a packet of raw nuts. She'd read somewhere that if you ate a small handful of nuts every day, you protected yourself from just about every disease known to man. At least that's what the article had claimed, but, more to the point, it was a good excuse to buy nuts. She loved nuts, but Denise – obsessed with her fitness and her figure – refused to have them in the house, calling them 'fat pills', due to their high calorific content.

The house was dark, when she let herself in, and blissfully warm. Kicking off her boots, she padded into the kitchen, poured herself some wine, and took her glass and the nuts into the living room, where she switched on the TV. Her head felt slightly muzzy from all the travelling, her body tired from the stress of her meeting with Stephanie Legrand. Taking a long pull of wine, Jay relaxed into the sofa and gave a sigh. It felt good to be home.

She'd barely sat down for ten minutes though when the doorbell rang. She gave a groan. Struggled up. Caution made her check through the kitchen window. A small man stood facing the door, waiting expectantly. He wore a smart blue overcoat and held a briefcase in one hand, a bottle of wine in the other. He looked slightly embarrassed, like someone who'd arrived home, but couldn't find his keys.

Jay ducked out of sight, cursing silently. What was Jim Turner doing here? She stood quietly, wondering what to do. She didn't trust him enough to let him in. Not when she was on her own.

The doorbell rang again. Then he knocked on the door. A polite rap. Tap-tap-double tap. Did he know she was home? Jay slipped back to the living room and sat in front of the TV without seeing it. Whether Turner knew she was home or not didn't matter, since she wasn't going to let him in. She took a sip of wine, and at that moment she heard the distinctive sound of a key in the front door lock. She bolted upright, wondering if she'd imagined it, but no. The door made its usual scraping sound as it opened.

Jay scooted across the room for the phone, fully intending to dial 999, but then Angela called out, 'We're back! And there's someone to see you!'

Relief flooded her. She wasn't alone any longer.

'Who is it?' she called back, pretending she hadn't already seen him.

'Jim Turner,' he called. 'I just want a quick chat. I won't be long, I promise.'

Jay stepped into the hallway, where the girls were taking off their coats. Both of them had already kicked off their shoes, which now lay haphazardly with Jay's boots, alongside bags of shopping.

'Sorry to trouble you,' Turner told Jay, peering past the girls. 'I know it's presumptuous coming to your home, but I want our conversation to be private.'

Both Angela and Denise glanced at him, then at Jay. Jay finally invited Turner inside and introduced him to the girls. She didn't take his coat. She didn't want him to make himself at home.

'I brought some wine,' said Turner, vaguely waving it in the air.

Angela pounced, saying, 'Thanks. Why don't you come into the kitchen and I'll pour you a glass?'

'I'd like to talk to Jay privately.'

Again, caution reared. Jay said, 'Whatever you want to say, you can say in front of Denise and Angela.'

Turner surveyed the girls, who surveyed him steadily back.

'How much do they know?' he said eventually.

'Pretty much everything,' she lied. The girls knew about the Garrison, but not its purpose. At least, not yet. She'd fill the girls in later.

'I see,' he said. He raised his hand and rubbed his forehead, suddenly looking weary. 'I'm sorry, but I still need to talk privately.'

While the girls headed to the kitchen, Jay led Turner to the living room and switched off the TV. She moved to the mantel-piece, preferring to stand. Turner stood at the other end of the mantelpiece. Neither of them said anything until Angela returned with the wine. She gave them each a glass and placed the bottle on the mantelpiece between them.

'Thanks,' Jay said. Angela nodded and walked out. She didn't close the door behind her, but left it slightly ajar – her signal that she was going to eavesdrop. If Jay shut the door, then the girls would leave her alone. Jay left it where it was. It would save her having to explain the conversation later.

'So,' Jay said. 'Why are you here?'

Turner shrugged out of his coat and placed it over the back of a chair. He took a long draught of wine. He said, 'I saw Blake this afternoon. He tells me you met Stephanie Legrand. That you have samples of drugs being analysed. That you know who kidnapped you, and that Alison Drake heads your kidnapper's chapter of the Garrison. You've also uncovered what could be a particularly unsavoury aspect of the Garrison running through the prison system. You know a lot, Jay. So do Blake and Nick, Dr Cole, and now your housemates . . .'

Jay remained quiet.

'I'm worried you know too much. I'm worried for all of you. Which is why I want to lay a trap.'

'For what?' Jay asked.

'The assassin.'

Out of nowhere, Jay pictured two of the photographs that had been laid on the floor next to her in the cold brick room.

I wonder which she'll fear more: losing her sight or her speech?

Jay gave a shiver. 'You know who the assassin is?' she asked. She could have told Turner. Blake could have told Turner too, but she kept quiet for the moment.

'I believe there's more than one. But one is all we need for our purposes. That's why I want to capture them. Then, we can interrogate them. What I'd really like is to turn the assassin. Have them work against the Garrison, for us. If the organization is as big as I think it is, it will take some time to bring it down.'

'What if they don't turn?' She didn't think Nahid could be persuaded to do anything she didn't want to.

'We'll have them on film,' Turner said. 'Collecting the drugs at the Musée d'Orsay, where Legrand will have left them. We'll follow them. We'll gather enough evidence to put them away for a long time. I think they'll be open to persuasion if we offer them a deal.' He gave a confident little smile. 'They'll turn.'

'But what if they don't?' Jay was insistent.

He frowned. 'Then we'll cross that bridge when we come to it.'

Jay twirled her wine in her glass. 'How are you going to trap them?'

'By sending a coded message. Blake tells me you cracked the code?'

Jay nodded.

'Clever,' he said on a half sigh.

She remained silent. She wasn't about to tell him a twelve-year-old had done it.

What sounded like a pan crashed to the floor in the kitchen, followed by a clatter of cutlery. Both of them glanced at the door, then away.

'I have the phone number of one of the Garrison's assassins,' he said.

Jay felt her senses quicken. 'How did you get it?'

This time, he looked at her straight. 'I'm a member of the Garrison and have been for a while. I'm trusted. Nobody suspects I joined with an ulterior motive – to learn about the organization, to see how far reaching it was, and, hopefully, to expose it. When the time was right.'

'You're undercover?'

He sighed, and as he did so, the lines deepened on his face, making him look old. 'Yes.'

'Who else knows this?'

'Just you and Blake. And I'd rather it stay that way, or . . . Well, you can imagine what might happen to me.'

Jay recalled Major Wayland, his overturned Audi, the bullet in his head. Turner's earlier warnings now made sense. He'd tried to deflect her from digging any deeper, not just to pro-tect her and Blake, but to prevent himself from being exposed to the Garrison. She surveyed him at length. Although his previous behaviour had been explained, she still didn't trust him. She supposed it would take time before that happened.

'If the Garrison trusts you,' she said, 'can't you get evidence that Blake was set up?'

He shook his head. 'I can't access the chapters in France, or any chapter other than my own. Only the head of the Garrison can do that. All I've managed to glean about the man is that he uses the name Brown – nice and innocuous – and that he's the only person who knows what's happening where. Brown is the one controlling the organization, the person who contacts the head of each chapter and gives the commands to his foot soldiers.' His jaw flexed. 'The Garrison is like a giant spiderweb, with a commander at its centre. If we crush or disable the spider, the web will begin to fracture and eventually break up. I want to know who the spider is, Jay. I want to find Brown. And I need your help to do that.'

Although Jay wanted to take a slug of wine, she refrained, in order to keep a clear head.

'How?'

'I want to send a code to the assassin. An order to kill you.'

'You *what*?' Jay stared at him in disbelief.

'We'll set it up so that when they come for you, you'll be one hundred per cent protected. There will be a crack team of Special Forces looking after you. You'll be covered every step of the way, I promise.'

She worked her mouth. 'How do you know your crack team isn't part of the Garrison?'

'Because of where I'm positioned in the Garrison – and also in MI5 – I have a list of everyone in the military who belongs to the Garrison. I will, of course, choose a team without any of these people. It will be a top secret mission, conducted ruthlessly on a strict need-to-know basis.'

'Can't you use your list to expose the head of the Garrison?'

'Nobody knows who they are.' He spoke slowly and carefully, as though to a particularly stupid student. 'They only know their own chapter members, and the head of their chapter.'

'Doesn't the head of each chapter know who their boss is?'

He shook his head. 'Communication is by electronic means only.'

'Surely GCHQ can track them?'

'GCHQ is riddled with Garrison members.'

'Jesus.'

'I want that assassin, Jay. I want you to draw them out.'

Another clang from the kitchen. Neither Turner or Jay gave any indication they'd heard.

'Does Blake know about this?'

'No. And I don't want him to know either. He'll want to be with you during the operation. Which means he'll break his bond, and get thrown into jail.'

She couldn't think what to say next, she was so stunned. Turner wanted to use her as *bait*?

'I'll talk to Stephanie Legrand,' Turner continued, seemingly unaware of Jay's horror. 'Blake tells me you sent him damning evidence of her involvement with the organization. I'll get her to provide the assassin with an innocuous serum that won't do you any harm, but I'm hoping it won't come to that. I'm hoping we'll grab them long before they get near you.'

'No,' Jay said.

'I'm sorry?'

'No, I won't do it. I won't be your bait. I won't risk my life for this.' She crossed the room and picked up his coat, handed it to him. 'Find someone else.'

'But you're perfect.' Frustration crossed his face. 'The Garrison already knows you're a threat. When the orders come through to dispose of you, the assassin won't turn a hair. It will make perfect sense to them.'

'Why don't *you* do it?' she said. Her tone was hard. 'Why don't you let the Garrison know – accidentally of course – that you've been undercover all along? You'd make an even more perfect target than I would.'

Turner dipped his eyes for a moment. He said, 'You're right.'

Jay saw him out. Neither of them offered to shake hands.

TWENTY-SIX

Predictably, the girls were agog.

Jay had been correct; they'd eavesdropped. While one of them banged and clattered in the kitchen, the other had listened at the living-room door.

'The Garrison runs a bunch of assassins?' Wide-eyed, Denise poured them all wine. Neither she nor Angela had touched a drop while Turner had been in the house. They hadn't wanted to take the edge off their reflexes in case Jay needed them. She couldn't wish for more loyal friends, Jay thought, and not for the first time she sent thanks to God she shared a house with them.

'Like how many?' asked Angela. 'Half a dozen? A hundred?'

'I don't think Turner knows,' Jay replied.

'You did good, girl,' Denise said over her shoulder. She was beating eggs with a fork while some onions and sweet peppers sweated in a pan. 'You don't want to be putting yourself on the line like that. What a little turd, thinking he could use you. You were right to suggest he offer himself to be served up on a platter.'

They sat at the kitchen table sharing Denise's giant-sized Spanish omelette, along with garlic bread and a green salad.

'It's a good idea, though.' Angela spoke around a slice of chorizo. 'Trapping one of the assassins like that. You can't fault it, really.'

Jay wondered if Turner would offer himself up as bait. She wasn't sure if he had the guts to do it. He appeared to be more of an office man, with his neat suits and soft hands, rather than an agent comfortable working the streets. She couldn't picture him in a fight.

They were washing up when the phone rang.

'Yo,' Blake said.

'Yo, yourself.' Her exhaustion dropped away on hearing his voice.

'Turner called and filled me in. Said you had a bit of an altercation.'

'Did he tell you he wanted to use me as bait?'

'Yup. He won't be doing that again.' His tone was tight, making Jay wonder what Blake had said. 'He's putting himself up for the job.'

'Top man.'

'I didn't give him much choice,' Blake said. His tone was dry.

She wondered what powers of persuasion Blake had used and decided not to go there.

'Doing anything in particular?' he asked.

'Washing up.'

'What, on a Friday? You should get out more.'

'I would if I wasn't so knackered.'

'You fancy coming over tonight? I've lit the fire. I also have a bottle of Chateau Lafite that needs sharing.'

'Which year?'

'Two thousand.'

'I'm on my way.'

Jay yawned her way home on Saturday. Although Blake had a home gym in his house and had, apparently, been using it to keep himself fit, he still had a lot of energy to displace from being cooped up at home. Not only had he made love to her thoroughly and at great length during the night, but he'd wanted to talk. Not about work, his job, or anything remotely to do with the Garrison, but about his sister. Since it was the first time Blake had opened up about his personal life, Jay had

firmly glued her eyelids open. He hadn't told her where he and
Emilie were brought up, or anything about their parents. He'd
just told Jay stories about him and Emilie. Like that one hot
summer, when most people had driven around with their car
windows open – air conditioning wasn't a standard feature back
then – they'd used to fill balloons with water and lob them at
the drivers. He and Emilie would then run away, hysterical with
laughter at the dripping, furious adults screaming abuse behind
them.

One day, however, Emilie had got caught. She was only six,
but she'd sworn blind her brother hadn't been involved. Instead,
she'd named a boy at the end of the street, who had once teased
her.

'You're a lot like Emilie,' Blake had told Jay. 'Loyal to a fault.
I like that in a person.' He'd kissed her lips. 'I like it a lot.'

Now, Jay beeped her car shut and made her way to her local
Café Nero and a double-shot cappuccino. She desperately needed
some caffeine to give her a jolt of energy. Making love all night
was all very well, but she needed to catch up on her sleep. She
felt wrecked.

While she waited in the queue – it was always busy around
eleven on a Saturday – she gazed at the street outside, settling
her mind on ordinary, domestic things and making a mental list
of things to do. She hadn't rung her mother recently, or her father.
And what about her niece and nephew? She could barely
remember what they looked like. She was way behind with her
washing, hadn't balanced her bank account in ages, or settled a
multitude of bills with the girls. It would be a weekend of admin,
she decided. Squaring things away.

Sunday brought wind and rain from the east. Almost a month
had passed since Sol had died, and as she listened to the church
bells calling worshippers to the morning service, she wondered
about his family, and who would be missing him, grieving for
him.

Having arranged to drive to Putney to lunch with her brother
and sister-in-law and their children, Jay grabbed a bottle of wine
and her handbag, wrapped herself in a long coat, and stepped out
of the house, automatically glancing up and down the street. She
spotted the woman walking her little white dog, both looking
bedraggled, and an elderly woman shuffling nearby with a walking
stick in one hand and a Sainsbury's carrier bag in the other.

Jay was digging in her handbag, searching for her car keys, and, without looking up, sidestepped the old woman so they could both pass on the pavement. Jay was level with the old woman when, suddenly, the old woman tripped, and before Jay could move aside, toppled towards her. Instinctively, Jay put out her arms to try and break the woman's fall, and at the same time she took in the gold chain around the woman's neck. The tiny mole at the corner of her mouth. Her man's watch. Its sturdy brown leather strap.

Sol's assassin.

Nahid.

Jay reared back before the woman could touch her, but Nahid came after her. Her eyes were bright and alive behind her wrinkled rubber mask, her lips drawn back over twin rows of strong white teeth. She was hissing as she lunged for Jay, a hypodermic needle in her hand.

Jay's bottle of wine shattered on the pavement as she turned and ran. Behind her, she heard a curse, strident breathing. Nahid's footsteps tearing after her.

Christ! You've got to run faster!

Sprinting to the bottom of Redcliffe Road, Jay swung left, and as she turned, she risked a glance behind her. She nearly stumbled. The street was alive with Special Forces. They wore jeans and windcheaters, but they were unmistakable to Jay. Three men were hot on their heels. All carried guns, but nobody was shooting. Two vehicles were rocketing along the street. They were coming to capture the assassin. Nahid didn't appear to have a gun. Just the hypodermic needle.

No time to think.

Run! Get away!

Jay charged down Fulham Road. Her long coat hampered her, but she couldn't afford to stop and shed it. Nahid was just yards behind. Jay lengthened her stride. Her legs were longer, and she was fast. She had to outrun the assassin. She kept racing, trying to plan her route. Tried to think how to shake her attacker. She tore past a bus stop full pelt, almost colliding with a couple who chose that moment to walk into her path. They reared back in shock, the man choking out, 'Hey, watch it!'

Breathless, she skidded around them, her boots slipping on wet leaves, but although she didn't fall, she'd lost a handful of seconds.

Can't make another mistake.

Approaching Evelyn Gardens, she risked a quick look behind her on her right, saw a gap between a car and a bus on the other side of the road, and darted between them. Horns blared. Brakes squealed. She raced on to the opposite pavement. A quick glance over her shoulder showed Nahid had been forced to wait for the traffic to clear. Two Special Forces guys were closing in on her, but Nahid wasn't looking at them, she was concentrated on Jay. Totally focused.

Jay dived around the next corner, losing valuable time as she ditched her coat. She'd dropped her handbag with the wine in Redcliffe Road, but they were the least of her troubles. She could hear Nahid's footsteps as she sped after her.

Jay ran south, her eyes latching on to a café midway up the street, where she knew there was a back yard and a wall she could scale to drop into a private garden. She ran harder, her breath rasping in her throat. Rain began to fall. The morning seemed to darken. She heard a helicopter's buzz approaching. She heard a man's shout behind her, but all she cared about were Nahid's footsteps, racing behind her.

A car roared up the street. It slowed in the centre of the road. A man shouted, 'Jay, get in!'

She was stunned to see Jim Turner waving frantically at her from the rear seat. Breathing hard, she kept running, the car keeping up with her. She glanced frantically over her shoulder to see Nahid twenty yards away. She didn't appear to be making any headway, but all Jay needed was to trip or stumble and Nahid would be on her in a flash, ramming that needle into her, killing her.

She wished the SF guys would shoot Nahid, take her out, but that's not what Turner wanted. He wanted the assassin alive.

'Jay!' Turner yelled. 'For God's sake!'

Could she trust Turner? Her priority was to stay alive. The only person she trusted right now was herself.

She reached the café. She dived inside and slammed the door shut behind her. Rammed the bolts home. Ignoring the shocked looks of the customers, the startled shout of a waitress, Jay pelted through the café, past the cake displays, the chill cabinet, until she came to the door at the rear. Yanking it open, she raced outside. Two women smoking cigarettes beneath an umbrella stared as Jay dashed past and leaped for the wall, hooking her fingers on to the top tier of bricks and scrabbling for purchase with her boots. Beads of sweat merged with the rain on her face. With a heave, she hauled her torso over the wall, swung her legs over, and dropped to the other side.

She sprinted up the garden. There were walls on either side, leading to more gardens. She ran for the house dead ahead, for its French windows, praying someone was home, that the windows weren't locked, or she'd be forced to break in . . . or, worse, hop from garden to garden, meaning Nahid – lither, more agile – would catch up with her.

The helicopter's buzz increased. She glanced up to see it was around five hundred feet, straight up. It would be Turner's heli, watching the chase unfold and reporting where she and Nahid ran.

Jay reached the French windows. Yanked the brass handles. She didn't expect them to open, but to her astonishment they did. She slipped inside, closing the doors behind her. The doors had a brass key in their lock, which she turned, securing them. She then took the key out and shoved it to one side. Creeping across the carpet, she heard classical music playing. Could smell coffee and pastry.

She was tiptoeing along the corridor, heading for the front door, when a man's voice said, 'What the hell—'

Jay turned, palms raised, to see a man in his forties. He wore jeans and a blue shirt and was holding a mug in one hand.

'I'm being chased,' Jay gasped. 'It's my boyfriend's ex, and she's gone insane. She wants to kill me.'

His mouth opened.

'We were having a coffee at the café when she turned up.' Jay gesticulated behind her. 'She went berserk. She tried to stab me with a cake knife. I ran away. My boyfriend called the police, but I don't want her to catch me. She's insane.'

He made a faint choking sound.

'It's OK. I'm leaving . . .' Hands still raised where he could see them, she slowly began to edge towards the front door. 'I'm sorry to have startled you. She says she wants to kill me. She's mad. Really crazy . . .'

At that moment, there was a thunderous pounding on the French windows. A woman yelled out. 'Anyone there?'

Jay felt the blood drain from her head. Nahid was so close!

'I've got to get out of here,' she said.

There came a splintering crash. Nahid was forcing her way inside.

The man put down his mug and strode past Jay, to the back of his house. Jay raced to the front door, tried to open it, but it was deadlocked. She tore to the next room, for the sash windows, but they were locked as well. Frantically, she tried the other downstairs windows. The man had crap security at the back of his house, but the front was a different matter. She was trapped inside.

She heard the man speaking. He sounded angry. Jay tiptoed into the kitchen, grabbed a knife from the block by the stove. She hid behind the door. Her heart was thundering, and she was pouring sweat.

Please God, don't let her find me. Please.

'I've called the police,' the man said. His voice was clipped. 'So you may as well go now. Break into someone else's home.'

'Where did she go?' Nahid's voice was soft. Jay nearly moaned. She was yards away!

'She ran out the front.'

Jay heard rapid soft footfalls as the woman padded down the corridor.

'It's locked,' the woman said.

'Of course it's bloody locked now, to try and keep people like you out.'

'Open it again.'

'With pleasure,' he snapped.

There came the sound of metal on metal, and then the *clunk* as the door opened.

'And don't fucking come back!' the man suddenly yelled, which Jay hoped meant Nahid was well and truly out of the house. She heard the man slam the door shut. Distinctive sounds of it being locked.

'Jesus,' he said.

Jay continued to stand behind the door, clutching the knife. Her heart was still thundering, her pulse through the roof.

'Hello?' he called. 'Are you still here?'

Jay didn't move.

'She's gone, I promise. Jeez, what a morning. I don't suppose you're going to pay for the damage she made to my windows? Hello? Hello?'

Still Jay remained silent.

Finally, she heard him sigh and mutter, 'Jesus,' again. He came into the kitchen. He was rubbing his face. He appeared to be alone. Cautiously, Jay inched around the door. He looked around. 'Fuck,' he said. His eyes were glued on the knife.

'Thanks,' she replied. 'You saved my life.' Ditching the knife, she ran back through the house and out through the French windows, over the neighbouring wall and into the next garden. She didn't want to exit via the café in case Nahid backtracked. Garden by garden, Jay tortuously began to make her escape.

TWENTY-SEVEN

Jay paused at the fourth garden. Only two to go and she'd be back on the Fulham Road, where she'd grab a cab and get the hell out of the area. Scratched and torn from scaling a trellis covered in climbing roses, she was balanced on top of the wall, unsure whether to jump down or not. She'd spotted a dog bowl set on the patio outside the rear door of the house. A *big* dog bowl. She glanced up and down the garden to see a couple of large bones, bleached and gnawed at the knuckles.

'Here, doggy doggy,' she called softly.

Nothing. Was the animal in the house? Was it out on a walk? Again, Jay called. She was about to drop down when a huge male mastiff appeared from behind a rhododendron, ears cocked. He was black and tan with a cropped tail and looked perfectly innocuous until he spotted Jay. It was as though a switch had been flicked. He took a deep breath and lunged at her dangling legs.

'OK, OK,' Jay snatched her legs out of the way.

He leaped up at the wall, scratching furiously. He was barking fit to burst. Big deep and angry barks, enraged, alerting everyone in the vicinity he'd just found an intruder.

Shit.

There was no point trying to tell the animal to shut up; it was hysterical. She hurriedly dropped out of sight, but the barking didn't stop. What to do? Heart thudding, she scanned the area. Should she try returning to the café? Where were the

Special Forces? Ever since she'd pelted through the café, they seemed to have vanished.

Jay decided to head back in the opposite direction. Perhaps she could call on the man she'd disturbed in his house to help her? Use his phone to call Nick? She was tiring rapidly, and the man had seemed to be on her side . . .

The dog continued its berserk barking. She tried to put it out of her mind. She had barely climbed the next wall – more scratches, this time from some brambles – when she heard a yelp, and the dog fell silent. She glanced behind her. Her stomach hollowed. Nahid was slipping over the wall, heading straight for her. She'd ditched her disguise. Panic flooded Jay. If the dog hadn't stopped the woman – it had been fucking *huge* – she didn't stand a chance.

Jay tore across the next garden and flung herself at the next wall, scrambling desperately to haul herself over. She had to get into the man's house again. He was her only hope. She could hear the helicopter's endless buzz above. Where were the Special Forces? Why hadn't they caught Nahid?

The noise of the helicopter caused people to peer out of their windows. Jay kept racing, but the assassin was faster than her. Much faster. Behind her, she heard shoes on brickwork, the crackling of vegetation. She tried to run faster, climb faster, but she still had two gardens to go before she reached the man's house. She was running across a patch of wet lawn, spraying muddy water up her legs, when she heard Nahid drop into the same garden behind her.

A shriek of panic burst from her lips.

Faster!

She heard a shout to one side. Then another. A man rose from behind a scrubby bush. He held a rifle. He was looking through its sights. He wasn't aiming it at Jay. He was aiming behind her.

Crack.

The single shot echoed against the brickwork.

Jay spun round. Nahid was still coming for her. Expression narrowed, she didn't seem to see two more men appear in the garden. She was concentrated on Jay.

Then she stumbled. As Jay watched, the woman slowly toppled forward, collapsing as though from within. She hit the grass with a soft thud. Her face was twisted to one side. One arm lay beneath her, the other was flung across the grass. She lay as though dead.

Jay stood gasping, hands on her waist, as two men raced to the inert figure. One checked the assassin's pulse at her throat, while the other pulled her hands behind her back and hand-cuffed them. Only then did Jay approach. The man with the rifle followed.

'Is she dead?' she asked nobody in particular.

'Nah,' said the shooter. 'Tranquillized.'

The strength went out of Jay's legs. She crumpled to the ground. *Fuck*, she thought. *That was close.*

'You OK?' asked the shooter.

'I guess.' She had started to tremble.

'One hell of a job,' he told her. He reached out a hand, and she let him pull her up. His grip was warm and strong, hers sweaty and pathetically weak. 'Turner told us you'd be good, but we had our doubts. You're a civvy, right?'

'Yes,' she agreed. 'I'm a civvy.' And she'd run like a civvy too, unfit and with the stamina of a two-year-old. Her legs began to shake.

'Sorry it took me so long to get a clear shot. You did good to keep your distance from her. Bravo.' He shook her hand.

'Could you repeat what you just said?' she asked him.

'Which bit?'

'What Turner said about my being good.'

He gave her a strange look, but complied. 'He said you'd volunteered to draw this piece of shit into the open.'

She nodded. 'Thanks,' she said. She didn't have the energy to feel any anger, but she had no doubt it would follow.

'What are you doing?' a tremulous voice called. An elderly man was peering at them through his downstairs window.

'Making an arrest, sir,' said the man with the rifle.

Above them, the helicopter banked and began to fly away. Mission accomplished. More soldiers appeared, accompanied by the elderly man, who was thrilled at having a criminal arrested on his lawn. He didn't seem to think it strange the 'police' were dressed head to toe in black with no insignia. Jay counted a dozen men. Quite a decent sized operation. Each SF guy had a look at the small form sprawled on the grass. They wanted to see what they'd been after.

'Like greased bloody lightning,' one man remarked.

'I thought she'd be a slant-eye,' another said. 'A Ninja.'

'Doesn't mean to say she wasn't trained by them,' the shooter said. 'She was good.'

'But not fucking good enough.'

The men cursed and talked, unwinding after a tense op. After five minutes, no more, a stretcher arrived. Jay watched Nahid being loaded and strapped down. They even gave her a neck brace.

'Where will you take her?' she asked.

'Sorry,' said the shooter, with an apologetic shrug. 'Need to know.'

She followed the men out of the garden and through the elderly man's house. On the street, she watched the soldiers climb into a variety of cars. Turner climbed out of a shiny Mercedes and walked to the van where they were loading Nahid inside. Jay didn't want to talk to him. She was afraid of what she might say, or do. Melting back to Fulham Road, she headed for a phone box.

Jay waited for Nick near the corner of Sydney Street and Fulham Road, just opposite Oakley Street, which led to the Embankment. She'd chosen it because it was a dog-legged crossroad, giving her lots of options should she need them. Despite the fact Nahid had been caught, she didn't feel safe.

She nursed a cup of coffee in Cinq, the little deli-cum-café on the north side of Fulham Road. Rain poured down the windows. She couldn't drink. Her nerves were still jumping, her heartbeat picking up every time someone appeared on the street. She couldn't believe Turner had gone ahead and used her as bait. What a snake. She was glad she hadn't jumped into his car. She might have hit him.

'You mind if I join you?'

She glanced up to see a man in a suit holding a cup of coffee. Since there were only two tables, and all the chairs bar the one at her table were taken, she gave a nod. Fixed her gaze back on the street.

She thought about Nahid. Talk about wily. She hadn't just worn a wig, she'd disguised herself with a liquid latex mask. And her movements . . . They'd been perfectly staged. Jay hadn't suspected the old woman was half her age, and nor had Turner and his SF boys. They'd all been duped.

'Nice day for it.'

Jay glanced across. The man in the suit was smiling.

'I love the rain,' he said, looking her up and down. 'How about you?'

She was half drowned from running in the downpour, her skin scratched and torn and probably reeking of fear and sweat, yet the man was trying to pick her up? Unbelievable.

'I'm sorry,' she said coolly. 'But I'm all out of small talk. Why don't you try someone else?'

He flushed. 'Oops,' he mumbled. She didn't respond.

Her heart gave a bump when she spotted Nick's tall frame appear at the door. He pushed it open, stepped inside. He didn't look at her as he strode forward, eyes clicking from the customers to the deli counter and back. She knew he was checking the joint. It didn't take long. It wasn't a big place. He disappeared down the stairs – marked *private* – and reappeared ten seconds later, apologizing profusely.

'I thought you might have a Gents down there,' he was telling the chef. 'Sorry. Can I have a coffee?'

The chef gave a snort. 'What sort?'

'Double espresso.'

Nick came and stood over the man who'd tried to chat to Jay. He said to Jay, 'OK?'

She gave a nod.

The man looked up at Nick, who looked back, face expressionless.

'I was just going,' the man said. He scurried outside. Nick took his seat.

'You look like shit,' he told her.

'So would you if you'd been running for your life. She scared the crap out of me.' Jay shuddered. 'She was so *close*.'

Nick put a hand over hers. 'You're here now. You're safe.'

His hand was warm. She squeezed it briefly before releasing it. His coffee arrived. He said, 'Tom's been trying to get hold of you. It sounds urgent.'

'My phone's in my handbag. I dropped it when Nahid attacked me.'

'Use mine.' He passed it over. 'His number's in the Call Log.'

Jay turned away as she dialled. When Tom answered, he said, 'Nick?'

She said, 'It's me.'

'Jay.' It was a gusting sigh that sounded oddly like relief.

'What's wrong?' she asked.

'Nothing. Everything. I don't know . . . Can we meet?'

Her lips felt stiff as she spoke. 'I thought you wanted a break.'

'What are you doing today? Can I drive over and see you?'

'I don't think that's such a good idea.'

'You're with Blake?' His tone was even, as though he was talking about the weather, but Jay knew what an effort it would have taken.

'No, I'm with Nick.'

'Why can't I come over?'

'It's complicated.'

'I don't care how complicated it is. I don't care if you've been taken to the moon and back for a joy ride, or that you've suddenly discovered you gave birth to twins ten years ago. I want to see you. I *have* to see you.'

If he'd called her yesterday, her emotions would have run riot, but after being chased by Nahid, she felt peculiarly distant. She said, 'I'll ring you when I know what I'm doing.' She couldn't think of anything else to add.

'OK.' He sounded defeated.

Jay hung up. Returned Nick's phone. Nick said, 'Let's get you to Blake's. Safest place I know.'

She was grateful Nick was being cautious. Blake had a perimeter alarm around his property, as well as alarms all over the house and an arsenal of weapons in his gun cabinet.

'Let's go,' he said. 'I'm parked on a meter in Pond Place.'

He hooked her arm in his and walked her down Bury Walk to the horseshoe curve near the bottom of the road. Jay climbed inside his car. Leaned back in the seat and closed her eyes. Nick tuned his radio to Classic FM and Jay dozed to the sounds of Debussy and Mozart, accompanied by the rhythmic swish of the windscreen wipers. She awoke when Nick's car began to bounce over the rough track that led to Blake's house. Leaves were blowing through the air, and trees lashed from side to side. Rooks flapped clumsily, tumbling in the wind. She stretched and yawned. Looked at her watch. Three p.m. Had so little time passed?

In front of Blake's house stood an old Honda. Nick reached across to the glove box and withdrew a handgun. Primed it.

'Nick?' she said, startled. 'Where on earth—'

'Blake loaned it to me the last time I was here. Just in case.'

'Jesus.'

He said, 'He'll let us know if it's safe or not.'

Blake appeared at one of the front windows. Jay saw he was holding a pistol. He wasn't taking any chances either. Nick made a circle with his thumb and forefinger. Blake did the same.

'All clear,' Nick said.

When Nick and Jay entered Blake's house, the gun was gone. Blake scooped Jay close. Held her for a long time.

'I'm OK,' she told him. Her words were muffled against his chest. She squeezed her arms tighter around him. He felt *so* good.

'No thanks to Turner,' he murmured. 'When I meet the man . . .'

'Prick,' said Nick. 'I'll punch him when I see him.'

'Stand in line,' Blake told him.

She became aware of Blake's scent, of lemon and something spicy, as though he'd been making a hot toddy. She dreaded to think what *she* smelled like.

'I need a shower,' she said.

'Go for it, hon. You know where it is.'

TWENTY-EIGHT

Jay took her time. Blake had the best power shower on the planet, and after washing her hair she switched the nozzle to pulse and let it pound against her neck and back until she felt her muscles begin to relax. When she eventually emerged, her skin was pink, and even though she was tired, she felt a little more human. As she padded into his bedroom, she paused, astonished. Spread neatly on the bed lay a pair of new but faded jeans, a soft cotton shirt and a cashmere sweater, all in her size. Three pairs of undies, a matching bra, and three pairs of socks were set to one side – again, all her size.

At that moment Blake appeared in the doorway with a tube of antiseptic cream for her scratches, and another of arnica for her bruises, which he gently applied. When he'd finished, he pressed his lips against her neck. 'OK?'

'Very OK, thanks,' she said.

'Turner got a guy to return your handbag. It's in the kitchen.'

'Great.'

He glanced at the clothes laid out on his bed. 'Got everything you need?'

She hugged him. 'You're a magician.'

'Hardly. It's having a cleaning lady who'll drop everything at a moment's notice and go shopping for you.'

Jay had never met Blake's cleaning lady – didn't even know he had one – and now she said, 'Who is she?'

'Mrs Doubtfire.' His eyes gleamed.

'She's a man?'

'Yup. An ex RAF batman. Geoff Ryman. But he's known as Tash. I gave him your sizes. Luckily, he's a man of taste.'

He could say that again. The cashmere sweater was as soft as a kitten's underbelly and in one of her favourite caramel shades, which brought out the chestnut highlights in her hair. 'Tell Tash thanks from me.'

'You can thank him yourself. He's in the laundry, doing the ironing.'

Curiosity got the better of her. After she was dressed, Jay headed for the laundry and ducked her head around the door. 'Hi,' she said.

'Hello,' Tash replied. He put the iron down. She could see why he'd got his nickname. A handlebar moustache the size of a ferret nestled on his upper lip. He was a small man, wiry, with vivid blue eyes and an easy smile.

Jay said, 'I just wanted to thank you for going shopping for me.'

'No problem. With Mr Blake unable to leave the house, I'm his legs, so to speak.'

'Nice to meet you.' She suddenly felt embarrassed. The man had, after all, chosen her underwear. There were only two men who'd done that for her, and both were in this house. Blake and his cleaner. How weird was that?

'Nice to meet you too.' He picked up the iron, letting Jay wander to the kitchen.

While Blake prepared something to eat – Nick had announced he was ravenous – she texted the girls, letting them know where she was and that she wasn't sure when she'd be back.

Angela texted straight back: *U R staying WHERE? What's happening? Where's Tom?! Come home soonest so you can explain all. Luv x*

Taking a stool next to Nick, Jay ran through what had happened. Both men let her talk until she'd finished, and then the questions began. Where were the men positioned when the woman first attacked her? Why weren't they covering the Fulham Road when she ran that way? Why hadn't they captured the assassin when she'd left the man's house through his front door? Where had the helicopter been at the start of the chase? How come the assassin went back for Jay in the gardens?

'Because the dog gave me away.'

More questions. Why were Special Forces in the gardens? Why weren't they covering the road on the other side of the houses? How come they hadn't shot Nahid sooner?

'He couldn't get a clear shot before then.'

By the time Nick had devoured a giant ciabatta toasted cheese and ham sandwich – Jay was too tired to eat – they'd fully debriefed her and she felt as though she'd been through a wringer. She didn't think she had the energy to react to anything, but when Nick's phone rang, she jumped a mile, her pulse racing. Her nerves were wrecked after the morning's chase.

'Yes?' Nick replied. 'Sure. Yes, she's here.' He held up the phone, eyes inquiring. 'It's Tom.'

She held out her hand. Took the phone. 'Hi.'

'Hi.'

She struggled to remember what they'd said earlier. She said, 'I'm at Blake's.'

'Can I come and see you?'

She flicked a glance at Blake. 'I don't think it's a good idea. Besides which, I'm so exhausted I can barely think straight.'

'What's been happening?' His tone lightened. 'Been chased by bad guys again?'

'Just an assassin who wanted to wipe me off the face of the earth.'

'You're kidding, right?'

'No.' The word came out as a sigh. 'It was the same woman who killed Sol. But I got away. She got caught . . . Tom, I'm knackered.'

'Oh, Jay.' His tone held dismay, affection and exasperation in equal measures. She was flooded with love for him. She wished he was with her to tuck her into bed and spoon her, hold her close. She closed her eyes. She was with a man who already did that. Who made her feel safe. Being in love with two men wasn't the best recipe for a happy, uncomplicated life.

'I want to see you,' he said.

'Not now, Tom.'

'When?'

'Tomorrow would be better. After I've slept for a hundred years.'

'Where does he live?' Tom asked.

Her eyes opened. Blake was watching her, expression neutral. 'I can't tell you that.'

'Why not?'

'Because I can't give out people's addresses willy-nilly and without their consent.'

'I won't cause a scene, I promise. I just want to see you and—'

Blake stepped across the kitchen and whipped the phone from her hand. He spoke into the receiver saying, 'I live at The Beeches . . .' He rattled off the remainder of his address, giving directions for the final part of the journey. 'Sure. See you tomorrow, ten or so.' He hung up and slid the phone along the counter, back to Nick, who was looking much like Jay felt: startled.

'OK?' said Blake to Jay.

'Er . . .' She couldn't quite believe her current lover had invited her ex to his place.

'I want to brief him about what's been happening,' Blake said. 'Best to do it in person, given that the spooks might be listening in. He's in the Garrison's firing line. He needs to know.'

'Sure,' she said, but despite his reasoning, her mind was still boggling.

After Nick left, Jay spent the remainder of the day sprawled on Blake's sofa watching TV. He'd lit the fire, and from time to time she nodded off, coming to with a jerk, adrenalin pumping until she remembered where she was. Early evening, Blake served wild mushroom soup in earthenware bowls with hot garlic bread, which they ate while half-watching the Channel

4 news. Afterwards, Jay curled into his arms. It felt strange being domestic with Blake, and she wondered how things would have panned out if he wasn't under house arrest. For some reason, she couldn't imagine things being as cosy. She could picture her waiting interminably for him to come home from some dangerous mission, trying not to worry about him, and then, when he arrived, him being unable to talk to her about what he'd been up to because it was classified.

This was never a problem with Tom. He shared his day without a qualm: which criminals he was chasing, the station's politics, who was pissed off with who. Unlike Blake, Tom wasn't a great cook, but he was steady and reliable, and she always knew where he was and who he was with.

She drifted off, unable to stop comparing the two men. Tom, who got irritated with her for not being a 'normal' woman. Blake, who thought she was entirely normal. Tom, who had a tricky daughter. Blake, who had no baggage – at least not that she knew of. Jay dozed, thinking she didn't know Blake well enough yet. Tom had proven himself to her, but she hadn't proven herself to him, hence the bust up.

Jay didn't think she'd be in the mood to make love to Blake with Tom looming so large in her mind, but when they were in bed, the instant he laid his lips gently on her bare skin, she melted.

She slept with her limbs interlaced with Blake's all night.

The next morning, she surfaced briefly to see morning sun slanting through the blinds. Blake wasn't there, but his side of the bed was still warm. She rolled over, feeling the aches in her body from the previous day's stress. She yawned, closed her eyes. She thought she heard men's voices, but she paid them no heed. She sank back to sleep.

'Jay.' Blake's voice was soft. He was crouched by the bed.

'Hi,' she said, blinking, still sleepy.

'I brought you some tea.'

She struggled up. Reached for the mug. 'Thanks.'

'Tom's here. When you're ready—'

'Tom's *what*?' A rush of heat fled over her body. She glanced at the bedside clock. Eleven o'clock! In a flurry of limbs, she flung back the duvet. 'Jesus, Max, you could have told me!'

'I just have.'

She grabbed a robe and raced for the shower. No way could she see Tom when her skin was covered with the scent of Blake. She scrubbed every inch of her body furiously before quickly shampooing her hair. She didn't bother blow-drying it; she didn't want to leave the two men alone for longer than she had to. Part of her wondered if Blake had let her sleep in precisely for this reason. What were they talking about? Please God, they weren't discussing her.

Jay pulled on her clothes, her skin barely dried, her hair still dripping wet, and raced for the kitchen. Tom stood at one end of the counter, Blake the other. When she entered the room, Tom stepped forward as though to embrace her, but then stepped back. He raised a hand briefly, saying, 'Hi.'

'Hi.'

Both of them looked at Blake, who was watching them, face inscrutable. He said neutrally, 'If you want to go for a walk, it's a nice day outside.'

They took the hint.

Not having a winter coat with her, Jay was forced to choose between staying dressed as she was and freezing, or wearing something of Blake's. Since she found it almost impossible to think clearly when she was cold, she grabbed one of Blake's fleece-lined skiing jackets from one of the hooks. She followed this with a fleecy hat to prevent her hair turning into ice. Tom didn't say a word. Just followed her outside.

Frost lay in the shadows, where the sun had yet to reach. The temperature was hovering on zero, and their breath made clouds in front of their faces. Rooks cawed from the trees, and Jay spotted a squirrel hopping along one of the lower branches.

'Jay.' Tom's voice was gentle. He held out a hand. She put hers in his. He turned it over. 'You're scratched.'

'I had a bit of an action day yesterday.'

'So Blake said.'

She took a breath. 'What else did he say?'

'That an assassin was sent after you. That you've been to Paris. That you've found your kidnappers and uncovered a lot of what's been going on with the Garrison. That you're in over your head – not that he said that, but I can read between the lines. You are, aren't you?'

'They killed my old boss, Major Wayland.'

'Yes. Blake told me.'

'And Madeleine Gal.'

'Yes.'

'I couldn't let them get away with it.'

'No. I can understand that.' He gave a wry smile. 'I know what you're like.'

Jay withdrew her hand from his, suddenly uncomfortable, in case Blake was watching.

'Walk with me?' Tom asked.

'Sure.'

Side by side, they walked along the rutted track. Some puddles were still frozen, others seeping water where they melted in the sun. They didn't say anything for a while. Finally, Tom paused. Blake's house was hidden around several corners and part of the beech wood. They were alone.

'I'm sorry,' Tom said.

'Me too.'

He gave a twisted smile. 'You drive me crazy, but I should be used to it by now . . .'

'I should have called you,' she said. 'Instead of the girls.'

'Calling the girls was good, they were closer. But the fact you kept me out of it for so long . . . Taking Nick with you to the police, rather than me. It made me wonder what you really thought of me. Why didn't you ring me sooner?'

She recalled her agony when she'd thought Blake was dead. 'Because I went a bit crazy after the kidnapping,' she said. 'I didn't want you to see me like that.'

He frowned. 'You know I wouldn't mind what state you were in.'

Although she'd promised herself to be truthful, she decided it would be more prudent at this point not to tell him exactly why she'd kept him at a distance. 'I know,' she said. 'I'm sorry. Sometimes I don't always act the way you want, but it's the way I am . . .'

Tom glanced over his shoulder, towards Blake's house, then back.

'Do you love him?'

'I care for him,' she prevaricated. 'A lot.'

He bit his lower lip. 'And me?'

'Oh, yes,' she said. 'I love you.'

His eyes flared, bright blue. 'Will you come back?'

Jay turned her head to watch a blackbird hopping through

the undergrowth, pecking beneath frosted leaves for a morsel. 'I thought we were on a break.'

'Well, we were.' He looked uncomfortable. 'But it's been six days . . .'

Long pause.

'Look,' he said. 'I spoke to Sofie. She admits to lying.' He looked up at the sky. 'I'm sorry I didn't listen to you . . .'

'She's your daughter,' Jay sighed. 'But I can't pretend I didn't feel hurt.'

'Christ, I've missed you.' His words came in a rush. 'I don't care if you don't want to get married. I don't care if you run around like a maniac, attracting trouble. I just want you, Jay. I want you in my life. You drive me nuts, but life without you isn't the same.' He swallowed. 'We're good together, aren't we?'

'Yes,' she agreed. 'We are.'

Another long pause.

Tom cleared his throat. 'So,' he said. 'Can we start over?'

'Not right now,' she said. She didn't want to face Nahid on Tom's doorstep, brandishing her hypodermic needle. But it wasn't just about her terror of Nahid. She pictured Blake bringing her tea in the morning, the way he kissed her, held her close. His intense concentration when he made love. How he held himself, calm, always in control. The humour that occasionally gleamed in his eyes. His energy. She didn't want to leave him, she realized. Not just yet.

'It's just that Blake's got such a safe place,' she added. She wanted to give Tom an explanation that wouldn't hurt him unnecessarily, but what about Blake? What if she walked back into Tom's arms right now? How would Blake feel about that? Without warning, a lump began to form in her throat. She didn't think she'd ever felt so torn, so conflicted.

'After Nahid trying to kill me, I feel safe here,' she mumbled. 'He's got perimeter alarms, cameras . . .'

Both of them glanced around as though trying to see if they were being watched.

'You don't feel safe with me?'

'Of course I do.' She rubbed her temples. 'But it's not you as much as the guys we're up against.'

'I see.' Despite his relatively neutral tone, she could see the effort it took. His jaw was tight, his hands clenched.

She wanted to touch his face, reassure him, but she couldn't do that when she'd woken in Blake's bed barely an hour ago. She didn't want to hurt Tom, but she didn't want to give him any false promises either. Nor did she want to betray Blake.

'Give me some time,' she said miserably. 'Until this works its way out. Until we find a way to release Blake. Bring the Garrison down.'

'And while you try to do that, you'll stay with Blake.'

Suddenly, Jay felt intensely weary. 'I don't know, Tom.' Her answer came straight from the heart. 'I honestly don't know.'

They walked back to the house in silence, and when he drove away, she felt an emotional pain she'd never felt before. Red, hot and deep as any chasm; it was her heart being sliced in two.

TWENTY-NINE

When Nick returned mid-afternoon, he wasn't alone. Filling the passenger seat of his Volvo was the hulking shape of Dr Cole.

'Nice place,' he remarked as he climbed out.

Blake led the way into his living room. Nick took the armchair on one side of the fire, Dr Cole the other. Jay sank on to the sofa, while Blake stood by the fireplace.

'Nick tells me you had a bit of a rough day yesterday,' Dr Cole said to Jay.

'Just a bit,' she admitted.

'I've been telling Nick about the samples you gave me.'

Jay shuddered inside at the memory of Nahid lungeing for her. She'd lost another life. She had to be five lives down now, at least.

'The heart attacks are caused by a designer drug that, once it's inside the body, acts fast. The victim dies within minutes of it being administered. However, the drug also degrades rapidly, which is why the toxicologists looking at your victims found elements of the degradation products rather than the actual drug. I have alerted the prison authorities to this fact, and they will be forwarding my report on to the relevant departments.

'Now, to the virus. As I thought, it's transferred by mucosal surfaces. It's massively aggressive, really nasty stuff, but fortunately it's not transmissible. I'm impressed that your sister's still hanging in there.' He sent Blake a sympathetic look. 'She's obviously one hell of a fighter.'

'She is,' Blake agreed. 'She opened her eyes four days ago. The nurse thought she was coming round, but nothing else happened. She fell back into the coma. Any chance of her recovering?'

'Perhaps.' Dr Cole appeared to choose his words carefully. 'The virus will have stopped replicating. She's still fighting it. That's good news. There's a possibility she might come round again and remain awake.'

'A possibility,' Blake repeated.

'She hasn't given up yet,' Dr Cole said. 'Her body might just need a little more time.'

Nobody said anything for a while. Finally, Dr Cole said, 'For these drugs to have been created, there would have to have been a team of people working together. A research institute, perhaps, with chemistry and virology departments. An animal unit for testing the viruses. Know about anything along these lines?'

All of them shook their heads.

Jay said, 'If the virus is passed via mucosal surfaces, how come the assassin doesn't get infected too?'

'I've been giving this a lot of thought. If what you say is true about this organization, then I'm inclined to think that each dose is tailored to the person targeted.'

'Like how?'

'If the victim suffers from asthma, then their inhaler could be swapped for an identical-looking one that contains the virus. Should the victim use contact lenses, then their contact lens solution could be contaminated.'

'Madeleine Gal wore contacts,' Jay said. 'How awful.' For some reason, the idea of having the virus introduced by the eyes made her feel squeamish.

'You could be quite inventive if you wanted,' Dr Cole continued. 'You could contaminate a victim's eyeliner and lipstick, mouth gel, or shaving stick. Items that would be unlikely to be shared with others. You could even contaminate a woman's tampons if you wanted. A man's hair tonic. You get the picture.'

'Where could this research institute be?' Jay wondered.

'Anywhere you liked. It might be under one roof, or could be several scientists working secretly in their own labs. However, given the inventiveness of the drugs, and the methods of killing the victims, I'd be more inclined to believe they're working together.'

How to find the research institute? Would Nahid know where it was? Jay doubted it, considering the elaborate efforts to keep members of the Garrison apart. Still, Jay put the question to Blake, who moved next door to call Turner, who was currently interrogating Nahid. He was gone for a while, during which time Nick and Dr Cole tried to think of a way of uncovering the Garrison's research lab.

'What about Stephanie Legrand? Wouldn't she know where the drugs came from?'

'Possible,' said Nick. 'I'll check it out.'

'And I'll call on some old Porton Down friends. See who's left, and who's still working where. Bespoke drugs like these are sophisticated. I wouldn't be surprised if one of them is involved. Then I'll check to see if anyone's published something in the medical journals,' said Dr Cole. 'Maybe they're talking about suxamethonium, a neuromuscular blocking drug used to induce anaesthesia . . . That could tie in with your victims' heart attacks . . . Or perhaps they've published an article on inventive ways to administer drugs to patients who can't swallow . . .'

Jay tuned out. She wondered whether, if they found the laboratory, they would find the evidence to nail the Garrison. Who paid the scientists? Who briefed them? Would the scientists turn witness in exchange for legal clemency? It was possible. The more Jay thought about it, the more she realized the lab could be their main chance to hang the Garrison.

When Blake returned, he said, 'Nahid says she doesn't know anything about a research institute, but Turner's going to push her. Turner's toxicologists have confirmed Nahid's hypodermic needle contained nothing but an innocuous serum.' He looked at Jay as he spoke. 'If she'd stabbed you, you would have been fine.'

Somehow, Jay remained unconvinced.

'Nahid has told Turner that she's a freelance operator. She's Israeli. She doesn't work exclusively for the Garrison and is involved with other organizations and individuals who require her specialist services. She doesn't know who in the Garrison gives her her orders. Initially, she was contacted by phone, by a man she's never heard from again, who ran through how they would work together. She receives a coded message on her phone, and, after confirming she can undertake the mission, she goes to Paris to collect the drugs from the Musée d'Orsay. She's paid by electronic transfer to an account in Turks and Caicos.'

'She's been remarkably forthcoming,' Jay remarked.

'She's not stupid.' Blake moved to take up his position beside the fireplace. 'She knows if she doesn't cooperate, she'll be in serious trouble. So, what's next?'

With Dr Cole covering the medical side of the hunt, and Nick going to talk to Stephanie Legrand to see if the woman knew where the drugs came from, Jay considered leaning on her kidnappers and their chapter head, Alison Drake.

'Not unless I'm there,' Nick said.

'I'll wait until you're back from Paris.' She glanced at Blake. 'I'll hold the fort at the office. With Nahid out of the picture, I should be safe.'

'I'd rather you remained here,' Blake said. His eyes sparkled. 'Where I can keep an eye on you.'

Since Jay was still bruised and tired, she didn't make a fuss. She said, 'Well, just for today then.'

In fact, she stayed at Blake's for the next couple of days. It was only when her housemates texted on Friday morning, telling her they were planning a slap-up meal that night, that she conceded it was time to go home, get back into the real world.

'Nahid's locked up,' she said to Blake. 'And since nobody's come looking for me here, wanting to do me harm . . .'

'Watch your back,' he warned before tucking her into his arms. He was freshly shaven, and his hair was slicked back, seal damp. He was dressed in combats and boots and a black sweater, and if he hadn't just devoured every inch of her in bed that morning, she might have been tempted to drag him back inside.

Blake's cleaner and odd-job man, Tash, drove Jay home in Blake's ancient sludge-green Discovery.

'Thanks,' she said when he pulled up outside her house.

'No problem.'

She climbed out and, despite knowing that Nahid was safely under lock and key, she checked the street, wary of little old ladies coming to attack her. The street, however, was empty, aside from a man over six feet tall, wearing a trilby. No way could Nahid make herself a foot taller. She waved Tash goodbye and let herself into the house.

Jay spent the remainder of the day catching up on work, and in the evening she drank wine with the girls and filled them in on the last few days. She was grateful they didn't give her too hard a time over Blake, just voiced concerns over the possibility that, one day, she might lose both men. The thought had crossed her mind, and she wondered how life would be without either Blake or Tom in her life. Uncomplicated, that's for sure. Perhaps she'd fall for a nice, safe accountant, who wouldn't mind her charging around the countryside rescuing trafficked victims. But then pigs might fly.

Saturday brought more clear, icy cold weather, just the sort of day Jay loved. Dressed in sweatpants and top, she pushed her feet into her trainers and went for a run. Being chased by Nahid had made her realize how soft she'd become, and she resolved to get fitter. She didn't push herself too hard, just allowed her muscles to warm, her breathing steady into a good rhythm for a couple of miles or so, before heading for home and a shower.

In the kitchen, a coffee and Saturday's *Times* to hand, she answered a call from Blake.

'Good news and bad news,' he said.

She pushed away her coffee. 'Fire away,' she said.

'Emilie's vanished.'

'What?' Jay felt her eyes widen.

'When the nurse went in to see her this morning, she'd gone. Her handbag, which was stored in her bedside table along with her clothes and personal stuff, was also gone. She left a note for me. It's an old code from when we were kids. It means she's gone into hiding. She hasn't contacted me again, and nor will she. She knows my phones will be bugged. She's on the run, Jay. She knows the second the Garrison finds out she's alive, they'll come after her.'

'Wasn't she in a coma?'

'I think she came out of her coma last week, when she opened her eyes. My guess is she pretended to remain unconscious while she gathered her strength to get away.'

'That's one hell of a thing to do.'

'She's in fear for her life, Jay.'

'Well, that's good news. I mean, that's she's alive.'

'She's given me an RV point in Brussels. She doesn't know I'm under house arrest. I need you to go and meet her. Bring her to my house.'

Jay briefly closed her eyes. Of all the things she had considered doing this weekend, going to Brussels to meet Blake's sister hadn't been one of them. Once again, she was being railroaded by Blake. If he'd *asked* her to pick up his sister, she might not be hesitating as much. It was the way he put things into action *without* asking that irritated her. His assumption she'd do his bidding.

'Tash is already on his way to you with my car. I want you to drive it over. I don't want Emilie travelling by train. She'll be extremely weak, and extremely vulnerable.'

Jay pictured herself in a city crawling with assassins who were hunting Emilie.

'Won't the Garrison be on to her?'

'That's why you've got to go today.'

Paranoia made her add, 'What if they're listening in to us right now?'

'Impossible. I'm using a jamming system.'

She covered her eyes with her hand. 'No, Max. I can't do this.'

'Tash will have some euros for you both and a false passport for Emilie. I don't want her getting pegged when you leave France.'

'And me? What if *I* get pegged? Won't they come after me if they think I know where Emilie is?'

'Tash will bring a passport you can use, if you want.'

'Emilie doesn't know me. How will she react when I approach her? Won't she run away?' *Or attack me*, Jay thought, but didn't add this particular concern.

'You'll be carrying something of mine that Emilie will recognize. Something from our childhood that only she and I know about. If she asks for a name, for confirmation, say the name Maria. She won't run, I promise.'

Jay visualized herself standing in some freezing Brussels square, clutching a tatty old teddy bear called Maria.

'Max, no.'

'I know I'm asking a lot, Jay.' His voice dropped. 'I'll make it up to you, I promise.'

'That'll be hard if I wind up dead. Look what happened when you sent me to Paris to meet Sol. He was murdered, and I ended up being snatched by the DCRI.' The memory of waking in the windowless, damp room with tape across her eyes sent a chill across her skin. Nahid may have been caught, but Tivon was still around. 'I'm sorry, Max. I can't do this . . . Not on my own. Not again.'

The line fell silent.

'Max? Are you still there?'

'What if someone came with you?' he said.

'Like who?'

'Give me ten minutes.'

With that, he hung up, leaving Jay with an urge to hurl her coffee mug across the kitchen.

Tash arrived twenty minutes later with a copy of the car's insurance papers – Jay's details added in Blake's neat handwriting at the top – a Eurotunnel ticket and two passports. Jay checked both. Where Emilie's actually had a picture of Emilie, Jay's picture was of a woman who looked older, with much darker hair and thinner lips.

'I can't use this!' she exclaimed. 'It doesn't look anything like me.'

Tash had a look. 'Actually, it's pretty good. I've known people cross borders with far worse.'

'I'm not going. Didn't he tell you?'

Tash didn't say anything, but continued to brief her. The item Jay was supposed to carry to the RV point wasn't a stuffed toy, but an Italian cookbook. Curious, she peeked inside, but there was no *happy birthday* or *with love from* inscribed on the title pages. It was pretty old too, and well used – some pages loose, some marked with splodges of oil and food. Perhaps Emilie had given it to him?

Tash finally passed her a money belt, which was, predictably, stuffed with euros. 'Emilie and I could go around the world with this,' Jay remarked.

'He wouldn't mind,' Tash said. 'As long as you were both safe.'

'But I'm not going!' She practically wailed the words, but

Tash didn't seem to hear. He wished her luck, and without further ado, handed over the BMW's keys and walked down the street, heading for the tube.

Jay turned the keys over in her hand. She'd have to put the car on a meter or it would get towed. Frustrated, still angry, she was continuing to look at the keys when her phone rang. Briefly, she hesitated when she saw who it was, but she couldn't think why she shouldn't talk to him. She loved him, dammit.

'Tom?'

'A little bird tells me you're thinking of taking a mini break. To get away for a bit. Have a rest.'

Jay stood, momentarily stunned. Blake had been talking to Tom?

'Fancy some company?' he asked. 'If you're going by car, I can share the driving. If you're going by plane, I can carry your bags. Should you get a puncture, I'll change the tyre. If the plane gets a puncture, I'll entertain you while someone else changes the tyre.'

Jay was speechless. Blake had rung Tom and asked him to join her on her trip to Brussels?

'Jay?'

'Er . . .'

'I heard you wanted to leave today. Will you wait until I get there?'

'I guess so.'

'Great. I should be there in two hours.'

THIRTY

Jay hung up and stared at the phone in disbelief. As she stared, it rang again.

'Hon,' he said.

'Tom's coming with me?'

'Would you rather someone else?'

'Well, no. It's just . . . a bit odd. I mean . . . with you and me. And Tom . . .'

'Emilie's my priority right now,' Blake said. 'We can sort out the personal stuff later.'

He had to have emotions of steel. Which was why he made such a good MI5 officer, she supposed, with his ability to put emotions aside for the mission in hand. Which was to rescue his sister.

'But isn't it a bit—'

'Put it this way,' Blake said drily, 'I trust the detective with your life. Not many people around who fit that particular bill. Look, my lawyer's just arrived. Keep safe, hon.'

Unsure how long she'd be away, she wrote a note for the girls, called Nick – already briefed by Blake, of course – and then called her mother.

'Tom's taking me on a surprise trip,' she said, glad her mother couldn't see her. She could always tell she was lying when they were face-to-face.

'Any idea where?'

'No. Isn't it fun?' Jay felt her cheeks heat as she continued to lie.

'Perhaps he's going to set your wedding date,' her mother suggested brightly. 'Present you with an engagement ring.'

'Perhaps he is.' Jay's tone was wry, but her mother didn't seem to notice. After they'd hung up, Jay packed. Travelling by car had its advantages, and although she normally travelled light, this time she didn't let weight or bulk bother her. As usual, her father's hip flask went in her day pack, along with her Swiss Army Knife. She added her own passport as a precaution.

Bags ready by the front door, Jay paced the house, waiting for Tom. The last time they'd travelled together had been when they'd gone to stay on her father's farm in Scotland in the summer. For a week they'd fished, hiked across heather-clad hills, and picnicked beside peat-brown burns. Remembering their contentment, their ease in each other's company, she found it hard to believe they'd split up.

Tom arrived just after two p.m. He looked lean and hard in washed-out jeans and a butter-soft black leather jacket. His dark-brown hair was newly cut. His boots in need of a polish.

This time he didn't hold back. He came straight for her and swept her into his arms. 'Missed you, beautiful.'

'Missed you too.' Which was true. She belonged in his arms. It was the simple truth. But what about Blake? Didn't she belong in his arms too?

'Blake's booked us on the four o'clock train,' Tom told her. He swept to gather her bags. 'But if we're late, it's not a problem. Blake's sorted it. We're taking his car, I gather?'

'Yes.'

'Better get cracking then.'

She was grateful for his no-nonsense approach, and after they'd dropped Tom's vehicle at Goose's, who promised to store it off the street to prevent it getting towed, they headed east, for Folkestone. When they picked up the M20, Jay felt the same sense of disbelief wash over her. The last time she'd been on this motorway, she'd been with Blake, returning from Paris.

'This is weird,' she finally admitted.

'Yup.' Tom rolled his head against the headrest to look at her. 'But I'd rather have weird *with* you, than without you.'

'I'm glad you're here. I couldn't do this on my own. Not after the last time.'

He reached out a hand and gently stroked her cheek. 'I'm glad too.'

They made the Channel Tunnel with thirty minutes to spare, thanks to the BMW's 507 horses beneath its bonnet. Jay had never driven a car like it before, and she could see why men went weak at the knees over it. The M5's power and performance were awesome, and the seats were the most comfortable of any she'd experienced, cradling her in leather. She wanted to compliment the car, share her appreciation for the machine with Tom, but there was no way she could do that. It was Blake's car, fifty thousand pounds plus worth of gleaming metal, and remarking favourably upon it would only make Tom glower. His three-year-old Vauxhall wasn't a bad car, by any stretch of the imagination, but it was nowhere near the league of the M5.

When they arrived in Calais, they took the E5 north-east, past Bruges, and then hooked south-east, skirting Gent and Aalst. Tom plugged his iPod into the Beemer's system, and they hummed along to a variety of songs as the car devoured the expressway. Darkness gradually fell, and Jay turned on the headlights. She didn't rush her driving. Emilie's RV wasn't until ten in the morning. Emilie had told Blake she would be at the Sucré Salé café in Ixelles at ten a.m. and four p.m. every day for the next week. When they reached the outskirts of Brussels, Jay got Tom to switch her watch an hour forward to local time.

Jay followed the BMW's satnav's directions to the Hotel Chambord on Namur Naamse, which Blake had booked for them. Set just inside the inner ring road, the area was prosperous, filled with graceful stone houses with grilled balconies. But on the other side of the ring road, Jay saw the cheap pizza and burger houses of what was locally known, she learned from the hotel receptionist, as little Africa.

'Two single rooms?' the receptionist queried.

'Yes,' said Jay, at the same time as Tom said, 'A double would be nice.'

Jay hustled Tom aside. 'I can't sleep with you,' she hissed.

He widened his eyes. 'You've done it before.'

'Not when . . . you know. I'm kind of with Blake. It wouldn't be right.'

He studied her at length.

'I will not sleep with you,' she insisted.

'OK, OK.' He raised his hands. 'Two singles it is.'

In her room stood a beautiful floral arrangement. Strands of freesias scented the air, reminding her of summer. She picked up the note propped against the vase.

Sleep tight, it read. *Max*.

She smoothed the card between her fingers. *Max, Max, Max*, she thought. *What to do with you? What to do with Tom?* She took a shower to wash away the journey, resolutely keeping her mind from both men by thinking about Emilie. Where was she staying? In a hotel? A hostel? Was she using her credit cards to pay for her accommodation? Were the Garrison able to track them? Boy, she was glad Tom was with her. She didn't want to face the Garrison on her own.

Tom knocked on her door at nine as they'd arranged. They ate at an Italian restaurant just down the road. Small and cosy, with candles on the tables, it was the sort of place Jay liked. They settled in the corner. Jay ordered pasta with artichokes, Tom roast *sanglier*. Wild boar.

Afterwards, he walked her to her hotel room door. 'Can I kiss you?'

'I'm sorry, Tom.'

He gave a wry smile. 'Sleep tight.'

Jay walked up the Chaussée d'Ixelles alone. They didn't want to spook Emilie by having Tom there as well. Blake reckoned

that after Jay had explained things to Emilie, Tom wouldn't
be a problem. The café Emilie had chosen stood between a
bus stop and a patisserie. Small, bare-bricked, there were rows
of freshly baked ciabatta and croissants behind the counter.
Jay took a seat by the window, where Blake's tattered old
cookery book could be seen clearly. She drank a cappuccino,
half-reading her newspaper. She waited for an hour before
leaving.

Jay returned at four in the afternoon, but still no Emilie.

The next morning, still no Emilie, nor that afternoon.

Finally, on the third day, at three minutes past ten on Tuesday,
a woman walked into the café. A thin, gaunt woman, with skin
the colour of curdled milk. For a second, Jay didn't recognize
her. But then she took in the dark curly hair, now lank and life-
less, and the strong chin.

Emilie looked straight at the book, then straight at Jay. She
gave a little wave, like a girlfriend would to another. Jay waved
back. Emilie walked over.

'Hi,' Jay said.

'Hi.' Emilie ducked down and brushed a kiss against Jay's
cheeks. The waiter hovered. Emilie ordered a latte. She said,
'Whose book is that?'

'Max Blake's. Your brother's.'

'Who did it belong to?'

Jay remembered what Blake had said: *If she asks for a name,
for confirmation, say the name Maria.*

'Maria.'

Jay hadn't realized the woman had been tense until it drained
from her shoulders. She slipped on to the chair next to Jay.

'Where is he?' Emilie asked. She picked up the book, put it
in her day pack.

'It's a long story.'

'It would have to be, to keep him from coming to me.' Emilie's
eyes coolly assessed Jay. They were the same colour as Blake's,
chocolate brown.

'He's under house arrest,' Jay told her.

'That's as good a reason as any.' Emilie appeared unperturbed. 'What for?'

'A murder he didn't commit.'

She said, 'Who are you?'

'Jay McCaulay.'

'Who's the man I've seen you with?' Emilie's tone was sharp. 'The tall good-looking guy with the leather jacket?'

So, Emilie had been tracking them, checking them out.

'He's my ex.'

'Doesn't appear to be an ex, the way you look at each other.'

'We're on a break.'

'Not for long, I hope.'

'Hmmm,' Jay murmured non-committally, thinking it best if Blake's sister didn't know the complexities of her love life and that her brother was involved.

The waiter arrived with Emilie's latte. Emilie poured four sachets of brown sugar into the cup and stirred. 'I need my calories.' She gave a grim smile. 'To help build me up.'

'You're the only survivor that we know of,' Jay said. 'Nobody else seems to have been able to fight the virus like you did.'

'How many had it?' Her gaze was curious.

'We suspect around thirty-three, but it could be much more.'

'And they're all dead?'

'Yes.'

Emilie closed her eyes briefly. She took a deep breath and exhaled. Stirred her coffee, shaking her head slightly. 'So, what's the plan?'

'Max said to drive you home. To his place.'

'Where's the car parked?' Emilie asked.

'At the Hotel Chambord.'

'What are you driving?'

'Max's BMW.'

Emilie blinked. 'The M5?'

'Yes.'

The woman suddenly leaned forward, her expression intent. '*Ku ka jetuar vëllai im?*' she said. *Where does my brother live? What's his postcode?*

It took a second for Jay to realize the woman had spoken in Albanian, a language Jay and her brother Angus had learned as children. Jay could count on one hand the people she'd met who spoke such an obscure language – including Blake and, now, Emilie.

'*Në Beeches, vetëm jashtë Londrës,*' Jay replied. *At the Beeches, not far from London.* 'I don't know the postcode off by heart, sorry. Will his phone number do?'

'It really is you!' Emilie's voice rose with excitement. 'Sorry,

I had to make sure . . .' Grinning, she rose, leaned over, and gave Jay a hug. 'Max has told me so much about you. Your escapades in Macedonia and Albania. And what about Russia? God, how you put up with him on a mission, I don't know. Bossy as hell, never listens. Just orders you around.'

'Don't I know it,' Jay agreed, grinning back. It was as though a switch had been flipped the second Jay had spoken Albanian. Emilie had come alight.

'God,' Emilie exclaimed. 'I feel so much better now I know I'm in safe hands. I know Max wouldn't have sent anyone he didn't trust to collect me, but even so . . .'

'I can understand your caution,' Jay said. 'I'd feel the same.'

'I take it the ex is DI Sutton?'

Jay looked away, feeling wrong-footed that Emilie knew Tom's name. 'Yes.'

'Max worked with you guys on the warehouseman case.'

'Yes, he did.'

Emilie sipped her coffee before ordering a pain au chocolat. 'I didn't feel like eating before. Too nervous.'

Jay joined her. The pastry had been warmed, and soft rich chocolate oozed from it.

Emilie told Jay about waking up in the hospital. 'I've never felt so weak. I thought I'd been unconscious for a day or so, but when I heard the radio announce the date, I just about died. I'd been out for a month. A *month*! Can you believe it? I've lost a month of my life, but it beats being dead, believe me.'

'When did you wake?'

'Thursday. Twelve days ago.'

When the nurse first reported Emilie had opened her eyes.

'How did you hide the fact you were conscious for so long?'

Emilie grimaced. 'It was one of the hardest things I've done, to lie there and let them fiddle with me. Refill my tubes. Bathe me. But I was so weak to start, my limbs so soft . . . I got up at night. Padded around. Tried to build up my strength.' She tucked into a second pastry. 'What set you and Max on to the Garrison?'

Unsure how Emilie would take the news of Sol's death, she broke it as gently as she could.

'He was trying to save me?' Emilie asked. Sorrow filled her eyes.

'Yes.' By the time Jay had filled Emilie in on everything

from Sol being an assassin, to Blake being framed and Dr Cole's diagnosis of the methods of assassinations, they'd drunk another coffee each and it was past twelve.

'Poor Sol.' Emilie sighed. 'Bad guy turned good. But it didn't save him, did it?'

'Why did they want to kill you?' Jay asked.

'I overheard something I shouldn't have. I was in one of the conference halls, tucked up at the back. Everyone else had gone, or so I thought. I'd been translating for my boss for most of the day, but I still had some paperwork to do. I heard two guys discussing one of our senior ministers, but didn't take it in, not until one of them mentioned the minister was being difficult and asked what this other guy could do about it. The guy said that the Garrison would "dispose of" the difficult person, no problem, and that the toxicology report would state they'd died from a heart attack. There was no way I could be mistaken. I was listening to people organizing the death of a senior EU minister . . .

'I wanted to sneak out of there, but didn't dare in case they noticed me. I put on my headphones, pretending to be listening to the day's tapes. It was only when they made to leave that they saw me. One of them came over and asked if I'd overheard anything. I denied it, and in all honesty, I really thought he'd believed me.' Her mouth twisted. 'Obviously, I was wrong.'

'Did you know him?'

'Oh, yes. He's Max's boss. Jim Turner.'

THIRTY-ONE

'Jim Turner?' Jay felt breathless, as if her lungs were being compressed.

'Yes.' Emilie twisted a paper napkin between her fingers. 'I rang Max immediately. I knew I was in terrible danger, but I didn't dare say much on the phone. I was terrified Turner might be listening. I didn't want Turner to know I really *had* overheard his conversation, and I certainly wasn't going to risk mentioning his name. I wanted to talk to Max face to face. But before he got to me, I was already ill. I could barely talk.' Her gaze turned distant. 'I can't even remember what I told him.'

'But Turner trapped Nahid.' Jay was having trouble computing Emilie's information. 'To find out who's running the Garrison. He gave us Stephanie Legrand's address. Gave us samples of the drugs. I don't get it.'

Emilie's mouth tightened. 'From what you say, a lot of people know about the Garrison now. The police, your ex, that doctor, your housemates, Blake, you, me . . . It's not containable any more. I bet he's pretending he's undercover, so that he looks squeaky clean. But he's not. He's the boss of the Garrison. The one who pulls the strings of the organization.'

'Are you sure?' Jay couldn't help the doubts crowding her mind.

'Oh, yes. I'm sure. And I'm the only witness. Who he tried to eliminate.'

Jay reran every conversation she'd had with Turner. How at their first meeting he'd warned her off, and when she hadn't taken heed, and had involved the girls, Tom, and Nick, he'd switched to helping her and Blake. What about Turner's assistant, Brian Keith? Now, Jay took out her wallet and withdrew his card. He'd written his mobile number, and what could be his home number, on the back. He'd also scribbled, *Battle of Britain Monument, Embankment*. Why? Was it an RV point? A coded reference of some sort?

Did Keith know his boss was part of the Garrison? He certainly knew about the organization . . . She remembered Keith shielding Turner from Nick, but how, when *she* had rung, Keith had made an immediate arrangement for her to come to Thames House. But Keith had seen her *himself*. He'd said Turner was in a meeting. And when Turner had turned up, Keith hadn't been comfortable. Keith had, she realized, wanted to see her on her own. Why?

Jay wanted to call Brian Keith, but distrust made her circumspect. Hadn't he warned her about using his numbers? She tried to remember what else he'd said, but too much had happened since, and the memory evaded her. Besides which, she'd better use her phone only when she was back in the UK, she thought. She didn't want the spooks to home in on her and Emilie.

'I think we should go,' Jay said. The sooner she, Tom, and Emilie reached the safety of Blake's home, the better.

'Fine by me.'

All three of them were jumpy on the return journey. Even Tom, who was pretty imperturbable, kept glancing round, keeping an eye on the traffic. If Turner knew Emilie was alive – which he had to by now – he'd be pulling out the stops to get to her.

At Calais, Jay hoped they'd be waved straight through when they showed their British passports, but no such luck. They were pulled to one side, along with two other vehicles, for an apparent spot check. Two uniformed cops gave their car a perfunctory search.

'Tom,' she hissed. 'Should I use my false passport?' She showed it to him.

'It looks nothing like you,' he said.

'Quite. What if they think that too? The last thing I need is to be stuck behind bars.'

A cop tapped on the window asking for their passports.

'I'd use your own,' Tom said. 'I am.'

'I'll use Max's,' said Emilie. 'I've used it before, so I know it's OK.'

Jay handed all three passports over: two genuine, one false. Her pulse picked up as the cop studied Emilie's closely, peering at her in the back seat. Emilie smiled. He didn't smile back. Instead, he took their passports to a booth at the end of the lay-by and made a phone call. He glanced their way a couple of times, and dread settled in Jay's stomach. Was Turner being alerted to them being at the tunnel? She could practically feel his hot breath on the back of her neck as he hunted them down.

The cop returned. He said, 'This passport –' he held out Tom's – 'is due to expire in a week. I suggest you get a new one.'

'Will do,' Tom said.

The cop returned all three passports and waved them through.

'Phew,' said Emilie.

But it wasn't over yet. After they had driven off the train at Folkestone, and were back on the M20, Jay pegged a motorbike that seemed to have been following them since they'd disembarked. She exited at the Ashford junction to see if it

followed, but it continued straight on. Two cars joined her at
the roundabout. Tom made a note of their makes and numbers
before they rejoined the motorway.

It wasn't until they began to skirt the south of London that
Jay saw the motorbike again, lurking behind several trucks on
the inside lane. All the hairs on the back of her neck rose.
'We're being followed,' she said. 'I'm sure of it. He's using a
team.'

Tom cursed. 'We'll have to ditch Blake's car.'

'What if,' Jay said, 'I drop you guys off without them seeing,
and you make your way to Blake's while they follow me on a
wild-goose chase?'

'No,' said Tom. His voice was firm.

'Or I could drop you guys off . . .' Emilie said.

'No,' said Jay. 'Your brother will kill me if I leave you on
your own.'

'We stick together,' Tom said.

'How?' Jay asked.

'Give me a minute.' He was frowning as he thought. Jay kept
checking the vehicles all around, and not just the ones behind.
Now she knew they were being tailed, she was sure she recognized the grey Volvo ahead of her. It had dropped back a
couple of times and would, no doubt, pull forward at some point
to confuse her. These guys were pros. No wonder it had taken
her most of the journey to peg them.

'Right,' said Tom. 'We go to Goose's, borrow his car.'

'How do we do that without them seeing?'

'First,' said Tom with a grin, 'we visit Scotland Yard.'

After parking Blake's BMW on a meter around the corner from
St James's Park, they walked up Dacre Street to New Scotland
Yard. Tom flashed his police ID card at the security guards and
asked if he could speak to DI Lark. Luckily, DI Lark was free,
and within three minutes all three of them were ensconced in
the reception area. Jay felt the muscles along her spine relax
a little now she was surrounded by cops – and what she hoped
was bulletproof glass.

'Goose.' Tom introduced them. Goose was a big man, carrying
a roll of fat that bulged over his belt. He had a warm smile
and humour in his eyes. He gave Jay a peck on the cheek,
shook Emilie's hand. His nickname, Jay already knew, came

from his colleagues teasing him he wasn't anything like a lark, but more like a goose being fattened up for Christmas.

'Of course you can borrow my shit heap of a car,' Goose said. 'It's actually at the garage, but it's been fixed up. Should take you anywhere you want to go. You can pick her up now, if you like.'

'Great,' said Tom. 'But we need one more favour before we do that.' He glanced through the tall glass windows. 'We need to get out of here without anyone seeing us.'

'Trouble?'

'Oh, yes,' said Tom.

Goose's eyes lit up. 'Can I join in?'

Tom considered it. He said, 'Could you smuggle us out? We don't want to be seen.'

'This to do with our phone conversation last week?'

'Yup.'

'I think we'd better have a word.' Goose glanced at Emilie and Jay. 'You OK to stay here for a bit?'

'Sure.'

Jay watched Goose and Tom vanish through the security barriers. Although she knew Goose, and knew that Tom trusted him with his life, Tom had also said he trusted Superintendent Clarkson, but Clarky had warned Tom off. Was Goose part of the Garrison? While Emilie took a chair in the corner, Jay paced the reception area, unable to stop worrying. She paused by a leather-bound book in a glass case, which listed officers who had lost their lives in the line of duty, but she couldn't concentrate enough to read anything. As the minutes ticked past – ten, twenty, thirty – her nerves tightened. Was Goose setting a trap with the Garrison? She looked outside, letting her eyes run over the pharmacy opposite, the newspaper kiosk, but couldn't see anything out of the ordinary. Not that that meant much. The entire place could be heaving with Special Forces, and she wouldn't know it. They were consummate at camouflage.

She wished she had Emilie's patience, and then realized the woman had fallen asleep. She'd only been out of hospital for five days. Little wonder she was exhausted. Jay didn't disturb her, but let her rest.

After an hour had passed, Jay was ready to grab Emilie and flee. She was convinced Goose had Tom in handcuffs, and that

Turner's troops were approaching. When Goose and Tom finally appeared, she was as skittish as a racehorse at the starting gate.

'Take it easy,' Tom told her. 'I had to fill him in. He made a recording. He's on our side, Jay, I swear it.'

Only slightly mollified, she was still jumpy as Goose led them into the underground car park. Fortunately, Goose had a nice large Vauxhall Insignia, so ducking out of sight didn't pose too much of a problem. With Emilie tucked low in the front passenger seat, almost buried in the footwell, Jay and Tom hunkered down on the back seat.

Nobody spoke as Goose drove up the ramp, paused at the barrier to insert his card, and exited Scotland Yard's car park. After a while, Goose said, 'You can sit up now. I can't see any tail.'

All three of them scrambled upright. 'Thanks, mate,' Tom said. 'No probs.'

Just past five, the streets were dark and dampened with a fine mist. Goose parked outside a garage in Clapham specializing in renovating classic cars. 'I'll bring it out for you. Wait here.'

Jay joined Emilie and Tom on the pavement. She stretched and yawned. The air was cold and smelled of diesel. She said, 'I don't think we should go to Blake's. They'll have his place covered.'

'Agreed,' said Emilie. 'Do you have some change? I'm going to ring him.' She indicated a phone box at the end of the street.

Jay passed Emilie a handful of coins and half-watched her go into the phone box, dial, and begin speaking on the phone. She wondered what Emilie and Blake were saying. Was Blake telling his sister that he'd been sleeping with Jay? He'd already told Emilie about their missions, and about Tom. What else had he said?

She turned when a gleaming red Jaguar XJ6 purred out of the garage. Goose hopped out, passed Tom the keys.

'It's not a shit heap,' Jay said. 'It's beautiful. Are you sure you don't mind us borrowing it?'

'Bought her from my brother-in-law last month for two grand,' said Goose with a grin. 'If you trash her, you owe me three. She's just had a brake overhaul, including front calipers and new shock absorbers. I even got her front bumper re-chromed.'

'What year?' asked Tom. He looked as though he was admiring the car, but Jay knew him better. From the way his head was tilted, his gaze moving across the street then back, he was thinking about something else. Something was bothering him.

'Nineteen seventy-one. Look, she's still registered in my brother-in-law's name, so Turner shouldn't be able to track you.'

'Great,' said Tom, shaking Goose's hand.

'No worries. Let me know if there's anything else I can do. When you've got a plan, count me in.'

'Thanks.' Tom bit the corner of his lip. Turned to Jay. 'Look, I'm not sure how to say this . . .'

Jay watched him cautiously, wary of what was coming.

'So I'm just going to come out and say it.'

She nodded her head. Licked her lips.

'You need to know that I rang Sofie from Goose's office. She's OK, but I'm worried for her. She says she saw a dark-haired man hanging around after school yesterday. When she pointed him out to Heather, he vanished, but he was there this morning.'

Tivon? Dear God, no.

'Tom, you've got to go to her. Make sure she's not in danger.'

'I don't want to leave you.' His face spasmed. 'But I don't want to leave Sofie either . . .'

'Of course you don't.' She stepped forward, took his hands in hers and gave them a squeeze. 'She's your child, Tom. She needs you. I'm an adult, OK? I'll be fine.'

'I hate it when you say you'll be fine.' His mouth twisted into a wry smile. 'Because you rarely are.'

'In that case –' she smiled back – 'I promise I won't say it any more. Go to Sofie, Tom. She's your priority.'

'If anyone comes asking about you, I'll tell them you've got a family emergency in Scotland. How does that sound?'

'Fine, as long as Turner doesn't send his goons up there,' Jay said.

'Doubtful, but if he did, he wouldn't find anything but your Dad and his cows.'

Emilie returned, looking pale and fragile. 'She needs to rest,' Jay told Tom.

'We can't take her to my place,' he said. 'Nor yours, nor Blake's . . . Turner will have them all covered.'

Emilie spoke up. 'Jay knows a safe house. From their last mission. Max said to use it. Jay knows where the key's kept.'

A rush of relief washed over Jay. Blake's safe house, set deep in the countryside east of Canterbury. Brilliant.

'You'll stay there until I get things sorted?' Tom said. 'Keep your heads down? If Turner doesn't know where you guys are, you're safe . . .'

He paused in front of Jay. His hands were balled into fists, and her heart went out to him. He was in much the same place as she'd been when she'd watched him drive away from Blake's place. His heart was torn in two, between her and Sofie.

'We'll stay at the safe house and not make a peep,' Jay assured him. 'We'll use the village phone box to stay in touch.' They quickly made up a code for two rendezvous points and another set of code words to alert the other to any potential dangers.

Tom hugged Jay close. 'I hate to leave you.'

'I know.'

This time, she kissed him on the lips. Immediately, his arms tightened around her. He slid his hand to her nape. He let his breathing mingle with hers. Gently, he lowered his head and deepened the kiss. Her fingers clutched his shoulders as a rush of heat filled her.

It was Tom who broke the kiss. He looked down at her, his eyes as dark as midnight.

'I want you,' he told her. 'I want you in my life.'

'Yes.'

'Take good care.'

While Tom walked to the tube, to catch a train to Paddington and then on to Bristol, Jay drove Goose's Jag out of London, joining the M2 east, which then turned into the A2, a dual carriageway. After they passed Canterbury, Jay took the A28 towards Margate, and soon afterwards ducked right on to a country lane. She recognized a farm as they passed, then a river, and by the time she drew up outside the small brick cottage it was nine p.m.

Jay climbed out of the car. The air was cold and smelled faintly of dung. She could hear water flowing nearby, which she knew was the river they'd crossed earlier. She'd only stayed here once, but oddly it felt as though she was coming home.

Jay walked to the front porch, plucked a key from beneath

a flowerpot, and opened the front door. She went to turn on the heating while Emilie pottered round the cottage, snapping on lights. Nothing seemed to have changed. Same simple tones on the walls, faded pinks and beiges, the furniture neutral. Same three bedrooms, one bathroom, and a downstairs loo. Kitchen cum dining room, and a cosy living room with wooden beams and an open fire that was already laid with logs and newspaper. Using the matches on top of the mantelpiece, she lit the fire.

'I'm going to bed,' Emilie said. She looked dead on her feet.

'You should eat first.'

'In the morning.'

Jay followed her up the stairs. Made sure she had towels and was warm enough. She was about to leave, when Emilie said, 'Jay.'

Jay paused in the doorway.

'I can't thank you enough for coming to get me.'

'It's OK.'

'I owe you.'

Downstairs, she opened a can of tomato soup and heated it in a pan. Toasted some bread from the freezer. The cottage was better stocked than her kitchen, but that was Blake for you, she thought. Always well prepared. Blake had rustled up a Thai curry out of seemingly nowhere when she'd stayed previously, which had been delicious.

After her soup, Jay poured herself a brandy from Blake's supply in the living-room cupboard. Rémy Martin, only the best. She didn't turn on the TV. Just sipped and gazed into the fire. Finally, after making sure the house was securely locked up, Jay washed her underwear and put it to dry over the radiator. It was the best she could do since she didn't have a change of clothes – they hadn't wanted to show themselves unnecessarily, and possibly for the second time, to the cameras outside Scotland Yard, and had left their overnight bags in the back of the BMW.

As she drifted to sleep – the smell of the countryside seeping through her open window, the sound of the river in her senses – she dreamed she was swimming with Blake somewhere warm and tropical, with a full moon and silver sand. They were both naked.

THIRTY-TWO

Jay awoke with a start. She'd heard something, she was certain. She sat up in bed, blinking, trying to clear her vision. She'd left the curtains apart to allow fresh air to enter the room, but there was no moon, and she could barely make out the dark shape of the river at the bottom of the garden.

Quietly, she rose and pulled on her shirt. Padded to the top of the stairs.

Who else knew about this safe house?

Cocking her head, she held her breath and listened. Distantly, she could hear the rush of the river, but nothing else. No traffic, no aircraft.

What had woken her?

Instincts on full alert, Jay tiptoed down the stairs. When she reached the bottom, she felt a cold breeze curl around her bare legs. Someone had opened the back door . . . Had she locked it? She was sure she had. She didn't dare shout to warn Emilie, because then she'd give away her position. Feeling vulnerable, she considered the weapons available. Carefully, she began to creep for the living room and the fire poker by the grate.

At that moment, a black-clad figure loomed in the hallway, right in front of her.

Jay stepped back, a scream in her throat.

'Jay,' the figure whispered urgently. 'It's me. *Me.*'

'Max?'

When he came to embrace her, she stepped back. 'You scared the shit out of me!'

'Sorry.'

'Why didn't you ring the front doorbell like a normal person?'

'I didn't want to wake you guys.'

'Jesus.'

And then his arms were around her, his lips searching for hers.

'Max, wait . . .'

He paused.

'What are you doing here?' She glanced down, but it was too dark for her to see if he was wearing his electronic anklet.

'The detective rang me.'

He began to nuzzle her neck.

'And?' she prompted. God, sometimes it was like getting blood from a stone.

'He said he was concerned about his daughter and was returning to Bristol.'

His fingers drifted down her spine to the small of her back.

'If he wasn't with you . . .' Blake softly kissed the hollow of her throat, while his hands moved to brush her bare thighs. 'That meant you were on your own . . .'

'Emilie's here,' Jay gasped.

'Hmmm. Which bedroom are you in?'

'Same as last time.'

'Mind sharing?'

She didn't reply. Simply took his hand and led him up the stairs.

Later, Jay stroked his bare feet with hers. He wore no electronic tag. He'd removed it the instant he'd heard Tom wasn't with her and Emilie any more. The cottage might be safe, but Blake had thought it would be a hundred per cent safer with him around. Jay didn't protest since he was probably right.

'Weren't Turner's men watching your house?' she asked. They were curled together, limbs entwined who-knew-where, her head cradled against the firm pad of his chest. 'Didn't they see you leave?'

'They don't know the area like I do,' he murmured. 'They don't even know I'm gone yet.'

'What about the Discovery? Won't they pick you up when you drive it again?'

'I have more than one set of number plates.'

Like he had several IDs. And several passports and mobile phones. The man sure knew how to slip in and out of life. He was a bit like Batman, crossed with the Invisible Man.

'You'll be in terrible trouble,' she said. 'You've broken your bail. They'll chuck you straight into jail when they find you.'

He tucked her hand in his. Pressed a kiss against her wrist.

'They won't find me.'

They slept tangled together like a pair of meerkats deep in their burrow.

*   *   *

The next morning, after tea, bacon, and scrambled eggs on toast – supplies freshly delivered out of Blake's Discovery – the three of them gathered in the sitting room to form a plan. Outside it was grey, still damp and cold, and Blake crouched by the grate to reset the fire.

'Have we enough evidence for the police to nail Turner?' Jay asked.

Blake shook his head. 'Aside from Emilie's testimony, it's all circumstantial.'

'What about Stephanie Legrand?' asked Jay. 'And Stewart Bradley, the guy who kidnapped me?'

'They don't know Turner is Brown,' Blake said. 'He's covered his tracks.'

'Max is right,' Emilie said.

She'd recovered some colour overnight, and Jay could finally see the resemblance to the happy, carefree woman who'd gone sailing with Blake.

'If I accuse him of being the head of the Garrison, he'll simply deny it, saying he's undercover. He's highly respected. At the top of the pile in MI5. We need something irrefutable to tie him in.'

Jay told them about Brian Keith giving her his private numbers and a possible RV point. 'He may be one of the good guys, but I'm not sure.'

'If he's on our side, he'll be invaluable,' Blake said. He put a couple of logs on top of the kindling and held a match against the newspaper beneath. 'Why don't you ring him? See how the land lies?'

The nearest public phone box, Jay knew, was in the next village, less than half a mile away. 'I'll do that now. I could do with a walk.'

She left Blake talking to Emilie about what she'd overheard in the conference room. He was hoping to turn up something that might give them another lead.

The road was muddy and covered with leaves. Branches stood stark against the gloomy sky. A tractor passed Jay, hauling logs. Then a Land Rover, spilling straw. A collie dog leaned out of the passenger window. It only took her ten minutes before she reached the village, its houses built out of soft red brick. There was a pub and a cooperative shop, opposite which stood the phone box. Jay raised the receiver and pushed in her credit card.

Dialled Brian Keith's mobile number. It was engaged. She
didn't leave a voice message. She walked into the shop, had a
browse. Organic, locally grown vegetables, milk and bread, and
a handful of postcards of trout fishermen standing knee deep
in the river.

She returned to find Keith's number still engaged. She bought
some supplies for the cottage, along with a newspaper, which
she read propped in the phone box while she resolutely rang
the man every three minutes. Finally, he answered. His tone
was cautious. 'Hello?'

'It's me.' She wondered if he'd remember her voice. 'I'm
not sure if you remember. We, er . . . met last month—'

'How could I forget?' he said smoothly. 'Delighted to hear
from you, my darling. You know where to meet? It's on my
card. Eight o'clock tomorrow night convenient for you?'

'Sure.'

'Come alone. I want it just to be the two of us, OK?'

'OK.'

After they'd disconnected, Jay turned the card over and reread
his inscription. *Battle of Britain Monument, Embankment.* Had
Brian Keith guessed she would contact him again? If so, he
was a man who planned well in advance. She tried to recall
his expression when he'd given her his card, but all she could
picture was his alabaster skin and the tightness in his eyes. He
wasn't her idea of an ally, but it was worth exploring.

Returning to the cottage, she found Emilie resting in bed
and Blake making soup from ingredients he'd dug up in
the garden: carrots, butternut squash and onions. Jay put the
kettle on and made tea. Taking a chair at the breakfast table,
she drank while she watched him chop and dice and sweat
the vegetables. She told him about her call to Keith and where
they were to meet.

'I'll drive you,' he said. 'Keep an eye out.'

'Great.'

They spent the rest of the day doing what Jay could only
term pottering. While she finished reading her newspaper by
the fire, Blake fixed things around the cottage. One of the
upstairs window catches needed replacing, and the shower door
had broken off its hinges completely. Curtains needed rehanging,
where they'd been pulled off their runners. A damp patch in
the hall needed seeing to.

Jay watched Blake quietly. Finally, she said, 'Who owns this place?'

He didn't look at her. Simply removed a nail from between his lips. 'I do.'

'Since when?'

He didn't reply.

'Max?'

He glanced across, then away. 'Since the owner died.'

She waited a while, and when he didn't say any more, let him be and went for another walk. She felt discombobulated, uncertain. She hadn't seen Blake in such a domestic light before. She'd had an unrealistic view of him, she supposed, taken from when they first met. He'd been undercover with the mafia in Macedonia back then, hard and uncompromising seemingly in every aspect of his life. But even MI5 officers need time out, she thought, to make love and fix the shelves. They couldn't be heroes every minute of every day.

When she returned, he was in the kitchen replacing a fluorescent light bulb. He turned and gazed at her, his expression intent. He put down the bulb. His gaze didn't waver from hers.

'What?' she said.

In four long strides he crossed the room and slipped his hands around her waist. 'Christ,' he murmured against her hair. 'Jesus Christ.'

She stroked his head. 'Max?'

'Emilie's having a nap.' His gaze turned urgent. 'You want one?'

Just after six p.m. the following day they departed for London, leaving Emilie in the kitchen, making herself an omelette. Blake had decided on using his Discovery, despite the Jag being registered to Goose's brother-in-law.

'The Disco's prepped,' he said. 'Besides, the Jag stands out.'

They arrived early and scouted the area for ten minutes before Blake decided on parking six hundred yards from the monument, between a red Met police van and a white police van with *police dogs* printed on its side.

'I'm a cop too,' he said.

Jay climbed out of the Discovery and pulled her coat close to her throat, trying to keep out the chill. Traffic rushed along the Embankment, a broad four-lane road running alongside the

Thames. The Houses of Parliament were lit soft yellow to her right, and across the river, way past the London Eye, Jay could just make out the distinctive dome of St Paul's Cathedral.

She walked to the monument. She appeared to be alone. She pretended to study the bronze aviator scrambling for his Spitfire, sculpted in relief to make the figure look as though he was about to run right past her. The bronze included observers, mechanics and riggers, women engineers; every aspect of the RAF was depicted.

She heard footsteps approaching. Immediately, she turned and recognized the slender and androgynous form, the ghostly white skin. He looked like a vampire looming in the dark, and she had to force herself not to take a step back.

'Mr Keith,' she greeted him. She didn't hold out her hand.

'Brian, please. If I may call you Jay?' He didn't offer to shake either.

'Sure, Brian.'

He glanced around briefly before gliding alongside the monument and coming to pause beside an engraved list honouring men and women who had died in the war. Jay moved with him, and immediately lost sight of Blake in the Discovery. She wondered if Brian Keith had pegged Blake. Whether he had or not, where they now stood made it far more difficult for them to be seen from the road.

'Why are we here, Jay?' Keith asked.

She took in the way he stood, wary as a cat, his eyes constantly moving, flicking past her and over the wharf, the public benches along the pavement.

She said, 'Why did you meet me last month, and not Nick?'

He considered her question for so long she thought he wasn't going to answer, but then he said, 'Mr Morgan was an unknown quantity.'

'And me?'

'You're known to be a friend of Max Blake's.'

'That makes you trust me?'

His eyes met hers, and stilled for a moment. 'I don't trust anyone.'

'I see,' she said. 'Why did you give me your card?'

'Why do you think?'

Jay glanced aside briefly. Lights twinkled and swam in the darkness of the river, which looked as black as coal.

She said, 'You know about the Garrison.'

His eyes narrowed into slits, but he gave a nod.

'Do you know who runs it?' she asked.

His alabaster skin seemed to tighten across the bones in his face. 'Even if I did, I would never admit it.'

'What if I was prepared to speak out?'

'Then I would suggest you hide somewhere very safe, for a very long time immediately afterwards. Preferably until you died of old age and with another name.'

His remark confirmed to Jay that he knew how deadly the Garrison was. What she had to do now was find out on which side of the fence Keith stood. Was he a stooge of Turner's, wanting to find out where Emilie was and what her plans were? Or was he a desperate employee who knew what was going on with the Garrison and needed help to stop it?

Jay walked to stand by a street lamp that had two iron dolphins wrapped around its base. She couldn't think of anything clever to say. No way to trap him into revealing himself. She decided to be direct. 'I need to know which side you're on before I decide what we do next.'

His gaze strengthened. 'If you don't know which side I'm on, then what are you doing here?'

'You could be trying to get information on where a certain someone is.'

'Ah. I see.' He glanced past her, into the inky black of the Thames. 'Then there's only one thing for it, isn't there?'

Jay watched the side of his face, the tension in his muscles.

When he spoke, his voice was so soft that she thought he was whispering to himself. 'I'll have to trust you.'

With a swift movement, he brought up his hand and pushed it inside his overcoat, reaching into one of his inner pockets. As he made to bring out his hand, a man spoke from behind him. He said, 'Don't move.'

Keith went so white that, for a moment, Jay thought he was going to faint. He was staring past her, his eyes bulging like a petrified rabbit's.

'Bring your hand out, slowly,' Blake commanded Keith. 'No sudden moves.'

Keith inched his hand into the open air. He showed Jay what he was holding: a bunch of three keys on a simple brass ring. One Chubb, one Yale, and another that could belong to an alarm.

'I brought . . . for you,' he said. He was swallowing reflexively and looked as though he might be sick.

'Whose are they?' Jay asked.

'Who is behind me?' He closed his fingers around the keys and raised his arm, making to throw them into the river.

When Blake stepped into view, Keith's shoulders slumped in relief. He swayed slightly as he ran a hand over his face saying, 'Christ, you have no idea . . . Thank God. Officer Blake . . .'

Blake put out the flat of his hand. Keith dropped the keys into his palm. Keith's hands, Jay saw, were shaking. Blake gave Keith a look.

'If you get caught,' Keith said, voice trembling, 'you get rid of them. You don't tell anyone where you got them.'

'Agreed,' said Blake. 'Address?'

Keith carefully brought out a pen and wrote something on the inside of his wrist. Jay leaned forward to see it was an address in Buckinghamshire – *Royal Burston Farm, Aston Abbots* – followed by a four digit number, 1491. 'The alarm code,' he said.

When Blake read the address, he stilled.

Keith said, 'He changes the alarm code each week.'

'Yes.' Then, 'Thanks.'

Keith licked his forefinger, wet his skin, and scrubbed it clear of ink marks. 'Goodbye,' he said. He looked at them each in turn. 'You won't see me again.'

They watched Brian Keith walk away, his footsteps quick and light.

When Jay suggested they follow him, Blake put a hand on her arm. 'Let him go,' he said.

THIRTY-THREE

Sofie put down her fork in order to read a text message that had just come through. Her mum had been in a filthy mood ever since they'd got home. Supper was late, and she'd bitched non-stop. She obviously didn't want Tom there and was making her feelings clear.

'Everything had better be back to normal tomorrow,' her

mum said. Her tone was low and angry. 'I've got better things
to do than sit at home with Sofie all day.'

'I'll stay with her,' said Tom. 'Or she could come to the
police station with me. She'll be as safe as houses there.'

'Like that makes everything better. I can't believe this is
happening.' Her mum flung up her hands. 'I knew it was a mistake
contacting you. If it hadn't been for Sofie falling ill . . .'

Tom pushed away his plate. 'I'm sorry I'm making life difficult for you. But Sofie's safety is my priority and—'

'You're nothing but trouble.'

Tom had insisted on staying overnight in case that guy showed
up again. The guy who'd watched her take delivery of Jay's
package that day. She'd spotted him after school, hanging
around, and when she'd told Tom, he'd freaked and pulled her
out of school. *For protection against a possible threat.* Which
was brilliant – her classmates were agog. Her email had been
flooded, and she hadn't had a single nasty text from anyone.
Just messages dying to know what was happening, if she was
OK. No one had mentioned her weight.

She hoped Jay was all right. When she'd asked, Tom had
gone tight-lipped and anxious. Not that he meant her to know
he was worried, but she could tell. She couldn't believe she'd
been so horrible to Jay. And she couldn't believe she'd wanted
her mum and Tom to get married. Having seen them together
this evening, she knew it would never work.

She wondered if Jay and Tom would take her to Disneyland.
Even Disneyland Paris would be awesome . . . She clicked *view
message* on her phone to see the text was from Jaz, asking if
she was OK. Grinning, she began to text back.

'Sofie!'

Her mum was glaring.

'I've told you before not to text at the table.'

'OK, OK.' She pushed her phone aside.

'Pass it over.' Her mum held out her hand.

Sofie quickly grabbed the phone and shoved it into her Ugg
boot.

'It's gone, OK?' She held up both hands.

'And what about the lessons she'll miss?' Her mum rounded
on Tom. She was off again. 'How is she supposed to catch up
on such basic learning? Education is all about building a strong
foundation . . .'

Sofie rolled her eyes. Anyone would think World War Three had broken out the way she was carrying on. Fed up with listening to her mum's diatribe, Sofie pushed away her plate and said, 'Please, may I leave the table?'

'Not until you finish your vegetables.'

Sofie knew better than to argue and shovelled down the peas and carrots as fast as she could. 'Finished,' she announced and bounded to her feet. She felt her phone vibrate against her ankle as another text came in, but she didn't risk bringing out her phone. Thank God she'd put it on Silent. She didn't trust her mum not to confiscate it.

'Put your plate in the dishwasher . . .'

Sofie obediently went to the kitchen and shoved her cutlery and plate into the machine. She was about to head for the peace of her room when she heard a scratching sound outside.

Smokey the cat, wanting to come in.

Sofie went to the back door and undid the latch, opened it, but the cat was nowhere to be seen.

'Smokey!' she called.

Tom had warned her not to go outside, so she hesitated on the doorstep. At the far end of the yard, she saw a slinky black shape emerge and then sit watching her, tail flicking.

'Come on, Smokey . . .'

The cat didn't move.

Sophie looked around. Everything was quiet. No tawny owls calling to one another. No foxes barking. There wasn't a breath of wind.

Wanting his furry company with her in her bedroom, Sofie began to walk to collect the cat. Her phone rubbed against her ankle, and as she bent down to retrieve it, she heard footsteps rushing towards her.

Startled, she looked around, but it was too late.

The man was upon her before she could move.

One hand went over her mouth. An arm clamped around her ribs.

He heaved her into the air.

She screamed, but the sound was muffled. Legs kicking, she tried to wriggle free, but he held her in an iron grip. He began to jog across the yard.

Panic set in, and she put all her effort into freeing herself. His grip intensified.

Mummy! Tom!

He rounded the stables and increased his pace. Sofie continued to scream, but no sound escaped. She tried to bite his hand, but couldn't get a grip. He was running down the drive, Sofie bouncing against his hip. He was panting.

A sob ripped through her chest.

Help me, help me!

The man raced through the gates. Ran for a car parked up the road. As they approached, the engine started. A pair of headlights were switched on. A woman slipped from the driver's seat and jogged towards them.

No! Please, no!

It was the same woman who'd delivered Jay's envelope.

The instant the woman neared, the man took away his hand from Sofie's mouth, but before she could take a breath to scream, the woman rammed a cloth over her mouth and nose. Sofie sucked in some air, but it tasted funny, sickeningly sweet . . .

Then she didn't know any more.

THIRTY-FOUR

B lake started the Discovery and pulled out between a small van and a black cab.

Jay said, 'Do you know whose address it is?'

'Yup.'

'Max! Come on!'

'It's Turner's address in the country.'

For a moment she was silent. No wonder Brian Keith had been petrified, she thought. Turner would eat Keith's entrails if he discovered his assistant was betraying him.

'I've been there,' he said. 'Went for Christmas drinks last year. Nice place all up.'

Instead of crossing the river and heading south-east as she expected, towards the safe house, he pointed the car north.

'Where are we going?'

'Turner's place.'

She turned to stare at the side of his face. 'What?'

'I haven't been cat-burgling in a while.' His teeth gleamed

briefly in an oncoming car's headlights. 'You can be my lookout. I quite fancy checking out his laptop. Bet it's got loads of stuff we can have fun with. Might even have details of the research centre.'

'No way! What if he's at home?'

'He stays in London during the week, Monday through to Friday. The farm is his weekender.'

'What about his wife? He has a wife, doesn't he? He looks as though he does. And what about dogs? Every farm has dogs. Usually big ones with lots of teeth . . .' Jay trailed off. She wished she could have prepared. She wasn't even wearing black. Or a pair of running shoes.

'Why the rush?' she asked. She hated doing anything – especially something potentially dangerous – unprepared.

'Because if they pick up Brian Keith, they'll be on to us in a flash.'

Jay shuddered. 'Let's hope they don't pick him up.'

'Plus, it's Thursday today. Turner will probably be at the farm tomorrow. My guess is that he changes the code on Sunday night. It's tonight or never.'

Jay shifted on her seat. Despite his logic, once again she felt railroaded. What had Emilie said? *How you put up with him on a mission, I don't know. Bossy as hell, never listens. Just orders you around.*

She turned her head to look at him once again. 'When did you last go cat-burgling?'

'When I picked the locks of your house to install some listening devices.'

It had been just before they'd met, she remembered, eighteen months ago. She said, 'That was a while back.' Her tone was sceptical.

'Yup.' He made a small circling motion above his head. 'Can't you see what you've done to me? You've given me a halo.'

Blake's halo wasn't anywhere to be seen when he parked his Discovery out of sight behind a Dutch barn. Hidden in the rear panels of the car were two weapons: a standard police-issue Glock and a Beretta. He passed Jay the Glock and a handful of ammunition, and although she didn't want to take the gun – she hadn't fired a handgun in four years – she knew she'd only regret it if the chips were down.

She was glad he'd given her the Glock, which made her more comfortable with its automatic safety mechanism. She could throw the thing over a wall, drop it from a mountain top, and it wouldn't go off. It would only fire when she pulled the trigger, and immediately afterwards the safety would automatically re-engage.

Blake strapped a hunting knife to his ankle. Pushed more ammo into his pockets, along with a length of fine wire, a torch, and two pairs of slim-fitting latex gloves. He passed Jay a black flak jacket. It was way too big, coming down to her knees, but it would help camouflage her and, since she was on lookout duty, keep her warm. He tucked a small metal disc into each of their inner pockets.

'Tracking device,' he said. 'In case we get separated and things turn nasty. I want to be able to find you fast.'

'How do I track you?'

'You switch on the laptop.' He showed her a neat little Sony tucked in the rear seat pocket and told her the password and which icon to access. 'A map will come up straight away, showing both our positions. If we're miles apart, it will flip between the two.'

'Did you know we would be on a mission tonight?' He seemed remarkably prepared.

'I prepped the Disco with Tash two weeks ago.'

When he'd been released on bail. Talk about a man who liked to be ahead of the game.

He blacked out both their faces. His touch was firm and warm and all business. Then he locked the car, stowing the key in a magnetic strip near the chassis. Jay's mouth was dry, her nerves hopping and jumping. Glock in hand, Jay followed Blake around the side of the Dutch barn. A clear sky filled with stars lit the scene into pale greys and blacks. She could see a handsome Tudor farmhouse ahead, the stripes of its beams stark against the plasterwork. There was a duck pond to the left, and two thatched barns flanked the gravel drive. She couldn't see any vehicles, and the house was dark. She prayed nobody was home.

'Where do you want me?' she whispered.

'Stand on the corner,' he murmured, pointing at one of the barns. 'Where I can see you from the front of the house. You'll be hard to spot by anyone who doesn't know you're there. Stay in that position if all's OK, but if you move out of sight, I'll know something's up. If nothing occurs, I'll meet you back at the car in an hour. If things blow up, I'll see you at the safe house.'

He melted into the darkness ahead of her, his boots crunching softly on the loose stones, and she followed close behind. When they came to the edge of the barn, he held out a palm and she stopped. He pointed at a window set in the barn wall. They both had a look to see it had a concrete floor, stained with what could have been a couple of oil marks. A garage. Thank God it was empty.

Blake gave her the thumbs up. She did the same.

With her back against the barn wall, she watched his figure slip across the drive to the front door. Within seconds, he was inside, the door shut silently behind him. Pulse humming, she listened for the alarm – had Keith given Blake the right number? – but all remained quiet. She prayed the house was empty, and that he'd come out safely.

Jay was still praying to a God she wasn't sure existed when a light showed in the farmhouse. Second floor, third window from the right, it glowed briefly behind a pair of curtains.

Was it Blake's torch?

Breathing shallow, Jay watched, but no figure appeared.

The light went out.

The minutes ticked past. Ten, twenty.

Jay stood quietly and waited. She could smell wet leaves and the faintest hint of creosote oozing from the barn wall. One day, she'd quite like to live in the country. Have a dog, a cat, and a big garden where the kids could play. Trees they could climb. She wondered if Blake wanted children. Whether he ever thought about settling down . . .

At that moment, she heard the distinctive sound of gravel crunching. It sounded as though it had come from the other side of the barn. It hadn't been close, but it wasn't far away either. She would never have heard it if the night hadn't been so still.

All her senses came alert. She held her breath. Let it out slowly, silently. Held it again to hear another scrape of gravel.

Someone, or something, was moving around.

Could it be a wild animal? A deer, or perhaps a badger? They were big animals and could easily sound as large as a human.

She hesitated before she moved, surveying her options.

Check it out.

With the Glock held in readiness in both hands, she crept

around the barn wall. Peeked around the corner. Nothing. As soundlessly as she could, her boots now squelching mud, she scouted the area, past an old plough and a rusting tractor with spikes on its metal wheels. Another two tractors stood behind the relics, and behind them stood a car.

Her breathing shallowed when she saw the gleaming black Mercedes: a big sedan. Was it the same car she'd shared with Turner in London? She didn't like the fact a car was there. Was Turner around? If so, why wasn't his car parked in the garage? Why out here, in the mud? Something was wrong. Every instinct screamed at her to get out. She decided not to return to her position by the barn. She wanted Blake out of there too.

Gun held in readiness, Jay hastened back to the Discovery. Blake would join her the moment he saw she'd moved from her post. Cautiously, she checked the area around Blake's vehicle. As she approached, a scurrying sound alerted her that she'd startled a small animal, maybe a rat. The Discovery was as they'd left it. Jay paused briefly, but nothing moved. The night was silent. She reached beneath the chassis and plucked free the key.

Before she could open the car, a sharp pain in the back of her neck made her flinch. She immediately swung round, the Glock searching for a target, but there was nobody she could see. She put up her hand to feel something small and hard just below her hairline, and she was about to pull it out when everything began to lose focus, and she reeled, toppling sideways on to the ground.

Jay came round to find she was lying on her side, her wrists bound with baler twine and tied to the Discovery's front bumper. A yard away sprawled the form of Blake. He appeared to be unconscious.

Her head was muzzy and thick, her mouth dry; after-effects from what she guessed had been a tranquillizer dart. She hoped she hadn't received the same quantity of the drug as Blake, who was much bigger, or it might take her hours to get moving. She twisted her head from side to side, searching the area. All was still, quiet.

'Max,' she hissed. She scrabbled round and reached out a foot. Prodded him. He didn't move. She prodded him again. 'Wake up, Max.'

'Ah,' a voice said. 'You're awake, Jay.'

She jerked around to see Jim Turner step into view. He wore corduroys tucked into long leather boots and a thick tweed coat. In his right hand, he held a tranquillizer gun.

He said, 'You can explain things to Blake, when he wakes.'

Her vision of him was blurred, and she shook her head to try and clear it, but it had little effect.

'I'm sorry the dose was a bit strong,' he went on smoothly. 'But I couldn't risk not knocking Blake out.'

'What are you going to do with us?' Fear edged her voice.

'Oh, don't worry. The last thing we need is your dead bodies to be found and cause a witch hunt. Much better to have you alive and frustrated in your efforts to get a handle on the Garrison. Which will be impossible once I disappear.'

Jay ran her tongue dryly over her lips. She said, 'How did you know we were coming here?'

He gave a chuckle. 'Brian Keith, who else? I've kept an eye on him ever since he saw you at Thames House. I couldn't be sure how much he knew, but the fact he met you without me that day had my alarm bells ringing. And then you kindly dropped your handbag, the day Nahid came for you. I had a little look. I saw he'd given you his private numbers. He wouldn't have done that without an ulterior motive.

'He's been a cunning little spook, leaving no evidence that he might betray me. When you met this evening, for instance, he didn't speak my address aloud – we were listening in, of course – and immediately afterwards he vanished. We still don't know where he is.'

Jay licked her lips. Clever Brian Keith.

'We followed you instead, you see.'

Jay was sure Blake would have seen a tail, especially at night, and said so.

'You didn't look for a helicopter, though,' said Turner. 'Did you?'

Automatically, Jay glanced into the sky.

'Oh, it's long gone now that it's no longer needed. The wonders of modern science.' Another chuckle. 'You never knew it was there. That's why it's called the Stealth Helicopter. The moment you turned on to the A421, I knew you were headed to my farm. So I put my car out of sight and made sure the floodlights were switched off. You thought nobody was home, didn't you?'

He sounded so smug, Jay longed to slap him.

'All I have to do now is disappear. When I vanish, everyone will assume the Garrison has had me assassinated as payback for spying on them. The only people who know the truth are inconsequential.'

'You call a DI inconsequential?' Jay tested her bonds and, as she did so, noticed that some energy was returning to her limbs. 'Too many people know what's been going on. There's Ruth Wayland and Colonel Greene. My housemates . . .'

'It's all hearsay. There's not a shred of evidence.'

'And Emilie? Blake's sister?'

'The same,' he sneered. 'It's her word against the establishment.'

'But with so many people singing from the same hymn sheet, don't you think others might start singing too?'

'I won't be around to witness it.' He gave a dismissive shrug. 'I'll be living miles from here. Still directing the Garrison, of course. I'm not giving it up just when it's gaining real strength. Now, if you'll excuse me, I have some last-minute packing to attend to.'

Jay watched him walk away. As soon as he was out of sight, she tried to work her hands free from the baler twine, but it was tied tightly, the knots secure. Once again, she prodded and poked Blake's unmoving form.

'Max! For God's sake, wake up!'

Nothing.

Jay continued to try and wake him to no effect. She glanced at her watch. Nearly ten o'clock.

She kept working on her bonds, occasionally prodding Blake. She'd always been determined, stubborn, and sometimes it paid off, but not tonight. Blake remained firmly out of it, and her wrists remained firmly tied.

Twenty minutes later, she heard the crunching of tyres on gravel, then the smooth purr of the Mercedes' engine. Turner climbed out of his car. He left the engine running. He came over to Jay. He said, 'I don't want you and Blake trying to follow me. Here's a little disincentive for you.'

He held a mobile phone to her ear.

'Hello?' Jay said.

'Jay?' The voice was hoarse.

Jay's heart went cold. She said, 'Sofie?'

'I'm so scared . . .'

The girl's voice faded.

'Sofie?'

'I don't know where I am.' She started to cry. 'They grabbed me from Mum's. I'm in a car and . . .'

Her voice vanished.

'Sofie!' Jay yelled.

Turner snatched the phone away. Said, 'Everything's going as planned?'

All went quiet while he listened. 'Good. Now, I want you to speak to Jay McCaulay, so that she knows who's looking after sweet little Sofie.'

Turner placed the phone back beside Jay's ear. She remained silent until a soft female voice said, 'Jay?'

Jay closed her eyes. 'Nahid,' she said.

'Yes.'

In the same calm tone, Jay said, 'If you harm a hair of Sofie's head, rest assured that I will hunt you and your family down and—'

'Enough.' Turner whipped the phone aside. 'Nahid, darling,' he said. 'Just to reiterate. If you don't hear from your sister confirming I have arrived safely by midday tomorrow, you will kill the child and dump the body where it will never be found.' Without another word, he hung up.

'What?' The blood left Jay's head. 'I thought you weren't going to hurt us!'

'The girl is an insurance policy. Nahid's sister is waiting for me. She will tell Nahid whether I arrive safely or not. If anything goes wrong – like you and Blake preventing me from getting airborne – the girl will die. If I arrive safely, Nahid will let the girl go. The real catch here, Jay . . . You are listening, aren't you?'

She nodded desperately.

'The catch is that I can't call Nahid off. She will only release little Sofie when she hears from her sister. Do you understand?'

Horror flooded every cell. 'But what if your airplane crashes? Or something else happens that's not our fault?'

'She'll become a casualty of the situation.'

'But she's only twelve!' Jay was shouting. 'She's just a little girl!'

'Goodbye, Jay,' he said. He pocketed the mobile phone and turned towards his car.

'What about her father? DI Sutton?' She was almost gasping.
'Where's Tom?'

'Oh, he's safe and sound with Sofie's mother. They've already
rung the police, but it's too late. Nahid and Tivon are long
gone. Now, I need to release you both. It won't do to have you
both tied up when the local plods arrive. I want Max Blake
back in jail, you see. Where he belongs.'

Jay's hopes leaped briefly, until he went to his car and
returned with the tranquillizer gun. He raised it to his shoulder
and pointed it at her.

'No,' she said. She tried to wriggle beneath the car, get some
cover, but it was no good. She was in full view and helpless.
'Please.'

He pulled the trigger.

As the world turned soft, distorted, she heard him calling
the police.

'I have intruders at my farm. Please, come quickly.'

THIRTY-FIVE

Jay blinked several times. She was in a bed. Her head ached,
and she felt terribly thirsty. She tried to work out where she
was. The walls were pale green, the floors a dull grey
linoleum. Her gaze lengthened to take in the flimsy looking
curtain surrounding her bed. The sounds of beeping. Soft shoes
shuffling. Muted voices.

She was wearing nothing but a pale-pink robe that gaped at
the back.

She was in hospital.

Carefully, she levered herself upright. Her vision wavered.
She swung her legs over the bed, let her body adjust to the
movement. She felt slightly nauseous and off-balance, but
nothing too serious. She wondered how long she'd been
unconscious, and as her mind began to function more clearly,
everything came flooding back.

Sofie.

She had to find out what was happening. Find Blake.

As she slid off the bed, she spotted the black jacket Blake

had loaned her, set to one side on the floor, along with her boots. Her jeans were neatly folded on top of a bulging carrier bag. Jay had a quick look through to find everything was there, except her handbag.

As quickly as she could, she dressed and pulled on her boots. She felt shivery and weak and wondered how long a double dose of tranquillizers would take to disperse from her body. She'd heard somewhere that a simple anaesthetic for a minor operation took two weeks and hoped it wouldn't be that long.

Cautiously, she pulled back the curtain. She was in a huge horseshoe-shaped ward with beds and machines lining the walls. A nurse's station was set at the bottom of the horseshoe. A&E. Where? Which hospital? Some beds were curtained, like hers had been, but others were in full view. She couldn't see Blake anywhere.

Jay walked to the nurse's station. There were three nurses and they were all on the phone. She glanced at the clock set on the far wall. One a.m.

A male nurse, in his twenties, hung up the phone. Although she moved to stand directly in front of him, he didn't look up, but continued scribbling on a form.

'Excuse me . . .'

'Yes?' He still didn't look at her.

'I was brought here this evening, probably along with a male friend of mine. Where is he?'

The man finally looked up. Glanced across to her bed – empty – and back. He rose to his feet. She took in the white plastic badge on his smock: Dr Stachiewicz.

'You need to go back to bed,' Stachiewicz said. 'We need to check you over.'

'Where's my friend? He's six two. Dark hair. Very fit . . .'

He frowned. 'I don't remember anyone like that being brought in. You came in alone, sorry.'

'Which hospital is this?'

'Stoke Mandeville, Aylesbury.'

Aylesbury was the nearest major town to Turner's farm and, at this time of night, less than an hour's drive to the West End of London.

'Who brought me in?'

'The police . . .'

At that moment he looked aside. His expression stiffened. Jay switched her gaze to see two sharp-eyed young men in suits approaching. They introduced themselves to Jay. The taller, who had sandy hair and pale skin, was Damien Rose, his side-kick Michael Dunn. Both were government agents. Rose was holding Jay's handbag. She put out her hand, and he passed it over. She had a quick look. All her credit cards, cash, and her mobile phone appeared to be there.

'We found you unconscious at Royal Burston Farm,' Rose said. 'What were you doing there? It belongs to a high-security govern-ment official, who has since vanished. We need to know—'

'I'm sorry,' Dr Stachiewicz interjected, 'but before you begin your questions, I need to check the patient over.'

'We're here on government business,' snapped Rose.

'So you've already said,' the doctor said stiffly. He glanced at Jay. 'It was the police who found you and arranged to have you brought in.'

'Then they contacted us,' Dunn chipped in. 'And we want to know what an employee of TRACE was doing—'

'Stop there,' Stachiewicz said. His cheeks began to flush. 'I appreciate you have a job to do, but so do I.'

Rose raised his hands in a placating gesture. 'Just make it quick, would you?'

As Doctor Stachiewicz ushered Jay back to her bed, the agents followed. The doctor pulled back the curtain and gestured for Jay to sit on the bed. He raised his stethoscope. He said, 'What happened to make you lose consciousness? You were out for a long time.'

'I was tranquillized with a dart gun.'

He gave her a startled look. 'That's a first.'

'Could you take some blood to confirm this is what happened?'

'Sure. I'll do that in a moment.'

He checked her blood pressure, her heart, her breathing, and her nerve responses. 'You're looking pretty good to me.' He shone a light into her eyes. 'Excellent,' he murmured. 'You're free to go.'

'Blood test?' she prompted.

'Oh, yes. Back in a tic.'

He slipped through the curtains.

While she waited, Jay checked her mobile phone to see she

had six messages. One was from her mother, one from her housemates. The next three were from Tom, his voice frantic. Sofie had vanished from Heather's. He'd alerted the police, Special Branch.

'Call me, Jay. *Now*.'

Breathing tight, Jay listened to the last message, which was from Blake.

Gone after Turner. Sit tight, hon. I'll have him before breakfast.

Dread flooded her. Blake didn't know that Sofie was in danger. That if Turner didn't arrive safely at his destination, Nahid would kill her. Jay immediately dialled his number.

The second it connected, she heard it ringing in time with another phone nearby. Both ringing tones stopped simultaneously when Blake's messaging service kicked in. Jay peeked through the curtain to see Dunn was holding an iPhone.

Dear God. Was it Blake's?

Jay disconnected and tried his number again.

At precisely the same moment her phone connected with Blake's, the phone in Dunn's hand began ringing. Jay ducked back and hung up.

If anything goes wrong – like you and Blake preventing me from getting airborne – the girl will die.

She checked her incoming calls. The number Blake had called her on was listed as *number withheld*. Suddenly, she felt like weeping. How was she going to stop Blake? She couldn't. Not unless he rang again.

She had to find Sofie.

She peeked outside again to see Dunn was still prodding Blake's phone. Dr Stachiewicz muscled the officer aside. He was holding a syringe and kidney bowl. 'Blood test,' he said.

Dunn stepped back. Obviously frustrated, he shook the phone at Rose, 'We'll never break the fucking pass-code.'

'You really think it belongs to Turner's kidnapper?' Rose asked.

'That's what the police reckon. They'd already patted him down and taken away his phone and weapons before he came round.'

'What a mess,' Rose said.

'They said he was like a fucking lunatic.'

'Yeah, I know. Can't blame them for letting him go.'

Jay gazed at the curtains while the doctor drew blood. 'All done.' He stuck a plaster on the inside of her elbow.

'Thanks.'

'I have to let the officers know you're OK,' he told her in an undertone. He looked oddly uncomfortable.

She gave a tired smile. 'I understand.'

'TRACE looks like a decent organization,' he remarked.

Jay looked at him in surprise.

'I googled it when the agents mentioned it. I was curious.'

'It also gets me into a lot of trouble,' she said.

'So I read.' He smiled.

'Let me know the results of the blood test.' She gave him one of her cards, which showed her mobile number.

'Of course.' He pocketed the card. 'I'll ring you myself. I'm curious to know what was used.'

No sooner than the doctor swept back the curtain and said, 'She's all yours,' than the agents swooped and hustled her out of the ward and into the corridor.

Rose made an ushering motion in front of him. 'Our car's outside,' he said. 'We'll take you wherever you want to go.'

Like hell you will, she thought.

'One minute,' she said. 'I need the Ladies' first.'

He glanced at Dunn, who gave a nod.

Jay scooted back inside the ward. Three nurses were busy at their station. None of them looked up as she passed. As she walked, she checked who was watching her. Most patients were asleep. She changed direction. Ducked behind a patient's curtains. An elderly man lay asleep, mouth open. He was snoring softly. Jay scurried to the curtain, peeked outside to see the agents were waiting at the corridor entrance. She checked her watch. One twenty a.m.

At one thirty, Rose walked into A&E and spoke to one of the nurses. The nurse looked at her watch, shook her head. Rose's face heated. The nurse rolled her eyes, got to her feet, and walked to the toilets, disappeared inside. Three seconds later she reappeared, shaking her head.

For a second, Rose and Dunn stood in disbelief. Then they bolted for the toilets to check for themselves. The instant they vanished inside, Jay slipped from behind the curtain and legged it across A&E. She was barely halfway across the room when Rose shouted, 'Stop!'

Jay lengthened her stride and hit the corridor at full speed. She ran past two male nurses and dived right down the next corridor. She could hear Rose and Dunn's footsteps hammering in pursuit. She tried the first door she came to, but it was locked. She tried the next, which opened. She dived inside, closed it behind her. It was dark, but she didn't turn on the lights. She waited until the agents' footsteps pounded past before she slipped outside and headed in the opposite direction. She didn't run. She didn't want to draw attention to herself.

At each corridor junction, Jay paused and peered cautiously around the corner before committing herself. The hospital was quiet. Few people moved around. She followed signs for the staff car park. She didn't think the agents would have parked there. They would have parked out the front. After five minutes, she came to an automatic door and stepped outside. She walked to the staff car park. In the shadows, she dialled directory enquiries and asked for a local taxi firm.

'My car won't start,' she told the dispatch office.

'You poor creature.' The woman was sympathetic. 'I'll have a driver with you in under ten minutes. He knows where the staff car park is.'

While she waited, Jay kept an eye out for the agents, praying they hadn't called the local cops for backup, but nobody appeared. The taxi arrived in seven minutes, driven by a man who had to be at least twenty stone.

'Where to, love?'

For a moment, Jay couldn't think. Then she said, 'Bristol.'

THIRTY-SIX

When Jay arrived, Heather's house was ablaze with light. Wall-to-wall cop cars. Searchlights everywhere. Heather was sitting on the sofa, chalk white. A female police constable sat next to her.

Jay went to Tom, who was obsessively checking his mobile phone. 'She had her phone with her,' he said. 'She stuck it in her Ugg boot. Why doesn't she answer? I keep ringing . . .'

Jay didn't say the kidnappers had probably found it.

'She went outside. That bloody cat . . . I told her not to. *I told her not to go outside.*' His voice shook.

'Have the police put a trace on her phone?'

'Of course.'

Jay had to pray Sofie's phone was on, and that a member of the Garrison wasn't sabotaging the process.

'Tom,' she said. 'We need to talk. A lot's happened tonight . . .'

He turned a blank gaze on to her.

'Blake's gone after Turner.'

She spoke hurriedly, in an undertone. 'Nahid will only release Sofie if she hears from her sister that Turner has arrived safely at his destination. She can't be called off.' Jay swallowed. 'Blake's gone after him, but he's off the radar. He doesn't have his phone. I can't contact him.'

'Blake . . .' His tone was strangled. If Blake was with them, she knew Tom would have torn him limb from limb.

'We have to find Sofie,' said Jay. 'Before Blake finds Turner.'

'How, Jay?' His gaze turned cold. 'How do we find Sofie?'

She swallowed. 'Keep ringing her.' She couldn't think of anything else. She moved away. She spoke to the cops, and to a hostage negotiator. She was interrogated by Tom's colleague Mac. She made and drank endless cups of tea. The minutes crept past.

Jay paced, unable to sit still. Praying for Blake to ring.

Praying for a miracle.

THIRTY-SEVEN

Sofie's consciousness crawled to the surface to hear a soft, female voice.

'She's still asleep.'

Out of nowhere, Sofie heard Jay's voice. *I played dead so they'd leave me alone.*

She mustn't let the woman know she was awake. She mustn't move an inch.

'I want her to wake up. I want to play.'

'It's my turn to go first,' he protested. 'Come on, Nahid. You promised.'

'Why don't we share her this time, Tivon?' Nahid said. 'Like we did with Stein's daughter?'

Please! Oh, God, don't hurt me!

Tivon said, 'Let's check on her in an hour.'

'We don't have to release her, do we?' the woman purred. 'Turner will never know. She could just . . . disappear.'

'I suppose she could.' The man's tone turned musing. 'We could keep her here for days . . . weeks.'

'I knew you'd come round.' The woman's voice was smiling. 'Come. I want to fuck. Right here, right now.'

God, don't move. Be still, still.

The sound of clothes rustling as the woman moved away.

'Ahhh.' The woman sighed. 'You're already hard, Tivon. Was that because you were thinking of what you wanted to do to little Sofie here?'

'Yes,' he whispered.

The chinking of a belt. More soft rustles.

'Bend over,' he rasped. 'On your knees.'

Quiet, quiet!

'Christ,' he said. 'You're wet. You bitch. You fucking . . . bitch . . .'

Wet sucking, slapping noises.

A sob surged up Sofie's throat. Desperately, she swallowed it.

'Harder!' the woman commanded. 'Fuck me harder! Fuck me like you're going to fuck sweet little Sofie!'

More repulsive sounds.

'Fuck . . . fuck . . .' Nahid was gasping.

Sofie felt nausea rise. Her body trembled.

'Sofie . . .' he moaned. 'Sweet . . . little . . . Uggggh . . .'

Silence.

The chink of a belt. Rustling of clothes.

Then the sound of their footsteps. A door being shut. A lock being turned.

Please God, they've gone.

Cautiously, she opened her eyes a crack.

She was alone.

She had plastic cuffs on. She was chained to the wall. No light showed through the dirty window. It was still night.

Sofie struggled to loosen her bindings. The plastic cut into her wrists. She tested the chain and the link, the padlock. She couldn't free herself.

Tremors rocked her.

And then she remembered her mobile phone. That she'd shoved it in her Ugg boot to prevent her mum from taking it.

With trembling fingers, she brought it out. Saw she had over a dozen calls, countless texts. They were all from her parents.

Fear and hope fired through her veins.

She dialled Tom's number. He was a cop. He'd save her.

There was a click, then a woman's voice intoned, *Le numéro que vous avez appeléz est faux.*

Sofie tried again.

Then she tried her mum's phone. Her grandfather's. Her school friends. But the same voice came on the line.

Le numéro que vous avez appeléz est faux.

THIRTY-EIGHT

Three a.m. and Jay prowled around the kitchen. She'd washed out all the mugs, cleaned the sugar and milk spilled, wiped down all the work surfaces. She wanted to do something, but couldn't think what. The police had the phones tapped in case Nahid or Turner rang. A hostage negotiator was standing by.

At that moment, Tom paced into the kitchen. Like Jay, he couldn't keep still. His eyes were rimmed red and held a haunted, desperate look she hoped she'd never see again. She watched him try Sofie's number for what had to be the hundredth time. Halfway across the kitchen, he stopped dead. He stood as though electrified.

He said, 'Sofie?'

Goosebumps flashed over Jay's skin. *Sofie was on the line?*

'Oh my God,' he said. 'Sofie, are you all right? Where are you? Please, God . . .'

Jay raced to his side.

'It's OK, sweetheart. Take a breath . . . Yes, I'm here. I'm not going anywhere. I promise . . .' He gripped the back of a kitchen chair with his other hand as though to stop himself falling. 'I'm here, sweetheart.'

Jay could hear the tinny sound of Sofie's hysterical voice, her sobs.

'Sofie, darling. Breathe,' Tom told her. '*Breathe.*'

More sobs.

'It's OK, sweetheart . . .' Tom continued to soothe the girl until finally the sobs began to lessen.

'Sofie, we need to know where you are, so we can come and get you . . . What? In *French*? . . . You have to dial the country code . . . Yes, that's right. You dial double zero for an international line, then four-four for England, then my number, but without the zero in front . . . Yes, that's right . . . Now, I need you to be really grown up and focus. Tell me where you are.'

Jay's skin bristled as Tom told his daughter how to dial from overseas. Nahid had taken Sofie abroad?

'You're in an empty room. It's cold . . . Brick walls and floor . . .'

Jay leaned close. Tom turned the phone so they could both listen.

As Sofie described the room, Jay felt a combination of disbelief and excitement. Had Nahid taken Sofie to the same farmhouse? Was that the reason why the police hadn't been able to pinpoint Sofie's position? Because she was in France? She looked at her watch, trying to work out timings. Sofie had vanished at nine p.m. The Eurotunnel operated twenty-four hours a day. Trains departed regularly throughout the night . . .

'Ask her what she can smell,' said Jay.

Thankfully Tom didn't question her request, but put it straight across. Sofie's response was swift.

Animal poo. Like a farmyard . . .

'Oh my God,' Jay said. 'I think I know where she is.'

Tom's eyes flew to hers.

Jay said, 'Tell her I'm on my way.'

'Sofie?' Tom said. 'Did you hear that?'

The girl had fallen quiet.

'Sofie?' Tom said urgently. 'Sofie?'

'Daddy?' Her voice was small, trembling.

'Sofie! Please!' His voice cracked. 'Oh. Yes. Yes, I'm still here . . . Look, Jay's coming to get you. She knows where you are . . .'

Silence.

'Sofie?' Tom said urgently. 'Sofie?'

The girl had gone.

Fingers trembling, Tom redialled. The phone rang and rang.
'Come on!' he hissed. 'Come *on!*'

When Sofie didn't reply, he raised his face to the ceiling.
Anguish was etched in every muscle.

'Tom,' Jay said. She had to force herself to keep her voice
level. 'I think she's at the same farmhouse Nahid held me.'

He blinked. 'In France?'

'Yes.'

He pushed the phone into his pocket, began striding for the
back door. 'Let's go.'

'No.' She caught his arm. 'You have to stay here.'

He shook himself free, opening his mouth to protest, but Jay
quickly shushed him.

'What if one of the cops here is with the Garrison?' she
whispered. 'If you leave, they'll want to know where you're
going . . . It'll look really odd if you don't stay with Heather.
What if they tell Turner, who tells Nahid? She'll only move
Sofie, and then we might never find her.'

'Christ.' He ran a hand over his face. '*Christ.*'

'I'll take Nick. The girls . . .' Jay brought out her phone and
started dialling. 'I'll be in France before dawn . . . Can I use your
car? It'll be far quicker than flying, then hiring a car. Besides
which, the airports don't open for another couple of hours.'

Jay prepared as fast and unobtrusively as she could. A couple
of sharp kitchen knives, a pair of wire cutters, a torch, water,
and some duct tape. Pathetic, really, but better than nothing.
She wished Blake was with her, along with his Discovery filled
with kit. But he'd vanished. God only knew where he was now.

Tom stood in the front doorway as Jay drove down Heather's
drive. He didn't raise a hand or wave. Just watched her go.

THIRTY-NINE

'Y̶ou're a very naughty girl.'

The woman stood over Sofie with an admonishing
expression.

Sofie's entire body shivered. 'Sorry,' she whispered.

The man's fingers twisted through her hair, forced her head

back. 'Who else did you call?' he demanded. His breath was wet and warm against her face and reeked of cigarettes.

'N–nobody.'

'She didn't know how to dial overseas,' the woman said. 'Didn't even know the country code, did you?' She laughed mockingly. 'Daddy had to ring her.'

Sofie whimpered.

Please, Tom. Please, Jay, come and save me.

'The McCaulay woman's on her way. I don't know if she'll be alone or not.'

'Should we move?'

'No. I'll go and keep a watch. If she brings people with her, we can be away in minutes.' Her rich chuckle echoed through the empty room. 'But if she's alone . . . Now, wouldn't that be nice? We'd have two girls to play with. You'd like that, wouldn't you, Tivon?'

Twisting her hair, the man forced Sofie's face to his. He licked her cheek. Sofie cried out, trying to break free of his grip, but he held her fast.

'Yes,' he murmured. 'I'd like that.'

Sobs erupted from her throat. Tears poured down her face.

The man released her hair. 'Later,' he whispered. 'We'll have fun later.'

They walked out of the room, their footsteps brisk on the stones. Eventually they faded, were gone.

Why hadn't she listened to Tom? He'd told her not to go outside! She was *so stupid*!

Sofie curled on to her side, sobbing.

Jay was walking into a trap.

They were both going to die.

And it was all her fault.

FORTY

Jay was speeding for the M4 when her phone rang.

Private number. She said, 'Hello?'

'I have Turner.'

Her heart clenched. 'Max?'

'I put a tracking device on his car.'

'No, no! You've got to let him go . . . He's got Sofie, Tom's daughter—'

'So he says.'

'Nahid will kill her if she doesn't hear from her sister. If Turner doesn't arrive at his destination safely.'

'Any idea where the girl is?'

'I think she's at the same farmhouse where I was held. I'm on my way there now.'

Long silence.

'Max! I won't be there for five hours at least! You have to let him go!'

'We're at Manchester Airport.' His voice was curt. 'He has a private plane ready.'

'Let him go!'

'Once he's gone . . .'

Jay knew what Blake was saying. Once Turner was in the air, he could fly anywhere in the world. Although the plane would have filed a flight plan, that could change once they were under way. Turner could switch to Europe, Africa, or South America. He'd vanish.

'We can't risk Sofie,' she begged. 'We *can't*.'

'Find the girl, Jay.'

Click. He'd hung up.

She was drenched in horror. Surely Blake was going to let Turner go? He wouldn't risk a little girl's life, would he? *Would he?*

Jay put her foot down. She didn't care about being done for speeding. She had to get across the country as fast as she could. As she drove, she rang Nick. His phone went straight to his messaging service. Jay left a lengthy message, which included directions to the farmhouse. Then she rang the girls. Nobody answered. She tried Angela's mobile.

'Hello?' Angela, sleepy, fuddled.

'It's me. I need your help.'

With the girls galvanized and hopefully catching the same Eurotunnel train, Jay continued speeding east. After she'd ducked on to the M25, she rang Nick again. She didn't leave another message. She'd already left two. She made the three twenty-eight train with ten minutes to spare. Although she wanted to cat nap through the thirty minute journey, she was too wired. Had the girls managed to catch the same train? Sod's bloody law that they hadn't been in London tonight, but in Oxford, having a piss-up with an old army buddy. She had to pray they weren't far behind.

Once she disembarked, Jay sped down the E402, past Boulogne-sur-Mer, before switching south on to the A16 for Amiens. Rain poured, making it hard to see. She was forced to slow. No point in wiping herself and the car out. Better to arrive in one piece than not at all.

It was still dark when she peeled west, barrelling through Beauvais, then down the D44 past Cauvigny. Dawn was over two hours away. The rain continued to pour. At last she came to Ully St Georges. She blasted through the tiny village, eyes hunting for the small road where Michel Fuduli and his dog, Aceline, had picked her up all those weeks ago. There! She swung left, following the sign for Foulangues, and a quarter of a mile along she spotted the lumpy, potholed track that led to the farmhouse. Hastily, she pulled over and switched off her headlights, killed the engine.

Rain continued to pour.

She peered along the track. She could see nothing. No lights. Not even a pinprick.

She rang the girls. 'Where are you?'

'Somewhere called Ercuis,' said Denise. 'Sorry, we overshot the turning . . .'

They were twenty minutes away.

'I'm going to do a recce.'

Ripping off a strip of duct tape, Jay quickly strapped a wickedly sharp kitchen knife to the small of her back. Put her phone on to vibrate. Slipped out of the car. She wanted to wear a waterproof, but decided against it. The plastic might be noisy. She'd have to get wet. She walked straight up the track, rain trickling down her face, her neck. The track was the quickest route, and it was so dark that she doubted anyone could see her. As she approached the farmhouse, she paused, listening. All she could hear was rain pattering, dripping. There were no cars that she could see.

Carefully, she walked around the periphery of the yard. Still no cars. No lights. Nothing.

Shivering now – it was icy cold and she was getting soaked – she fumbled her way through the mud to the outbuilding.

Unlatched the door and let herself inside. Closed the door behind her. Switched on her torch. As quietly as she could, she crept down the corridor until she came to the door at the end. Shone her torch over it.

She stared at the bolts on the door.

They weren't engaged. The door wasn't locked.

Dismay in her heart, Jay pulled open the door and swung her torch round.

The room was empty.

Immediately, Jay backtracked. Crossed the yard for the farmhouse. It didn't take her long to ascertain it was empty as well.

Shit, shit, *shit*.

In the kitchen, dripping muddy water on the flagstones, Jay rang the girls.

'No go,' she said.

'You're kidding.'

'Let's RV at Ully St Georges. At the bus stop.'

'Are you sure?'

'Yes. There's no one here.'

Jay hung up. Pushed a lock of wet hair from her eyes. What next? How to find Sofie? They'd have to start a house-to-house, barn-to-barn search. There was no other way. Instinct told her Sofie wasn't far. Nahid knew the area, she'd feel comfortable here. But where were they?

Jay jogged back along the rutted track, splashing mud and water up her calves, her thighs. She stumbled and almost fell a couple of times and forced herself to slow. She didn't need a sprained ankle. Gradually, the rain eased into a drizzle, but it was still icy cold.

Shuddering, soaked to the skin, she beeped open Tom's car. As she put her hand on the door handle, someone said, 'Jay.'

The woman's voice was soft. All the hairs on the back of Jay's neck rose.

'I see you came looking for little Sofie.'

Nahid appeared on the other side of the car. She held a gun. A pistol, aimed at Jay's chest.

'Throw me your phone.'

Jay threw it to one side, where it fell on to the ground with a soft splash. Nahid didn't move to pick it up.

'Your weapons.'

Jay chucked down her two paltry knives.

'Dear, dear.' Nahid clucked her tongue. 'You are such an amateur. Now, get in your car. We're going for a little drive.'

FORTY-ONE

Jay drove east, as instructed. Nahid was in the back of the car, the pistol trained on Jay.

'Did you really think we'd be stupid enough to keep Sofie at the same place we kept you?'

Jay shrugged.

'But you couldn't sit around doing nothing, could you?'

Another shrug.

'I'm so glad,' Nahid purred. 'Tivon's really looking forward to seeing you again. Little Sofie's going to hate what I'm going to do to you. And you're going to hate what Tivon's going to do with little Sofie.'

Jay refused to let the woman's words disturb her. She mustn't be distracted. She had to keep her concentration sharp.

They passed a sign for Chantilly. Angela and Denise would be going nuts by now, Jay thought. They would be at the farmhouse, trying to work out what had happened, where Jay had gone.

Nahid leaned forward and stroked Jay's hair. Jay jerked her head aside. 'Don't touch me,' she hissed.

Nahid gave a soft laugh. 'I've been so looking forward to this, I can't tell you.'

Jay downshifted for the corner coming up and as she turned into the corner, Nahid leaned back. She said, 'Next left. Just after the bend.'

Jay slowed the car to turn on to another rutted farm track. Another farmhouse looming ahead. A barn. Some stables.

'Sofie's here?'

'She's waiting for you with baited breath,' Nahid purred.

It was all Jay needed. She took a breath, clenched the steering wheel, and shifted the gear down into second. Rammed her foot on the accelerator. The rev needle spun into the red.

Briefly, the tyres spun in the mud, then gripped on stones.

Engine roaring, the car shot forward.

'What the . . . Stop!' Nahid commanded.

Jay ignored her. Aimed the car straight at the ancient brick wall of the house. Forty yards away, maybe more.

'I'll shoot you!' Nahid yelled.

Jay kept her foot on the accelerator. The car's engine was howling, the vehicle bounding and rocketing forward. She rammed the gear into second without taking her foot off the accelerator. The wall loomed closer.

BANG!

The windscreen crazed. Jay couldn't see. She kept her grip tight on the steering wheel. Kept the wheels straight. Willed the car to go faster, dammit. *Faster.*

'Stop!' Nahid screamed.

Jay ignored her. The farmhouse was barely twenty yards away. She pushed her foot harder on the accelerator.

'STOP!' Nahid shouted. 'You fucking . . .!'

The car hit a pothole and, at the same time, Nahid fired again. *Bang!*

Jay felt something punch her very hard from behind. Like someone had hit her shoulder blade with a hammer.

Oh shit, she thought. *I've been shot.*

The car slewed sideways, but she yanked it back on course. She felt a strange calm descend over her, but she didn't take her foot from the accelerator. They were roaring straight for the farmhouse. Just seconds away now.

'NO!' screamed Nahid.

Yes, she told Nahid. *I'm wearing a seat belt. You're not.*

When the three-year-old Vauxhall hit the ancient wall, the bonnet crumpled like newspaper. The windscreen exploded. Glass flew everywhere. Metal shrieked and groaned. Jay's vision became enveloped in the white mushroom of an air bag. Briefly, she lost consciousness.

She came round to the sound of steam hissing.

Nahid lay sprawled across the central console. Her head had smashed into the dashboard. Blood was everywhere.

Fingers trembling, Jay undid her seat belt. Fought to open her door.

It wouldn't budge.

She wriggled backwards, dragging her legs clear of the tangle of metal. The effort made her go dizzy. A wave of numbness washed from her shoulder and into her lungs.

Don't stop. Keep going.

She forced herself sideways, struggling to get herself clear of the driver's seat.

Suddenly, she smelled burning.

Get out!

She clambered, fought her way over Nahid's inert form. Every movement made her vision sway, the numbness across her shoulders deepen.

The smell of smoke thickened.

A tongue of flame flared from beneath the bonnet.

Faster.

She increased her efforts to crawl into the back seat, kicking against Nahid.

She heard a shout. The passenger door was tugged open. A rush of clear air swept inside.

'Nahid!' Tivon screamed. 'Nahid!'

Jay fell into the rear footwell.

Tivon continued to scream. 'Nahid!'

The numbness spread from her shoulders to grip her neck, but Jay kept pushing herself.

Must get out. Get to Sofie.

She pulled the door handle. Nothing happened. She heaved herself on to the seat. Put her shoulder against the door and tried again. The door opened with a groan of metal. She tumbled outside, fell to her knees. The ground kept moving. Her vision wavered.

Flames and smoke poured from the engine block.

Tivon was fighting to get Nahid out of the car.

After three attempts, Jay managed to stand.

Now, walk.

Jay stumbled away from the car. Where would Sofie be? The main house? The stables?

She'd barely reached the stables when a wave of nausea broke over her. Her skin turned cold. She found it an incredible effort to put one foot in front of the other.

Keep going!

In tortuous slow motion, Jay checked the first two stables. Empty. She was staggering for the third when she heard a soft *whoosh*.

BOOM!

The car erupted into an inferno.

She didn't pause to see where Tivon was. She couldn't waste the energy. She checked the final stable. Empty.

She had to get to the house.

It seemed to take hours to cross the yard, days to stumble through the front door. Hands against the wall, Jay stumbled down the corridor. She paused as another wave of nausea overtook her. She staggered, suddenly light-headed.

Mustn't stop, she told herself, and then she heard a thin, desperate sound echoing from somewhere deep inside the house. It was Sofie. She was screaming, 'Help, help!' over and over again.

Jay tried to shout back, but all that came was a whistling sound.

She followed Sofie's shouts to a door near the rear of the house. It was bolted from the outside. She unlocked it. Opened the door. Began to shuffle down the stone steps.

The numbness crept past her neck and down her chest. Her breathing rasped.

Mustn't stop.

With fierce concentration, she made it to the bottom.

A single bulb lit the cellar. Sofie was tied to the wall. Tears streaked her face.

The numbness turned cold. Ice cold, its fingers spread into her lungs, her heart.

Sofie.

Jay's legs slowly collapsed. She toppled to the cellar floor. She could hear Sofie shouting at her to get up.

It's OK. I'm coming.

She began to crawl for the girl.

I've got a knife . . . It's taped in the small of my back.

The ice put its hand around her heart and began to squeeze.

Oh, God. Let me free Sofie first.

Her eyelids fluttered.

Bugger it.

She was dying.

She could hear Sofie shouting at her, but her voice was growing smaller and smaller.

And then she couldn't hear it any more.

FORTY-TWO

Jay tried to swallow. Her throat was dry and sore, like it had been scraped with barbed wire.

She tried to open her eyes, but they seemed to have been glued shut.

She tried to move her arms, but they refused to budge.

Fear seared her.

Was she paralysed?

Flashes of memory fired into her brain. The Vauxhall exploding. Her collapsing in the cellar. Sofie's tearful face.

A repetitive beeping entered her consciousness. Soft shoes shuffling. Muted voices.

She was in hospital. At least she hoped so.

Open your eyes!

Finally, she forced them open a crack.

A ceiling. She could see a ceiling. Great. She tried to roll her head to one side and extend her vision, but she couldn't move.

'Hey.'

Dark eyes met hers.

Blake.

'Hey,' she managed.

His hair was awry and he looked unusually pale. 'You scared the hell out of me,' he said.

'Sorry.'

'You nearly didn't make it.'

'But . . . I did,' she whispered.

He gave a ghost of a smile. 'Yes.'

She licked her lips, but she had no saliva.

Blake vanished. Reappeared with a paper cup and a bendy straw. 'Here,' he murmured.

This time, she managed to move her head. She rolled it slightly to the side and sucked greedily. 'Mmmm,' she said. 'Thanks.'

More flashes of memory. Turner climbing into his car. Tom pacing Heather's house. Sofie's thin cries for help.

'Where's Sofie?' she said.

'She's with the detective. He flew in yesterday—'

'I've been out for a day?'

'Yup.'

She thought further. 'I'm in Paris?'

'Yup.'

'I'm OK? Not paralysed or anything?'

A glimmer of a smile. 'Not paralysed or anything.'

'Max.' It was an effort to speak. 'Fill me in.'

He gave a nod. 'There's a lot of debriefing going on. Between the Paris and British authorities. Nahid and Tivon's bodies were found burned in the detective's car. The girls saw the explosion. Found Sofie running along the road to get help for you.'

'What?' She was bewildered. 'How did Sofie get free?'

'You told her where to find your knife.'

'I did?' She thought back to when she'd struggled across the cellar floor. She didn't think she'd spoken out loud. Wow. The mind sure played tricks on you.

'What about Turner?' she asked.

Blake looked away.

'Max?'

The muscles in his jaw bunched. 'I let him go.'

For a moment, she didn't take in what he said. 'You what?'

'When you told me the set-up with Nahid and her sister, I let him go. I had no choice.'

'But you . . . You told me to *find her*.'

His expression cleared. 'And you did.'

'Jesus, Max. If you'd told me you'd released Turner, things might have been different.'

'You weren't answering your phone.'

'Oh.' She guessed he'd rung after she'd chucked her mobile into the mud. 'Will you be able to find him?'

He didn't respond in any way; his expression didn't change.

'So how can we prove you're innocent of killing Sol? That you didn't shoot Major Wayland?'

'Brian Keith's come forward. He knows where the research centre is. The cops are there now. Also, Alison Drake, the chapter head of the guys who kidnapped you, is turning witness. Stephanie Legrand is also onside. Loads of evidence for the defence.'

'You're cleared?'

'Yup, I'm clear.'

'That's fantastic.'

A commotion sounded outside. Blake went to the door, cracked it open. 'Visiting hour's started.'

She smiled inside. How typical of Blake not to stick to the hospital's regime.

He came and gently tucked a lock of hair behind her ear. 'People are waiting to see you. You up for it?'

'Like who?'

'Like your parents, for starters. Your mum's nice. She asked me over for Christmas lunch.'

'She *what*?'

Strength flooded Jay, giving her the energy to shuffle upright a fraction.

'I like that kind of generosity,' he mused. 'All I told her was that my parents were dead, and—'

The door opened. Blake switched his head round.

'Can I come in?' Sofie flashed a grin at Jay.

Jay felt Blake's warm fingers close around hers. 'I'll see you at Christmas,' he murmured.

'But that's two weeks away!' Bewilderment fell. 'Where are you going in the meantime?'

'I have a criminal to catch, remember?'

Swift press of his lips against hers, and then he was gone.

'Jay.' Sofie rushed to stand at her bedside.

Jay stared at the space where Blake had been.

'You made it!'

She forced herself to look at the girl. 'Thanks to you running hell for leather for help.'

Sofie's face was alight. 'I ran as fast as I could. Angela and Denise picked me up when I was on the road. I fell over twice, it was so dark . . .'

Jay relaxed against the pillows, listening to Sofie relate the final stages of the story. How the girls had raced to the farmhouse to find Jay in the cellar. How they'd called for an ambulance and the police, and then kept her alive until the paramedics arrived.

When Sofie came and gave her a hug, tentatively so as not to hurt her, Jay kissed the girl's forehead. Things had changed so much over the past few weeks. She wasn't the same any more. Something inside her had changed. Something primary, something fundamental.

Tom appeared, clutching a bunch of roses that looked almost as exhausted as he did. Behind him were her mother and father. Angela and Denise, and Nick. Even Tom's parents were there. Everyone crowded inside the room.

'Jessica, you scared us half to death,' said her mother.

'Sorry.'

'I came as quickly as I could,' said Nick. 'I got your messages, but too late to help . . .'

'The girls rang me the instant they found Sofie,' said Tom. 'I got on a plane . . .'

'And Tom rang me,' said Jay's father. 'I drove straight to Inverness airport . . .'

The babble continued, but Jay was barely listening.

She loved these people, her friends, her family, but her true heart was no longer in this room.

It was with the man who had already left.